SHAWNDIREA

AETHEAON CHRONICLES: BOOK ONE

LEONARD D. HILLEY II

Copyright © 2014, 2019 by Leonard D. Hilley II

ISBN: 978-1-950485-12-3

Cover art by Ellie Douglas

All rights reserved.

No part of this book may be reproduced in any form or by any electronic or mechanical means, including information storage and retrieval systems, without written permission from the author, except for the use of brief quotations in a book review.

❧ Created with Vellum

ACKNOWLEDGMENTS

A special thanks to my beta readers: Carol Ann Murrell, Michelle Lump-kins, and KC Riley-Gyer. Thanks for your encouragement and taking this journey with me.

To Christal: Without you, these stories may never have been told. Much love always.

Disclaimer:

Just a note: the spelling of Vyking (for Viking) and Faery (for Fairy) are intentional for the Realm of Aetheaon and this series.

Aetheaon
Misty Seas of Reus
Isles of Welkstone
Snowton
Breezfar
Nunlee
Highvale Plains
Icebourne
City of Hoffnung
Sparrows Point
Nagdor
Cyress point
Forvale
Wordvost
Haunted Forest of Darian
Ul'thanel
Glacier Ridge
Jordan River
Isle of Frozen Tears
Glasslyn Lake
Mothalla
Bridgeshadow
Vylan
Baybourne
Falls Lake
Syllantium
Evendale
Black Chasm
Wordnog
Westovyna
Taurin
Spellhaven
Kingdom of Legoland
Shadeport
Kingdom of Oculoth
N
W — E
S

CHAPTER 1

The early autumn sun blazed over the freshly cut hayfield in Cider Knoll, Kentucky. Ben Whytten rested his butterfly net against the rusted barbed wire fence and then wiped sweat from his brow with the back of his hand. Sweat soaked his shirt and blue jeans. Although fall had officially begun, the outside temperature didn't indicate it. Sporting near ninety degrees, summer refused to let go of the climate and turned what should have been a pleasant Saturday afternoon into an intimidating taunt, daring anyone with partial sanity to remain outdoors in the sweltering heat.

After he unscrewed the canteen cap, he tilted it back and took a long drink of cold water. Beads of water dripped down his short brown beard. He sighed and twisted the cap tightly. His piercing brown eyes studied the sky. Not a cloud in sight. No breeze to help combat the hellish sticky heat.

Ben combed his sweat-matted brown hair from his eyes with his fingers. He picked up the butterfly net and looked across the straw-colored field at the small grove of pastel leafed maples that lined a winding stream. The shade was inviting, and he guessed a good ten degrees cooler than the open field. He took a deep breath and trudged across brittle grass stems that crunched beneath his hiking boots.

Collecting butterflies during autumn was better than spring or summer because the diversity of species increased. The fall forms of butterflies were generally brighter, larger, and fed in greater clusters on the ironweed, milkweed, and clover. Brilliantly colored swallowtails puddled along the creek beds. Plump moth larvae were also easier to find as they searched for places to spin cocoons or burrow beneath the soil to pupate before the colder temperatures set in.

"If colder weather ever settles in," Ben thought, *"Hell will have truly frozen over."*

Long narrow grasshoppers jumped and took to flight as Ben crossed the field. Their wings buzzed as the alarmed insects glided and drifted downward, landed, and propelled themselves into the air again.

Reaching the shade beneath the maple branches, Ben leaned against a thick tree trunk and closed his eyes. The shallow stream trickled softly. Cicadas hummed. In the distance a woodpecker rapped the bark of a massive dead pine. Weather had stripped away sections of the rough pine bark, revealing the smooth yellow wood underneath. The soothing sounds of nature relaxed him, and he was thankful to be outside, alone.

Dr. Isaac Deiko had planned to collect insects with Ben this particular Saturday, but at the last minute, he called and said that he couldn't go. Deiko had to help set up tables for a gun show in a neighboring town.

The news didn't disappoint Ben. He'd rather collect butterflies and other insects alone. The outdoors was a place where he gathered his thoughts and meditated about life. The forests, bluffs, and meadows were the best places where he felt at peace. Leaving the fast-paced, bustling technological-craving addicts for a calmer, slow-paced life without all their distractions was worth more than millions of dollars to Ben. He'd give up all the instant gadgets for the tranquility that his grandfather and great-grandfather experienced while working on their farms.

Ben kept a serious outlook on life while Dr. Deiko spent more time playing practical jokes on their colleagues and students, which often irritated and infuriated Ben. He knew if Deiko came on this field trip, the collecting possibilities would be little or none simply because Deiko was clumsy-footed and boisterous.

Ben had never extended an invitation for Deiko to join him in the first place. In fact, Deiko had *invited* himself when he found out about Ben's collecting plans for the weekend. Although Deiko was a biologist like Ben, Deiko was more concerned with uncovering a discovery to make him famous, whereas Ben loved science and didn't care if anyone other than his students knew he existed. Of course when final exams rolled around, most of his students would rather he *didn't* exist. Other than giving his students field trips from Hell, his tests were considered harsher than rigorous ten mile hikes through steep mountainous terrain.

Ben looked back across the field and chuckled. He had traipsed hundreds of acres through forests, caves, and fields when he was still in middle school. He had done so voluntarily, without a word of complaint, and yet, today's college students voiced disdain over the least thing. The challenge wasn't getting them to learn; it was getting them to do anything that didn't require the pacifying need for their technology.

His inner frustration brought more heat to his face. He was seconds from rehashing how he wished computers and cellphones weren't so controlling until the soft bubbling creek caught his attention. The gentle soft sound of water allowed his mind to leave the tensions of the classroom and return to the natural calm surrounding him. He expelled a long sigh and refocused himself.

Tall narrow blades of grass covered the sandy banks of the shallow stream. Small drab satyr butterflies fluttered lazily from grass blade to grass blade. Ben shook his head. After two hours of walking the fields and woods, he had hoped to capture a few new specimens to add to his collection. But with each species he encountered, he already had at least a half-dozen of those pinned inside glass-top boxes at home. In many ways, he believed he'd have done himself a greater service by staying home.

But regardless of what he deemed bad luck, his life was about to change. Forever.

He removed his backpack and set it down. Slowly he lowered himself and sat back against the tree trunk to rest. He set down the canteen and placed the net handle across his lap and watched the gentle stream flow. A few minnows darted back and forth beneath the water as water striders skimmed like polished skaters across the water's surface.

Ben was drenched in sweat and drained from the heat. A cool breeze stirred along the stream, which seemed an invitation to relax a while longer. His eyes ached to close for a nap. He fought the urge to doze even though the place was so comforting and peaceful. But, if nothing interesting presented itself soon, he was going home. He dreaded walking across the dry pasture to his SUV.

Ben took his hunting knife from the sheath attached to his belt and then picked up a dried oak branch. He whittled and shaved away bark.

Perhaps it was the extreme heat that kept the most brilliant butterflies in hiding, but he still didn't see any within the grove or along the sandy banks. Later in the evening he might have better luck, but he refused to stick around that long. He slid the knife back into its sheath and rubbed his tired eyes.

Sunlight filtered through the leafy canopy. Several birds flew low across the stream and through the trees. Seconds later two yellow butterflies glided to the edge of the far bank and landed. A larger butterfly caught his attention. At first glance he thought it was a giant swallowtail, but instead, it turned out to be an oversized tiger swallowtail.

Ben's fingers tightened around the net handle. He pushed himself to his feet. He stepped lightly and headed toward the stream to get a better look at the butterflies. Near the bank, a blur of metallic bluish-green streaked past him.

"Damn!" he said, watching the zipping wings catch the breeze and glide.

With incredible speed, it darted up, down, left to right, and along the stream's edge. Perhaps the sweltering heat or near dehydration was playing tricks on him, but he was almost certain glittery dust trailed behind it.

Ben hurried after the butterfly, a prize unlike any other in his collection.

Few butterflies in this part of Kentucky had such metallic colorings. One he thought of immediately was the White M Hairstreak, but this one was too large and flew much swifter. Another butterfly with similar colors was the long-tailed skipper, but the sheen sparkling off the butterfly following the stream was too bright. Its flight was also more erratic. The skipper stayed near gardens, and he doubted any strayed this far into the woods since the larvae food plant was the leaf of various beanstalks.

Ben realized he had just discovered something new. Excitement shot through him.

He hurried along the stream and jumped over a fallen tree. His sudden pursuit had not gone unnoticed. The iridescent creature darted downward and swept through the tiny branches of a shrub. But Ben moved faster.

As the beautifully winged specimen shot through the other side of the bush, Ben arced the net sharply and captured his prize. The end of the net pulled and stretched while his captive struggled to fight free.

Quickly, Ben clamped his fingers near the end of the net, but by the time he did, the struggling ceased.

He opened the net and looked inside. His eyes widened.

"What the hell?" he asked.

At the bottom of the net lay a gorgeous creature, but not what he had expected to capture. Her wings were tattered, frayed. Unconscious, he hoped, but he feared she might be dying or already dead. Broken scales and wing fragments covered her nearly nude body.

His excitement of the chase suddenly turned to regret and dread.

A faery?

Ben dropped to his knees and gently set down the net.

"God," he whispered. "I hope I didn't kill you."

He carefully placed his left hand beside her unmoving form. He nudged her into the palm of his hand with the tip of his finger. She breathed, but her eyes remained closed. Her radiant face was more beautiful than any woman he had ever met.

A door slammed and echoed near the pasture gate where he had parked his SUV.

Ben looked over his shoulder but couldn't see who had driven up.

"Ben!" Deiko shouted. "Where are you?"

"Dammit," Ben grumbled under his breath, looking back over his shoulder. "What the hell are you doing here?"

He hurried to the tree where his pack lay. He curled his left hand gently around the faery's limp body while reaching into the pack.

"Ben!"

Ben took a wide-mouthed dark plastic bottle, set it between his knees and unscrewed the hole-punched lid. Glancing back over his shoulder he saw Deiko's lanky figure jogging toward the grove. Deiko smiled and waved when their eyes met. His jog turned into a sprint as he headed toward Ben.

Ben placed the faery into the jar, turned the lid, and wrapped the jar inside a white cloth before setting it back into his pack. No sooner had he placed it there and zipped the pack shut, Deiko's thundering footsteps stopped beside him.

"Catch something nice?" Deiko asked.

"No," Ben replied, looking up but not making eye contact with Deiko. "Not much activity out here today. I blame the heat."

Deiko smiled broadly. "You caught something. Something *special.*"

Ben shook his head, picked up his pack, and stood. "Look around, Isaac. What do you see?"

Deiko glanced around but then his eyes focused on Ben's backpack again. "I agree. Not much flying around. But you got something."

"What makes you think that?"

"Your eyes. It's the same with poker players who have a great hand and haven't conditioned themselves to suppress their excitement or like kids that find money on the ground after someone drops it. Hell, I noticed people at the gun show who bought guns from people far cheaper than the owners knew the guns were worth."

Ben's eyes narrowed, and he chose to change the subject. He said, "How was the gun show? I thought you'd be there all day."

Deiko shrugged. "That had been the plan. Not much going on there, either. Got a couple good deals though. Like this Ruger."

He pulled a handgun from the back of his belt.

"Nice," Ben replied. Carefully he slipped his pack over his shoulder and headed toward the hay field.

"Well?" Deiko said. He tucked the gun behind his belt and stepped in front of Ben. "Aren't you going to show me?"

Sweat dripped from Deiko's black hair and beaded on his brow. Ben studied the determination set in his colleague's dark eyes and his firm muscular jaw. Within seconds, Deiko's boyish face had hardened into that of a fierce murderous villain. Physically, he had no weight to put behind his facial threat. He was tall and quite bony with slender arms. And although Deiko was probably fifteen years younger, Ben had no doubt if he was forced to fight that Deiko would be the one sitting on the ground looking up and rubbing his jaw. But, then, there was the gun issue. Isaac was armed and all Ben had was his knife. Even those odds didn't stand in Isaac's favor.

"Show you *what?*" Ben asked.

"Your prize. It must be something nice since you still refuse to show me."

"How many times have I told you that I haven't found anything?"

"You and I should play poker sometime," Deiko said. "I'd make a fortune."

"Being as I don't play cards, you're probably correct with that assumption."

"Oh, come on, Ben," Deiko said. Hostility loomed in his voice and darkness narrowed his eyes. "Why are you afraid to show me what you found?"

Ben studied him for a moment. Never had he seen Isaac behave like a demented spoiled brat. He had his moments, but Dr. Deiko generally didn't keep a quiet and intimidating tone. But out here, away from others, Ben suddenly saw the violence that hid deep within the botanist, and it was creeping to the surface. Knowing that Deiko lusted for fame, for a discovery beyond what man had seen or could fathom, Ben knew he could never show the faery to Deiko. The second he did, something horrible would happen. To Ben and the lovely faery.

Deiko had not only shown the gun as his grand prize from the gun show, he had established his subtle threat by revealing he had brought it into the field. Hunting season was still a few weeks away, and no one needed a gun to collect butterflies. He had shown the gun for a reason— either as a bullying tactic or simply to exhibit dominance.

"I think the heat is getting to you, Isaac," Ben said, shaking his head and stepping around his colleague.

"Put down the pack," Isaac said.

"What?"

Ben froze when Isaac inserted the magazine into the gun and snapped the gun's chamber back and forth.

"Put down your pack. I want to see what you're hiding inside."

Ben turned. He looked in Isaac's eyes, then to the gun.

Isaac shook his head. "Uh-uh. Just set it down."

Ben frowned and slowly lowered his pack to the ground. He held his hands before him in surrender. "You're making a big mistake."

"So you did find something."

"And if I did? You going to kill me for it?" Ben asked.

Isaac chuckled. "Depends on how good a find it is."

"Seriously?"

Isaac didn't reply as he stepped closer to the backpack. He held the gun steadily aimed at Ben, and by the ease he carried the weapon, Ben knew Isaac had a lot of experience using one. Isaac's hand didn't shake or tremble. His cold gaze indicated a side of him Ben had never seen, and he wondered what further words might make Isaac squeeze the trigger.

And over *what*?

Ben thought it odd that Isaac was bent on knowing what was inside the backpack. His timing couldn't have been better planned. He had run into the grove within minutes of the capture. Without being told, Isaac automatically assumed Ben had some spectacular discovery. But how? And why? Then Ben noticed the set of binoculars hanging around Isaac's neck. Had he watched Ben catch the faery?

Isaac tugged at the zipper on the pack but with only one free hand, he couldn't unzip it. His building frustration with the zipper troubled Ben. Isaac seemed seconds away from an outburst that might turn deadly.

"Put the gun away," Ben said in a calm, almost apologetic, tone. "I'll show you what's inside the pack."

Isaac peered up unconvinced.

Ben smiled and outstretched his hands while offering a slight shrug. "Look, the old zipper sticks anyway. Almost have to use a combination of tugs to pry it open."

Isaac sighed and regret overshadowed his face. He tucked the gun behind his belt. "I don't know what came over me," he said.

"Yeah, I don't know either."

"I'm sorry. Just playing around."

"That's not how I view it," Ben said in an even tone.

Ben reached down for the pack, but instead of grabbing it, he spun around and swiftly planted his boot between Isaac's legs. Isaac's eyes bulged. He clutched himself, bent forward, and collapsed face-forward onto the ground. Ben grabbed the gun and the backpack.

Looking down at his gasping colleague, Ben grinned and said, "I'm not a fan of guns. I'd rather use my hands and feet. Or knives."

Isaac groaned and writhed in pain.

"You shouldn't play with guns," Ben said, turning to walk away.

"It wasn't loaded," Isaac said, forcing out the words. "Hell, you know I pull pranks all the time."

"You're very lucky you're not dead. I could have dropped you with my knife in less than a few seconds."

"You knew the gun wasn't loaded?"

"No, but it wouldn't have mattered if it was. I could have hit you with the knife *before* you pulled the trigger."

Isaac rolled to his side and said, "You actually considered doing that?"

"Yes."

"Can I have my gun back at least?"

"I don't want it, but what makes you believe *you* deserve it?"

"I bought it."

Ben shrugged. "I'll leave it on your truck. But one thing you need to remember."

"What?"

"Never ask to come hiking or collecting insects with me. In fact, never speak to me again. Burn it, no, *brand* it into your mind. Understood?"

"Sure, no problem," Isaac stuttered between painful gasps.

Ben turned and walked away.

"Then whom do I tell about your winged woman?" he asked. "I guess faeries do exist."

Ben stopped walking.

"I thought so," Isaac said. He took a couple of deep painful breaths and continued, "You did catch her. My eyes weren't playing tricks on me."

"I don't know what you're talking about," Ben said.

"The world will know about her," Isaac said. "I'll get the proof I need and let everyone know."

Ben hurried to his SUV.

"I saw her!" Isaac insisted. "You have her. You can't keep her hidden."

Ben opened the pasture gate and yelled, "The heat is making you delirious, Isaac. I suggest you find a place to cool off and rehydrate."

He disassembled the bullet-less gun and tossed the pieces into Isaac's truck bed. Then he climbed into his SUV. He started the engine, turned on the air conditioner, and quickly unzipped the pack. He took the jar with the faery and placed her where the cooler air could reach her. His guilt was heavy enough. He had already injured her with the net. The last thing he wanted was for her to die due to suffocating heat inside the jar.

CHAPTER 2

*B*en drove his SUV up the steep winding road to his house at the edge of a bluff. His garage was built into the rocky mountain-side. He parked the SUV and took the jar with the faery into the house.

He carried her into his study where he kept his vast insect collection. The walls housed built-in mahogany-stained bookcases. Glass-topped cases covered the black Formica tables. He kept a microscope and spreading boards at the center table. A stack of *The Journal of the Lepidopterists' Society* journals lay neatly placed near his lamp. After flipping on the desk lamp, he opened the jar and looked inside.

The faery lay sprawled across the bottom of the jar. She breathed softly, but she still hadn't awakened. Her tattered metallic wings wilted around her near nude form. Colorful scales covered her breasts, her butt, and her pubic area.

Ben gently slid her from the jar and placed her onto a thick square of cotton.

Admiring her beauty, and pained by the damage he had inflicted upon her, he whispered, "I'm so sorry."

Ben took another piece of thick cotton and a pair of scissors. He cut out a circle and tapped the cotton into a glass gallon jar. After he finished, he set her on the cotton layer and covered the top of the jar with cheesecloth. He used a thick rubber band to hold the cloth in place.

He turned his attention to a pinning board where several large cecropia moths were spread to dry. He picked up the board and inspected the moths.

Ben left the room for a few minutes to get live crickets to feed his two tarantulas in the terrarium. He dropped several crickets into each spider

10

cage. The large tarantulas quickly pounced the crickets and chewed through their soft stomachs while rolling the squishy insects between their large fangs.

"Murderer!"

Ben turned and looked at the gallon jar. The faery stood with her arms crossed. She watched him. A rigid frown creased her beautiful face. She pressed her hands against the glass and her fingertips glowed green. Her broken and tattered wings hung like ribbons down her back.

He set the board down and turned to face her.

"Murderer!" she said, fuming.

"What is your name?" he asked.

She glared at him. Her emerald eyes beamed with fury.

"Look," Ben said. "I'm sorry I hurt you. I never imagined something like you existed."

She crossed her arms and her eyes narrowed even more.

"What is your name? Could you please tell me?"

"Shawndirea," she replied in a sour tone.

"A beautiful name."

"Am I next?" she asked.

"For what?"

"To die."

"Why would you say that?"

Shawndirea nodded toward the pinning boards. "You killed *them*. And you're holding me prisoner inside this . . . this glass bottle. I don't see why you'd spare me."

"I never intended to hurt you."

"Your intent was brutal . . . nonetheless."

"I know. I thought you were a butterfly. I never would have imagined you were a . . ."

"Faery?"

"Yes. I'd never hurt you. I wouldn't have captured you. You're more beautiful than any creature I've ever seen."

"And yet, you kill all these without remorse."

"They're not like you."

She held a piece of her tattered wing out for him to see. With wide eyes, she shrugged. "No?" she said.

Ben sighed. "They are insects. You're much more than that."

"Am I? So you're saying these butterflies and moths are *less* than I?"

"Of course."

The piece of tattered wing slipped from her fingers. She crossed her arms again and said, "Humans. All of you think such foolish nonsense. You think all other creatures are beneath you. You're more savage than you realize."

Astounded, Ben said, "You actually consider insects equal to yourself?"

"We all have our place."

"I agree, but you're the only faery I've ever seen."

Shawndirea frowned. "So not seeing one doesn't mean I don't exist, does it?"

"I can't deny your existence, but why don't we see more of your kind?"

"Because we choose not to inhabit your realm, and with good reason as you can see." She held her arms up to shoulder height, showing the shredded ribbons of her once glorious wings. A tear trickled from her eye and streaked down her cheek.

Ben's eyes moistened with tears. "I truly am sorry. I don't know how to make this up to you."

"Obviously, there isn't anything *you* can do to reverse my situation."

"Can you?"

"No."

"So faeries cannot do magic?"

"We can. Just not on ourselves."

"There must be some way to repair your wings," he said.

"Not in this realm."

"I could take you back to yours."

"I'd suffer greater punishment for bringing back a human than the damage you've already inflicted on me."

"Again," Ben said, extending his hands.

"No more apologies."

Ben leaned closer to the jar. He stared into her beautiful angry eyes. As she studied his, the coldness in hers softened. She looked away, somewhat surprised and startled.

"Are you okay?"

She wiped tears from her brilliant, green eyes.

"I mean, other than the loss of your wings?"

"I'll survive, if that's what you're asking," she replied in a soft, sad voice.

Ben gave a slight nod. "You . . . you won't bleed to death or anything?"

"No."

"Listen, I'd be happy to take you back to your homeland, if you'll allow me. Of course, you'd have to show me how to get there."

"No," she replied. "The risks are too great for you and I."

"I'm afraid they are greater for us if you remain here."

Shawndirea turned and faced him at the slight sound of worry in his voice.

"Why?" she asked.

"I'm not the only one who knows about you."

"So?"

Ben shook his head, took the jar in his hands, and held her inches from his face. "No, you don't understand. The man who knows about you would probably kill me to take you."

"Oh, I'm not that important."

"To him you are."

"What makes you believe that?" she asked.

"Because he pulled a gun on me earlier."

"But you possess me."

Ben shrugged. "His gun was unloaded, but once he finds out where I live, he'll bring a loaded one."

"I doubt he'll be that persistent."

"If you saw the greedy glint in his eyes, you'd believe me. He's well capable of murder in his present state of mind."

"And if he took me, what would he do to me? You did enough dam—" she shook her head and waved her hands. "Sorry. You apologized. Anyway, what harm do you believe he'd do?"

Ben swallowed hard, and then he took a deep breath. "Worse than what I've done with these butterflies and moths."

Shawndirea's eyes widened slightly. Her face paled. Her shoulders drooped.

"Getting to my realm isn't easy. There are dangers you've never encountered. Horrible things you've never imagined. Creatures unlike anything in your realm."

"Maybe so. But I *owe* you."

"You owe me nothing . . ." Her eyes stared questioningly. "You never told me your name."

He smiled. "Ben."

With a slight frown, she shook her head and said, "That name doesn't suit you."

"You have a better one?" he asked with a slight grin.

Shawndirea folded her arms and tapped her chin with an index finger. "I'm sure one will come to me over time."

Ben chuckled. "When it does, tell me. I'm curious what you'd pick."

"Oh, I will. But you don't owe me anything."

"I will get you home."

"Don't make a pledge you cannot keep."

Ben's smile parted his beard. "I will get you home."

Nervousness and concern reflected in her deep green eyes. "We shall see."

"I guess I should find you a place for the night. This room probably makes you uncomfortable."

"No, this is fine."

"Here?"

Shawndirea nodded.

"These dead insects obviously disturbed you earlier. Why would you want to be here with them?"

She shrugged. "For spiritual reasons."

Ben set the jar down and with a look of confusion, he asked, "You're sure?"

She nodded.

"I can't leave you in this jar," he said.

"It's fine. I'll be okay."

"I don't want you to feel like I've imprisoned you."

She shook her head. "With my damaged wings, I'm actually safer *inside* the glass than outside."

"From?"

"Mice, spiders, or whatever else might frequent your home," she said with a wry smile.

"I get it. I don't clean a lot. But the house isn't infested with rodents. Spiders, *maybe*, but no mice or rats."

She laughed. "Without wings to fly, I really am safer inside this glass enclosure."

Ben smiled. "I'll get you out first thing in the morning."

CHAPTER 3

eiko paced his apartment living room floor. From the moment he first saw Ben capture that faery, Deiko was possessed with a strange, sudden desire to have her for his own. Never had a feeling gnawed inside him with such overpowering urgency. He didn't understand, nor could he attempt to explain *why* he had to get her at all costs. He couldn't shake the dark force controlling him.

He ran his fingers through his black hair and uttered a low growl of frustration. He picked up his cellphone off the end table and scrolled through his contacts. He touched the screen and autodialed the biology department head.

"Dr. Thorsom, this is Isaac."

Thorsom audibly yawned and said, "This better be important. It's terribly late for you to be calling me."

"Sorry. Could you tell me how I can get in touch with Ben?"

"Ben Whytten?"

"Yes."

"At this hour? Why?"

Deiko closed his eyes tightly and bit his upper lip. Releasing a pent up sigh, he said, "It's a personal matter."

"Is it urgent?" Thorsom asked with agitation.

"Yes. I believe so."

"Have you tried calling him?"

Deiko replied, "He doesn't have a cellphone. Anyone on campus *knows* that."

"Landline," Thorsom said firmly.

"It's been disconnected. At least that was the reply I received when I tried the number."

"Then I don't know what else to tell you. I don't have any idea where he lives."

"You've gone hiking and fishing with him."

"So?"

"And he's never taken you to his house?"

"Never. And what business is *that* to you?"

"It just seems odd, that's all," Deiko said.

"Ben is a private man. He tends to keep to himself, other than where his teaching priorities demand; I haven't a clue as to what he does during his spare time. Take a few lessons from him and quit prying into other people's lives."

Veins popped up on Deiko's forehead. Unfamiliar rage surged. Right when he started to yell into the phone, he realized Thorsom had disconnected the call.

"Dammit!" Deiko shouted.

How he wished he had been talking on a landline phone, so he could slam the phone down. His rushing anger made him almost throw his expensive smart phone at the wall, but he caught himself a second before releasing it.

Fuming, he walked to his computer and typed in Ben's name, job description, and college position, hoping the search engine brought up an address where he could find Ben.

Very little information surfaced.

Deiko suspected that Ben lived under an alias because the Internet notoriously tracked people. Detailed personal information files were often too easy to find. But Ben's steps seemed to have been erased.

"Why don't you have a trail to follow?" Deiko whispered.

He attempted a couple of updated searches but still nothing new came up.

In his mind he pictured the small iridescent faery that Ben took from the butterfly net. He wanted the faery. He *needed* the faery. Once he had her, everything he dreamed of achieving fell into place—notoriety, money, and success. He'd be known as the man who unveiled a fictional myth as genuine truth. But that wasn't his only drive for getting her. Something more profound pushed his mind and made her the target of his deepest desires.

But first he had to find where Ben lived. He wouldn't rest until he found him and took the faery for himself. Tossing his cellphone onto the sofa, he grabbed the Ruger he bought at the gun show.

Ben knew more about guns than what he wanted Deiko to know. Otherwise, Isaac reasoned, Ben would not have disassembled the gun so quickly. In fact, he probably would have just tossed the gun in the truck bed and left.

Once Deiko got home, he cleaned the gun and put it back together. The systematic process passed without much thought, almost as if he worked while entranced. When the pieces were in place, he stared at the gleaming metal and smiled. He released the clip and set the magazine on the coffee table. He opened a box of bullets and counted out ten. He held them in his hand until their coldness faded, and he calculated their weight. With methodical movement, he inserted nine bullets. He held the last one between his thumb and index finger, and stared at it.

Again he pictured the flying faery and the exoticness to have such a creature for his own. The more he thought about her, the less interesting the money and fame became. Of course, he wanted all that as well, but owning her seemed more important.

A few moments later the sharp pain in his groin made him wince. Anger boiled inside him as he thought about the cheap shot Ben had taken when he kicked him. The severe kick had dropped him hard and hours later, the pain continued radiating from his severely bruised scrotum. He feared he had suffered a rupture and needed to see a physician, but he couldn't brave the task of having a stranger inspect the injury. Such was too embarrassing. But if the pain persisted . . .

His eyes locked on the brass bullet. Amazing that something so small could end a man's life. Quick death if the shot was successful. Agonizing otherwise.

For the pain Isaac suffered, he wanted his colleague to suffer worse agony. He placed the last bullet into the clip and slapped it into the Ruger. Had he discovered Ben's whereabouts, he'd end it tonight and get the faery. Now, though, he had to wait until Ben went to campus and then follow him back to his house. Until that happened Deiko's fury intensified.

CHAPTER 4

*B*en turned off his alarm clock five minutes before it was scheduled to wake him. He had a hard time sleeping through the night. He kept thinking about Shawndirea. Her stunning beauty made his heart beat harder. He fought the urge to return to the room where she was because he didn't want her to feel threatened by his presence. He thought of different things to tell her, to ask her. Although she was tiny, she intimidated him. He struggled to find the proper words to say to her as if he was practicing to ask a gorgeous woman out for a first date. He couldn't quite figure out why she made him feel inadequate, but his pulse increased and sweat coated his hands whenever he thought about her. Nervousness quaked his stomach.

Her beauty captivated him and the perfection of her face was etched in his mind. Even with damaged wings, she held herself with elite regality. He wished he could somehow shrink to her size, but even if he could, he didn't believe she'd ever forgive him for the damage he had done to her wings.

Ben grieved over her injuries. He tried to imagine how beautiful her wings were *before* she happened across his path.

He dressed quickly. Through the narrow hallway he crept. In apprehension and a bit of excitement, he approached the study where she was. Never had such a mixture of emotions pulsed through him. Turning the doorknob slightly, he gently eased the door open. The room buzzed with soft, rasping sounds.

A quick feathery flutter and scrape hit the edge of the door. He opened the door wider. Stunned, he couldn't believe what he saw. His eyes widened and his hands dropped to his sides.

Flying around the room was every butterfly and moth he had collected and mounted in the glass-top boxes. The thousands in his shelved cases were flying as well.

Miraculously they were alive and gently fluttering through the air.

Shawndirea sat on the cotton pad in the jar bottom with a broad smile on her face. Her smile was the most beautiful smile he had ever seen. Her eyes brightened and her face glowed. The curl of her lips was perfect. His heart raced. Her charm flowed more graceful than the butterflies and moths drifting through the room. Her smile alone was enough to make him cherish his next breath, his next heartbeat. A world without the life of her smile was tarnished, dark, and filled with gloom.

For the first time in his life, he knew he could give his heart and life's devotion to someone else. Although she was a faery, he felt his soul reach for hers. He had no doubt his unexpected desire edged with love and destiny. They had been brought together for a reason, and he believed it was something more than getting her to her homeland.

Butterflies drifted to the edge of the glass bottle and tapped the glass with their antennae as though they were paying homage to their queen. Each time one did this; she blew a kiss in its direction and giggled. The butterfly drifted upward and hovered lazily.

Ben cleared his throat.

Shawndirea turned with a start.

"What have you done?" he asked.

When she looked at his surprised face, she gave a little shrug and crinkled her nose.

Ben's eyes glanced from butterfly to moth to butterfly as he asked, "*How did you do this?*"

She smiled. "How else?"

"Magic?" he asked.

"Of course."

A day before he'd have been frantic, possibly gone *insane*, if something happened to his collection. But the warmth of her smile luring the butterflies to her made him realize these were more than just trophies to kill and display. They had identities that Shawndirea recognized and that he hoped one day to identify as well. She had a way of communicating with these glorious insects. For some odd reason, they *knew* her.

Hearing her laughter as each butterfly greeted her prevented Ben from looking at the ordeal as a loss, and incredibly, he was anxious to see what other surprises the little faery might reveal.

Species he had collected over a ten-year period floated through the room. His dated and detailed collection data were now useless. Some biologists lost their minds when fire or floods destroyed their lifetime collections. Laughter crept inside him. He didn't feel loss at all. Only one word explained what had taken place overnight.

Magic.

That was the only way to define what had occurred. All that remained in the insect boxes were the insect pins that had resembled thin stainless steel daggers through their hearts. But the moths and butterflies flew all around the room. They had been dried and brittle. He watched them glide, gently and quietly, and suddenly he saw them differently. As they recognized and greeted the little faery, their connection, their bond, was unlike anything he understood. Each was unique and had personalities that he had previously failed to recognize. Although he couldn't communicate with them like she could, he coveted the ability. Instead of destroying, he wanted to preserve.

The sly grin that curled her lips brought a broad smile to his face. A few seconds later, he found himself laughing.

"You're not mad?" she asked.

Ben shook his head. "No."

"I'm surprised," she replied.

"Why?"

"Most humans would be furious at losing their *prizes*."

Ben shrugged. "Perhaps. But I'm not like most humans."

Shawndirea offered a small smile. Her bright eyes peered into his, and she said, "I'm beginning to sense that, which will help better determine a more suitable name for you."

"Oh? You haven't come up with one yet?"

She firmly planted her hands on her hips and said, "As you can see, I've been a bit busy, but it won't take much longer."

Ben smiled. "So *this* is why you wanted to stay in here last night."

She nodded.

"I thought your reason was more spiritual."

"Can you think of anything more spiritual than creatures being brought back from the dead?"

"I suppose not. I see that you didn't free the tarantulas."

"Spiders don't respect our kind. Releasing them would place the butterflies and myself into grave danger. I can't allow that."

"I see."

"So," she said. "What will you do now that your collection has taken flight?"

"Let me show you."

Ben walked carefully across the room to the window. Several butterflies fluttered against the pane trying to get out. So many large moths had attached themselves to the curtains that the cloth was barely visible. He unlocked the window and gently raised the glass. With a quick, solid punch, he knocked the screen out.

"Really?" she said. "Just like that? You're letting them go?"

Once the outside breeze flowed into the room, the freed butterflies drifted through the open window by the dozens. The lazy moths clung to the curtains.

"What do you expect me to do?"

"Reclaim your collection."

"I couldn't." He shook his head. "I can't."

"Even after all the time you've invested?"

"No. I'm afraid I can't kill them again."

"If I were able to teleport back to my world? Gone in an instant? Never to be seen again? Would you try to catch them?"

His heart ached more at the thought of her vanishing than seeing the collection return to the wild. For a moment, he couldn't speak. Finally, he cleared his throat and said, "I find it hard to believe I'd ever say it, but I think you've ruined me. I couldn't kill any of these. Here or elsewhere. I'll have to burn my collecting nets."

"Good," she said with a nod. "That's more than noble. Now I know I can trust you."

"For?"

Shawndirea smiled. "To take me back to my homeland."

"I told you that I would."

"I know, but I believe you'll do everything you can to protect us."

"The fact that I keep your existence a secret from the world should be enough to let you know that I'd protect you. It's also a reason why I need to get you back home before my colleague finds us. His lust for wealth and fame gives us little time."

Concern furrowed her brow. "You really believe he'd kill you to obtain me?"

"I wouldn't put it past him. I certainly don't want to chance it."

"I doubt I'll ever understand humans."

Ben nodded. "I am one, and *I* don't understand my species, either."

He reached down into the jar. Shawndirea stepped onto his palm. He lifted her out and let her step onto the tabletop. Several of the remaining butterflies swooped low and politely kissed her cheeks with their tongues.

She rubbed the sides of their faces and whispered what Ben assumed were blessings.

Shawndirea raised her arms above her head and outstretched her fingers. She closed her eyes and spoke in a language Ben didn't recognize. Green light glowed around her feet and radiated through her body. Seconds later, the light glimmered from her fingertips. The moths on the curtains awakened and lazily flapped their wings. They unlatched their legs from the curtain and clumsily flew out the window.

When the greenish hue that surrounded her faded, she drooped like a wilted flower and slowly fell to her knees, exhausted. She kept her eyes closed, laid back, and curled into a fetal position.

"You okay?" Ben asked.

"I'm fine. Just tired."

"What did you do?"

"I sent them to return to the wilderness with my blessings. They still have time to reproduce before the leaves are gone."

"The record hot temperatures have held steady far longer than normal this year. Winter will be late."

Shawndirea opened her eyes slightly. When she noticed Ben watching her, she gave a weak smile and sighed.

"You're pale. Are you sure you're okay?" he asked.

"Very weak," she whispered before closing her eyes.

Ben rolled a cushioned desk chair to the edge of the table and took a seat. "What can I get you to eat or drink? I have no idea what faeries eat."

"Honey mixed with water. Any fresh fruit will do."

"Rest," he said, rising. "I'll bring some fruit and something for you to drink."

"Thanks," she said with a weak smile.

"After you regain your strength, you must tell me how I can get you home."

"I will."

"I'll be right back."

SHAWNDIREA WANTED to rise to her feet but dizziness prevented her from doing so. Just barely lifting her head made her stomach sicker.

This human surprised her more than any she'd seen before—here in this realm or in her homeland. Although he had been the one responsible for her injuries, she recognized the sincerity and remorse in his words and facial expressions. He truly felt sorrowful for what had happened, and she wished he was of her species and not human.

Few male Fae suppressed their arrogance long enough to show compassion like Ben had. Bringing him back to her kingdom wrought possible repercussions from her own race, but she had few alternatives since her wings were shredded. Trusting a human with her life was safer than being at the mercy of what predators she'd encounter at ground level. Faeries were blessed with wings and meant to fly. They were too vulnerable on foot but lightning fast in flight.

"Most of the time," she whispered, thinking about how she'd failed to avoid Ben's swift net.

She hardly remembered being captured, other than when she slammed into the end of the netting and thrashed her wings into ruined tattered ribbons. The instant pain that tore through her body had knocked her unconscious. She suddenly realized that had it been someone else that had captured her . . . she might be dead.

Shawndirea groaned as she repositioned herself. She opened her eyes slightly and watched several butterflies flutter into the wind. The way they stretched their wings to catch the morning breeze and drifted upward with the wind's current, she knew she had done what she was destined to do. She had given back life to those who had been killed prematurely. So being captured by Ben had not been a mistake. Fate had crossed their paths.

Edging closer to falling asleep, she wondered if their meeting was meant for something more, something deeper. Was he supposed to pass through the Underworld to where her kind and other creatures lived? Could he offer a solution to the dark unrest that sought to control her world and its inhabitants? It certainly appeared that way.

BEN HURRIED to his small drab kitchen. Old green wallpaper peeled from the walls. Most of his old appliances had somehow outlived their warranties by twenty years. He opened one of the maple cabinet doors above the sink and took out a small bottle of honey. He measured out a tablespoon and mixed it into a tall glass of water. Not certain how much honey to water mixture he needed, he hoped she found it palatable.

From the old refrigerator he took a fresh blueberry from a pint cup, grabbed the honey mixture, and hurried back to the study. Shawndirea's chest rose and fell in soft breaths. Her eyes remained closed. Ben wondered how much using magic taxed her. At last count he had over twenty-five hundred butterflies and moths mounted in display boxes. That had probably required a massive amount of magic for the faery to bring them all back to life. Not to mention she also had to open each insect drawer and sealed glass-topped box that contained specimens. She did all that *after* having suffered the injuries from her capture.

Ben set the blueberry on the table and balanced a spoon filled with the honey mixture, angling it where it wouldn't tip over.

"Here," he said.

Shawndirea's nose twitched slightly. Her eyes opened, and she smiled. She scooted closer to the spoon, cupped the honey water in her tiny hands, and drank.

"I wasn't sure how much to mix," he said.

"It tastes fine. The sweeter the better though."

Ben turned and took a step toward the door. "I can get more honey," he said.

"No, this is fine. I'm just letting you know that you don't have to worry about making it too sweet."

"Sweet tooth?" he asked with a grin.

"Faeries *thrive* on sugar."

"Noted," Ben said. "How did you get to our world?"

Shawndirea sat back and crossed her legs.

"Had to pass from one dimension into this one."

Ben frowned. "How?"

"You have to find a weak spot in the dimensional wall in order to pass through. There aren't many rifts."

"What about the one where you came through? Can't I take you back there?"

Shawndirea shook her head. "Unfortunately, no. The thin veil somehow reinforced itself after I went through. I believe it was intentional."

"I don't understand."

She pursed her lips. "Someone wants to keep me trapped here."

"Why?"

Shrugging, she said, "It's a long story."

"Have you passed through before?"

Shawndirea nodded. "Only once before. Almost didn't find my way back."

"With that possibility, why would you return to this realm?"

She shrugged. "Curiosity, I suppose. Other reasons, too, because my world is in unrest."

"Why? What's happening?"

"Darkness is spreading through our lands. Evil has taken root and threatens everything we hold sacred."

"Since the veil you passed through sealed shut, how do we find a hole through the dimensional wall?" he asked.

"Caves are the best places to find a rift."

"There are several in this area."

Shawndirea tilted her head to the side and thought. After a few seconds, she said, "Any of them have deep passages?"

"One on my brother-in-law's property, but it is supposedly haunted."

"Haunted?"

Ben nodded.

"Then that's the one we should take."

"Why?"

"It's *not* haunted."

"I don't know. I've been in there. You *hear* voices. Shadows move. I've been touched, shoved, and heard my name whispered many times, but I've never seen anyone or anything."

"The passages must connect to a major rift or pass through one."

"Why would that make a difference?" he asked.

She smiled. "Because some sprites like to frighten people and can quickly move back and forth through the veil to enact mischievousness without being seen. Other creatures are much worse."

"Worse?"

"Some abduct humans and enslave or torture them to death."

Ben shook his head. "People have vanished in this cave. It has become known as Devils Den."

"Not an appropriate name. A devil doesn't cross through a veil like that."

Ben's eyebrows rose.

"Trust me," she said. "I know. There are procedures."

He gave a slight shrug. "I'll take your word for it."

"On the other side of the veil, you'll understand a bit more."

"Maybe. But I'm not certain seeing will clear my thoughts about it."

"How much time would it take to get to the cave?" she asked.

Ben shrugged. "About forty-five minutes. Not more than that. But you should get some rest before we go there."

"No. My strength is coming back. But the time we get there, my energy will have returned. I'll be refreshed."

CHAPTER 5

*D*eiko had parked his car at the far end of the campus parking lot where Ben wouldn't see it. He stood at the window of his second floor classroom and peered through the half-open blinds, watching Ben's parking spot impatiently and eagerly.

"Hi professor," Jim Mathers said, entering the room and taking a seat. "Why are you here so early?"

"Just admiring the early morning while I await Dr. Whytten. Most days he's already here by now."

"Yeah. I think he gets here before the sun rises and checks for moths around the campus lights," Jim replied.

"Well, not today," Deiko replied in a low, slightly agitated, voice. "His vehicle isn't here."

Jim chuckled, "I'd say give him a call, but he swears off using or owning a cellphone."

"I know."

"I guess I can understand why he doesn't own one though."

Deiko turned and faced the student. "Why?"

"His house is out on that ridge. Probably couldn't get any type of reception way out there anyway."

"You've been to his house?"

Jim shrugged. "All of his Field Botany and Entomology students have been there. Great place to collect plants and insects. Some hard to find Lobelias grow along that wooded area. We had a great time, a cookout—"

Deiko took heavy steps crossing the room and towered over Jim. "Which ridge does he live on?"

Jim was a husky young man and more than able to defend himself under the right circumstances, but Deiko's dark glare startled Jim. The gruffness in his voice took Jim by surprise, making him cower in his chair. The sudden closeness caught Jim off guard, creating the false impression that the intimidating professor was even larger than he was.

Deiko noticed the fear in Jim's eyes and smiled. An advantage of being in the authoritative role was knowing most students feared striking a professor or a coach because of the difficulty proving what actually had happened. Without solid proof most colleges allowed leniency for an instructor that had no marks on their record. The same held true for outstanding students, but it depended upon whose story the administration believed.

"Which ridge?" Deiko repeated with a more threatening tone.

For a brief moment, Jim could have sworn that the whites of Deiko's eyes turned black.

Almost stuttering his words, Jim said, "Boykin Ridge. At the very top of the hillside. His house is where the road dead ends."

Deiko turned and walked to the marker board. He took a dry erase marker and wrote: "Today's class is cancelled."

He snapped the cap on the marker and grabbed his satchel off the desk. He glanced at Jim who didn't seem to know whether to leave or stay.

"You're dismissed," Deiko said evenly. "Unless you want to stick around and let the other students know the message *isn't* a joke."

With his eyebrows raised, Jim said, "Whichever you prefer."

Deiko headed toward the door. "It doesn't matter to me."

A FEW SECONDS after Deiko's footsteps faded down the hallway, Lacy stepped into the classroom. Jim politely waved, a bit more nervously than normal, and then he pointed at the board. Although he smiled, his face was pale and his eyes, haunted.

"No class?" she asked with overwhelming excitement. Her blue jeans were tattered with holes in the knees. She walked toward Jim's seat and lowered her book bag.

Jim glanced nervously into her eyes and quickly looked away. He cleared his throat and said, "Yes. Odd, huh? But true."

"Is everything okay?" Lacy asked, standing beside his desk. She flicked back her blonde ponytail. Her bright, blue eyes peered into his. "You look upset."

"Me? Nah, I'm fine."

"No, you're always energetic and chipper. What happened? You look frightened."

Jim stood and grabbed his backpack. After he slung it over his shoulder, he ran a hand through his black hair and shrugged. Gazing down at the floor, he walked toward the door and said, "Maybe a little startled, but not *frightened*."

"Why?" she asked. "Did you encounter a road-rager on your way to campus? Or did something happen here this morning?"

He explained Deiko's questioning, the professor's bizarre behavior, and how Deiko quickly cancelled the class once he found out where Ben lived.

"What do you think it means?" she asked.

"Not sure."

"You don't think he'd try to harm Dr. Whytten, do you?"

"I hope not," Jim said. With a bit of timidity, he glanced both directions down the hallway, fearful Deiko might return. "But he seemed highly agitated. I've never seen him behave like that. He's such a cutup that I never imagined him to have violent tendencies."

"Me either. Should we contact Whytten and warn him?"

"I don't know how we can. He doesn't have a cellphone. The only way to give him a heads-up would be to go to his house."

Lacy smiled and with a voice that was overly cheerful due to the circumstances, she said, "Well, we don't have class. Want to drive out and make certain everything is okay? Dr. Whytten needs to know."

"I suppose that would be the best thing to do."

CHAPTER 6

*B*en put on rugged hiking boots, thick jeans, and brought a light jacket. From previous explorations inside Devils Den, he understood the cave's temperature was much cooler than the outside sweltering heat. He tucked a hunting knife into each of the jacket pockets. He hooked two knife sheaths to his belt and inserted two sharp throwing knives into them. Not certain what Shawndirea feared on the other side of the veil, he didn't want to take any chances. Perhaps she teased him about the dangers, but he doubted it. The more he thought about it, the more he believed her warnings were worth heeding and giving the utmost respect and precautions.

Her eyes not only flirted with him, which he found flattering, but occasionally the fear of returning to her homeland flickered in her eyes. He stared at her, studying her closely. Her attitude was drastically different than the day before. Her injuries were more than enough reason to despise him and question his motives, but she had transformed from the day before, almost warming up to him far quicker than he could have imagined.

Ben liked that she wanted to give him a new name. What she chose indicated the true feelings she held for him—whether detestable or respectable.

One reason he seldom dated was that he found it difficult to read women's hints when they were interested in him. He didn't like the pressure of trying to figure out what a woman's smile indicated. Was she flirting, interested, or simply being polite? He preferred direct approaches. Straightforward conversations. Subtle hints left him clueless.

That's why Ben pursued science and favored collecting specimens because those answers were readily available in scientific books and journals. He might have to invest long hours into research, but the information was out there. Guessing what a woman *might* be thinking placed him into awkward situations. If he misread a smile that he thought indicated interest when the lady was only being polite, he set himself up for an embarrassing moment. He had suffered enough of those.

Shawndirea sent all the signals that she liked him and perhaps was interested in him. But she wasn't human. She was a faery. Hell, she wasn't even the same *height*. Was she flirting just to torment him? Or, like times past, was he seeing only what he wanted to see?

Now wasn't the time to mentally wrestle through the dilemma. Getting her home required his devoted attention to detail and the ability to sidestep any threats of danger they encountered. Their journey would answer most of his questions, but only if they both survived. That meant they had to get to Devils Den quickly. The first danger was getting there before they encountered Deiko, provided the clown professor was smart enough to figure out where to find them.

Ben had never given a lot of personal information to Deiko, or anyone else for that matter, and with good reason. The less people knew about him, the easier it was to maintain a low profile. He never used credit cards. He paid his bills with cash. And he didn't trust phones.

Cellphones had trackers. He refused to buy a vehicle that had installed OnStar. He genuinely distrusted people and believed using such devices allowed people access into his personal life. People violated privacy. Always.

No longer was it enough for people to call someone at home. They seemed to *need* to be able to find others wherever they were at any given time of the day. Cyber-stalkers. People were *always* texting or talking to someone. Although he wasn't a hermit, he loved his privacy.

In a sense, getting Shawndirea to her realm meant discovering a new territory free from the technology he didn't want to be a part of. He wondered if entering a cave he knew was haunted was something he should do. And what if the veil they crossed *trapped* him on the other side? In some ways, he liked the idea of never returning, but the uncertainly of the new life he would live in another realm left unanswered questions he wanted answers to. Unfortunately, the faery only supplied vague answers.

"Only one way to find out," he thought to himself.

Devils Den.

Ben's sister, Lib, and her husband, John McKnight, owned the property where Devils Den surfaced. For years, Ben had tried to map out the passages of Devils Den many times, but each time he journeyed inside, the pathways were different than he had last drawn. Having drawn out the passageways, he knew it wasn't memory lapse, but he didn't exactly know how it had occurred. Something dark and possibly sinister possessed the cave.

Ben had not lied to Shawndirea, either. He had heard voices many times. Several times Ben's name had been whispered, but he never found the person or *being* that called his name. He wondered *how* they knew his name.

He wasn't a jumpy person, but he did believe menacing creatures moved about in the dark recesses of the cave. Even using the brightest lights he could buy, he never found anyone lingering in the cave. With Shawndirea's information of the mischievous creatures passing back and forth between realms, he realized that he had never been alone in that cave. Whatever they were, they didn't want anyone to see them. With the rift they had the ability to remain concealed. Some other creatures were there, and not being able to see them made them that much more dangerous.

He wasn't about to travel inside without some form of protection. Knives worked well in tight places. A gun would be too dangerous. One misplaced shot could ricochet and kill him or Shawndirea. And besides, he hated using them.

Older folks in the area feared the cave and warned John and Lib that they should prohibit anyone from venturing inside. So many haunted rumors circulated through the community that church members drew the conclusion that demons or devils hid within the dark passages and the cave was a portal to hell.

Ben believed their conclusions were ridiculous. But superstitions seemed to go hand in hand with some of the religious country folks, although they'd never openly admit to it.

"Block it up," Old Man Harper had told John at the general store on many occasions. "Seal it shut with cemented blocks to prevent the devils from surfacing from hell. Our world is evil enough."

John had laughed off the remarks many times, but several times he told Ben about his plans to block the passageway. Ben kept convincing John to ignore the old wives' tales, but he didn't know how long John would allow the cave to remain open. John didn't hide his uneasiness and fear too well. He wore his emotions on his face when it came to supernatural stories. Genuine fear creased his wrinkles far more than age ever could.

"But the devils," John said. "Don't you think there's the possibility?"

"Do you?"

John wiped sweat from his brow with a handkerchief. "I don't want to, but several people have vanished inside there. They are documented by the sheriff's department."

"I've been inside many times, John. I'm still here. I've come back each time."

"I know. Did you see any signs of them?"

Ben shook his head. "Never, and I've thoroughly searched the passages."

"And you believe it's safe leaving it open?"

"Believe me. If I suspected such things existed in there, I'd be the first to tell you."

"Wonder what became of the people who never came back out?" John asked.

"Hard to say," Ben replied. "There's always the possibility of drop offs or wild animals. You never know. Maybe they had come out a different way, got lost, and died where no one would stumble across their bodies?"

"I suppose that's possible."

"Some caverns run for miles underground."

John shook his head. "But that sounds so horrible to die without anyone able to help. And worse for their surviving relatives not knowing what happened to them."

"I agree."

John sighed with frustration. "I've had over a dozen church folk out here this week begging me to seal off the cave."

"You don't go to church."

"I know."

Ben shrugged. "It's your property. Don't let others scare you into something you don't *have* to do."

John chuckled. "Everyone at Harper's Grocery now calls the cave Devils Den."

Ben smiled. "I kind of like that. That will keep people from trespassing."

"Or just attract crazier types out here."

"That's true, too."

John shook his head and said, "Devils Den."

Soon the name Devils Den stuck. All the elderly men that gathered at Harper's Grocery every morning added even more myth to the cave than fact. If a cow died, or an odd weather occurrence happened, the blame was cast that another demon had escaped from the cave.

The expanding tales were so vivid that John refused to enter the cave, and he owned it. Ben was glad that John didn't go inside. He hated to lie to

John about not encountering anything in order to keep the cave open, but John had been shaken enough without Ben adding to his worries.

The haunting stories had a different effect for Ben.

The idea of people being afraid to go near the cave thrilled him. Their fear allowed him to keep the place to himself. And in spite of the whispering voices that echoed inside, he kept returning. Nothing bad had ever happened to him while exploring. No major injuries. Had he lost blood or limb, he'd rethink his logic and gather at Harper's Grocery to add more spice to their tales. In many ways it was like a curious person playing with an Ouija board. Some bizarre things might happen, but it seldom deters one from seeing what might happen the next time.

Ben had often wondered whether the cave actually led to another world, and with Shawndirea telling him it did, he was mentally prepared to follow the path until they discovered a breach in the veil to cross to the other side. He'd like to know what the pranksters that had toyed with him on previous visits looked like. Of course he might *not* like discovering what they really were, and again, they might flee once they discovered he could see them after crossing the barrier. At least he believed he might be able to see them.

As he thought about that, he wondered if he'd actually *want* to see them.

Ben tucked a narrow, pointed letter opener made of silver behind his belt buckle. He shoved a Swiss Army knife into his front pocket. For some odd reason, this seemed a rather needed necessity.

He grabbed his backpack and went to the kitchen. He poured honey into a half full bottle of water, tightened the lid back on, and shook it vigorously. From the table, he tucked several apples, a blueberry, and some hard cheese into the pack. Sliding open a drawer near the sink, Ben took a flashlight, some extra batteries, matches, and a piece of flint. After placing these inside the pack, he took several candles as a last option should he need them. He opened the cabinet under the sink and grabbed a small First Aid Kit.

Confident that he had enough essentials, he went to his mudroom and took his canteen off a nail. He rinsed it and filled it with fresh water. He took a quick inventory of everything once more.

Once he was certain that he wore suitable clothes and had ample weapons to protect them, he returned to the study. Shawndirea sat at the edge of the table and swung her feet back and forth. A black swallowtail glided above her. Her lips moved, but he didn't hear any sound. He smiled and wondered if she possessed the ability to speak in such a high frequency that the insects were capable of hearing and understanding what she said.

The butterfly seemed to dance on air and encircled her several times before making a final spiral and drifting to the open window.

"Amazing," Ben said.

Shawndirea turned in surprise and grinned. Her face was more beautiful than he remembered. And her smile. The glorious shape of her lips took his breath. So much came with the brightness of her smile. All worry seemed to vanish. He'd fight the most dangerous creature in the world to protect her. He'd give his life to ensure hers was spared.

Her energy must have returned. Radiance glowed from her. Her emerald eyes gleamed and twinkled.

"They are drawn to you," he said. "They honor you."

She laughed softly.

"What?"

"You'll understand soon enough."

Ben thought of those words and couldn't tell if she hinted a subtle threat or that she'd reveal secrets untold.

CHAPTER 7

$\mathcal{J}$im drove slowly through the campus parking lot. He stopped, looked both directions, and pulled out onto the highway.

Lacy texted on her hot pink cellphone. She hit 'send' and a broad smile curled her lips.

"I see why Dr. Whytten hates cellphones."

Lacy playfully slapped his arm and said, "Oh now, I see you on yours all the time."

Jim winced and rubbed his arm. "You over exaggerate."

"Now, Jimmy."

"Jim," he quickly corrected. "I hate being called Jimmy."

"Why?"

"Because it makes me sound like I'm a six year old kid."

"Aww," she said. "I bet you were cute then."

He scowled.

"Oh, I don't mean that you're *not* cute now." Her face reddened, and she quickly looked out the side window. "I should shut up."

He glanced at her and noticed her embarrassment. This side of her he had never seen before. Normally she was a bit loud and never at a loss for words, but seeing her shy and a bit awkward made her more down to earth. He liked that she was comfortable enough to let her guard down.

Jim refused to allow their brief silence to escalate.

He cleared his throat and said, "It's just that my father always called me Jimmy or Jimmy Boy when he tossed softball with me at the park. Then one day he split. He left my mother and me. He abandoned us. From then on I insisted that she called me Jim because I was the man of the house."

"I'm sorry."

"Don't be."

She glanced at him. "So how old were you when he left?"

"Probably around eight."

"Do you ever see him?"

"No. I don't particularly want to, either. We're actually better off since the deadbeat left."

Lacy noticed the conversation was making him uncomfortable, so she changed the subject. "Who do you text after classes? Your girlfriend?"

"No."

"Sorry. I'm being nosy, aren't I?"

"It's okay. I text my mother. I have to check in on her every few hours."

"Why?"

"She's in hospice care. She has cancer."

Tears formed in Lacy's eyes. She looked away.

"She insists that I don't drop out of college. She made me swear that I wouldn't because she wants me to be successful. After classes I head straight to where she is and study for hours."

"That has to be hard," she replied.

"It was much harder several weeks ago. She was in so much pain," Jim sighed. "Since she's in the last stages of bone cancer, they've given her a morphine pump. She stays too doped up to feel the pain, which is sad because I miss talking to her. I read my notes and books aloud so she knows I'm near. Most of the time she's too incoherent."

Lacy placed her hand atop his and squeezed. He didn't move his hand. The warmth of her fingers made him take a quick breath. He turned his hand slightly, and without hesitation their fingers entwined.

He glanced at their hands and then to her eyes.

She smiled. "Things will be okay."

Jim felt his throat tighten. He fought tears. "I don't think she'll live much longer."

"Sometimes we lose people," Lacy said, squeezing his fingers with hers. "Everyone faces this. Sometimes it's way sooner than it should be. We question, but there really isn't a good answer. It happens."

"I know. I've sort of accepted it. The prognosis is too clear to ignore. And I know it sounds bad, but if she dies, she won't suffer anymore."

"I understand."

"It still hurts."

Lacy nodded and wiped away her tears with her free hand. "No matter the end result, you're a strong person."

"Let's just figure out why Deiko is bent on finding Dr. Whytten," Jim said with a shaky voice. "I need this distraction."

"That makes sense."

"I can't see any reason why Deiko would suddenly become angry with Dr. Whytten."

"That's where the mystery is," she replied.

"Solving a mystery is a great way to occupy my mind. Besides, I like puzzles."

Lacy smiled. "Me, too. But of all the professors we have, Dr. Whytten is everyone's favorite. He makes biology fun to learn."

"I know. Do you think Whytten may have pulled a revenge practical joke on Deiko?"

"If he did, Deiko definitely deserved it. Although I have found him funny at times, sometimes his bizarre sense of humor is more aggravating than amusing."

"I agree."

They looked at one another and smiled.

"So who do you text?" Jim asked.

"A couple of my friends."

"On campus?"

"No, from high school. They decided to go to other universities. I miss them."

Jim nodded. "A lot of my friends did the same. My best friend went to a college in Louisiana. Too far away to come in for the weekends."

Glancing at him and looking into his eyes, she said, "I'm glad I decided to stay in state."

"I'm glad, too."

Several miles from the campus, the roads narrowed. Trees shrouded overhead, making the morning light dimmer. As he drove, they continued talking. This was the first time he ever really talked to her. Until today, he thought her to be one of the snobby girls because she was much too pretty to be interested in a nerd like himself. But being alone with her, he found his prejudice had been wrong. She was someone he really wanted to be around. He was certain those feelings were mutual.

However, he didn't realize how much danger they were about to get into.

GRAVELS CRUNCHED beneath Deiko's feet as he trudged heavily across Ben's steep driveway. Set with unshakeable determination in his stride, he held his Glock tightly in hand. This time the gun wasn't empty. This time what he planned wasn't a joke. He intended to take the faery for himself and kill Ben if the need arose. At the very least he'd make Ben suffer as much pain as he had for the cheap groin shot.

Science had solved many mysteries and myths over the generations, but some things science could never touch, never explain. The faery was one of those. For hundreds of years many cultures had written about seeing them, their magic, and their mischievous pranks. It wasn't coincidence that so many had written records of such encounters. Faeries existed, and he sought to claim the discovery for himself.

Through his binoculars, Deiko had watched Ben capture one. And if there was one faery, there had to be others. But where? That's the answer he sought. Once he had her, he'd find out where she came from and much more.

Deiko never thought he'd ever find himself capable of killing another human simply because he loved interacting with people and making them laugh. After his confrontation with Ben, something inside Deiko snapped. A dark entity or force sought to control him. Thinking back to when he held the unloaded gun on Ben, Deiko loved the surge of adrenaline and power that rushed through him. He had never felt such control over another person. For a brief few minutes, he thought Ben would hand over the faery or at least tell him that he had caught her. Deiko *might* have considered sharing the discovery spotlight with Ben if Ben had not chosen to be so stubborn.

However, Ben had fooled him. He had never really shown any fear of the gun, but Deiko truly thought he had the edge, even with the unloaded gun. When Ben had told Deiko with such cool smugness that he could have thrown a knife and dropped him before he pulled the trigger, Deiko actually believed Ben was capable of doing so. He had no doubts that Ben could have delivered on that statement.

This meant that had Deiko not put the gun away, Ben would have killed him instead of inflicting severe bruising in Deiko's groin area. After a quick wince, he wondered if death might have been a favorable relief.

He found himself loathing Ben and wanting to hurt him. That urge continued to grow, and now he no longer resisted. He longed for vengeance. Taking the faery from Ben was probably the most pain Deiko could inflict on his colleague. Death meant no suffering. The faery was Ben's prize possession. That's why he wanted to keep her a secret and keep her for himself. Taking her would hurt Ben in the worst way, but Deiko understood Ben would pursue him, and when he did, Deiko had no choice but to kill him. He didn't know when he'd have to kill Ben. It wouldn't be days away. Not even hours. It probably would happen minutes after Deiko stole the faery, and he found that acceptable.

From near the house a feathery whispering sound rustled softly. The noise caught his attention and brought him back to reality.

Deiko clicked a round into the gun chamber and headed around the side of Ben's house. One side window was fully opened. Easing closer, he listened for activity inside, but no loud sounds or talking indicated anyone was inside the house. However, the strange whispering continued, but he still wasn't able to locate exactly where the noise radiated.

His heartbeat increased as he held the gun with both hands. Suddenly faced with the possibility of another confrontation, his tightening throat felt drier than cotton. Sweat trickled down his back. Taking a deep breath, he braced himself and mentally talked up his confidence. The gun provided less certainty than he had expected.

Deiko scanned the hillside, down the drive, and seeing nothing, he closed his eyes and took another deep breath. No one had the drop on him as best he could tell, but that was only in the area where he had direct sight. What was around the corner? Who might be waiting for him to make a move and then shoot him?

He could not wait any longer. The gamble was his to make. Gritting his teeth, he pivoted around quickly and aimed the gun through the window into the room.

No one.

Somewhat relieved, Deiko lowered the gun and whispered, "Dammit."

Even though Ben wasn't waiting for him, shock widened Deiko's eyes. On the tables were all of Ben's insect boxes. They were empty.

"What the hell?" he whispered.

Ben was obsessive with collecting butterflies and moths. Nothing on earth would have made the man destroy his collection. Deiko figured Ben would kill someone before he let anyone steal them.

Leaning his head partway through the window, he listened for the slightest sound or movement to reveal where Ben might be. Nothing stirred inside the room, but the whispering echoes grew louder. More intense.

Above his head the soft quivering noises rose.

Looking up, Deiko saw them. Hundreds of butterflies and moths rose in a swirling motion, drifted higher and higher, and slowly the cloud of wings moved like a delicate shimmering tornado being summoned by an unseen force.

"What's going on?" he asked.

They seemed controlled by . . . magic. In disbelief he stood and watched until they floated into the tree canopy and separated outward in different directions. Although his expertise lay outside entomology, he was certain a lot of those butterflies were only found in the tropics. Their bright metallic blue wings let him know that much.

Deiko tucked the gun behind his belt, braced himself on the window-pane, and pulled himself into Ben's study. Lying beneath the window, he took deep breaths as his heart pounded. The fast rhythm of his heartbeat thudded in his ears. Sweat trickled from his brow. He suddenly found himself even more afraid. He feared that at any moment Ben was going to charge into the room to defend his home. Knowing that Ben didn't fear him was enough to make Deiko extra cautious. He wondered if he could fire the gun precisely and fast enough before Ben made a move.

Deiko lay still. His eyes checked every corner of the room, the two doorways, and even in the dim lighting, he believed he was alone. No noises stirred in the house other than his labored breathing. His heartbeat ringing in his ears was nearly deafening. At the height of his tension, he feared he'd suffer a heart attack before finding Ben and taking the faery for himself.

Satisfied the house was empty, he slowly rose to his feet and pulled the gun from the back of his belt. He took several deeps breaths, held them, and exhaled gently. He stepped to the edge of the nearest table and noticed that all the insect pins were still stuck into the bottoms of the boxes, as were the paper data labels. It was odd.

Wing scales were scattered along the tabletops like a fine layer of metallic dust. Looking around the room, he noticed a couple of large moths attached to the curtains. These were nonnative to the country. Rare species like those required permits to import into the country unless they were papered specimens. Living foreign moths were illegal to own without specialized permits.

So why were they here? Ben certainly would have pinned these and stored them in a box with the rest of his collection. Allowing them to be free in the room risked significant damage to their wings. No professional lepidopterist would chance such loss.

But where were his collected specimens? The boxes were empty, and as he inspected closer, there were faint outlines where the fat moth bodies had once rested.

The whirlwind of moths and butterflies that had vanished into the autumn forest didn't make sense. Never in the wild would any entomologist be fortunate enough to stumble across a small cloud with such a vast number of glorious specimens. It seemed, again, like magic.

On another table set a large gallon jar with a thick wad of cotton in the bottom. A cut blueberry had tiny bite marks. Nearby a spoon filled with dark water was balanced close to the jar. His eyebrows rose from the sudden insight.

"The faery!" Deiko gasped.

Somehow she had done this miracle, which meant she couldn't be too far away. The massive resurrection of butterflies and moths had to have happened within the past hour. Surely no more than that. That explained why the insect pins were still in the boxes and the butterfly funnel cloud outside, but where were she and Ben?

Deiko stepped out of the study and into the dark, long narrow hallway. The aged floorboards creaked with each step he took. Still a bit paranoid that Ben might be somewhere in the house, Deiko tried to step lightly, but no matter how softly he stepped, the boards whined beneath his modest weight. At the end of the hall, he came to the living room. He paused to inspect the room before stepping forward.

A small fireplace was on the far wall. The couch and sofa chairs were cluttered with various scientific journals and magazines. Deiko shook his head. Ben really *didn't* have a social life, he thought.

Making his way to the fireplace, he noticed framed pictures on the mantle. One was of a couple that he assumed were happily married by their smiles and the look in their eyes.

At the base of the picture frame a card was still tucked inside its Hallmark envelope. Curiosity got the best of him, so he pulled out the card and opened it. Neat handwriting frilled beneath the typed message: "Great to have a wonderful brother like you."

It was signed, "Your sister, Lib."

Deiko turned over the envelope and found the McKnights' address neatly written on the front. He smiled.

He took the envelope and hurried through Ben's house. He unlocked the front door and stepped out onto the porch. An oak swing rocked slightly in the breeze. The old chains creaked. A gust of wind tossed a wave of leaves into the air. More leaves spiraled from the limbs overhead. Two squirrels played chase around a maple tree trunk.

Caught in the moment, Deiko understood why Ben lived here. He could think of no better place for an entomologist to thrive. Everything Ben loved lived here within reach. He only had a few neighbors nearby, and possibly seldom ever had visitors. Until today.

The gun weighed heavy in his hand. He looked at the address on the envelope and wondered if they could tell him where Ben was. He doubted Ben would actually be there, but the possibility existed.

Way below on the driveway entrance at the bottom of the ridge a car slowed. The brakes squealed. A couple seconds later, the motor revved as the driver headed up the winding drive.

Deiko walked to the edge of the porch. At this distance, he had no idea who might be headed up the ridge toward Ben's house. It could be a neighbor that lived off the side road on a lower side of the ridge. Perhaps it was Ben, but Deiko's guess was that it wasn't, not unless Ben had ditched his SUV for an older car. As he thought it over, the possibility was something Ben might do to throw Deiko off his search to get the faery. It was a drastic decision but not unheard of. After all, there had to be a reason why Ben hadn't shown up at the university this morning, and why he wasn't at home.

The car increased its speed, so Deiko pulled Ben's front door shut and then sprinted across the wide porch, down the steps, and ran through crunching layers of dry orange, yellow, and red leaves to get to his pickup.

Glancing down the driveway, he realized the drive was too narrow for two vehicles to pass one another. He'd have to wait for the oncoming vehicle to reach the top before he could even attempt to drive his truck downhill.

Instead of waiting for the visitor, Deiko tossed his handgun onto the truck seat, climbed inside, and turned around on the paved area outside the garage. While he waited for the car to come into view, he quickly typed the McKnights' address into his GPS locator.

"Twenty-five miles?"

Going there was a great gamble unless Ben had actually gone there. Otherwise, Deiko stood to lose a good half hour or more on a feeble hunch.

With an exasperating sigh, he glanced toward Ben's house. The old cottage almost blended into the rugged trees and leaves. During the summer, other than seeing a driveway headed up the hillside, most people probably wouldn't know a house rested at the top of the three-mile ridge road. The garage held its own camouflaged wonder since it had been carved into the side of the narrow mountainside.

Deiko had parked his truck near the side of the house where it wouldn't be noticeable until the driver was right upon it, so he had the upper hand.

He left the engine running, the door open, and stepped out with the gun in his hand.

The car crept up the winding path, much too slow for Deiko's patience. He glanced toward the garage and back down the drive.

The front of the car came into view. Not Ben. The driver didn't have a beard and looked much younger.

Deiko raised the gun and aimed. He couldn't have any witnesses that he had been at Ben's estate. He squeezed the trigger and fired.

~

AT THE BASE of the three-mile ridge road, Jim stopped the car for a moment and pointed.

Glancing at Lacy, he asked, "This is the right place, isn't it?"

She looked up the winding drive that seemed to disappear around a massive tree and shrugged. "I think so."

"Me, too. It looks so different."

"Lots of leaves. Everything looks a bit different once fall sets in."

"Ah, look," he said, pointing. A rusted sign for Boykin Ridge Road was slightly covered by an oak branch.

Jim backed the car and then proceeded up the road. Lacy held his hand. She had never loosened her hold on his hand during the entire trip. With a day that had started so troubling and hopelessly overcast by the constant fear that his mother might pass away any day, Lacy had somehow lessened his pain and lightened his load.

And while he would lose his mother to her devastating disease, he wouldn't be alone afterwards. He believed she would be there for him to lean on. That's what he hoped and what he truly needed.

Jim gently squeezed her hand. She took her free hand and cupped it around the other side of his, surrounding his hand between hers. He looked at her, and she smiled. Her radiant eyes sparkled. He had no words. From the look in her eyes, he didn't need them. Nor did she. It was the only time in his life when he knew uttering words was useless. Words were a total loss. Here, at this moment, mutual expressions and emotions rendered far more value.

He didn't want to break their eye contact, but the road was narrow and the hillside was steep. He reluctantly placed his attention ahead of them. Something large moved at the edge of the road.

Jim hit the brakes.

A doe sprinted from the trees and darted across the road just a few feet ahead of them.

"Whoa!" he said, shaking his head. "She came out of nowhere."

"Deer are fast."

"And plentiful."

Lacy nodded. "Yes, when you see one, there are usually others nearby."

He waited a moment before easing off the brake. When they were satisfied that no more deer were alongside the road, he drove on.

Approximately one mile up the winding road, a narrow side driveway angled off. A new doublewide trailer set crossways between some massive trees. Flowerbeds encircled the trailer. Orange and yellow marigolds were the size of small shrubs. No cars were in the little parking spot near the road.

"This area certainly has some beautiful places to live," Jim said. "I doubt I'd put a trailer out here, though."

"I love it out here. It's always nice when you are away from the overpopulated areas. The only noises are the sounds of nature."

"Those places are getting harder to find."

"I know."

Jim pressed down the accelerator. The motor roared and stubbornly climbed the incline.

"One steep hill," he said.

"Yep."

He shook his head. "I'd hate to drive up or down this slope after the winter snow hits."

Lacy laughed. "You'd slip and slide trying to get to the top, but you'd *ski* down."

"I believe that."

Jim would never admit he owned a clunker, but he couldn't exactly deny it after its poor display pulling the winding driveway. Embarrassed, he put the car into third. The engine revved and inched forward as they passed the only other driveway that shot off the ridge road. This driveway separated and two small brick houses occupied this area of Boykin Ridge.

Cars were parked in each drive, but no one was outside either home, which made Jim feel a bit more at ease. The way the car's motor whined, he didn't want to further add to his embarrassment of others hearing and watching it pull the hillside.

After he drove another quarter mile, Ben's house came into view. Lacy said, "We're almost to the top."

"Thank God," he whispered.

Coming around the last bend, a harsh TWACK! echoed. Flakes of glass burst into the car. The back glass exploded. Lacy screamed.

"What was that?" Lacy asked.

"A gunshot!"

Jim glanced toward Ben's house.

"Get down!" Jim shouted. He pulled her over toward him, and quickly put the car into reverse.

"What's going on?" she asked.

"Deiko. He has a gun."

"You *see* him?"

"Yeah."

Jim gunned the engine. The car shot backwards. A second bullet fired and lodged into the radiator.

Trying to maneuver the vehicle while he looked over his shoulder was impossible. He kept looking at Deiko, unable to take his eyes off the crazed professor, fearful of another round coming through the windshield and killing one of them.

Steam rose from beneath the hood. The punctured hose sprayed antifreeze onto the hot engine. The smell of burning antifreeze crept through the air vents.

Jim veered to the left to keep the car on the narrow road. He hoped he could manage the car long enough to turn into one of the lower drives downhill, but that was a good distance yet to go. When he glanced ahead, Deiko aimed again. Jim panicked and pushed the gas pedal to the floor. The car spun and weaved side to side.

"Stay down," he said when she tried to lift her head.

The back passenger tire slipped off the road's edge and spun. Jim attempted to slow the car by slamming the brakes, but it was too late. The loss of traction caused the car to dip and leave the road.

Lacy screamed.

"Hang on!" he said, trying to hold her close.

The car tipped over the edge, dropping slowly onto a row of saplings. Their thickness only held the car for a few seconds before the weight of the vehicle splintered them. The bottom scraped rock and tree stumps, which slowed its momentum slightly but didn't prevent the inevitable. The plummet down the hillside happened quicker than he imagined.

Lacy screamed as the car rolled over and over. Then she was quiet. Jim hit his head and everything went silent, black.

～

Deiko aimed to fire the third time, but to his surprise, Jim slammed the accelerator. Killing Ben was one thing Deiko had planned to do. Killing a student wasn't something he wanted to do, but the kid had seen him. As much as he liked having Jim as a student, Deiko couldn't let any witnesses escape.

And why in the hell was the student here? To warn Ben? Deiko realized that it really wouldn't have mattered if the opportunity to kill Jim happened today or not. He had forced Jim to give Ben's address in the classroom, which meant that Jim could lead the authorities to Deiko once news surfaced that Ben had been murdered. He would have had to find and kill Jim before that happened. He couldn't believe his fortune.

He ran after Jim. Rounding the next bend, he aimed and fired, but the car left the roadway. The shot struck a small hickory tree and rocked, teetering over the edge.

Preparing to fire again, he noticed the car tilt and slide off the embankment. Within a minute, the car rolled and bounced down the side of the ridge. He stepped to the edge of the drive and watched. The car struck a large boulder and came to a dead stop. A cloud of dust puffed over the car and slowly filtered downward.

Deiko glanced at his watch and waited. On his way up the long road, he had not noticed any neighbors outside their homes. Should any of them be home, he expected the thunderous crash and gunfire to draw them outside. Such a raucous would raise anyone's curiosity.

After five minutes, no one inside the car moved, and he didn't see any neighbors rush to the side of the ravine to check out the crash. Confident only he and nature had heard the incidents, he sprinted up the winding hillside and got into his truck. He dropped the truck into neutral and coasted down the sloping, curving driveway. He needed to find Ben. The McKnights' address was the first place where he could start looking.

He rounded the curve where Jim's car plummeted and stopped. He wasn't for certain, but he thought he saw movement. He grabbed the gun, shut off the truck engine, and watched the crumpled car at the bottom of the ravine. Although finding Ben was his top priority, he thought it best to make certain he left behind no witnesses. While he waited, he took out the gun clip and inserted more bullets. The best that could happen would be for Ben to drive up the hillside where Deiko waited.

Time would tell.

CHAPTER 8

*A*fter the long series of rolls, the crumpled car stopped upright. When Jim opened his eyes, Lacy's face was covered with blood. Her head was slumped to the side and her eyes were closed. Shock tore through him. Quickly, he unfastened his seatbelt and reached for her. She was breathing and her pulse was strong. He let out a deep breath of relief.

"Lacy," he said, gently rubbing her cheek. "Lacy?"

Blood trickled from a small cut on her scalp. The injury wasn't life threatening, but he knew from CPR training that any cut on the scalp could bleed profusely. She also had a goose egg bump on the side of her head.

He opened his dash compartment and got his first aid kit. Taking a gauze strip, he applied pressure to the cut to help stop the bleeding. As he held it in place, he tried to get his bearings.

The last he remembered was going over the ravine and the first couple rolls the car endured before he lost consciousness. He gazed through the splintered windshield, which looked more like a glass spider web than anything else. The car had stopped in a dry rocky creek bed.

Jim removed the gauze for a second. The bleeding had stopped on her head and a soft scab was forming.

"Lacy?" he asked.

He patted her cheek gently.

Lacy's eyes opened. She blinked erratically. Her eyes fought to see clearly.

"Are you okay?" he asked.

She looked around, shook her head slightly, and then she gave a slight nod.

"I think so," she said. "Where are we?"

"At the bottom of the ravine," Jim replied.

She gave a confused smile.

Jim looked into her eyes and smiled. "You had me worried for a few minutes."

She noticed the bloody piece of gauze in his hand. She asked, "Will I be okay?"

"Just a small cut. Are you hurting anywhere?"

She shook her head. "No. Well, I have a bit of a headache."

Their faces were inches apart as they looked into each other's eyes.

Jim said, "Look, I'm so sorry . . ."

Lacy kissed his lips. Her advance caught him off guard for a few seconds, but then he kissed her back. When they separated, their faces flushed red.

"The crash wasn't your fault," she said, hugging his neck tightly.

"Maybe not, but I feel like it was. My driving isn't that great, as you can see."

"We were being shot at. You reacted like I would have. At least you got us out of his range. I might have driven us *up* a tree."

Jim wanted to smile, but he remained serious. "Deiko may still be around. I tried to see where we were, but the only way I can really find out is to get out of the car."

Lacy shook her head. "No. That's too dangerous."

"But he may be headed downhill anyway. I have to check."

"Be careful."

Jim pushed against the passenger door but it was wedged against a large boulder and wouldn't open.

"Damn," he said. "Let me try the other one."

The crumbled door wouldn't budge when he pulled the handle and shoved his weight against it. The side windows were shattered, so their only option was to crawl out.

"Wait right here," he said.

"What are you doing?"

"Going to see if he's out there."

Jim cautiously peered through the window. With the distance the car had tumbled and rolled, he was surprised they had not been seriously injured or killed. He scanned the side of the rocky ravine. He couldn't find a clear path that looked safe enough for them to attempt to reach the top, which indicated Deiko didn't have an easy way to get down to them, either.

Jim placed his hands on the top of the car and pulled himself through.

His feet dropped to the smooth rocks on the dry creek bed. A second later a shot echoed through the small valley. The bullet struck and ricocheted off the top of his car.

Jim ran to the rear of the car and squatted behind the trunk. Through the trees along the ridgeline, he was unable to see where Deiko was positioned.

"Are you okay?" Lacy asked.

"Yeah. He missed. Otherwise, you'd hear my powerful girly scream. No offense."

"None taken."

He took out his cellphone and shook his head. No bars. He tucked it into his back pocket.

"You have any phone reception?" he asked.

"No. Not here."

"I don't either, but that happens a lot in the mountains."

Jim eased around to the driver's side window, which was out of view for Deiko, provided he was still on Ben's driveway. Crouching low, he leaned through her window. She eased closer to him.

"I need you to climb out on this side. He shouldn't be able to see us at this angle."

"Then what?" she asked.

"We follow the creek bed until we find help."

Lacy nodded. "Okay."

She extended her arms to Jim. He remained below the car's top, so Deiko didn't have a clear shot. He helped Lacy out and supported her so she didn't fall face first onto the rocks.

Once she was crouched beside him, he pointed and said, "Stay low. We run for those willows. They should provide a little bit of a blind to prevent him from getting an easy shot."

"All right."

"If I had my deer rifle and scope, though, we wouldn't be running," Jim said with a smile.

"You wouldn't want that on your conscious," she said.

He shrugged. "Maybe not, but right now, I'm a bit pissed."

She placed her hand to his cheek and smiled. "I understand."

He took her hand in his and on the count of three they ran to the willow grove. No more shots echoed. The sound of Deiko's truck winding down in low gear while descending Boykin Ridge Road let Jim know that Deiko was leaving. Glancing ahead at the creek bed that meandered through a shady forest, he wondered where they'd end up. Without being able to find Ben, he wondered if Deiko had killed Ben before they got there. He didn't know, and now he worried.

Not even noon yet, and the sun's intense heat loomed over them, making the humid air thick and difficult to breathe.

"Wait," Lacey said, stopping suddenly and leaning over. "I'm dizzy and sick to my stomach."

Jim looked around for a moment. "Here, lean against me."

She did, and he supported most of her weight as they walked.

The best thing Jim could do until he found out whether Ben was dead or alive was for him to keep Lacy safe. She was his top priority. He was convinced she liked him as much as he liked her. And if so, theirs was the most unusual first date ever. Nothing like having a car wreck and being shot at to liven things up.

Once they reached the shaded area that shadowed the creek bed, Lacy slowed and sat on a fallen tree.

"I need to rest," she said. "Everything's spinning, and my head is splitting."

"Okay, sure. Hold still, let me look at your head again."

Jim gently examined the cut on her head. The bleeding had stopped, but dried blood covered her forehead and the left side of her face. The knot seemed the same size, but her dizziness indicated she might have suffered a concussion.

He ripped a piece of cloth from his shirt and tried to clean off some of her dried blood.

"Wonder what's wrong with Dr. Deiko?" she asked.

"I really don't know. But there was craziness in his eyes."

"You don't think he . . . killed Whytten, do you?"

Jim shrugged. "The thought has crossed my mind. The only way to really know is to go up there."

"Then we should," Lacy said. "We need to follow the creek until we get to the road. We can walk the road back to Ben's house."

"That's three miles straight up the ridge. I'm not certain you're able."

She smiled. "I'm a trooper. I'll be okay."

The uneasiness in her eyes and the uncertainty in her voice indicated she was trying to act tough. He feared she might have a concussion; so taking their time getting to the road was safer than hurrying in the outrageous heat without water. If she passed out, he'd have to leave her to find help, and he didn't want to be faced with such a possibility.

"Maybe we'll get some bars somewhere so we can call for help. A ride up that ridge would be better than walking. Besides, I didn't see any trails back up from where the car went off the road that we could take."

"A ride would be nice."

"Yes. But if we have to walk," Jim said, "Deiko should be far from here by the time we get to Whytten's house."

He took her hands into his and smiled at her. She blushed.

"I'm glad that you're okay," he said.

"I'm glad that you are, too," she replied. "I'm okay. We should go. At least our day didn't end in tragedy. Let's hope the best for Dr. Whytten."

Jim took her hand. She slipped off the side of the tree. Together they walked down the dry creek hand in hand.

CHAPTER 9

*B*en drove along the back roads. Shawndirea stood on the dashboard and stared through the windshield. Showers of whirling leaves fell from the maples and oaks and skidded across the blacktop.

So many thoughts went through Ben's mind. He glanced at the faery. Her radiance glowed on her face. Her beauty was beyond anything he'd ever seen. Looking at her wilted, tattered wings, he winced. How it hurt to know he had done such damage to her. He hoped her wings could be magically repaired once they returned to her realm.

She smiled when songbirds flew across the road.

Her smile continued to captivate and lure him. The perfectness of her face enraptured him, making it nearly impossible at times to not stare at her.

"Lovely countryside, isn't it?" Ben asked.

Shawndirea nodded. "It's attractive, but not nearly as lush as the forests in my world. Not near the dangers here as there, either. Don't say you weren't forewarned."

"I won't."

Her eyes focused on the blacktop. She shook her head and said, "I'm afraid I'm not too fond of your realm."

"Why is that?"

"All the damage you do. These black scars that cut through forests, fields, and cross over waterways. Your roads diminish what might otherwise be spectacular."

Ben nodded. "You won't hear me argue against that. The advancements of technology greatly bother me, too. It has for a long time."

She turned and faced him, studying his face. "You wouldn't simply say that to impress me, would you?"

He frowned. "Of course not."

She studied his eyes intently for several moments.

"I believe you. How much farther?" she asked, changing the subject.

"A few miles. Maybe ten minutes."

"Good. I sense I'm needed."

He frowned. "Even though the veil separates you?"

She nodded. "Our world is connected to yours. A magical barrier doesn't shut off nature's pain. Evil lurks beneath the surface and travels through realms inflicting as much damage as possible. Its tendrils reach far."

"Evil exists here, too."

"On a different level."

"How so?" Ben asked.

A thin smile curled her lips. "In your world, most individuals and creatures have a conscious that keeps them in check. Of course, there are always those here who abandon restraint to kill, rape, or mutilate. In my realm, some creatures are bred and born without a conscious. They exist solely to inflict pain and destroy."

"Like demons?"

"Some are spawned from demons. But sorcery has contaminated the souls of many races in my world. Even my race."

"I will get you where you need to go."

Shawndirea studied his determined face for a few moments and shook her head. Sadness filled her eyes. "Perhaps it's best that you don't."

"Why not?"

"You don't understand how others will view it if I bring a human into our kingdom."

"I refuse to abandon you after what I did," Ben said.

"There are others who can get me home."

"No. For damaging your wings, I need to make this right. It's my obligation."

"We don't exactly have peaceful terms with humans," she said softly.

"Aren't there humans in your realm?"

"There are. That's where the contention lies. Amongst other things."

Ben frowned. "I don't understand."

"And you won't. Let's just say that treaties were broken between our species."

"But I've no part of that."

"No," Shawndirea said. "But they won't care *where* you're from. They will only see you as a human. To them, *that's* all that matters."

Ben smiled. "Then I'll have to prove myself to them."

"Not a task so easily done."

Ben slowed and turned onto a dirt road.

"We're getting closer," he said. "At the end of the road is where we can get to Devils Den."

Ben glanced toward the McKnights' farmhouse as he passed. No one was outside, which was good. He didn't want to talk with John at this time. Doing so meant that he'd have to hide Shawndirea, and with everything she had endured, she didn't need cramped out of sight.

John never had a problem with Ben parking his vehicle on the property while he explored the cave. That was usually for only a few hours or a day at the most. But Ben had no idea how long he might be in the other realm.

Should he leave the SUV parked too long—days or perhaps weeks—John might panic and get authorities to organize a search for him. The last thing he needed was more attention on Devils Den with someone *mysteriously* disappearing again. The community was already slated against John for refusing to block the cave. Should Ben be gone longer than normal, they might take matters into their own hands and seal the cave *without* John's permission. Ben needed Devils Den to remain open. It might be the only passage he had to return to the surface.

Ben parked the SUV, gathered his jacket, his pack, and then he extended his palm for Shawndirea to step upon. She did so elegantly.

"Where is the cave?" she asked as he opened the pasture gate.

Ben pointed and said, "Through those trees on the other side of the pond."

The sun disappeared behind thick dark clouds. The area darkened. Crows cawed from the trees surrounding Devils Den.

Her vivid eyes scanned the forest line and widened slightly.

"What is it?" he asked.

"It *is* a place where evil surfaces," she said softly.

"As rumors and superstitious wives tales have stated," he chuckled.

"No rumor or wives tales," she said with a serious tone. "Yes. It dares us to enter."

"Ahh," Ben said with amusement in his tone.

"That's *not* a good thing."

"We have to enter."

Shawndirea nodded. "We do, but be prepared."

"I am," he said, placing his hand on his knife.

"No. Your weapons are useless with some of these creatures."

"Then how?"

"My magic."

Ben replied, "I'm not exactly equipped that way."

"I know."

"Are you strong enough?" he asked.

"I have to be."

"I believe you're trying to frighten me."

She smiled. "Fear is sometimes the best respect you can offer."

"It can also get you killed."

"I won't deny that," she said with a firm gaze toward the cave. "But when an enemy senses fear, they tend to drag out their torture before they kill you."

Ben frowned. "And how is that good?"

"Gives you an opportunity to make an unexpected attack."

"I'll try to remember that."

Ben hurried across the pasture, around the dam of the pond, and into the shade of the forest. The mouth of the cave was dark, much darker than normal. Cool air seeped out. The coldness radiated farther than it should.

"Wait," Shawndirea said.

"What is it?" he asked.

"Not sure."

While they watched the cave, several bats fluttered out.

"This place doesn't feel right," Ben said. "Something's different."

"Good. That means you're awakening to understand what lies beneath your world."

More bats exited and shrieked.

"It taunts us," she said.

Thunder rumbled overhead.

"What's happening?" Ben asked. "The sky was clear before we got here."

"It's a warning for me to stay here."

"I've never had anything like this occur before. I've come and gone freely. Sure, there's been days of strange things *inside* the cave, but never outside."

"That's because you are human and cannot perform magic. I'm the one he wishes to keep out. I sense his presence."

"His?"

Shawndirea nodded. "A powerful sorcerer has placed his magical hold over this cave. Finding a rift to pass through won't be easy. He'll do everything possible to keep us from getting to the Underworld, so we can cross into my realm, Aetheaon."

"Aetheaon?"

She nodded.

"Why does he want to keep you here?"

She smiled. "I'm weaker on this side of the veil, and I cannot help my race when they need me the most."

"What is the urgency for your people?"

"In time you will understand."

Thunder bellowed.

"How is it possible for him to control the weather from the other side?"

"He's powerful, but he doesn't control the weather. He creates a good illusion though."

"No real thunder?" Ben asked, looking at the sky. The rolling black clouds swirled. Lightning flashed. Another grumble of thunder shook. "Looks real to me."

"Real if you believe it is."

"So do you know who he is?"

She shook her head. "No."

"Will we find out?"

"Let's hope not."

Ben walked to the mouth of the cave. Cold air funneled out, which felt good in the sweltering heat, but the cave temperature held an icy touch. Like death. Ben had been inside Devils Den dozens of times, but this was the first time he felt uncomfortable entering. He feared it might be his last time, too.

"I'm ready whenever you are," she said. "That is, if you still want to go."

Voices echoed from deep inside Devils Den. Ben had heard them before, but never quite this angry and never this close to the surface. Their undecipherable chattering vibrated off the walls. At other times it sounded like goats bleating. Even more disturbing were the painful moans from what sounded like tortured people.

He wondered what they might encounter once he stepped inside Devils Den with Shawndirea. Would he actually see these mischievous imps this time, and would their games no longer be playful? Perhaps now, they played for blood. But that was okay. He might bleed a little, but he was certainly going to try to make them suffer and bleed more.

Ben took a deep breath and said, "Let's go."

CHAPTER 10

*B*en's flashlight was bright. The wet walls shimmered in the light. But the cold was harsher than he remembered. No more than fifteen feet into the cave, and he had to put the jacket on. His breath made little clouds when he exhaled.

Shawndirea sat upon his right shoulder.

Moving through the cave tunnel wasn't easy. The atmosphere was thick, heavy, and for some odd reason, he felt like he was trying to walk through waist deep water. Lifting his foot was like tugging against an attached iron anchor. His boots seemed to weigh a ton. A cold invisible force also pushed against him. Never had he faced such opposition any time he had been inside Devils Den. She had not exaggerated about something or someone wanting to keep her out.

In spite of the bright flashlight, their visibility was limited to less than a few feet ahead of them. The darkness seemed to swallow the light, much like a black hole in space. The void was empty, quiet, and eerie. Each step he took made him wonder if it might be the last. Voices echoed deeper in the shadows beyond his light's reach. Occasionally, the walls moved and seemed to breath.

"It's never been this way before."

"It will get worse," she said.

Ben didn't doubt her prediction, but he wasn't inclined to turn back, either. What he had encountered many times in here was only from his side of the veil. He wanted to know what kingdoms lay beyond and what creatures he'd discover. Or perhaps after he gave it more consideration, he wouldn't. But at this particular moment, his curiosity had the better of him.

"This light has a longer range distance than this," Ben said.

He flashed the light against the wall for a moment. One of the protruding rocks suddenly turned into a hideous face. He stepped back.

"It's not real," Shawndirea said.

"You said that about the thunder."

She frowned. "Don't tell me you still think it was *real*?"

Ben shrugged.

Shawndirea shook her head. "I don't think our journey looks too promising."

"Why?"

"Because you're falling for the simplest tricks."

"Until you," he said, "I didn't know magic existed."

"Again, that's why I don't think we should venture farther."

"I imagine you'll teach me."

"There's not time."

Ben smiled. He loved hearing her voice directly in his ear. Her resonance was the most pleasant sound he had ever heard. Her soft tone and rich faery accent was alluring.

"Are you indicating that I could learn magic?" he asked.

"Anyone can. Some do and never know it. It's best to know the intent of your heart before you begin."

"How could someone perform magic and not know they're doing it?"

She whispered, "It depends upon how badly someone wants something to occur. Not all intentions are good ones. Some are pure evil."

Ben replied, "If I even considered learning magic, I don't know what I'd use it for."

"Just remember one thing," she said.

"What?"

"Using magic comes with a cost. There is *always* a price."

"And that is?"

Shawndirea replied, "Depends on the spell. Dark magic requires sacrifice. Blood or animal. Magic of the light is more complicated."

A low guttural growl rose further down the tunnel.

"But now isn't the time we should discuss it."

Ben nodded. "Sounds like we have company."

For a moment he thought that the sound might have come from the face on the wall. He took the flashlight and shone it upon the rock again. The face was gone.

"Told you," she said.

Stepping forward, Ben staggered as the floor shifted. He set his foot firmly upon the path. Had all these unusual things occurred when he was alone and without Shawndirea's warning, he'd have thought himself crazy and never returned. The fact that she knew strange occurrences would take place didn't make the situation much easier, however. He wondered exactly what she had *not* warned him about.

Ben crept through the cave corridor, and advanced slowly around the next curve. Here the light radius shrank even further, almost like the light retreated, but he knew that wasn't possible.

"How will we be able to know where the veil is? We cannot even see three feet ahead of us."

"It will be tricky."

"I could have told you that. I've been in this cave many times. Never have the passageways been the same twice."

"The sorcerer has great power."

Ben glanced toward Shawndirea, and a smoke-like image appeared outside the radius of the light near the moist cave wall. He turned the light toward it and it vanished. He had never seen a ghost, but he was certain that was what had loomed nearby.

"Did you see that?" he asked.

"No. What did you see?"

"Not quite sure. I'd guess it was a ghost."

Shawndirea shrugged and smiled. "You probably did, which means we aren't far from the veil."

"How can you be certain?"

"Spirits often wander before they find peace, especially if they died at the hand of this particular sorcerer."

"Why did it vanish?"

She replied, "Spirits shun the light."

Again, at the edge of the light, the spectral image drifted. This time Ben didn't turn the light toward it because he didn't want to lose sight of it. Training the flashlight on the opposite wall, he watched as two others soon joined the lingering spirit. These were more detailed, wearing tattered cloaks and robes. The first did not have an actual body outline. It was residual and simply hovered like a long stream of fog on a cold morning.

"Do you see them?"

She shook her head. "No."

"Then why do I?"

"Perhaps you're an empath?"

"Not that I know of. I've been here many times. Never seen a thing."

Shawndirea placed her hand to his cold cheek. "Then your guess is as good as mine."

Ben said, "Then what's your guess?"

"Exactly what I suggested."

He frowned, still watching the spirits slink through the corridor. "Why now?"

She leaned and whispered in his ear, "Maybe my magic has enhanced what you didn't know you had."

Chills shot through him as the formless being crept closer. He turned the light quickly. The spirit screeched and dissolved into nothingness. The other two retreated in slow, bobbing movements.

Seconds later, a low voice with an evil tone whispered, "Give the faery to me, and you may keep your life and flee."

"Never," Ben said.

"Then you shall die!" it hissed.

Shawndirea looked at him. His eyes were wide and searching. "What do you mean, 'Never?'"

"You didn't hear that?" he asked.

"No."

"Something has demanded I give you to them, and it will let me live."

Shawndirea stood on his shoulder, outstretched her hands, and said, "Be alert. Our challenges are about to begin."

She closed her eyes, whispered a chant, and green light glowed at her fingertips. Instinct brought Ben's hand to the hilt of his hunting knife. She thrust her hands forward. A blaze of greenish-blue flames shot across the cave path before them. The two retreating ghosts blazed into small balls of fire before vaporizing. The wet walls shimmered green as her fire rolled through the corridor. When her light faded, she stumbled and sat on Ben's shoulder.

"You okay?" he asked.

She nodded, closed her eyes, and took a deep breath.

At the curve of the corridor where the shot of her green flame ended, large burning eyes glowed. A deep growl reverberated and echoed toward them.

"You dare reveal my presence?" it asked. "Today you're both mine."

"Illusion?" Ben asked. "Or real?"

"Oh, it's very real," she whispered.

"So you *do* see it?"

"Unfortunately, I do."

$\mathcal{D}$eiko drove along the road that would eventually take him to the McKnight farm. The gun lay on the seat beside him. At some point he knew he had to find Jim and kill him before he contacted the authorities. His mind struggled with what he was becoming, but his growing obsession to announce his discovery for fame and whatever financial gain he might receive was consuming him. He no longer had a problem murdering people to achieve such goals. But a darker force pressed his mind to get the faery, to take her.

He glanced in the rearview mirror and gasped. His eyes were dark, strange, and never had his own reflection frightened him. He didn't recognize himself and quickly slowed his truck to a stop on the narrow grassy bank at the edge of the road.

Deiko looked closer in the mirror. His irises were black and what should have been the whites of his eyes were now ashen gray.

"What the hell?" His rage and need to find Ben subsided as shock rocked his soul.

He pried his eyelids wider apart with his fingers while staring in the mirror. He was horrified at what he saw. Little black tendrils, no larger than capillaries, pulsed in the corners of his eyes. Something was taking control of him. What exactly, he didn't know. This brief realization made him understand why he was so focused on acquiring the faery.

Deiko had never been a violent person. He enjoyed practical jokes that were often embarrassing and distasteful to others, but he never intentionally set out to inflict deliberate pain. But after seeing the faery, he found himself wanting to hurt, to kill, and to steal. That obsessive drive had turned him into something he didn't truly understand. His mind raced to recall exactly what he was doing, but there were gaps in his memory that made him uneasy.

It was almost like he had been . . . possessed.

And if so, where had this occurred? More importantly, why?

Deiko looked away from the mirror. About twenty yards ahead was a bridge. He opened the truck door, took the gun, and began walking. He didn't know why, but something inside him insisted he must. So he did.

Midway across the two-lane bridge, he stepped to the edge and looked down at the dry creek bed. Two people walked hand in hand directly toward him.

"Jim?" Deiko whispered through clenched teeth.

As the pair came closer, he recognized it was Jim. But he couldn't make out whom the other person was. Without thinking, he raised the gun and aimed. His finger tightened on the trigger. He fought the growing urge to kill. His hand shook.

"No," he said, trying to take control. "I won't do it."

Deiko tried to straighten his finger to prevent himself from pulling the trigger, but his finger was locked into place. The force controlling him squeezed the trigger tighter. His hand shook more violently as he fought to resist. Sweat covered his brow.

His left hand grabbed the shaky gun, but even with both hands, he couldn't lower the gun. His finger tightened. He pulled the trigger.

The girl with Jim screamed.

JIM AND LACY walked along the edge of the dry creek bed. He was careful not to walk too fast. Although she was walking okay, he didn't want to rush her and add to her fatigue. Her balance was good, she didn't seem confused, but he believed she still needed to see a doctor in spite of her protests.

Layers of dry leaves covered small rocks that tilted and turned when they stepped on them. Twice he came close to turning his ankle because he kept his focus more on her footing than his own.

"There's the bridge," Lacy said.

"Yeah, I see it."

"One second," she said. She stopped and leaned over to catch her breath. Sweat dripped down her face. She panted through her mouth.

Jim stood beside her and rubbed the center of her back. "Perhaps we should sit over there in the shade," he said.

"I'll be okay," she replied.

"You're pale. You need to rest."

He checked his phone. Still no reception.

"Come on," Lacy said. "Let's get beneath the bridge. I can rest there."

"We're a football field away," he said. "Are you sure?"

She smiled and nodded. "That's not really that far."

"But we were banged around in the wreck. You have a nasty knot on your head, and it's extremely hot."

Standing upright, she walked over and kissed him.

"I bet I can still beat you there," she said.

Jim took her hand and smiled. "Maybe next time. Let's just get there without passing out. Okay?"

She smiled, and then she pursed her lips. "That's cause you know I'd beat you."

"You're probably right. We'll find out later. I promise."

"I'll hold you to that."

Jim took her hand, and they walked toward the bridge. An approaching vehicle slowed.

"Listen," he said. "That sounds like Deiko's truck."

The engine stopped. They did, too.

"You really think it's him?" she asked.

"I hope not. But just in case, let's head to the trees for shelter."

Lacey nodded. Her bright eyes widened with fear. As they turned, she pointed toward the man on the bridge. "Is that Deiko?"

The man raised his gun.

"Yes!" Jim said, grabbing her around the waist. She screamed.

The gun fired. The bullet stuck the rock on the ground ahead of them, missing Jim's foot by mere inches. He scooped her into his arms and rushed into the tree line where they were safely out of Deiko's sight. In the trees, Jim lowered her so she could stand.

"You're not hit, are you?" he asked.

"No."

"Good."

"What about you?" she asked.

"I'm fine. He missed."

She sighed with relief and hugged him.

They waited in the trees until Deiko's truck started, and he headed on down the country back road.

Her beautiful eyes were tainted by uncertainty. "What should we do now?"

"We should wait here a little while longer. At least until we're certain he's not coming back. Had we been on the road when he came this way, we might both be dead."

"I know."

Lacey was clearly rattled. He believed his face revealed his terror as well as hers did for him. She was pale, frightened.

"I want to keep you safe," Jim said. "We wait fifteen minutes and see if he comes back. That also gives us enough time to rest, too."

She shook her head and smiled, taking his hand. He pulled her close and hugged her tightly. She held him, and her body shook. Warm tears wet his shirt. She buried her face against him.

"It will be okay," he whispered. "I promise."

Choking through the tears, she replied, "I want to believe you, but I'm so scared."

Jim rested his chin on top of her head and looked at the bridge. His promise was one he'd keep. He didn't have much left in the world, but what the future held. He wanted Lacy to be a part of that, so he'd make certain no harm came to her.

CHAPTER 12

*B*en stared into the shadows before them. The flashlight's glow didn't reveal anything more than the pair of eyes burning like red-hot coals.

"What did it mean when it said that you *revealed* him? Is that true?" Ben asked.

"Yes," Shawndirea replied.

"So he was there the entire time, and we couldn't see him?"

She nodded.

"How?"

"Magic," she said with a shrug. "Or it has the ability to move between realms. My guess would be magic."

"So this isn't the sorcerer?" he asked.

She shook her head. "No. It's his pet or minion."

"So that's good?"

"If you mean weaker, then yes. But quite dangerous, just the same."

Ben held his knife at his side. The hilt was clenched firmly in his hand, but he didn't remember removing it.

"Human," the creature said. "You do not belong here. This battle isn't yours. Release the faery to me, and I bid you your freedom."

"No way in Hell," Ben replied.

"Hell pales in comparison to what I will do to you," it said.

The flashlight in Ben's hand went black. He clicked the button on and off several times, but the light never returned. It was useless so he tossed it to the cave floor. Darkness cloaked them.

"Show yourself!" Shawndirea commanded.

Laughter bellowed from the darkness. "You have no authority over me, Shawndirea. Don't raise your voice to me."

Ben glanced at her. "He knows you?"

She shrugged and asked. "To whom do I speak?"

The fiery eyes vanished as the creature blinked. A second later, they blazed open and narrowed.

"Gouthan," the creature replied.

"And your master?" she asked.

"Has demanded I bring you to him," Gouthan said with a deep chuckle. His laughter rattled like rocks rolling down a hillside.

"His name?"

"That mystery you'll know when you give yourself to me."

Ben replied, "No. She stays with me."

"You'd die for her?" Gouthan asked amused.

"Yes. Without a second's thought," Ben replied.

"Interesting." More laughter rumbled in Gouthan's throat. "But will she, for you?"

Ben glanced at her from the corner of his eye. After the damage she had suffered because of him, he wondered how'd she reply. She had no reason to really protect him and certainly no reason to die for him.

"Return to your master and let us pass," Shawndirea said, "Or else you'll see the limits I'll go to protect him."

"You're an insolent little imp," Gouthan replied. "I shall end you here."

Shawndirea frowned. Her fury caused her fingertips to glow. To Ben, she whispered, "Be prepared. This may not work the way I plan."

"Nothing ever does," he replied.

She smiled and winked. "Then our worlds are more alike than most imagine."

"I'm beginning to see that."

Green-shimmering balls of light encircled her hands. The same light glowed around her feet. Warmth coursed through Ben's body as she drew her flow of energy from the earth beneath his feet. The two green orbs swelled and grew larger. She closed her eyes. Seconds later, the two orbs joined and fired straight ahead through the corridor.

The blast struck the creature and for a moment, Ben was able to see it. The thick massive black body somehow resembled a giant cat crossed with a lizard. Its head looked like a cat with long fangs. The short-legged body was stretched like a lizard, but it didn't have scales. Its fur was dark.

Possibly black. That explained why they weren't able to see it in the darkness. As it twisted in the air from the blast, the light displayed even more of its characteristics. Its tail was long and barbed at the end like a scorpion. Shawndirea's ball of light caught the creature square in the chest and flung it further down the tunnel.

After the green light vanished, the creature was no longer visible. Ben was uncertain if the magic Shawndirea hurled had hurt Gouthan or shoved him back through the veil. That is, until a vicious growl vibrated the walls.

"You are a fool, faery!"

Before the rattling echo of his voice faded, a blazing orange flame rushed toward them. Shawndirea thrust both hands forward. Just seconds before the flame reached them a green barrier shielded them. The flames angrily licked her energy shield but did not pass through and engulf them.

"Are you any good throwing those knives you carry?" she asked.

"Yes."

"Good. When his flame retreats," she said, "Throw the knife hard and for his throat."

"I will try, but I can't really see him."

"The receding flame is a direct path to his mouth," she said, gasping. "Use the fire line as your guide."

Ben smiled. "I can do that."

The flow of Gouthan's flame weakened, and as it slinked backwards, Shawndirea's shield slowly shrank. Whatever spell she had used not only blocked the flames, it blocked the heat as well. The cave was as cold as when they stepped inside. Colder perhaps. Frosty clouds puffed the air each time he exhaled.

Shawndirea collapsed on his shoulder and took the collar of his jacket in her hands to keep from sliding off.

"Now," she whispered.

Ben flung the knife hard and fast. As the flame vanished and the green shield disappeared, they were swallowed again by the cave's darkness. The blade chinked as it connected, but Ben wondered what it had struck. It sounded like metal hitting metal, but this creature appeared furry without any source of armor plating it.

Gouthan growled with a sputtering rattle in his throat. He hissed and spat, but no more flame sparked.

"I believe you hit him," she said.

"Are you certain?"

"He didn't shoot more fire."

Ben nodded. "No more threats, either."

"He *did* talk too much," she replied.

"Now what?" he asked. "The flashlight went out."

"Try it again. It may have used a spell to thwart light."

Ben squatted and grabbed the light. He clicked the button and the light worked.

"Let's go see what this creature is," he said.

"Careful," Shawndirea said. "It's still alive. Although injured, he's not defenseless."

Ben removed another knife. "I realize that, but I *do* want my blade back."

He aimed the flashlight and walked down the center of the tunnel. Gouthan writhed on the muddy cave floor. It used its front paws to tug and pull at the deeply lodged blade thrust in its neck. Its long claws prevented it from gaining a solid grasp. Blood oozed from its toothy mouth. Its fiery eyes narrowed as Ben stood directly in front of it.

Ben shone the flashlight across its face and body. The creature was spectacular and quite intimidating. The light revealed that the beast was parts from several different creatures sewn together. Suture scars were at the neck, the tail, and the clawed bird-like feet.

"What the hell is it?" Ben asked, setting the pack down.

"The sorcerer has made his own creation from different beasts."

"I thought when it shot fire in the darkness that it was a dragon."

Shawndirea cackled with intense laughter.

"What?" Ben asked.

"Dragons are one thing that you won't encounter in my realm."

"Really?"

"Yes."

"Did they ever exist?" he asked.

She nodded. "But they died out more than a century ago."

"That's a shame."

"Perhaps. But when most villages have thatched rooftops, you don't miss them that much."

Ben smiled. "I guess not."

Shawndirea slowly stood and peered down at Gouthan while Ben held the flashlight on the creature. "Your life is spared provided you name your master."

Gouthan grasped the knife hilt. Blood bubbles frothed from its catlike nose. He hissed and shook his head. Growling, he gnashed his teeth. Ben took a step back. The beast lunged and swung its barbed tail, narrowly missing him.

Ben lowered himself with the blade outstretched in his right hand. He had, unfortunately, fought another man with a knife before, so his stance prepared him for defense. However, that was with another human. This beast was more cunning and less predictable.

The long tail circled back and with lightning speed, it snapped forward. Ben moved a second before the barbed end would have stung him, but he wasn't quick enough to avoid the thick base of the tail as it slammed into his side. The impact knocked Ben into the air. He was flung to the right side of the tunnel and turned seconds before he would have crashed into the wall. The flashlight bounced across the wet floor after he dropped it. He quickly placed his left hand out to prevent himself from striking the wall with full impact.

Wingless Shawndirea lost her handhold on Ben's jacket collar and dropped to the cavern floor.

Ben grabbed a narrow cave column, swung around, and hit the ground. He rolled and came to his feet. He still held the knife tightly in his right hand. The flashlight stopped and spun with its light directed toward Gouthan. The strange creature moved rapidly across the cave toward Shawndirea in spite of its injuries. She ran toward the backpack.

Ben rushed toward Gouthan. His first fear was that the creature would take her, cross realms, and vanish. He couldn't allow that. Although it sounded premature, he knew his world would be lost without her. He had never been one to believe in destiny until he met her. Something in his soul let him know they needed one another. His purpose was not just to get her to her homeland, but it was for something far more. Perhaps he'd discover who he really was as well.

Gouthan scuttled across the mud. Blood coated his sharp teeth. It panted as it moved. And even though its injury weakened him, he was going to get to Shawndirea before Ben did.

Ben hurled the knife but his aim was off. Instead of striking a deathblow through the side of its head, the knife lodged into the creature's side. It snarled and turned to face him, swinging its tail madly and wildly at him. The sharp stinger dripped poison as it missed Ben and darted repeatedly into the cave floor.

Ben stepped further out of its reach. As the tail rose over Gouthan's back, Ben rushed forward and kicked the blade wedged in its throat as hard as he could. He moved back, crouched down, and grabbed Shawndirea.

Gouthan's eyes widened. He staggered side to side, trying to maintain balance. It sputtered for air, choking on its own blood. Collapsing forward, its legs twitched. Spasms reverberated throughout its body. Breathing stopped.

Blood spilled from its mouth and nose, forming a large dark pool on the cave floor. The barbed tail trembled. Poison dripped from the sharp tip.

Ben knelt and grabbed the hilt of his hunting knife. With a quick tug, he pulled it from Gouthan's throat. More blood gushed from beneath its throat. Ben stood and walked around to the other blade and pulled it loose, too.

The blazing eyes of the creature dimmed and extinguished. Seconds later, smoke rose from its empty eye sockets like the eyes were actual coals of fire.

Ben retrieved the flashlight and looked into Shawndirea's beautiful eyes. "Are you okay?"

"Yes."

He looked down at the creature and said, "I really believed it would be stronger and more difficult to kill."

When he gazed back at her, she smiled the endearing smile he had witnessed when she interacted with the resurrected butterflies in his study. Her eyes trained on him like someone deeply in love. She quickly looked away.

She stared at Gouthan's lifeless body and said, "For most, he would have been impossible to kill. Most would have died from fear."

Ben frowned. "If the sorcerer created him, why doesn't it have magical powers?"

Shawndirea shrugged. "It's a powerful beast with deadly abilities. Most wizards won't grant their pets access to magic for fear the creature will turn on them. I imagine Gouthan was difficult enough to control as he was."

Ben leaned closer to her and asked, "Do you wish to continue further? You look exhausted."

"We best head forward and quickly," Shawndirea said.

"Why?"

"Gouthan's master will soon know his pet is dead. Sorcerers seek vengeance for lesser offenses."

Ben sighed. "Let's go then. I'm not too fond of what other possibilities lay in wait for us in the darkness."

"Don't think it gets easier once we cross to the other side of the veil."

"At least there will be light."

"Don't be so certain."

Ben zipped open the backpack, grabbed the plastic bottle of honey mixture, and poured some into the lid.

Shawndirea smiled. "Thanks."

He grabbed an apple and took a huge bite. "Short break before we hurry forward."

CHAPTER 13

*D*eiko turned onto the dead end dirt road where the GPS indicated the McKnight farm was. Plumes of dust rose behind the truck as he sped toward his goal. Ben's SUV was parked at the end of the road. He parked beside it and looked into the mirror. His eyes were still dark but seemed to be returning to normal. Inside he quaked, fearful of what was bidding him to continue the dark quest to take the faery.

He had fired the gun toward Jim and a female, but he had also managed enough resistance to make the shot miss by a few feet. After his disobedience he found himself back inside the truck and driving fast. Most of the trip he didn't remember. In fact, he remembered less and less. He wondered why and *what* exactly had occurred during these recent mental blackouts.

The noise of the tractor motor approaching his truck startled him. He opened the door and stepped out onto the grass.

"Morning!" John McKnight shouted over the motor. He shut off the tractor and looked down at Deiko. He took the straps of his overalls in his hands and smiled.

"Good morning," Deiko replied, sliding his hand behind his back and repositioning the gun behind his belt.

"You here with Ben?" John asked.

Without hesitation, Deiko replied, "Yeah. Where is he?"

John grinned. "I'd say that he's probably already at the cave now."

Deiko looked around the pasture. "Where is it?"

"Just walk down past my pond there and through those trees. You'll see the mouth of Devils Den easily then."

"Devils Den?"

John nodded. "Yep. Reckon everyone around here calls it that now."

The name of the cave startled Deiko. He wanted to get into his truck and leave, but he found it wasn't that easy a task to do. Something pressed him to enter the cave and find Ben and the faery. The inner evil force sought complete control, and Deiko didn't believe he was strong enough to fight it.

"Well," John said, turning the tractor's ignition key. "I should be heading to my office today, but I've got a couple of dried out pastures to bush-hog first. You shouldn't have any trouble finding Ben. If he knows you're coming, he won't venture far inside."

Deiko nodded. "Thanks."

John nodded and smiled. He shifted the tractor into gear and drove through the open gate.

Deiko waited until the tractor was midway down the field before he headed toward the pond. When his eyes caught sight of the grove, he was compelled to pick up his pace. He tried to slow himself, but he had no control. An unseen force was drawing him.

Grasshoppers jumped and buzzed into the air. Brittle yellowish tan blades of grass crushed beneath his feet as he briskly walked to the trees. Crows angrily burst into flight and the dark shade welcomed Deiko.

Quickly his vision darkened when the mouth of the cave came into sight. Tunnel vision was all he had. Seconds later, his thoughts and vision were no longer his own. He pulled the gun from behind his belt and entered Devils Den.

EXHAUSTION OVERWHELMED Jim and Lacy by the time the truck stopped beside them. One of Ben's neighbors had seen them walking along the road and offered them a ride to Ben's house. Happily they accepted and climbed into the truck bed. They rode in the back of a truck up the winding, steep driveway to Ben's house.

Jim was thankful the elderly man had stopped. Each step they took along the highway made him ache. And although Lacy didn't complain, he could tell she had been a step from collapsing on the side of the road.

The gentle breeze that flowed over them while the man drove was a blessing. Covered in sweat, they had said little but continued holding hands, occasionally glancing at one another and exchanging smiles. Mud and grime coated their clothes, faces, and even their hair.

Along the way, they continued checking their phones for reception, but nothing had changed. No bars. No service connection.

The old man slowed the truck and the brakes squealed when they reached the top of the driveway. Stiff and feeling older than the driver, Jim stood and helped Lacy to her feet. He climbed over the side of the truck bed and his feet stung when he landed on the drive. He held a hand for her, she took it, and he helped her down.

"Much obliged," Jim said. "Do I owe you anything?"

The old man narrowed his eyes and said, "Two hundred dollars."

Jim's stomach turned. He didn't have that much money on him.

"Sir, um," he said, "I don't—"

The old man cut him off with a hysteric laugh and slapped his knee. "Works every time," he said. "Nah, I'm happy to help you out. Looks like the two of you have been through hell."

"Close," Jim replied.

"Say your car rolled off the side of this ridge?" he asked.

Lacy nodded.

"I saw the break in the trees back there. You two are lucky to be alive."

"I know," they both replied.

"You sure there's nothing more I can do for you?" he asked.

"No, but thanks. Dr. Whytten can help us if we need anything," Jim replied.

"Okay," he said, easing the truck forward and turning it around.

They waited until the old man was out of view, and then they nervously stared toward Ben's house.

"Should we check the front door to see if it's unlocked?" Lacy asked.

Jim shook his head. "We should probably check the garage first, just in case Deiko came back from the other direction."

He took her hand and headed on up the drive toward the garage.

"We would have heard his truck go up the drive if he had. Wouldn't we?"

"Probably," Jim said, "But I'd rather be certain he's not waiting for us."

Lacy forced a weak smile. "Me, too."

"Look, I'm sorry for bringing you out here. I almost got you killed. Twice."

"No," she said. "Coming to warn Dr. Whytten was *our* idea. And Deiko was the one who tried to kill *both* of us. Not just me."

Jim shrugged.

Lacy gave him a concerned look. "You don't think we should have tried to warn Whytten?"

"I should have. Alone."

"What? And let me miss all the excitement?" she said with a cute grin on her grime-covered face.

Jim tried not to smile back, but he couldn't help it. This beautiful young lady that chose to accompany him to Whytten's estate now had matted hair, dirt and grime on her cheeks, and dirt-caked clothes. She was a mess, and no longer the glamorous girl he had seen on campus day after day. This was the girl he never thought would give him a second glance. And after all they had been through, the car crash and the gunfire; she wasn't angry. She didn't blame him and incredibly, she was still capable of smiling.

He was amazed at how well she had bounced back. Or, he wondered, was she suffering from shock? He understood that extreme trauma or pressure could cause people to react with giddiness. Of course, she was probably a lot stronger than he expected. Maybe she wasn't as pampered as he had considered her to be from afar.

After he returned the smile, she brushed the hair from her eyes and stepped closer to him. She said, "And with everything that's happened today, I'm glad that you are the one with me."

Jim pulled her close and hugged her. After a couple minutes, he eased his hold and said, "Let's look around and make sure that Deiko didn't kill Dr. Whytten."

"Okay," Lacy said. "And then what? We don't have phone reception or a car. How do we get home?"

He sighed. "I don't know. We'll figure something out."

They quickly inspected the garage. Nothing seemed out of the ordinary. And better, Deiko's truck wasn't there.

The back door was locked, so Jim took her hand. They circled the far side of the house and walked onto the front porch. He checked the door. It wasn't locked. Once they entered, the house was dark, quiet.

"Might as well check each room," Jim said.

She nodded.

Every room was fairly clean. No sign of Ben. No traces of blood anywhere.

"Apparently Whytten wasn't here when Deiko arrived," Jim said.

"That's good."

"I know."

After they entered Ben's study, they froze when they noticed all the empty insect boxes. They exchanged surprised glances.

"What happened?" she asked.

"Not sure. But he'd never allow anything to happen to his collection."

"Exactly. It was sacred to him. I remember how excited he was when he showed the class."

"What the . . ?" Jim said, coming closer to the nearest box. "All the pins are in place. Just the butterflies and moths are gone."

"How?"

Jim shook his head. He was baffled. "I have no idea."

Leaves crunched underfoot as they headed toward the window. He looked outside and said, "I believe Deiko came through here."

"But the collection? You think he did that?"

"No. That would have taken too much time, and for what purpose? Pinned butterflies are very brittle. There would be no way to remove them without destroying their wings and bodies. No, if Deiko or anyone had wanted to steal them, they would take the boxes, too."

"Then how?"

"I really don't know," he replied. "Come on. Let's check the other rooms."

Jim flipped a switch on the wall. The hall light came on, so they headed back to the living room. The floorboards creaked beneath their footsteps. Entering the living room, he turned on a lamp. Usually a dimly lit room didn't bother him, but that was before Deiko had tried to kill them. He was a bit paranoid, overly cautious, and extremely tired. His adrenaline rush had crashed.

He sat on the couch, leaned back, and closed his eyes. Lacy sat beside him and rested her head against his shoulder. Neither said a word, but moments later, sleep overcame them.

CHAPTER 14

Queen Istrell, the Faery Queen of Elvendale, stared over her kingdom from the tallest tree. Rage flowed through her while she searched for her daughter, Shawndirea.

"Where is that girl?" she asked. "She's been gone for days."

Anger creased her aged brow. With her tiny, balled fists, she floated back inside a hollow opening in the massive tree. Luminous mushrooms lighted the narrow path that led deeper into her fortress. Around the next turn of the endless spiraling path, she stopped and stepped softly into another path that dead-ended. Attached to the tree were rolls of tall crystals that matched the array of rainbow colors. Slid into a tiny crack of the tree was a black-framed looking glass.

Istrell placed her hands on the crystals as she had done many times over the past few days. The crystals glowed brilliantly. She closed her eyes and drew upon their power, their energy. More energy flowed from the living tree, passed through her feet, and the growing sensation brought concurrent heat and chills to her.

The magic grew. Her head tilted upward. Her mind raced, floating through the tree canopies, through the valleys, dark forests, rivers and lakes, and through the kingdoms beyond hers.

Shawndirea was nowhere to be found.

"Where are you, child?" Istrell asked aloud. Pain echoed in her tone. Finally, exhausted, she released the crystals and drooped prostrate to the floor.

Sweat covered her. She shook uncontrollably, sobbing. Sadness ached her heart. Shawndirea was the next in line for the throne. She was gone. There wasn't any trace of her in their realm. Istrell didn't sense her spirit. Something blocked their magical connection and that alarmed Istrell. Especially since a new darkness had entered the Underworld and passed through to their realm Aetheaon. Its manifested evil disturbed her more than anything prior to its arrival.

And now, her daughter was missing.

She feared that Shawndirea might have been captured. Or, perhaps, she had been snared by whatever lurked in the center of their world and had not yet been identified.

Her daughter was often more curious than she should be. She was a stubborn princess, at times, but more suited to keep the kingdom in order than any other royal faery.

Istrell rose to her feet, shook her head, and flexed her faery wings. Her sadness was subsiding and soon to be replaced with anger once again. She seldom allowed her emotions to battle one another, but when it came to her daughter's well being, she lost control. She hoped that she was in her sad cycle when Shawndirea finally came home. Otherwise the harangue she unleashed on her daughter would be bitter and frightening.

She watched the power of the crystals dim. They grew cold. She reached to the side of the crystals and took the black mirror from its hiding place. She gazed at the cold mirror. The glass shimmered silver and came to life. The images that surfaced were of the darkening region in the center of Aetheaon where the new evil grew.

Smoke and thick fog swirled over this area. Istrell focused harder but the darkness prevented her from seeing into what lay beyond. She wondered what hid within, how it came to be, and why it concealed itself. Running her palm across the glass, the images disappeared. The glass grew cold again. Lifeless.

Istrell didn't entertain looking through the glass for longer periods of time. She feared that while she couldn't see what was within the black smoky region that it might see her and identify her whereabouts.

Regaining her strength, Istrell glided back to the tree opening to look out over Elvendale once again. She kept the mirror close, just in case she felt the urge to scan the area for Shawndirea.

Should something tragic happen to her daughter, not only would Istrell weep, all of Elvendale would weep.

If Shawndirea didn't return home soon, Istrell would have to call the High Court together and summon a search party to find and retrieve her.

She hoped it didn't come to that. Others in the court might view the loss of her daughter as a sign that someone new should be placed on the throne.

Holding the mirror with both hands, she whispered, "Where are you, my child? Hurry home."

CHAPTER 15

Shawndirea sipped the honey mixture from the plastic lid. Her energy was returning. When she finished, Ben took the lid and sealed the bottle shut. He placed her on his shoulder.

He stood and wiped the blood from his knife against the bottom of his boot. He held the knife and looked back at the Gouthan's carcass.

"One second," he said.

"What is it?" Shawndirea asked, quickly adjusting her seated position on his shoulder.

Ben walked back toward Gouthan and smiled. "Taking a souvenir."

He reached for the animal's ear, and the creature vanished.

"What the hell?" he said, looking all around. "Where did it go?"

"The veil swallowed it."

"Why?"

"To erase any evidence that magic has crossed to your side."

"But us? Why didn't it take us?"

Shawndirea smiled. "It doesn't work that way. Imagine what might happen if someone else happened upon it? The realms beyond the Under-world attempt to conceal its existence from those living in the Overlands."

"So what happens if you get stuck on this side of the veil?"

Worry wrinkled Shawndirea's brow. "Let's not speak of such a thing."

Detecting her fear, he asked, "What happens?"

"At some point, I will have to die prematurely," she said softly.

Ben frowned. "Why?"

Shawndirea shifted on his shoulder and released a long sigh. "Magic from the Underworld and beyond must not exist in your world. It creates an unbalance. If I stay too long, Veil-Watchers will be summoned to find and kill me."

"Veil-Watchers?"

She nodded. "Wraiths."

"Who summons them?"

Shawndirea offered a small shrug. "Once my magic is detected on this side of the realm for several days, they just come. I don't know what actually summons them. But like Gouthan, my body will return to my homeland."

"How did you get past them to cross the veil?"

"They don't stand guard. We can pass freely as long as we don't overextend our stay in your world."

"Then we get you back."

"Thank you," she said, smiling. "It's far more complex than I can explain."

"What about me?" Ben asked.

"What do you mean?"

"What if I were to stay in your world?"

She grinned. "You're human. We have many cities occupied by humans. They've been there for hundreds of years."

"So have people like me from the Overlands moved from this side of the veil to yours?"

"Of course, but they're generally kept as prisoners or slaves. They never rise to position."

"Why not?"

"They tend to die quickly."

"Rebellion?"

"No," Shawndirea replied. "Some go insane because it's difficult to adapt to a place they never believed existed outside their nightmares. That's why I'm trying to mentally prepare you for what we may encounter as we pass through the Underworld into my realm. It's easy for you to say that you understand, but you won't. Not until you've actually seen things you cannot explain."

Ben chuckled. "I have to admit the creature I killed is certainly something I'd never be able to explain to someone outside this cave. That's about the best eye-opener a man could encounter."

She nodded and gave a cute grin. "True. But, what I'm trying to convince you is that there are far worse creatures and beings than Gouthan. And don't insist that you believe me."

Ben nodded. "Okay. Seeing is believing."

"If that enables you to understand the uniqueness of possible dangers I'm stressing, then okay. But for most, seeing is only disbelief that makes them freeze and become vulnerable to unexpected attacks. Since there's no logic to what stands before them, they don't act until it's too late. Few humans from the Overlands survive in the Underworld."

Ben slid the hunting knife into its sheath and said, "Since I've nothing left to take from Gouthan as a souvenir, we'd best head deeper into the cave."

Shawndirea leaned closer to Ben and placed her hand upon his cheek. "Wait," she said.

"What is it?"

She held her hands above her head, closed her eyes, and spoke a quick spell in a language unfamiliar to him. A bright orb of light encircled them. If Ben didn't know better, he'd have thought they stood in an open field under the midday sun. The brightness lit up even the darkest crevices in the small cave room. On the ceiling amongst the icicle-like stalactites, tiny brown bats chirped and fled from the light's glow into the darker recesses down the tunnel.

She smiled. "There is something you get for killing Gouthan."

Puzzled, Ben looked around and finally asked, "What?"

"I have figured out what your name should be."

Ben gave a nervous side-glance and asked, "And what name have you chosen?"

"Roble," she said flatly.

"Roble?"

Shawndirea nodded. "It means noble with great strength."

Roble smiled. "I like it."

"In my realm, that is the name you must tell others when they ask who you are. From this day forward, you are no longer Ben. At least not there."

"Okay," Roble said. "But I don't understand why."

"Ben is an Overlander name. Using it in my realm will betray you. You don't want anyone to know you are not of my realm, Aetheaon."

"If you say so."

"No, I *insist*, Roble," she replied.

"Very well. Let's go."

She laughed. "Since I'm currently at your mercy and cannot fly, I go where you take me. Within *reason*, of course."

Roble glanced at her and said, "I'll never put you in harm's way."

She smiled. When she looked into his eyes, his stomach tightened.

Never had he seen a woman look at him with such trust and what he *hoped* indicated her love for him. It caught him off guard.

He took a quick breath, swallowed hard, and looked away.

"Is something wrong?" she asked.

"No."

Shawndirea shook her head.

"What?"

She giggled and smiled. "Your eyes give you away."

"Not the first time someone's told me that in less than a week."

"What troubles you about me?" she asked.

"Nothing really *troubles* me. It's just . . ."

She rose to her feet. "Tell me what it is?"

Flustered, Roble shrugged. "I'm probably reading too much into your glances."

"In what way?"

"Sorry. But . . . I've never been able to read women well."

Her perfect lips formed a sly, flirty grin. "You're afraid to tell me?"

"Not afraid. Just uncertain."

She stepped closer, kissed his cheek, and whispered into his ear, "You never know unless you ask."

The sultriness of her voice sent chills down his back.

"Say it!" Shawndirea said sharply and then playfully covered her mouth with her hands.

"Are you flirting with me, or are you really attracted to me?" he asked.

She quickly kissed his cheek again and stepped back. "Of course I'm attracted to you."

"Even after I damaged your wings?"

"I told you to let that go."

"I know, but it bothers me."

Shawndirea sighed. "I wasn't fond of you in the beginning, but you've proven yourself to me. I know your heart's intent. You're noble and strong, which is why I gave you the new name."

"But we're not even the same race," he said.

"And does that matter?"

Roble laughed and shook his head. "Wouldn't it?"

"Why should it?" she replied evenly.

"Our sizes, for one."

"Phht!" she replied. "Faeries have a great deal of magic. But even magic isn't stronger than love."

Roble turned toward her quickly. He held out his hand for her to step upon. She did. He brought her around before his face and stared into her eyes. "You're implying that you love me?"

"Too soon?"

"I would think."

Shawndirea crossed her arms. Her eyes sparkled from the encircling light's glow. "Your true feelings for me reflect in your eyes," she said softly. "Since the day I revived and released your collection, you've been unable to hide it."

"I wasn't about to admit it."

"Why not? You still blame yourself for hurting me?"

He nodded.

"I honestly don't hold that against you, Roble."

"Okay. I'm glad you don't. But you said that faeries and humans aren't getting along in your realm. Why would you let yourself consider falling in love with a human?"

"For one, you've never met any male Fae. Arrogance is something I detest, and they cannot suppress their loftiness for a second, which is why a majority of female faeries outlive our counterparts. Males foolishly get themselves killed because they believe they're invincible."

"Men are not much different," Roble replied.

Shawndirea pursed her lips. "*You* are different than most men. I don't detect greed or animosity in you. Modesty is perhaps a flaw you've inherited, but even so, you don't lack courage. You stand your ground. You willingly set your life as a sacrifice to protect mine against Gouthan. Few humans in the Underworld would entertain such an detriment."

"I appreciate the compliments."

"No compliments. Just the truth."

"Thanks all the same."

Shawndirea gave a slight shrug. "The first real test was releasing your collection back into the wild. You didn't protest like I expected one to do, which showed me that you're able to appreciate living creatures for more than prizes. Had you lost your temper and hurried to catch them all, that would have shown me an ugly side that I couldn't tolerate."

"So," Roble said, gazing into her eyes. "What *exactly* were you looking for when you crossed the veil? I don't believe it was your curiosity that enticed you."

She looked away.

"I answered your question. Now, please answer mine," he said.

"You," she replied softly. "I was looking for you. Or someone like you."

"Really?"

Her eyes met his. She nodded again.

"A human?"

"More than that. A life companion."

"And why not in your realm?"

Shawndirea sighed. "I already told you why."

"Yes, faery arrogance."

"You'll understand once you encounter a male of my race."

"Okay, maybe so. But how can we be life partners? It simply isn't possible."

"The height, size issue still bothers you?"

Roble shrugged. "It does present some major obstacles."

She smiled. "I can alter my height, but at a cost."

"And that is?"

Her gaze dropped. "I . . ."

The light that encircled them faded. The cave filled with darkness. Shrieks and screeches echoed deeper inside the cavern.

"We must go!" Shawndirea said sternly. "Now!"

"Back outside?"

"No, toward the noise."

Roble frowned. "*Toward*? You're certain?"

"There's no fleeing now. Our presence has been detected. We must find a way through the veil."

Before Roble could reply, Deiko shouted from the cave's opening, "Ben! I know you're in here! Don't make me come in after you!"

Deiko's voice sounded strange, dark, and hate-filled.

Roble looked at Shawndirea and started to reply. She quickly placed her hand on his lips. "There's no Ben here. Remember?"

"Yes."

She looked concerned. "That's the man?"

Roble nodded. "Yes, that's Deiko."

"We definitely need to find an opening in the veil immediately," she said.

"Why?"

"Because he's being controlled. He's not acting under his own power. Whoever wanted me trapped on this side of the veil has decided to use any method possible to kill me. You probably don't understand."

"Do you mean that he's possessed?"

"That is one way to put it."

"It makes some sense actually," Roble said. "When he pulled the gun to make me hand you over, he acted like a completely different person or someone with a split personality."

When Deiko got no immediate reply, he shouted, "I have you trapped, so might as well show yourself."

Shawndirea said, "You must hurry, Roble."

Roble hurried down the tunnel. Shawndirea cast a small wisp of blue light that floated ahead of them. The wisp wasn't bright enough that Deiko would see it from a distance, nor was it too dim that Ben couldn't see the cave floor. But the light didn't diminish the dangers of the wet, slick floor as he ran.

Rounding the next curve of the cave path, they came to a crossroads. He had seen this intersection a couple times he had ventured in, but it wasn't there each time he mapped the pathways. He stopped dead center of the crossroads.

"Which direction?" Roble asked. "I'm open to suggestions."

"I thought you knew the cave."

"It changes, like I told you."

The blue wisp shot straight ahead. Growls and shrieks came from the two side directions that the wisp ignored.

"Follow the light," Shawndirea said.

Ben sprinted after the light while she held tight to his jacket collar. She sat beneath his left ear. Her breathing was soft against his skin. He loved having her that close, and while he followed the wisp, he wondered what Shawndirea would sacrifice for them to be together. And *why*? Whatever it was must be precious because her countenance drooped the second he asked the cost and she considered her reply.

"Even if Deiko wasn't here, we still wouldn't be alone," she said.

"No need telling me. I hear the other creatures approaching."

"Those are minor to what I feel we're about to encounter."

"Damn," Roble said. "I was hoping we'd get somewhere safer."

"That will take some time."

"How much time?"

"Could be days," she replied.

The blue wisp stopped and hovered about six yards ahead of him. Roble slowed. His boots skidded on the slick cave floor. He reached out with his right hand, found a handhold in the wall, and held tightly. His feet slid from beneath him, and he dropped to the floor hard. He stopped inches from running off the edge of the path into a deep abyss. His feet dangled over the ledge.

Quickly, Roble looked around for Shawndirea. He didn't see her. Rolling over, he held himself on hands and knees.

"Are you okay?" he asked, still not seeing her.

Back down the path from where they had come the snarls of unseen beasts echoed.

"Shawndirea!" Roble shouted. His voice echoed through the fiery fissure below and across the open cavern that spanned at what seemed endlessly.

"Shh!" she replied.

"Where are you?" he asked softer.

The blue wisp hovered, turned, and glided to her. Above her head it floated. She sat with her legs curled beside her. "Here."

Roble crawled toward her. "Are you okay?"

In the glow of the blue light she nodded.

"A little shaken but I'm okay."

He held out his hand. She stepped onto his palm. "Sorry," he said. "I didn't know there was a drop off. The pathway has never taken me this way before."

Slowly, Roble rose to his feet and using the wisp's blue light as a guide, he made his way back to the ledge. Below, perhaps several hundred feet, the fiery stream flowed. Occasional bursts of flames shot upward, like tiny exploding gas-filled balloons. The harsh choking air reeked of rotten eggs. The temperature was no longer cold. Heat rose from the yellow-orange fissure. In the glow of the fire small winged creatures zipped back and forth.

"Where are we?" he asked.

Behind them, the pursuing beasts grew closer.

"No idea," she said. "It's your cave."

"Not *my* cave. This path I've never traveled."

Shawndirea smiled. "I tease."

"Normally I'd say that's cute, but we're in a rough spot. Whatever caught our scent at the crossroads is getting much closer."

"I realize that."

Roble stared down into the abyss. Jagged rocks lay on this side of the flame-filled stream. He didn't see a clear path from where they stood that led downward. He opened his mouth to speak when something caught his attention in the shadows below.

Pockets of fire blazed about every fifty yards. At first he thought the little fires were trapped within rock barriers or small outcropping rocks, but then a large wing stretched and flapped. Other winged creatures lurked near the edge of the stream. A larger one flapped its wings. Then another. Dozens of these dark beasts huddled around the fires but seldom did they move. They weren't restless, and he hoped they were asleep. As best he could tell, they weren't aware of their arrival, but with the snarling beasts growing closer, it was only minutes until a major confrontation occurred between them and the pursuing monsters or against the winged creatures below should they choose to venture into the vast abyss below.

"Do you see them?" Roble asked, pointing.

Shawndirea followed the direction of his finger. Several of the winged creatures stretched their wings.

She leaned close to his ear and whispered, "Back away, slowly."

Roble stepped back from the ledge and eased toward the left side of their path that opened into the dark abyss.

"What are they?"

"Minions."

Roble frowned. "Like Gouthan?"

She shook her head. "No, closer to demons."

"Really?"

"Yes. The name for the cave isn't wrong. This is a den of demons."

"Had I ever seen anything like this, I never would have returned."

She placed her hand against his cheek. "Nor would I."

"You didn't see anything like this?"

"No."

"So they are demons?"

"Or something like them. Underlings are vile creatures usually controlled by a stronger demon."

Roble said, "So did we miss the veil?"

"In a way I suppose we have, or we have been misdirected into a more dangerous place by whomever wishes to keep me from my homeland."

A loud hiss of flame blazed in the chasm. Shadows danced through the wide cavern. The growling creatures stood behind them at the head of the path, blocking their access to the way back to the crossroads. Their green eyes narrowed.

"We don't have any good options," Roble said softly.

"I know."

A man hidden in the shadows on the other side of the path near the overlook said, "I can lead you out."

Roble turned with a start. He placed his hand on his knife. "Who are you?"

"My name is Forcas."

Shawndirea waved her hand. The blue wisp shot across the path and shimmered brightly, revealing the old haggard man. He stood six foot tall, thin and frail. He leaned upon a gnarled staff. His long gray hair flowed into his beard, making it impossible to tell where they met. His tattered clothes were thin and sooty. His wrinkled face cringed tighter as the wisp dipped closer. Other than the staff, the old man didn't appear to have any weapons, but Roble understood the blue lighting had its limits.

Forcas held his right hand up to shield his eyes from the blue light. Roble slowly drew his knife from its sheath.

"How can you get us out of here?"

"There is a hidden path, but you don't have much time."

Shawndirea shook her head and whispered, "Don't trust him."

"Why?" Roble whispered back.

"It doesn't *feel* right."

"He's human."

She replied, "He *appears* to be human. Don't forget how things alter and change down here."

"You mind with the light?" Forcas asked, still blocking its glow with his hand.

"Sorry," Shawndirea said. The wisp's light dimmed but remained bright enough that they could see him should he rush at them.

Roble looked toward the two green-eyed beasts in the tunnel. They eased closer but stayed outside the glow of the blue wisp. They growled and sniffed the air. He guessed they were trying to get his scent.

Shawndirea turned and shot a small green ball of fire at them. The fire struck one, it yelped, and both fled further into the tunnel.

"How did you get here?" Roble asked.

Forcas coughed and cleared his throat. He spoke with a deeply strained voice. "I've been here so many years I cannot remember. I've wandered the passageways for so long that I've given up on finding my way back to the surface."

"And yet you offer to get us *safely* away?" Shawndirea said.

The old man shrugged. "Only from the direction that I just came, which is this path that leads downward."

"Down there?" Roble asked, pointing. "Where all those creatures wait?"

Forcas nodded and pointed a different direction. "The path goes away from them and over the fiery stream."

"Easy," Shawndirea said. "Something about him isn't right."

Roble watched the old man take a step back and turn away. He stepped to the side of the tunnel and headed downward, using his staff to balance during his descent.

"Very well," Forcas said. "Find your own way."

"Wait," Roble said.

Forcas stopped but kept his back to them.

Roble whispered to Shawndirea, "You don't trust him?"

"Not completely."

"But if he can get us past those underlings, we don't have to continue following."

Forcas cleared his throat. "I don't have an eternity to wait on your decision."

Shawndirea gave a slight nod and whispered to Roble, "Keep on guard. Never get within an arm's length of him."

"Well?" Forcas asked.

"We'll follow," Roble said.

"Splendid!" he replied. "Haven't had the pleasures of conversation for so long. Other than my own mindless ramblings, that is. Talking to another human is something I've missed."

Shawndirea leaned close to Roble's ear and whispered, "We cannot trust him. There's something dark about him."

Roble nodded. "I have that feeling, too. But what else can we do?"

"We watch out for ourselves," she whispered.

To the old man, Roble said, "You've wandered this cavern for years?"

Forcas stopped walking and replied, "That is what I said."

"So where did you come from?" Roble asked.

The old man took a step down the path, and then another. "Careful where you step," he said. "So many jagged rocks, holes, and strange creatures waiting for morsels like ourselves to feast upon. Don't snare yourselves in the rocks. No. Wouldn't be good. No good at all."

Roble gritted his teeth. "Forcas, where are you from? Your homeland?"

"A place you wouldn't know," he replied.

"Overlands or Underworld?" Shawndirea asked.

"Both, the same, each. Yes. Been many places. Seen many dangers."

"Babbling old fool," Roble whispered.

"Shh!" she said into his ear. "He may hear you."

Roble shrugged. "So?"

"He's far from harmless."

"Seems he suffers more from dementia than anything else."

Shawndirea shook her head. "You have a lot to learn about guise."

"Not quite certain what you mean."

"Many thieves in the Underworld disguise as different things simply to catch you off guard or guilt you into sympathy to give them coins."

Roble gave an even smile. "Spend some time in my realm, you'll find much of the same thing."

"Then why taunt him? None of those in the Overlands can bewitch you or cripple you with their magic."

Forcas took more nimble steps and descended about a dozen steps below them. His pace was quicker. Roble hurried to get closer. The temperature grew hotter, making him want to shed the light jacket he was wearing. Each step he took, the black stairs crackled, crumbled, and powdery ash rose. Not only was the air getting warmer, the smell of sulfur was getting worse.

Roble dared a glance from the stairs to look at Shawndirea. He shrugged and said, "That's true. So you detect he has magical abilities?"

She shook her head. "No. Not magical powers, but something dark."

"Maybe he's the master of Gouthan."

"No. If he were, I would know it."

The jagged path was dark, steep. One misstep and they'd barrel downward. The rough-hewn steps would slice through their flesh like little razor-tipped pins. While Roble struggled to see where to place his feet as he walked, Forcas moved with ease and almost seemed to glide down each step. Shawndirea's blue wisp stayed behind Forcas and drifted inches above the path so Roble could see where to step. The old man didn't seem to notice or care. He simply moved a step at a time. A burst of yellow flame shot from the meandering fiery stream. The brief explosion allowed Roble to see that the rock stairway descended a good quarter mile before leveling off, but he didn't see the bridge that Forcas spoke of.

Forcas muttered a string of words in jumbled phrases of several different languages. He amused himself, it seemed, by talking aloud and ignoring them.

"And how would you know if he was Gouthan's master?" Roble asked.

"The touch of control that Gouthan had would be much stronger on Forcas, if he was the master. I don't sense that at all. I'm certain that Gouthan's master seeks to find us and make us suffer for killing his pet."

"I have no doubt."

She smiled. "Creating Gouthan required a lot of time, a great deal of magic, and a major blood sacrifice."

"Oh?"

"Yes. That creature wasn't easy to give life to."

Roble shrugged. "At least he died easily enough."

"As we may, too, if we continue following Forcas."

Forcas reached the area where the stairs leveled off, and the path was smoother. Roble still had several dozen stairs to descend. Forcas stopped long enough to turn and face them. He laughed.

"You're certainly taking your time. You must want to wander these caverns like me," Forcas said, turning and continuing his stride.

"Wait," Roble said. "Forcas, wait for us."

Forcas stopped walking and stood with his back to them as Roble hurried down the steep, jagged steps. Plumes of black ash drifted and formed small clouds that hung in the acrid smelling air.

Roble stepped off the final step and walked toward Forcas. The old man turned and his eyes narrowed. He no longer appeared to be a frail old man. His face looked younger. The beard that had been twisted and long was now a neat, short mustache and a jet-black goatee. His eyes disturbed Roble the most because of the flickering blue glow that radiated in them.

Roble stood still.

Forcas smiled. "You know, there is something we failed to discuss earlier."

"What is that?" Roble asked, slowly placing his hand on the handle of his hunting knife.

Forcas' eyes flamed red for a second before turning icy white. "My price for leading you to safety. We never discussed that, did we?"

Roble swallowed hard. Shawndirea had warned him not to trust this man and nothing was exactly as it appeared in the Underworld.

"Did we? Remind me if we did," Forcas said.

"No, we didn't," Roble said. "What's your price?"

"Your lives."

Shawndirea raised her hands.

"I advise you not to, Faery. You have no idea who you're dealing with here. I'm more powerful than you, especially inside my domain."

Roble frowned. "Whom are we dealing with?"

"I gave my name," Forcas replied.

"I'm not familiar with it," Roble said.

"Nor I," Shawndirea said.

"It doesn't really matter. You won't ever forget it."

Forcas tightened his hands around his staff, lifted it, and then he drove it into the charred floor. The ground split, shook, and a rumble much like thunder echoed throughout the dark cavern. The fiery stream bubbled; fissures widened to both sides of it. The stream became a wide river of molten lava. The winged creatures took to flight, shrieking their deafening high pitch cries.

The thick lava flowed, spiraled, and balls of gas ignited into clouds of evaporating fire. The ground shook. Stalactites dropped like sharp daggers, bursting and shattering all around. Where they struck, holes opened.

Streams of smoke billowed up from these little cones. The sulfuric air reeked and choked them. Along the walls of the deep cavern previously unseen unlit torches flickered and blazed.

"What the hell?" Roble said.

Forcas smiled. "Your perception is quite keen."

Roble glanced at Shawndirea and whispered, "What is he talking about?"

She shrugged.

Deep rolling laughter echoed from Forcas. His human appearance retreated. A wicked smile crept across his demonic face. He pointed toward the flowing lava and said, "The river below is the River Styx. Welcome to Hell."

CHAPTER 16

$\mathcal{L}$acy awakened curled against Jim on the couch. He was still sleeping. Her head ached. She looked around the room and took a few seconds to remember where she was. While Jim slept, she slid her cellphone from her pocket and checked for reception.

Still nothing.

She shook her head. "I can't believe my silliness," she said.

Lacy dialed 9-1-1. The phone rang through.

"9-1-1, what's your emergency?"

She explained their ordeal, where they were, and that they had no means of transportation. She also stressed how much she feared Deiko would return to kill them.

"I'm sending out officers now."

"Thanks."

Lacy disconnected the call. She gently shook Jim's shoulder until he opened his eyes. He glanced at her with a confused expression.

"Police are coming," she said with a broad smile.

"How? Did you pick up bars?"

She shook her head. "No. I remembered that you can dial 9-1-1 even when you don't have phone reception."

"Really? I didn't know that, but glad it worked."

"Me, too."

She looked at her filthy hands and said, "Do you think Dr. Whytten would care if I washed up in his bathroom?"

Jim shrugged. "I don't know, but my guess would be that he wouldn't mind."

Lacy smiled. "Good. I can't stand all this dirt and grime. My fingernails are nasty. Be back in a little bit."

While she showered, Jim went back to the study where all the open insect boxes were and tried to make sense of how the butterfly collection was no longer there. The pins were, and although he wasn't an entomologist, he understood how brittle a dried insect was. Simply pressing down on the thorax to remove the pin would shatter a specimen.

The open window caught his attention and before he reached it, a vehicle screeched to a stop in the driveway. Jim moved to the side of the window and pressed his back to the wall. The vehicle didn't sound like Deiko's truck. Before the person got from the vehicle and slammed the door, voices came over the radio transmitter. He glanced through the side of the window and gave a relieved sigh. It was a deputy car. The lanky officer headed toward the side door.

When he knocked hard, he stated, "Sheriff deputy! We received a 9-1-1 call from this address!"

Jim hurried and opened the door. He noticed the name "Higgins" on the officer's uniform.

Deputy Higgins asked, "Are you the one that made the call?"

Jim shook his head and replied, "My girlfriend did."

"So what's the trouble?"

A smile spread across Jim's face as he realized he had called Lacy his girlfriend, which was the first time he ever had one.

"Something amusing here?" Higgins asked.

"No, sir. Sorry."

Jim stepped outside and explained where Deiko had started shooting at them and pointed where his car plummeted down the ravine.

Higgins frowned and wrote down the information while Jim told the events. When Jim finished, Higgins said, "And you're saying that this man is your professor?"

Jim nodded. "Yes."

"Any idea why he is bent on killing you?"

"None, sir. He's never acted like he even *disliked* me. He always has an odd sense of humor, but I've never thought he'd be a violent person."

The back door opened and out stepped Lacy. Her hair was wet and her makeup was gone. For a moment she looked startled, but then she offered a modest smile.

The officer glanced from Jim to Lacy and asked, "She was in the car, too?"

"Yes."

Lacy joined them in the driveway. She smelled of soap and shampoo.

Higgins asked, "Do either of you need me to call paramedics?"

Both shook their heads.

"It's surprising that the two of you walked away with your lives."

Jim replied, "I know."

"We do need a ride though," Lacy said. "I'm certain my mother is getting worried."

Higgins nodded. "Let me call dispatch and give them this information. At least we know who we're looking for. I'll put out an APB. Any idea where he might have gone?"

"No," Jim said. "My guess is that he's still looking for Dr. Whytten since there's no sign of him here."

"Okay," Higgins said. "I have other officers on their way. Once they arrive we will search the perimeter to make certain Dr. Whytten isn't still here. I'll find someone to get you home."

"Thanks," Lacy said.

~

FRUSTRATED, Deiko entered the cave, but not exactly willingly. Something forced his mind to obey. He had no control over his body. It was an odd sensation to attempt to move a certain way, but have no power to do so.

The building urgency to find the faery was no longer his own, but whatever had control of him. Several times he fought against this dark power, but he wasn't strong enough to thrust it away or wrestle free of its hold. He seemed to be watching from outside his body from time to time, and didn't know how to gain back his control. Now he wondered how much of the desire to get the faery was actually his. Whatever had taken over his body probably knew his desire for fame and wealth and over-magnified his lust in order to get the faery.

By granting this entity brief access to his psyche, the being flung open the door and took the reins to enact its own greed and lust.

"Ben!" Deiko shouted against his will.

Further into Devils Den he walked. Although he carried a flashlight, the light wasn't turned on. Oddly enough, he could see, but only through narrow tunnel vision that glowed with a yellowish tint. After a couple of twists and turns in the darkness, he didn't hear or detect that Ben was anywhere nearby.

Several more steps and his feet wouldn't budge. His legs seemed to weigh more than he could lift. His arms hung heavy to his side.

"Fool," the voice said in his mind. "You think you have more power than I? Your resistance comes at a great price."

Deiko tried to speak, but he was voiceless. In his mind he poised the question, "Who are you?"

"Elias."

"Elias who?"

"You have all you need to remember. I will haunt your dreams. You will never be the same."

Severe pain tore through his mind. Everything seemed darker. And without warning, whatever power controlling him suddenly left him.

As it ripped its way out, coldness rushed over Deiko. He braced himself against the cave wall and vomited. He staggered several steps in the darkness and collapsed to the chilly, wet floor. Extreme vertigo made his head bob and kept him unsteady.

He clicked the small flashlight.

"Where am I?" he whispered, trembling from the cold.

Rather than trying to stand, he put the flashlight in his mouth and crawled.

"Help," he thought. "I must get help."

Voices echoes from the dark tunnels behind him. Nervousness overtook him. He clawed and pulled himself through the cave following his light. Due to the dizzying sensation, his head kept lulling toward the right, and he crawled sideways. The feeling sickened him, making him dry heave until he nearly collapsed.

Wings fluttered around him. He screamed.

"Leave," Elias whispered in his ear. "Leave and never come back."

Deiko scrambled forward. His knees dug into the ground so hard while he crawled that he bruised them. He didn't see anyone, but invisible hands smacked him, clawed him, knocked the flashlight from his mouth, and then whispering voices echoed around his head like irritating mosquitoes. He stopped crawling and pressed his hands against his ears. Screaming, he hoped to drive away the voices, but when his screams ceased, their cries continued.

Darkness surrounded him. The shattered flashlight was useless. He pushed himself to his feet and ran. Without light he hit the cave wall, spiraled, and smashed his face into the opposite wall. The voices swirled around him.

Deiko placed his right hand against the wall and patted it, using it as a guideline to find the cave opening. His bruised face ached. The clawed cut marks all over his body burned. After ten minutes of running his hand along the wall, light broke through the darkness. He ran toward the opening and hurried outside.

He trembled all over. His hands shook, and he sat back against a large rock.

CHAPTER 17

John McKnight got off his tractor near Devils Den. As he approached the mouth of the cave, he noticed Deiko sitting outside on a large rock. The man trembled like a dog that had gotten the worst end of a raccoon fight. His eyes were hollow with fear.

Deiko didn't notice John step closer. Deiko's face was dark from a forming bruise. His hands were filthy from mud and grime. A couple of his fingernails were chipped and split. Strange claw marks covered his arms. Blood oozed from the cuts. Other than the bruising, his face was ashen white.

"Everything okay?" John asked.

Deiko replied with a short scream. He jumped to his feet and almost fell.

"Easy, now," John said. "Did you find Ben?"

Deiko's lips quivered. Endless babbling sounds were all that he could utter.

John shook his head and said, "Let me help you."

He gently placed his hand around Deiko's elbow. As Deiko stepped beside him, John noticed the gun tucked behind Deiko's belt. Slowly, John placed his hand on the butt of the gun and took it without Deiko noticing.

Deiko mumbled.

"Come with me," John said. "I'd say you're suffering from heatstroke, but you've been inside that cool cave for some time. So I know that isn't what happened."

Deiko's pale face beaded with sweat. His wide eyes searched erratically, never focusing on any particular object.

John studied his face for a moment and then asked, "What did you see in there?"

"Elias," Deiko whispered.

"Come again?" John asked.

Deiko's haunted eyes stared past John. Again, he said, "Elias."

"Let me get you to the house," John said, helping Deiko onto the tractor. "We need to get you to a doctor quickly."

The short five-minute tractor drive to the McKnight farmhouse didn't change Deiko's behavior any. He babbled endless strings of intangible words. John feared that the man had suffered a harsh stroke, but he didn't know.

John went inside to call 9-1-1 while Lib tended to Deiko on the porch.

When he stepped back onto the porch, the old screen door slammed shut behind him. Lib used a cool wet cloth to wash some of the grime off Deiko's face.

"Has he said anything?" John asked.

Lib replied, "The only word that I can make out is Elias."

John frowned and shook his head. "I don't know anyone by the name."

"Doesn't sound familiar to me, either," she said.

A half hour passed before an ambulance arrived. A few minutes after that a sheriff's patrol car pulled in. Deputy Higgins got out of the car. He opened the rear door and let Jim and Lacy out.

"You two stay here for a few minutes," Higgins told them.

The rear ambulance doors were open. Deiko sat on the bed while two paramedics examined him.

Higgins approached the ambulance. John came closer.

"Afternoon, John," Higgins said.

"Deputy," John replied.

"Got a call that Isaac Deiko is here."

John nodded. "That's him at the back of the ambulance."

"Where did you find him?"

"He came here to see my brother-in-law, Ben. They were going to explore Devils Den."

Higgins frowned. "According to the two teenagers I brought here, they said that he tried to kill them and that he might be planning to kill Ben as well. We're searching outside Ben's house for a body."

"Ben's truck is here. Deiko arrived well after Ben did."

Higgins sighed. "I guess we can stop searching at his house then. Have you seen Ben?"

John shook his head. "No. I found Deiko outside the cave . . . in this strange condition. No sign of Ben though, and if he went inside the cave, he hasn't come out."

"Has Deiko mentioned anything about Ben, or if he found him?"

"No. The only thing he mentions is a name. Elias."

"Elias?" Higgins said, frowning.

John nodded.

"Any significance?"

"None that rings a bell for me," John said.

"Thanks, John."

"Don't mention it," he replied. "I have to head to my insurance office soon."

HIGGINS WALKED to the rear of the ambulance, read the nametag of the nearest paramedic, and addressed her, "Patty? How is he?"

"I'm afraid he's not doing well at all," she replied.

"What's wrong with him?"

"He's delusional."

"Is he still not talking?"

Patty shook her head. "Nothing that's understandable."

"So asking him questions right now isn't a good time?"

"I'm afraid it wouldn't do you much good."

"Any reason for his condition?" Higgins asked.

"Not without taking him in for mental evaluation and testing, I don't know."

"I have two teenagers over there that have stated he tried to kill them earlier today."

Patty shrugged. "I suppose anything's possible. He's definitely not in a good state of mind."

Higgins motioned to Jim and Lacy to come over. They approached slowly, cautiously. Lacy kept her arms crossed and stayed a few paces behind Jim.

Higgins motioned toward Deiko. His eyes stared straight ahead. His body trembled. Higgins said, "Is this the man?"

"Yes," they answered in unison.

Lacy stepped closer and said, "What's wrong with him?"

Patty offered a slight smile and shrug. "We don't know, honey, but we're going to take him for a mental examination. He clearly needs medical help."

Jim frowned and looked at Higgins. "He didn't act anything like this earlier. Hell, he shot at us even after we survived the wreck."

"I have everything written down," Higgins said. "And after he goes for a mental evaluation, he'll be locked safely away."

Lacy looked at Jim, took his hand in hers, and then she looked at the paramedic. "Do you think his condition might be responsible for why he tried to kill us?"

"Hon, I'm not a doctor, but the odd things we see from time to time, anything is possible."

"El . . . El . . . Elias," Deiko muttered. His glazed eyes stared into nothingness.

"Oh," John said, coming back to the ambulance. He held the 9mm by the barrel and extended it toward Higgins. "I found this on Deiko when he sat outside the cave. I believe it's his."

"Thanks," Higgins said. To Jim and Lacy, he said, "Not much more we can do until he's evaluated by psychiatrists, but I have your report. Now we need to get you home."

John smiled. "I can take them home before I head for my insurance office."

Higgins nodded. "Much appreciated."

"Glad to help."

Jim looked at the cave and then to John. He said, "Where's Dr. Whytten?"

John shrugged and shook his head. "We've not seen him."

"Is he in the cave?" Lacy asked.

"That's my guess. He explores it a lot," John replied.

"Deputy," Lacy said. "Shouldn't someone go in and check for him? Dr. Deiko may have shot and killed him inside."

Deputy Higgins replied, "We'll have someone check it out. I assure you."

John glanced at the cave with nervous eyes and then motioned Jim and Lacy to follow him. "Come on, guys. Let's get you two home so your parents won't worry about you."

CHAPTER 18

*R*oble held Shawndirea in his left hand and pulled his knife with the other.

Forcas vanished.

"I told you not to trust him," she said.

"That you did. I didn't see much alternative at the time."

"I'm not blaming you. Our choices were few."

Roble nodded. "Any suggestions?"

"Watch where you step."

The black volcanic ground had numerous open pockets of bubbling lava. The winged creatures drifted overhead in the sulfuric, smoke-filled air. They were impressively massive creatures, but he didn't want a close up view of them.

Sweat poured from Roble's pores. He wiped his forehead with the back of his hand. He slipped off his light jacket and stuffed it into his pack.

"It's hot," he said, "But I would have thought Hell to be much hotter. Of course, I've never been one to believe such a place existed."

"All religions have a similar belief for eternal damnation."

"So we've been damned, I suppose."

She smiled. "Not if we find the veil."

"I thought that we have gone too far?"

"No. Not necessarily. No one knows the veil's boundaries."

Roble scanned the area around them. Styx flowed slowly. Shadowy creatures burst from the orange lava and were quickly pulled back under by what appeared to be massive chains. They cried their agonized protests, but whatever held them captive didn't allow them to break free.

Winged creatures flapped their massive wings. There wasn't a clear path for Roble to follow. After Forcas slammed his staff into the cavern floor, the stairs they descended vanished. The expanse that encircled them was barren. No large boulders or rocks to hide behind. They were almost dead center of the massive domed room where Styx cut through.

"So Forcas," Roble said, "Was a *what* exactly."

She shrugged. "Possibly a demon. I'm not certain. His dark aura makes me believe he is."

Chattering sounds echoed. Hissing steam rose from fissures around the domed chamber. Occasionally, rocks slides crumbled along the river's edge and splashed into the molten lava. The chatters of unseen creatures chilled Roble. His mind pictured nightmarish beasts that lurked within the shadows.

Hot wind howled and swirled, purposely sending the dry heat at them. Forcas had to be watching. Roble imagined their abandonment in the center of the flaming abyss added great entertainment for the demon's amusement.

Roble glanced at her and said, "I wonder if he'll return."

"He's probably watching us now."

"You think so, too?"

She nodded. "We are part of his game."

"What game?"

"Whatever one he wishes to play."

Roble looked away from the river. Going closer toward the river, the temperature would only grow hotter, and the creatures had an even better chance at seeing them. Moving to the outskirts might put them in less light and heat, but he feared they had already been noticed. Several of the flying gargoyle-like creatures now circled overhead.

"I do believe things are about to get heated, if you'll pardon the pun," he said.

"What do you mean?"

Roble nodded upward toward the circling creatures. "We've been located."

She looked up, and her eyes widened.

"Perhaps you should slip into my backpack."

"It's too hot."

"If one of those creatures attacks, I'm afraid I might accidentally crush you in my hand. I don't want to chance that."

"Put me in your shirt pocket."

"The same may happen," he replied.

"I can scramble out, if necessary."

One of the winged creatures shrieked and descended like a hawk.

"That may be the case. Hurry."

Shawndirea climbed into his pocket and held fast to the top border. He quickly placed the pack over his left shoulder.

Roble sprinted. Afraid to accidentally step into a hole filled with lava, he kept his attention on the ground ahead of him. He didn't dare look up, but this prevented him from seeing where the diving creature was. Its clawed feet grabbed the back of his shirt and lifted him into the air.

"Are you okay?" he asked.

"Fine so far. You?"

Roble gave a slight nod and tried to speak.

He gasped for air, which he quickly regretted since the air reeked worse than rotten eggs. His captor was a black demon. The space between its scales was fiery orange, which made it resemble a cooling piece of hot coal.

The creature's hold on his shirt tightened the collar around his neck. He was choking. He held the knife tightly, but the angle at which the beast pulled, prevented him from striking.

The sharp talons had partially cut into his shirt, making the material weaker. A slight ripping sound alerted him to the added danger of falling.

Shawndirea turned in his pocket, lifted her hands above her head, and spoke.

Roble shook his head and stuttered a weak, "No."

His face beamed red. Veins popped across on his brow. Death seemed inescapable. Either he'd choke to death, or he'd be dropped and land in the fiery river below.

Shawndirea's green fire zapped the creature's chest. Surprise filled its evil black eyes. Its hard brow narrowed in anger. The shot didn't do much damage, but enough that the black Hell-beast lost hold of Roble.

"Dammit!" he said, plummeting.

As they fell, the creature flapped and hovered for several moments, and then it quickly dove after them. Before it could recapture them, another winged demon zipped by and wrapped its claws around Roble's waist. This one's exoskeleton was as orange as the flowing lava. Black outlined its bright fiery scales.

The black Hell-beast grew angry. It growled and flung itself onto the orange flying demon in midair. It reared back its head and exposed its jagged fangs. Using the clawed hands on the tips of their wings, they battered one another. They flogged and snapped. The black winged beast wrapped its wings around its opponent and barrel-rolled.

Roble looked below. They were directly over Styx. He closed his eyes as the beasts spiraled. Neither creature was flying. They were falling. Their wings had entangled with one another. Both struggled to get free, and during their attempt to unhook their wings, Roble broke free of the demonic beast's grip and began his own free-fall with the faery trapped inside his pocket.

The two falling Hell-beasts growled and bit one another's throat. Their frantic battle to kill one another made them ignore their falling destiny.

Roble thought about Shawndirea and regret washed over him worse than ever about how he had destroyed her wings. If she were able to fly, at least she'd be able to survive, but each was doomed to fall into the burning river of fire and souls.

She held to his pocket tightly. Her sad eyes stared into his. He feared she'd read his thoughts and realized their possible fate.

The rush of heat encircled them as they fell. He was certain the temperature would incinerate them well before they hit the river of lava.

The two fighting demons tumbled and struck the lava, igniting in a quick burst of explosive energy that vanished as fast as they touched the river.

Roble opened his mouth to tell Shawndirea good-bye when the breath was knocked from his lungs by a third winged demon that grabbed him and swiftly flew over the river. It slowed and hovered over a small ledge on the opposite side of the expanse from the tunnel where they had entered from Devils Den. On the narrow ledge was a large nest.

"Careful," Shawndirea said. "This one is a female."

The she Hell-beast released Roble, and then she gently dropped Roble and Shawndirea into the nest. Three large eggs rolled. Roble ran behind one of the eggs to put some distance between them and the demon. Her massive wings folded behind her back. She reached to grab him, but he sliced her boney hand. Two of her three digits dropped from her hand. She hissed and narrowed her eyes. Yellow fluid flowed from where her long fingers had been.

She gnashed her dark jagged fangs. Drool dripped from the sides of her mouth. The dribble sizzled on the rocky ledge like acid. Small streams of smoke rose.

"Damn," Roble whispered.

The female demon lunged for him. He darted to the side and swung the blade again. The blade cut through the air with a swish but missed her.

A strange gurgling growl rumbled in her throat. Her narrowed eyes loomed with hate. She carefully paced side-to-side, studying Roble's movements and awaiting a proper chance to grab him.

Roble took a step backward, and bits of broken rock slid off the ledge. He dropped to a knee to prevent himself from falling over as well. Glancing back, he saw they were on a high perch set directly over a large pool of lava. Even if he were able to get away from the she-demon, he didn't see a quick way to flee. Had the pool been water, he'd leap over the edge to escape now. As it was, he was forced to remain close to this demon until either he killed her or she killed him.

The three eggs vibrated. One cracked. A pointed beak chipped and chipped at the hard shell from the inside. Flakes of the shell popped upward. A jagged crack branched down the side of the egg. Inside the shell, two odd shaped feet kicked, cracking the egg even more. The demon was minutes from breaking free.

Roble pushed the egg, which was almost equal to his size and weight. The egg rolled slightly, tipped into a slanted groove, and then tumbled over the edge. The she demon's eyes widened, and she growled in alarm. Her wings spread, she kicked upward, and took to flight. She dove over the ledge and screeched.

"What now?" Shawndirea asked.

"Not sure," he replied, moving closer to the wall of the cliff and pressing his back against it. He lowered the pack from his shoulder and set it against the cliff wall. The loss of the bag's weight helped, but he was a long way from recovering from being nearly strangled during the brutal flight across the large hellish cavern.

Roble panted for air. The overwhelming heat and undesirable rotten smell sickened him. He took his hunting knife and rammed the sharp serrated blade through one egg and then the other. After he pried apart the shells, he drove the knife through their soft skulls, killing them instantly.

A hot breeze drifted upward and the air pushed Roble against the wall. Shawndirea lowered herself into his pocket.

The she-demon rose over the ledge and planted her feet inside her nest. Her sharp-tipped toenails carved into the rocky surface. Shawndirea crawled from his pocket and scrambled down to the rocky ledge to hide.

When the demon noticed the two eggs busted and her dead offspring, she became infuriated. She roared and gnashed her teeth. She set down the other egg and rushed at him. Without hesitation Roble met her and leaped upward. He drove the blade through her tough exoskeleton and plunged it into her heart.

She flailed her long-fingered hands and smacked him. He held the hilt tightly. She pressed him against the wall, driving the blade deeper. Her acidic breath gagged him and made Shawndirea cough. She quickly covered her face.

The demon's strength weakened. Yellow blood oozed down her chest. Roble realized that if she died while pressing him against the wall, he'd died, too. He twisted the blade. Pain tore through her. She pushed back from the wall. Roble refused to let go of the hilt. He had few weapons, and he didn't want to lose this one. This was the best knife in his possession.

She staggered backwards, carrying him as she fought to stand, and due to her height, he dangled two feet above the ledge while gripping the dagger. Roble was unable to brace his feet against the rock to get leverage, so he wrapped his legs through hers and around the back of her knees. He yanked down on the blade, slicing through her chest into her abdomen. Life drained from her.

Roble pulled back on the blade. It made a sickening wet sound as it slid out. Once the metal freed from her demon flesh, Roble dropped to the ledge with the blade in his hand. The demon dropped backwards with a heavy thud.

He lowered to his knees with sweat dripping from his body. He ached for fresh air, water. Unzipping the pack, he watched the demon. Her shallow breathing stopped. Shawndirea peered out from behind one of the broken eggshells and hurried to him.

Roble took the bottle of honey mixture, opened it for her, and poured a capful into the lid. She closed her eyes and drank deep gulps. When she paused, she whispered words he didn't understand, but what he assumed, and hoped, were words of blessings.

He dug through the pack and grabbed the canteen. After opening it and turning it up, he nearly spit out the water. It was hot.

"Ehh," he said after forcing down the liquid.

"Make do with it," Shawndirea said. "I am."

"Sorry that it's hot."

"Not your fault. It is what it is."

Roble screwed the lid back on the canteen and placed it inside the pack. He rolled the last egg over the ledge and watched it fall hundreds of feet until it hit the lava pool. Beyond the lava pool a flash of light shot upward and exploded against the domed ceiling like a bottle rocket. Chips of stalactites showered down.

"What was that?" he asked.

Shawndirea strained to see. "Forcas."

The light flashed again. Roble traced from where it emitted. A dark robed figure stood near the area where the winged demons had snatched them off the ground.

"Come on," Roble said. "Time to find a way out."

Deep laughter bellowed through the cavern.

"Forcas seems pissed," he said.

She shook her head. "Drunk?"

Roble laughed. "No. Angered."

Shawndirea shrugged. "Let his anger consume him. All you need to do is get us to the other side of the river."

"Why?"

"Styx divides the realms. He cannot pass."

"But we can?"

She nodded.

"You shall not escape me!" Forcas' voice roared, echoed, and then like a small breeze, it whispered past them.

Shawndirea climbed onto his shoulder. Roble pushed himself close to the wall. The widest area of the ledge was where the demon had built her nest. On both sides of the nest, the width was only three feet at the widest. A couple hundred yards away was a lit torch. The path beneath the torch was wider. Unless the flickering light was playing tricks on him, there were crude steps leading downward.

"It's risky," he said, "But if I can get us over there, we should be safer."

"Look at me," she said softly.

Roble stared into her lovely eyes. They narrowed. He couldn't look away. She whispered words he didn't understand. When she blinked, he shook his head and looked down. He stood on the rough-hewn rock stairs beneath the burning torch on the other side of the lava pool.

"You cast a spell on me?" he asked.

Shawndirea shook her head. "No. I won't do that. I refuse to. I would never marry a man that I had bewitched."

Roble's heartbeat increased. He was stunned. *Marry?* he thought to himself.

"It breaks so many rules of magic," she said.

"Then how did we get here?"

"I only spoke words of encouragement to you in my language. I built your confidence by speaking to your subconscious. You did the rest."

"And seconds later, I'm here."

She placed her hand to his cheek and shook her head. "It took you over a half hour of careful climbing to get us here."

"But I was looking into your eyes."

Shawndirea smiled. "The important thing is that you got us here safely."

"No magic?"

"None. I vow to you that I'll never cast a spell on you. Never."

"Thanks. I appreciate that."

"If I did, honestly, I could not marry you."

Roble smiled. "And that's what you want to do? Marry me?"

"I believe it's meant to be. Although the news *won't* be taken well in my kingdom."

Roble took the torch and walked down the stairs. The light diminished.

"Because of the conflict?"

"That. And my mother."

"Oh?" Roble said. "Why?"

"Because I'm destined for the throne."

"Royalty. That's nice."

"I'm already known as the Butterfly Queen in my kingdom and throughout the Underworld," she said softly, "Which is why I had no choice but to do what I did with your collection. But I am also destined for the throne that rules my race."

"Can you have both?"

Shawndirea shrugged. "Anyone can hold two titles, but my marriage to you will void any right I have for my mother's throne."

"Then you shouldn't abandon that."

"For the future, our future, it is best. And should you prove your worthiness to them, perhaps that will end the quarrel between our races."

Roble frowned. "What started the division?"

Shawndirea looked away. "It's best I don't tell you right now."

"No, you should."

She replied, "And why should I?"

"You keep mentioning marriage and bringing me into your kingdom, then I should know exactly why your race hates mine."

"Very well," she replied softly. "You're right. I should, but it's so difficult."

Tears formed in her eyes.

She said, "My father was killed during his journey with a group of humans."

"I'm sorry."

She lifted a hand. "I don't believe he was purposely killed. I believe it was accidental. My mother is the one who declared our species no longer at peace with humans."

"What happened?" Roble asked, still carefully taking the stairs downward. The torch flickered and barely kept the stairs visible.

"He accepted the task of spying on a group of Dark Elves outside Kendrick Woods. It was believed that this renegade group had stolen gold from one of the Dwarven blacksmiths in Hoffnung, when that city was still thriving."

"And the elves killed him?"

Shawndirea shook her head. "No. He was able to sneak into their camp while they encircled the campfire. He hid in the brush and found where they kept the gold. He returned to the humans, told them, and they rushed the camp. They got the gold without having to kill one Dark Elf."

Roble stopped at the base of the rugged stairwell, held the torch high, and looked around. Although it was still quite warm for a cavern, the heat and light slowly dissipated. Unlike the entrance to Devils Den, where the walls were dripping wet, these walls were dry and caked with yellow sulfur. At least they weren't black ash and the rotten smell wasn't nearly as harsh.

He held the torch and looked at the opening of a small tunnel. It was too small for him to enter, so he searched the level area until he came upon another hidden stairwell.

"Did the Dark Elves retaliate?"

"No. The humans stripped them of their weapons and boots, and sent them to venture through the woods."

"Harsh."

Shawndirea shook her head. "No. They're thieves. They should have been killed on the spot. They went away. For awhile."

"So how did he die?"

"As most humans do when they collect a bounty from a dwarf, they celebrate in the tavern. These men did the same. The blacksmith invited them for drinks. And, of course, they didn't refuse."

Shawndirea sat on Roble's shoulder. The hissing torch flames danced as he motioned it back and forth and ascended the stairs.

"My father drank with them," she continued. "It was afterwards, when they left the tavern in the dark of the night that he was killed. By what, we're not certain. He was separated from the humans in the Haunted Forest of Dorlan."

"Haunted?"

She nodded. "Usually no one ventures there. But they needed a shortcut from Hoffnung to Belshast. Halfway through something grabbed my father and darted into the forest. The men took swords and pursued. They never found the creature, but they did find him. He was drained of all his blood, shriveled and lifeless. My guess is they took his magic first."

Roble walked up the stairs. He stopped with a frown on his face. "Why would a king join himself with others to pursue a band of thieves?"

"He wasn't king."

"I see."

"This was over a hundred years ago. My mother took the throne about ten years after his death. He never wore the crown, but in his memory, my mother swore that the Fae and humans be eternal enemies."

"So now I see why your mother will oppose us."

"Yes."

"Did she not believe what happened?"

"The men gave her their explanations, but she refused to accept it as an accident. She insisted they should have taken the long road around the Haunted Forest instead. Without fully knowing what attacked and killed him, she didn't risk sending out scouts to investigate for fear they would be killed in the same manner."

"Sounds like she believed them," Roble said.

"I am certain she does. The problem is she needed closure and not being able to gain that, she took out her harbored vengeance and blamed the human race."

"And why do you take a different stance?"

"Just because one group makes a mistake doesn't make all guilty. I talked with two of the men before they died of old age. Each gave the same explanation for what occurred. Both offered regret. Their remorse was real, and they blamed themselves, even though I believe there wasn't anything they could have done to save him."

"I'm sorry."

She smiled.

A quarter of the way up the long stairwell, Shawndirea said, "Stop."

Roble did so. "What is it?"

"Go back down."

"Why?"

She pointed and said, "The veil. It passes down there. I sense it."

Roble hurried back down the stairs.

At the base of the stairs, she closed her eyes. A frown creased her dainty brow. She pointed again. "Just a bit more over that way."

Roble stepped to where she directed.

Her fingertips glowed. "There."

He turned and took another step.

"Wait. A bit more to the left."

As he followed her directions, a massive flowing wall appeared a few seconds after her fingers touched it. The wall resembled a green tidal wave, but it never crashed forward. It stood like a wall of water.

"How did it appear?"

She smiled. "Magic detects magic."

"It's good that you found it."

"Yes," she said, "But I don't see a rift. No opening to pass through."

Roble wiped the lines of salt from his face where his sweat had dried.

"There must be a place to cross."

"I'm certain there is, but be patient. We're being too hopeful to expect to find the rift at the exact moment we find the veil."

Roble stared at the veil. The images floating within were distorted. When he caught a glimpse of his own reflection, it resembled what he might see in a funhouse mirror.

"Back up the stairs, quick!" She said.

Roble turned and headed upstairs. Midway up the veil now crossed the stairs. He had not seen it before, so why was it there now?

"There," she said, pointing. "There's a rift. It's small, but you should still be able to step through."

The veil looked dark and detached. To get through, Roble had to drop to his knees and crawl. "Are you certain it's safe?"

"There is never any certainty when you cross through the veil."

He tossed the torch through the veil before he entered the tear on his hands and knees. Immediately the wall swallowed him. The thickness gelled around him and moving was like trying to crawl through Jell-o. He held his breath for a half a minute until Shawndirea told him that it was okay to breath.

When he crossed through to the other side, he rose to his feet and looked around. The veil wall had vanished. Nothing seemed different. Still the same set of stairs and what appeared to be the same hellish cavern.

"It didn't work."

"We don't know yet," she replied.

"And how will we?"

She smiled. "Patience. We'll see."

CHAPTER 19

The heat from the lava pool began to fade as Roble and Shawndirea headed up another spiral rocky path. The temperature chilled to a familiar cave climate, and Roble was beginning to miss the heat they left behind. The farther up the winding cave tunnel they walked, the colder it became. For a while the coolness was a welcome comfort after sweating in the blistering temperature, but now he shivered. He reached into his pack and took out his jacket. After sliding it over his shoulders and putting it on, Shawndirea returned to his shoulder.

Even away from the heat, the glowing lava brightened the cavern, but that light was diminishing. He was glad he had taken the torch. If not for the many dangers of demons, sorcerers, and other strange beasts, he would have admired all the marvelous cave formations. Those spectacular natural speleothems were worthy to be studied, photographed, and documented, but not worth sacrificing limb or life for closer examinations.

At the top of the tier, the path ended at the wall that shimmered in the orange light. He placed his left hand against it. Ice? After he placed the torch in his left hand, he removed his knife and struck the smooth glassy ice. It chipped. He struck it harder. Pieces of ice fell and shattered at his feet. The ice chips slowly melted.

Using his knife like an ice pick, he jabbed and jabbed at the ice until larger pieces of ice broke free. Light filtered through a crack in the ice.

Roble pushed his right hand through the icy wall. The outer wall of piled snow crumbled and fell outward. Wind whipped through the opening and chilled him. He hit and kicked the ice until a large portion of it gave way and crumbled to the floor. He stepped outside the cave onto the frozen mountainside.

The harsh wind sucked the fiery life from the torch. The torch smoldered for a few minutes, and then it only held the burnt scar where the fire once thrived.

"Damn," he whispered. "Building a fire will be more difficult now."

Roble pulled his jacket tighter around his neck. The cold wind bit his bare hands and face without mercy and chilled him to the core.

"Did you expect this place?" he asked.

"I didn't know what to expect. Like Devils Den's constantly changing pathways, you have no guarantee where a rift in the veil might take you."

"But what are the odds we'd end up in a place so cold?" Roble asked, rubbing his hands together while huffing into them.

"Not much different than tossing a golden coin of fate," she replied.

"Seems a bit treacherous a choice." White clouds escaped his mouth as he spoke.

"Oh, there are much more crueler forms of fate."

Roble shook his head. "I suppose so. I never expected to go to Hell and back in order to get you to your home."

"That took me unexpectedly, too, I must admit."

"Seems we've gone from one extreme to the other."

"Damn, it's brutally cold," he said. "I never thought I'd have needed a heavy coat."

"We have to find shelter. Neither of us can survive this temperature for very long."

Scanning the thick forest of trees with twisted forked branches that stretched toward the gray overcast sky, Roble took several difficult steps through the knee-deep snow and pointed. "There's a trail," he said. "Something's been through here often."

"These tracks," she said, "look more recent."

Tall trees lined both sides of the dark path. Other than the line of thick firs along the outer edge of the forest, most of the trees were bare. Snow caked the sides of the trees; revealing which direction the storm had blown overnight. Over the valley below, spiraling waves of snow drifted upward onto the ridge where he stood. The wind pushed toward the forest. Wolves howled from the mountain on the opposite side of the vale. Their cries echoed with driving hunger. He was thankful they were too far to be an intrusive threat.

"Any idea where we are in your realm?" Roble asked. Snow crunched beneath his boots as he walked toward the forest.

"My guess is Glacier Ridge," she replied.

"How close is that to your village?"

She pursed her lips. Disappointment shadowed her eyes. "About one hundred miles."

The distance shocked him. On foot that was much farther than he expected he'd have to travel. In this extreme cold, they'd never survive.

Roble leaned forward to make himself a smaller target, which kept the harsh wind from cutting into them at full force. Stepping out of the open area and under the first intertwined branches that stood as the gateway to the icy trees of misery, he realized how much danger he was in. Even had Shawndirea known they would enter a frozen terrain, he'd never have believed such a forewarning. He foolishly entered Devils Den to find the Underworld based upon his masculine curiosity more than crediting the greater risks he might endure once he reached the other side of the veil.

Yes, she had warned him. *Seeing was believing.* Indeed rugged experience was the best way to learn, however, he had not prepared himself for every situation they might encounter. He feared their deaths here were on his hands. If they both died, which seemed the most probable possibility, his quest and pursuit to discover new creatures, terrains, and a hopeful future away from the Overland technology was doomed.

The icy wind blew sharper and howled as branches sliced its power. He stopped walking when a dull creaking sound out-voiced the wind. Pellets of snow and ice rode the wind, striking his face and stinging his exposed nose and ears. He was thankful that he had not shaved his beard weeks ago in spite of the abnormal sweltering temperatures in the Overlands.

Uncontrollable shivers ran through his body. He was losing valuable body heat. Shawndirea hid in his jacket pocket, not daring to peek out into the abrasive cold. He could feel her tiny body quiver against his chest. He pulled his jacket tighter to block the wind from striking her.

Creeeeaaak! Creeeeaaak!

Roble cupped his hands around his aching, red ears and tried to pinpoint from where this sound was coming from. He could no longer feel his nose. Cold ached through him. His lower jaw shook uncontrollably from time to time.

Creeeeaaak!

He massaged his ears, trying to warm them. The action sent a burning sensation through them. Frostbite wasn't far away. Wrapping his arms around himself, he knew Shawndirea was right. They had to find shelter, despite his want to discover the source behind the noise.

Creeeeaaak!

Ahead, less than ten yards, a dark figure hung and swayed back and forth from a large branch. He didn't have to look again to know it was a man. The dead man's weight sagged the branch. The wind forced the roped noose to cry its announcement of the justice or injustice poorly served.

Roble hurried to the man and looked up. The eyeless man didn't offer any gaze. Pock holes covered his face from vicious pecking, and whatever birds had done this were probably the ones that had taken his eyes from their sockets.

Blood speckles painted the snow crimson beneath this man's swinging body. Near the tree, Roble counted three distinct sets of large boot prints in the snow. The footprints were fresh.

There didn't seem to have been any struggle up to the point where the man was hanged. These prints led back to the path where massive hoof prints deepened the snow.

Three horses.

Perhaps following the riders' trail would lead Roble to a village. But was this a village he should seek? The hanging corpse might have been a victim they had robbed and then murdered. In which case, he should hope *not* to find these men.

Something else stirred in the tree limbs above him. When he located them, their appearance caught him off guard.

On a lower branch three white crows perched. Their feathers were snow white, and their eyes shimmered an icy blue glow. Blood stained their grayish white beaks. They cocked their heads to the side and studied him. As much as he regarded their strangeness to crows he was familiar with, he was certain they knew he didn't belong in their world. They weren't out of place. He was.

Their solid stern gazes indicated they wished him to leave their feast alone. Roble was unable to take his eyes off these fascinating birds. He truly wished he had a way to photograph them and show other scientists these birds' uniqueness, but they weren't unique here. They were probably commonplace.

Shawndirea brought her head up and looked out. "What is it? Why are you not moving?"

He nodded toward the hanging man.

"So?" she said. "There's nothing you can do for him."

"I know. Just a puzzle in this world."

"Worrying or trying to solve a puzzle in this horrid weather will be the end of us."

Roble nodded.

"But," Shawndirea said, "there is something you should do."

"What?"

"Cut him down."

Roble frowned. "Why?"

"Strip him of his clothes. He was dressed for this weather. You are not. Besides, your clothes immediately identify you as an Overlander. And depending upon who we may run into, your fate may be the same as his."

Roble didn't like the idea of taking a dead man's clothes, but she was right. The man's overcoat and robe were thick, which would insulate him from the cold winds and growing snow. He was also certain that his own clothes labels would draw immediate questions from people in this region. Setting down his pack, he looked around. He drew his knife, and then he studied the limb and the distance up the tree. The massive trunk prevented him from scaling the tree the ten feet he needed to reach the branch.

He sighed and shook his head.

"What now?" she asked.

"Trying to figure out how to reach the rope."

She released an aggravated little grunt. "Step back."

Roble took three steps back.

Shawndirea stood inside his pocket. Her shoulders and head were in direct view. She raised her hands, closed her eyes, and a green ball of fire shot from her fingers. The band of white crows cawed with alarm and took to flight. The fire hit the rope, setting it on fire. Soon the rope stretched, the fire grew a bit more, and the rope snapped.

The dead man dropped and hit the ground with a heavy thud. His body bounced and made a sickening crackling sound, which indicated one of two things. Either he had been dead a long time while the winter wind froze his corpse, or the plummeting temperature was severely cold enough to freeze flesh quickly, within hours. Although he hoped it was the former and the marauders were a safe distance away, he feared those responsible for the hanging lingered nearby in the forest because their tracks were fresh.

"Hurry," Shawndirea said, hugging herself tightly and snuggling against the pocket lining. "I'm freezing."

Roble unbuttoned the dead man's thick black trench coat. He stared for a moment at the silver medallion that fastened the gray cloak into place. He unlatched the medallion, which held the face of a horned dragon skull, and tugged the cloak out from the man's stiff carcass. He then walked to the man's feet and yanked off his leather boots. He looked at the man, feeling somewhat guilty for taking his clothes. The remaining flesh on the man's face was tinted blue.

"Sorry for this," he whispered to the dead man.

The tip of the noose smoldered from the remaining small flame. Roble took his knife and cut strips of cloth from the man's cotton undershirt. Quickly he placed them on the flame. The fire flickered, rose. While the fire grew, he pried the man's frozen arms out of place so he could remove the coat. He took the cloak and wrapped Shawndirea in the edge of the cloth to keep her out of the cold. After unzipping his jacket, he tossed it onto the fire, grabbed the heavy coat and pulled it on. There wasn't much warmth to gain since the owner was dead, but in time, Roble's own body heat would build inside the coat and warm him.

He removed the man's gray gloves and put them on. Although thin and fitting tight like a second skin, the wind no longer numbed his fingers. His hands became incredibly warm. He untied the man's belt and tugged off his pants. He held them close to the fire until warmth radiated through them.

"Now for the hard part," Roble said, bracing himself for the cold.

Unlacing his hiking boots and loosening them, he kicked them off. Mentally, he braced himself for the next task. He unbuckled his belt, dropped his pants and tossed them onto the fire. Shawndirea peeked out from the cloak and smiled. Her eyes widened. In lightning speed, he grabbed the fire-warmed trousers and pulled them to his waist, quickly tying the belt into place.

Roble took the knife and cut out a square of cloth from the bottom of the dark cloak. He cut a small hole in the center and handed the cloth square to Shawndirea. She put her head through the hole and pulled the cloth around her. Taking a loose thread, she used this as a belt to hold the cloth close to her body.

Pulling the cloak around his shoulders, he paused again to study the silver dragon skull medallion. He wondered what the symbol represented as he snapped it together to hold the cloak into place. He pulled the hood over his head to prevent the wind from frostbiting his numb ears. Without noticing, the cloak tightened and whipped around his legs.

Roble exchanged boots and tossed his old ones onto the fire. He took his Swiss Army knife and stared at it. Knowing the blades would never burn, he tucked the knife into the overcoat pocket.

"You realize the fire and smoke will reveal our position?" she asked.

He shrugged. "Maybe so, but it's best I destroy the clothes so no one discovers an Overlander has arrived. Besides, I think we could use a good fire to heat us before we move further into the forest."

She nodded.

Roble unzipped his pack, took out the plastic bottle of honey mixture and poured another capful for Shawndirea. While she drank ice formed around the cap and the liquid in the bottle solidified.

"I'm afraid this is the last of it for now. As much as I hate it, I must destroy all the evidence."

"You must," she agreed.

He stepped closer to the fire. Puddles of water formed from the melting snow. Black smoke rose off the burning rubber soles of his hiking boots. The inviting heat kept him close to the fire. Holding the pack by the handle, he tossed it onto the flames. The sides of the pack smoldered, blistered, and finally burst open as the fire ruptured it. All the contents vanished beneath the flame. He worried how they would find food, especially for her, in this weather.

The cold wind funneled through the trees. Large wet snowflakes swirled. His beard caught a lot of the passing snow, which slowly built a thin white layer and made his brown beard look frozen.

A good fifteen minutes passed. He was no longer cold. The weather didn't affect him at all. The clothes had incredible insulation and weighed less than the ones he had discarded.

With a long branch, he churned the fire to make certain no identifiable traces of clothing remained. He watched the flames settle, and as the clothes turned slowly to ash, the fire lost its power. Smoke pillowed and drifted through the ice-covered trees.

Wolves howled from a great distance across the valley. Their wails were desperate and agitated. Although he loved to hear their cries, he was thankful he wasn't in any threat of confrontation with them. Hunger might be their major motivation.

"That's the best of the fire," Roble said, marching toward the dark path that divided the forest. The wind whipped his cloak behind him as he walked. "I suppose we head on to see if there's a town nearby."

"I wouldn't be so eager to rush into any town near here," she said.

"Why not?"

"Your fate might equal to the man who owned the clothes you now possess."

Roble shook his head. "I'll be careful."

"You're in a different world now. You may have to defend yourself in a very aggressive way."

"I did that with Deiko."

She smiled evenly and said, "Have you ever killed a man?"

"No."

"The possibility may arise where you may have to do exactly that. Are you capable of killing someone?"

"I hope I never have to."

"We are near the ridge where bandits thrive, trade, and murder. There's no question a time will come where you will face an enemy that will kill you if you don't kill him first."

"Noted," he replied. "Now we must find safe shelter, even if that means renting a room from a poor family."

Thinking about the encounter with Deiko, he remembered how he debated on throwing the knife to end Deiko's life. At that moment, he knew he could throw the knife in self-defense, but the only drawback was the headache of dealing with law enforcement officials and possibly court proceedings. But the laws and rules differed here. Shawndirea was right. He didn't have time to debate dangerous situations he encountered, which eliminated any reluctance he might have in the Overlands.

He wondered, though, how his mind would cope should he find the need to end a man's life. Deep inside, he truly hoped he didn't have to find out.

CHAPTER 20

Queen Istrell stared over her kingdom from the highest branch in her tree palace. The sun faded behind the evening clouds, which turned the sky into a lovely array of pastel pinks, purples, and orange.

She wrung her aged hands. Warm tears streaked her cheeks. Then she felt it. A gentle rush of energy pulsed from the earth. Her eyebrows rose.

"Shawndirea?" she gasped. "I feel you. Where are you?"

Istrell hurried to the crystals and placed her hands upon them. Power surged through her. Immediately Shawndirea's face materialized in Istrell's mind. Her daughter's jaw shivered. Frosty clouds exited Shawndirea's nose and mouth. She was freezing.

As the imagery became clearer, she saw Shawndirea curled inside a dark cloak spread out on the ground. A human stood nearby.

Istrell's attention turned back to her daughter. With horror, Istrell's eyes widened. Shawndirea's glorious wings were tattered, destroyed. Tears from anger, frustration, and worry streaked Istrell's cheeks.

The human stood over the body of a dead man and seemed to be stealing the man's clothes. The man undressed and quickly put on the clothes he had taken.

Snow spiraled around Shawndirea, who sat shivering. The man picked up Shawndirea after fastening the cloak around his shoulders. She watched the man latch the silver pendant to hold the cloak into place. Istrell's stomach became uneasy. She recognized the pendant.

The Dragon Skull Order. *What* was this man up to? *Why* did he have Shawndirea?

The man cut material from his cloak and handed it to Shawndirea. After she placed the cloth over her head, she vanished. Istrell couldn't see her or feel her presence. The power from the crystals faded. She grabbed her mirror, but no images appeared.

Istrell's distaste for the human race enraged further. She had lost her husband due to reckless humans and now one was keeping her daughter from her place in the kingdom. Shawndirea's precious wings. What had happened to her wings? Istrell's fists tightened with rage.

"I will find you, my daughter," Istrell vowed. "And when I do, he shall pay dearly for what he has done."

CHAPTER 21

Shawndirea moved to his shoulder. The square of cloth from the cloak magically hugged her from neck to feet, detailing the perfection of her body. The black cloth even formed small boots on her feet. Sadly, her tattered wings hung loosely as a distraction that kept reminding him of his misdeed.

"Did you use magic to transform the cloth into those clothes?" he asked, gently touching her stomach.

Stunned, she examined her clothes and reached behind her head. She pulled a hood over her head that hid her pointed ears and smiled. "No. No magic at all. But their instant warmth is welcomed."

Roble stopped walking and took the cloak in his hands. He searched along the bottom hem to find where he had cut away the material, but there wasn't a gap at all. His eyebrows rose from his sudden surprise.

"What do you make of this?" he asked.

Shawndirea shrugged. "I haven't any idea."

"Magic?"

"Enchanted cloth perhaps. It's hard to say."

Roble frowned. "Enchanted by whom?"

"There's no way to know."

Roble flipped the cloak behind him and continued his stride down the path. Fresh falling snow was filling the three sets of hoof prints. In another half hour the prints would be gone.

"What do you know of the humans in Glacier Ridge?" he asked.

"Fae do not venture here. At least none from my kingdom."

Roble walked at a slower pace. The cold grew even less noticeable the longer he wore the dead man's clothes. "Why not?" he asked.

"For one, it's too damn cold. Even if I possessed my wings, I could not fly."

Roble nodded. "Some insects are like that."

She frowned. "I am *not* an insect!"

He shook his head. "I wasn't implying that. I was merely comparing it to what I've seen during winter at my home. Sometimes hibernating wasps or bees get exposed from beneath firewood, and they cannot take flight. They must generate enough heat for their wings to lift them."

"You *had* to be a scientist," she muttered.

"So the cold was one reason. What are others?" he asked.

"I get grumpy."

"No comment," Roble said with a smile.

Shawndirea's eyes narrowed, and she crossed her arms. A peevish expression darkened her face.

"Sorry," he said. "I didn't mean to anger you."

"Cold weather sours my mood. I am the Butterfly Queen. Flowers and butterflies aren't viable during winter, so I reside in a valley that never suffers cold. Otherwise I'd go insane."

"So your homeland never has winter?" he asked.

"No."

"Other than not being able to fly and your grumpiness, why don't your Fae venture here?"

"Bandits and assassins use this ridge as a gathering place. If someone wishes to hire an assassin, they know they can hire someone along Glacier Ridge, provided they're not killed before they make their offer."

"We need a horse."

She nodded. "And you need a better weapon."

"I have knives."

She smiled. "Most use swords or crossbows here."

Roble replied, "If I have the distance I can stop a man wielding a sword. But even the best swordsman is no match against someone with a crossbow."

Shawndirea cocked her head and gave a quick little nod. "True. But could you use a sword?"

"Never tried."

"Then you best learn," she said, crossing her arms and tilting her nose upward. "Otherwise I will be without you before long. I simply cannot have that."

He smiled at her statement, which implied she wanted to be with him. He asked, "You doubt my abilities that much?"

"I've seen a lot of death in this realm."

"And who will train me?"

She smiled. "I imagine you'll find someone who pities your lack of swordsmanship."

"Oh?"

"It is a major handicap."

"I imagine so."

"In a world that settles disputes by the blade, you have no idea. Please trust me."

Roble smiled at her. "I do. When such opportunity presents itself, I promise to hire someone to train me."

Smoke drifted across the pathway about a quarter mile away. Horses whinnied.

"Off the road," Shawndirea whispered.

Roble hurried off the path and stepped behind a massive tree. He waited several minutes, watching and waiting for riders to come toward them. No one came.

"Perhaps they're heading the other direction," he said.

"Perhaps. Proceed slowly but you might want to stay off the main road."

He shook his head. "No. The road is frozen solid. Even with the fresh layer of snow that's on it, it's quieter for me to walk along the road than try to step through frozen briars and foot deep snow."

"Be cautious," she said. "Remember thieves and assassins could be anywhere."

"I know. I'll be careful."

Roble stepped softly along the road, hoping to prevent any crunching sounds that gave away their position. Laughter echoed off a side path away from the main road. He followed the path for a few hundred feet until he noticed the smoke rising from a crackling fire. He leaned against a massive tree trunk and peered around. Three men sat on logs facing the fire. A fourth man sat opposite them. His hands were shackled together, and he wore clothes similar to the ones Roble now wore.

The other three wore brown leather pants. Their heavy fur coats were made from the hides of white wolves. One man took a long drink from a leather flask, passed it to the man on his right, and then he wiped his beard with the back of his hand.

They sat hunched forward, possibly to catch the heat of the fire. One spoke and the other two laughed at whatever he was saying.

"They hold the man prisoner," Roble whispered.

"Or for bounty," Shawndirea replied. "Don't forget where we are."

"I really wish you could fly," he said, placing his hands on his knives.

"You're not confronting them, are you?"

"Why not?"

"They appear to be rugged renegades. And the man they hold prisoner was probably in company with the man hanged back there."

Roble nodded. "I know, which is why I plan to free him."

"What? Why?"

"Right now we could use another ally."

"There's no guarantee that he will side with you and not attempt to kill you."

"I know," Roble whispered. His eyes studied the men closely while they talked. "But I have the feeling that he won't."

"Your odds are still three to one."

Roble smiled. "I learned to count years ago."

She frowned. "They learned to fight with swords while boys. You're not prepared to combat *one* of them, much less three."

"Where will you feel safest?" he asked.

"What do you mean?"

"My shoulder, in my pocket, or I can place you on this small tree branch," he replied.

"Your shoulder would be best. If necessary I can leap into the snow."

"Okay."

Roble took a step away from the tree toward the narrow path that led to the campfire.

"Remember that hesitation will be your death."

Roble studied the men a few moments longer, took another step and his foot snapped a branch. The sound echoed and immediately caught the attention of the three men warming by the fire. They turned and stood quickly, drawing their blades. The men were massive, in both muscle and their near seven-foot height. Their faces were covered with thick beards woven into neat knots that stopped at their belts.

For possible assassins or thieves, they looked more like Viking warriors. Their stature was unlike anyone Roble had seen in the Overlands. Oddly, he didn't fear them, although they should have intimidated him.

Roble put his hands out to the side and tucked his chin against his chest. When he lowered his head and headed toward them, their eyes widened with fear. Their blades lowered momentarily, and then they stood side by side to offer a solid defensive front. The man in the middle stepped forward and pointed the tip of his sword at Roble.

"How?" the center man said. He frowned and squinted, trying to understand what he was seeing. "We hanged you."

"There must be a sorcerer," the man to his left said, looking around the trees. "It's sorcery. It has to be. This one can't possibly be alive."

"But he is!" the third said, shifting his sword from hand to hand. "It's his ghost."

The leader turned, grabbed their prisoner by the back of his cloak and yanked him to his feet.

"Stay back whatever you are," the man said. "Or we kill your comrade!"

Roble's eyes narrowed. The wind whipped his cape behind him as he walked forward ignoring any potential dangers. There was no hesitation in his stride, nor did any fear attempt to consume him. Confidence set in his eyes.

The leader drew his dagger and pressed the sharp serrated edge against the prisoner's throat. The prisoner closed his eyes and clasped his hands together as if bracing himself for the slice of the blade. Or perhaps he prayed.

"No further," the leader said. "I swear it!"

The two blades left Roble's hands without notice. The blades sang a near whisper as they struck and delivered deathblows. One knife blade rammed through the leader's right eye before he could slit the prisoner's throat. The man's left eye widened from sudden pain. The serrated blade fell from his hand, landing point down in the snow. The prisoner dove to the ground, crawled through the snow and rolled over the large log to hide near the tied horses.

The second man clutched the hilt that stuck out of his throat. He dropped to his knees and fell face forward into the snow. Dark blood spurted from his neck and painted the snow crimson.

The third man glanced at his two dead comrades. He scrambled backwards, making his way to the horses tied to the trees. Roble didn't slow his step. He marched fearlessly.

"Roble!" Shawndirea whispered in his ear sharply.

Roble ignored her.

The man rushed to his saddlebag and fought to retrieve a bow. Roble pulled his last blade, which was too light to be thrown a great distance with much accuracy, so he sprinted through the crunching snow. White puffs of icy clouds drifted from his mouth and nose as he ran.

The large man loaded an arrow and right when he turned to face Roble, the small knife struck his shoulder. The man gnashed his teeth, growled, and yanked the tiny blade out. He stared at the blade for a moment. He laughed, tossed the knife in the snow, and smiled, pulling back the string.

"Roble!" Shawndirea shouted. "Watch out!"

The words never registered with him. He acted like he was in a world all to himself. He stood emotionless and braver than any fool could be.

The arrow went far to the right of Roble's head and sailed into the trees. He never flinched. The man who shot it was on the ground, growling in pain. The prisoner had kicked the back of his captor's knees, which knocked the man off balance and sent him to the ground. The prisoner then climbed on the man's chest and battered his face with his cuffed hands until the man's screams stopped.

"You damned bastard," the prisoner said to his dead captor before spitting on his bruised and bloody face. And for good measure, he swung another heavy blow.

Roble approached, and the prisoner rolled off the dead man. He backed away through the snow, beneath a horse, and toward the trees. His fearful eyes were wide. His lips trembled.

"What's wrong?" Roble asked.

"Don't kill me," the prisoner said, gasping for air as he pushed his back against the trunk of an enormous tree. His cuffed hands shook, and he held them up in surrender. He trembled like a scared rabbit.

Roble crossed his arms and shook his head. In a gentle tone, he said, "I'm not going to kill you."

"I tried to stop them from hanging you, Bausch," the prisoner said, pleading. "I offered my life for yours. Don't you remember?"

Roble frowned. The man spoke in a delirious manner. His eyes were haunted. Roble wondered what his captors had done to him.

"Please spare me, Bausch,"

"I'm not Bausch," Roble replied.

"Please. It's me, Lehrling, your friend and trainer since you were a lad. I'm not an old fool. We wear the Dragon Skull pendants. Death occasionally passes us, Bausch. You know that. Perhaps Death spared you and that's the reason for your confusion."

Roble held the silver Dragon Skull clasp between his left forefinger and thumb. He looked down at Lehrling. The man was barely five foot six with a plump gut. The lines on his face revealed he smiled more than he ever frowned, and yet there was hardness around his eyes, which showed he had dealt death to enemies in the past. His yellow beard and shoulder length hair looked well kempt except for the frozen spittle around his lips where he had frantically tried to negotiate with the three men to free him. Now he seemed to believe he must continue to beg for his life.

"I'm not Bausch," Roble said. "I wear his clothes since . . . well, I didn't see that he had any further need for them."

Lehrling frowned, shook his head, and then looked surprised. Sudden recognition calmed him. He said, "I could have sworn you were he. Are you his spirit coming back to seek revenge?"

"No."

"Then who are you?"

"Roble."

"From what land?"

Roble smiled. "No place you would know."

"Perhaps." Lehrling shrugged. "I don't usually travel this far myself."

Roble extended his hand. The man lifted his cuffed hands upward and clasped Roble's hand. Roble pulled the rotund man to his feet.

"Then why did you?" Shawndirea asked, standing on Roble's shoulder.

Lehrling's brow rose. "A faery? The surprises never end. How did you come to possess her?"

Her piercing green eyes narrowed. "He does *not* possess me."

"My apologies," Lehrling said, lifting his cuffed hands in surrender. The small chain that linked his cuffs rattled. "No intention to offend."

"We're on a mutual journey," Roble said. He went from dead man to dead man, patting them down.

"Oh, I see," Lehrling said softly. "And does that journey consist of robbing a hanged man of his clothes and pilfering through bounty hunters' pockets?"

"This is just a brief detour."

Lehrling laughed heartily. "No one detours near Glacier Ridge. It's the end of the mountain trail."

"For most," Shawndirea whispered in Roble's ear.

Roble patted the dead leader's vest, pulled out a small leather pouch, and opened it. It was packed with heavy gold coins. On the dead man's belt, he found a small key ring. He yanked the ring from the belt, examined the keys, and stood.

"We're on the icy plateau that overlooks the Vale of Frozen Tears," Lehrling said. "There's no path that leads down from this ridge into the valley. The only way in is from the other side but getting there is almost a guaranteed death sentence."

Roble took in the information and nodded. "Who were these men and why did they hold you as their prisoner?"

"They are bounty hunters," Lehrling replied.

Roble studied the dead men. "They're damn near giants."

"Aye. They invaded the ports by sea," Lehrling said. "Hundreds of them. They came at night, killing the port guards without being seen."

Roble said, "That would be difficult to defend against, I'd guess."

"Of course. But they had to have had some help from a traitor in Hoffnung."

"Why do you say that?" Roble asked.

"Because the port is a good thousand feet beneath the city. The city sits atop a rugged cliff. They use lifts to carry supplies and troops up and down. Someone from above had to have been signaled and alerted to their arrival for the lifts to be lowered before sunrise."

"Any idea where they're from?" Shawndirea asked.

"No."

Roble stood over one bounty hunter and knelt beside him. He lifted the man's right hand. His massive muscled hands had extra thumbs and unusual tattoos. Their fingernails curved like sharp claws. With their great size and odd hands, he wondered why they even sought to use traditional weapons. Up close these men stood to deal a lot of damage in normal hand to hand combat.

Roble had never thought he'd kill another human, and this happened sooner than he imagined. He wanted to feel some remorse, but it didn't come, which worried him. He should feel something for their loss of life. No, he *wanted* to feel, but he didn't. The quickness to attack also alarmed him. He wondered if Deiko's threat had come now rather than when it actually occurred, would he kill without question. In the Overlands, the closest he'd ever come to such violence was when Deiko had pulled the unloaded gun. However, Deiko had kept demanding to see what was in the pack. Roble didn't doubt that Deiko would have killed to possess Shawndirea. Should they encounter one another again, Roble had no doubt that he would kill Deiko to protect her.

Although Roble was good at throwing knives, he looked at these three dead men and marveled that he had such remarkable accuracy. The worrisome thing was that he didn't remember throwing any knives at all. Everything had occurred in a blurred rapid pace without any recollection, so perhaps that's why remorse did not register with him. He was alive, and they were dead. He didn't know what to feel. And he wondered had he actually thought about the confrontation, would he have hesitated and died?

He tugged his knife from the dead man's throat. The man's lower jaw dropped open, revealing sharp jagged teeth. Two large fangs were on the top row and two smaller fangs set on the bottom. His tongue was a dark blue, almost black.

Roble looked at Lehrling and said, "You're certain that you don't know where these men came from?"

"No."

Roble pointed at the man's teeth and showed Lehrling the man's strange tattooed hands. "Are there other people you know of that have these traits?"

Lehrling looked closer and shook his head. "No. I've never seen anything like them."

Shawndirea gasped.

"What is it?" Roble asked.

"The tattoos. Whoever they hold allegiance to has dark magical sorcery."

"You recognize them, faery?" Lehrling asked.

"Shawndirea is my name."

Lehrling nodded. "My apologies, Shawndirea. From where do you know these?"

She shrugged. "I don't know them. I sense the dark force that put them there."

"So demonkin?" Lehrling asked.

"Could be," she replied. "They look similar to the Vykings."

Lehrling nodded. "I was thinking the same except . . . their teeth and extra thumbs."

"That's what makes me believe they're demonkin," she said. "But why would they keep you for a reward? That seems odd."

"I know."

Roble looked at Lehrling and said, "So there's a bounty on your head?"

Lehrling smiled. "One for you, too, as long as you wear that armor."

"Why?"

"We're . . . I should say that *I'm* of the Dragon Skull Order, the Guardians for Queen Taube of Hoffnung."

"Taube is dead," Shawndirea said. "Her kingdom was overthrown six months ago."

Lehrling nodded. "Truth. You are correct. Bausch and I were scouting for her daughter."

"So Lady Dawn lives?" she asked.

"We pray so. Daily. She was never accounted for after her kingdom was invaded. No one found her body, and no one ever saw her leave the city gates."

Roble took the key and unlocked the cuffs. The heavy metal bands dropped into the snow. Lehrling rubbed his wrists and nodded graciously.

Roble walked to the next dead man and pulled his blade from his throat.

"Why take back your blades?" Lehrling asked, picking up the dead man's sword. "When you can claim their swords?"

Roble wiped blood from the blade before tucking it into its sheath. Without making eye contact, he replied, "I've never used a sword."

Lehrling's yellow bushy eyebrows rose. "Never?"

Roble shook his head.

"Boys are brought up learning how to use a blade efficiently," Lehrling said. "It's a means for survival. Any father worth a beggar's piece of bread places a sword in his son's hand by the time he is six years old."

"I guess I'm the exception," Roble replied.

Lehrling frowned. "How have you survived this long? The world is a brutal place."

Roble smiled. "By avoiding fights."

"You're damn good with knives, but you still should use a sword."

"He needs training," Shawndirea said.

Lehrling chuckled. "No need telling me. Anyone not trained to use a sword is a fool."

"Can you train him?" she asked. "You mentioned that you trained Bausch."

"Aye, but that was years ago. I'm much older and a bit slower."

Shawndirea smiled. "A modest man is rare these days."

"Me, modest?" he replied, blushing. "I've been called a lot of things, but modest isn't one that I've heard, especially after I've been drinking."

"If you were slow to use a blade," Shawndirea said, "You'd by no means be journeying across the countryside willing to engage in battle to find Lady Dawn."

"Oh, but to defend her crown, her rightful claim to the throne? I'd die a thousand times if necessary."

She said, "A modest man filled with valor."

Lehrling chuckled and stared at her. His laughter stopped. "My dear one," he said. "What became of your wings?"

Shawndirea's smile faded. She looked away. "An accident. It is why Roble carries me back to my homeland."

"Aye. Pity, young faery. Is there hope that you'll get them back?" he asked.

"Yes."

"That's good."

Lehrling picked up a bastard sword, held it at a downward angle, and admired the blade. "Here, Roble. This was Bausch's before they killed him. The blade's sound and well tempered. Lighter weight than most like it, which will aid you in combat."

Roble took the sword and said, "Thanks."

He maneuvered the blade in his hand and did a couple of practice swings. The weight of the sword felt good in his hand, and he liked the thought of mastering its use. And albeit strange, he felt like he had used it before.

"Not bad," Lehrling said, "For a man who's never used a sword."

Roble smiled, "Thanks. I guess."

Lehrling shrugged and retrieved the other two swords, their daggers, and their pouches of gold coins.

"I suppose I'm not the only looter among us," Roble said.

"As you said about Bausch's clothes, none of these demon-men will be needing these. Gold buys ale and hard liquor regardless of the coin's seal."

Lehrling cleared his throat, walked to the log near the fire, and set the weapons against the log before plopping down. Roble joined him, propped his blade against the side of the log, and opened the leather pouch of coins. He examined the gold coins one by one. All were imprinted with the same lettering and a king's image on one side.

"Okay, so why's there a bounty on our heads?" Roble asked.

"Over two dozen of the Dragon Skull Order combs the kingdoms and countryside looking for her. Lord Waxxon, the new ruler in Hoffnung, hunts for us, hoping that we have found Dawn so he can kill her."

"To prevent a rightful heir from taking the throne," Roble said.

Lehrling nodded. "Exactly. That's Waxxon's ugly face on the coins you're looking at."

"Queen Taube was loved and her charity was renowned," Shawndirea said.

"And her daughter was destined for greater," Lehrling added. "That's why we were scouting to find her."

"Or someone that may help you find her?" Shawndirea asked.

"Not exactly like that," he replied with a slight shrug. "We hoped that by visiting a few taverns along the ridge that we might overhear a drunken rogue reveal that he had found her and was trying to find a way to seek a ransom."

"Taverns in this area are dangerous," she said. "Competition between hired assassins leads to many deaths."

"I know. That's how Waxxon's henchmen found us."

"And what if you do find her?" Roble asked.

"We return her to power," he replied.

"Two dozen of you? Possibly even less, if any were captured and killed like Bausch."

Sadness claimed Lehrling's eyes. "We will rally the townspeople and peasants within Hoffnung's boundaries."

Roble shook his head. "That is hardly an army worth storming a city, especially if the troops you're facing are like these dead demonkin warriors."

"Waxxon's ascension to the throne was not welcome. Queen Taube's murder angered the villages, townships, and most everyone that knew Her Grace. People will want to fight."

"Perhaps," Shawndirea said. "But you may have a better chance if you gather assistance from the surrounding kingdoms. Since Taube was beloved throughout the regions, others will aid you."

Lehrling nodded. "I imagine they would, but getting to them is a difficulty."

Roble clasped Lehrling's shoulder firmly. "We have horses now. Choose one."

Lehrling shook his head. "No, they are branded with Waxxon's symbol."

"I don't give a damn," Roble said. "There's no way I'm leaving them here. I'm not walking through this miserable icy forest."

Roble stood and sheathed the sword Lehrling had given him. The snowflakes became bigger, wetter.

"Very well," Lehrling said. "We keep them until we can trade them for different ones."

"That's fine by me, but the weather's too harsh to walk through."

The horses were large and resembled Clydesdales. As they exhaled, long white puffs formed momentary clouds. Lehrling untied a bay horse.

"No," Roble said, shaking his head. "We should take the other two. Both are white and they'll blend in better with our surroundings."

"And what of this one?" Lehrling said. "Should I tether it behind the other?"

"Sure."

"Makes for a better trade."

Roble climbed upon the mountain of a horse and adjusted himself in the saddle. Shawndirea clung to his collar until he was steady.

"Mind if I ask you something?" Lehrling asked.

"Not at all," Roble replied.

"What did you do with Bausch's body?"

Roble sighed. "He's still beneath the tree where I cut him down."

"Before we head southward," Lehrling said, "I think we should properly set his body to rest."

"The ground is probably too solid."

Lehrling smiled and held up an ax that was tied to the side of the saddle.

"Okay," Roble said. "It still won't be easy."

"I know. The grave will be shallow. But I can't live with myself knowing his body is out for the animals to pluck clean."

"I understand, but you should know the crows had access to him before I came upon him."

Lehrling cringed and shook his head. He whispered some words that Roble believed to be a prayer. Regardless of what words were spoken, he believed that prayers weren't enough to protect them from dangers that awaited them.

CHAPTER 22

Deep in the maze of Devils Den, the Dark Chancellor sat on his throne made of skulls. His long gray beard flowed down the front of his black robe. He twisted a strand of his beard with a crooked index finger. His hood was pulled over his head and the shadows hid his face. His golden eyes glowed while he pondered about various disturbances that crossed through his magical cavern.

His control weakened across the depths of the cavern, especially since it continually expanded. With this he constantly sought to maintain stability but discovered that some of his prisoners had gained powers of their own. Unless he reined them in, the possibility of lesser creatures toppling his throne existed. However, he expended most of his energy channeling control over all the others.

The sacrifices of mortal prisoners no longer granted him adequate power to subdue those he feared would eventually challenge him.

His throne room was dark with the exception of blazing sconces at each corner. Their modest fires glowed. Darkness soothed him. That's where he gathered strength and what hid his reptilian facial features from sporadic visitors or accidental adventurers who stumbled inside.

In the center of the throne room hung a large teardrop shaped amethyst. The quartz shimmered, glowed, and the bright light forced the chancellor to shield his eyes with his hand. When the blast of light vanished, ten aged figures stood before him.

"Ah," the Dark Chancellor said in a hiss-filled voice. "Welcome, Ten Sages of Vylan!"

The eldest, dressed in an elegant crimson robe, stepped forward. In surprise he turned and looked at the other nine. He acknowledged each of his brothers with a slight nod. He was stooped as he walked. His red feathery hair and beard were bright like fire and flowed around his crow-like black beak. His beady eyes stared coldly, and he spoke with a shrill-pitched cry, "Why have you summoned us, Botis?"

"No time for proper greetings, Staven?" the Dark Chancellor, Botis, asked.

"You call us from our realm for what? To cackle? For a conference?"

"Now, you've offended me," the Dark Chancellor said, leaning forward on his throne.

Staven squawked. "You understand the delicate balance we hold in Vylan. Only one of us may be summoned at a time, and yet, you've called us all here at once."

"It's an important matter," Botis said, rising to his feet.

"It had best be," Staven replied in a sharp shrill. "What is this matter about?"

"Elias."

"The Overlander? What of him?"

"He's resurrected for the sixth time."

Staven's red eyes narrowed. "So? Why call us here? He's a product of your dark sorcery. Not ours."

"His power grows," Botis said with a concerned expression.

"Such a fool, Botis, for giving a mortal access to your power. Have you lost control of him?"

Botis hissed. "Not entirely, but his intent for immortality increases with each cycle of his resurrection."

"How long before he reaches immortality?" Staven asked, ruffling his feathery hair around his face and neck. He shook his wings beneath his robe.

"He will return to the grave one last time and resurrect again in twenty years."

Staven's eyes narrowed. "And his body? Its decomposition rate? How is it?"

"Better than I hoped. Somehow he has found a way to slow the rotting process. After all, I only granted him power because I believed his body would turn to dust well before he reached the fifth resurrection."

"There are no guarantees with magic, Botis. Even you should know that."

"That's why I sought your entire council."

Staven chuckled in half laugh, half chirp. "The best you can hope is that his body deteriorates too badly that he cannot walk to complete the next cycle."

"He has yet to offer his sacrifice of an innocent soul. Without that, he's doomed."

Staven nodded. "Then there is hope that he will fail."

"Yes. However, he did gain control of another mortal earlier today. But, that man lost track of what Elias sought."

"And that was?"

The Dark Chancellor gave a grim smile. "A faery."

"In the Overlands?"

"She was."

Staven shook his head and weighed the information. "You realize that had he captured and sacrificed her that nothing you did could rein him back under your control?"

"I know. But she has crossed through my cavern and the veil back to the Underworld. She had the help of a human."

"You need to take control of Elias before he gains immortality," Stark said.

"So will you and your brothers help?" Botis asked.

Staven shook his head. "No. This is your spell. Elias is your minion. You must deal with what you have created."

Staven turned and faced the other nine sages. "Come brothers," he said. "Vylan awaits."

"I do have an alternate solution," the Dark Chancellor said. "At least evaluate it and tell me your thoughts on whether it might succeed."

Staven stopped walking and sighed. "What does it consist of?"

"Follow me," he replied.

The Dark Chancellor led the ten sages into the adjoining chamber. At the center of the large room, a solid black staff levitated, which was held in place by magical currents. Shimmering violet light flowed from all four corners of the ceiling. The staff was a conduit that funneled the humming energy through and into the floor beneath it.

Staven leaned on his staff and watched the cascading magical energy that radiated through the black staff. "What strange magic is this?" he asked with a steady squall in his throat.

"This staff is carved from a black tree in Mortel," the Dark Chancellor said.

Staven glanced quickly at Botis in surprise. "Mortel? How is it possible? The darkness in that city is great."

"It was not an easy feat," Botis said.

Staven studied the Dark Chancellor for several moments. Unable to see the serpent chancellor's eyes, he said, "I imagine not. The stirring black mysticism that spawns from the earth in Mortel is why we should have never all been summoned at once."

The Dark Chancellor smiled. "You have fear of Mortel?"

"More a fear of *what* controls it," Staven replied.

Botis hissed with amusement. "Whom, you mean."

"You've met the sorcerer?"

"How do you think I came to possess this staff?"

"He gave it to you?" Staven asked. "But at what price?"

"The cost was acceptable."

The vibrating violet light shimmered. The droning whine it emitted was soothing, coaxing, and drawing.

The nine other raven sages focused on the flowing magic that buzzed and hummed throughout the chamber. Their eyes glazed a grayish-white. The violet beauty of electrical-like waves of energy captivated them. Slowly, one by one, they edged closer to the black staff. Staven noticed the power calling to his brothers and shrieked warnings, but the sages didn't hear.

"What is this?" Staven asked, turning his red-eyed gaze toward the chancellor. "What sacrifice did you offer to obtain this staff?"

"Not as heavy a price as you and your brothers will pay."

Staven's nine brothers encircled the staff. He squawked his protest in a high pitch call, trying to break the hypnotic draw of the magic, but their ears were deaf to his pleas.

"Stop this, Botis!" Staven said, pointing a feathered finger.

The Dark Chancellor hissed in a long subtle laugh. "Who's the fool now?"

A great flash of light expelled from the black staff and when the glaring violet light faded, the nine sages around the staff were gone.

Staven shrieked. "Where are they? My brothers, what have you done with them?"

"The same that shall be done to you, Staven," Botis said, raising his hands.

Staven lifted his magical staff like a shield and shivered behind it. "You have no idea what you've done. Vylan will fall, and it will be upon your head."

Botis laughed and his amusement echoed throughout the chamber. "Vylan is not of my concern. The Raven-kin are strong enough to survive without your protection."

"No," Staven said. "They need us. Without us to protect the mountainous forests, they'll have no safe place to nest."

"They are not my concern. No more than Elias was yours."

Staven's beady eyes widened. "Release my brothers, Botis, and we'll do whatever you need to stop Elias."

"You will anyway." The Dark Chancellor smiled and said, "Beirt noier valens."

A strand of violet energy shot out from the staff, looped around Staven's waist, and tugged him toward the staff. Staven fought and resisted. Loose feathers drifted in the static air and fell to the floor. His staff dropped from his hand to the floor. He squawked, fluttered, and protested, but in the end, the magic sapped and pulled him inside the ebony staff. Once the staff possessed the last of the Ten Sages of Vylan, the pulsing magical energy entered the staff and sealed it. The staff dropped from the air and clacked against the chamber floor. The Dark Chancellor walked over and claimed his prize.

He held the staff upward and admired it. Ten beady red eyes blinked from different knotholes, which now housed the sages and their magical power.

Botis chuckled and said, "Now, let's take back what once was mine."

CHAPTER 23

*A*fter they arrived at Bausch's frozen body, Roble took the ax from Lehrling and chopped into the frozen ground. Ice chips and frozen dirt flicked into the air. Roble pulled and pried with the ax handle to release the ax head from the ground's grip.

Wolves howled in the Vale of Frozen Tears below.

"Something disturbs them," Lehrling said. "Normally, their cries come near dusk, but it's only midday."

Roble buried the ax into the frozen dirt, pressed his weight against the handle, and broke free a chunk of the earth. He picked up the ice-solid earthen brick and tossed it aside where several other hunks lay. He swung the ax downward once more. The ax handle cracked. When he tried to pry it loose, it snapped.

"Dammit!"

"Here," Lehrling said, handing a hatchet to him.

Roble took the hatchet and glanced up at the solid gray sky. Swirling snowflakes dropped heavily. The clouds were so thick; there wasn't a hint of the sun. Almost like constant twilight hung over the mountainside.

"Midday, you say? How could you possibly know that it's midday when you can't see any trace of the sun?" Roble said.

"Trust me. Once the sun sets, darkness here is something even demons would tremble about."

"I see. So you really don't know the time?"

"Not exactly, no," Lehrling laughed and clasped Roble's shoulder. "But that's why we must hurry to where we can find shelter for the night."

Shawndirea sat beneath the protection of a snow covered fir branch.

She said, "That's possibly more dangerous than what lurks in this forest after darkness settles."

"Let's hope not," Lehrling said. "But with what happened to Bausch, we'd best remain cautious."

He looked at his comrade's frozen, eyeless face. Remorse weighted upon his facial features.

Lehrling whispered, "He was like a son to me."

"Did he die honorably?" Roble asked.

A tear edged from Lehrling's right eye. "He did. And he refused to utter a word to those demon-men. He kept his allegiance to Queen Taube and vowed Lady Dawn would assume the throne."

Roble stopped chopping the ground with the hatchet, stood, and looked at Lehrling. "I'm truly sorry for your loss."

"I appreciate that."

After fifteen more minutes of busting the frozen earth, the hole was deep enough to drag Bausch's body into and cover with branches, frozen dirt, and snow. Roble extended his hand to Shawndirea. She stepped onto his palm and he placed her on his shoulder.

"I wish I could do more for him," Roble said. "Not much of a grave."

Lehrling stared into Roble's eyes for a moment, gave a slight nod, and then he climbed upon the tall steed. "I sense you speak the truth. It will have to do. My thanks for giving his body a place to rest."

Roble swung upon his horse. "Again, my condolences."

Lehrling gave a weak smile. "He died serving our future queen, Lady Dawn. As will I should it deem necessary."

"Let's hope it doesn't come to that."

"Should we cross more men riding mounts like these, we will be forced to fight."

Roble smiled. "That might be a hell of a fight."

"You have no idea," Lehrling replied.

Shawndirea whispered into Roble's ear, "You need to have him train you."

"Here? In this weather?"

"No. When we get to wherever he wants us to stay the night."

Roble shook his head. "There's no way he can train me in a few hours what takes most men years to master."

"I agree," she said. "But he can teach you quick defensive moves that may well save your life."

"Very well. Once we find a place, I will discuss it with him."

Lehrling frowned. "What's all the whispering about?"

"She insists you train me," Roble replied.

"Sure. I can show you basic tactics, but you'll still need years of practice to be proficient."

"I understand that."

The snow fell heavier as they rode along the frozen dark path that divided the forest. The sound of the howling wolves faded. The trees stood like gray silhouettes across the white landscape.

Streams of smoky air puffed from the horses' nostrils as they walked. The third horse remained tied behind Lehrling's. The leafless trees provided little protection from the windswept snowflakes that blew from the west. In spite of the frigid climate, Roble didn't feel the cold due to Bausch's clothes.

Lehrling turned in his saddle and looked at Roble. "It's odd, but when I watched you approach the three bounty hunters, I could have sworn you were Bausch. I can't believe the resemblance you hold. Could it be that you're related?"

"Not possible," Roble replied.

"Where are you from?"

"Again, a place you wouldn't know."

"Entertain me with a name?"

"Cider Knoll," Roble said.

Lehrling frowned and said the name softly several times. He forced a frustrated smile. "You're right. I don't know of such a place."

"I told you."

"Trading town?" Lehrling asked.

"Far from it."

"Listen," Shawndirea said, interrupting them.

Lehrling pulled back on the reins, and Roble did the same.

Wailing echoed through the woods.

"Go!" she said, pointing ahead.

"Why?" Lehrling asked.

"You don't hear it?" she asked.

Roble and Lehrling shook their heads.

"Hurry!" Shawndirea said. "Or we may be attacked."

Lehrling tapped the flanks of his horse hard. The horse reared and then ran forward.

"What is it?" Roble asked. "What's going to attack?"

She frowned and pointed again. "Go!"

Roble kicked his horse's side with the heel of his boot. The horse shot forward and galloped to catch up to Lehrling.

"What are we fleeing from?" Lehrling asked.

"A spirit that seeks revenge," she replied. "Possibly Bausch."

"If it is he, he has no reason to harm us," Lehrling said.

Shawndirea said, "It depends upon what he remembers or sees as truth. You're both riding horses of the men responsible for killing him. And Roble wears his clothes."

"He knows me, faery," Lehrling said. "Even in the afterlife, he'd know me. I was a second father to him."

She nodded. "I understand, but I don't know that it is him. These woods are possibly littered with corpses since we are so close to Glacier Ridge. It could be any spirit."

"That's true."

Roble shook his head. "How do you defend yourself against a spirit? Especially when neither he nor I heard it."

She shrugged. "Death comes for someone is all I can say."

The large snowflakes clung to Roble and Lehrling's beards. Their horses plodded down the dark wooded trail. Mists of fog and blowing snow suddenly blinded them, making them stop riding. The horses' eyes widened. They shuffled their feet and stepped backward and then side-to-side.

"What's going on?" Roble asked.

"Something has frightened them," Lehrling replied, pulling his sword.

Shawndirea's fingertips glowed. She whispered, "Be prepared. Something has tracked us and seeks to prevent us from going further."

Roble unsheathed his knife and listened. The horses breathed heavily and whinnied, rearing up and stepping swiftly backwards. Lehrling struggled to hold his horse steady. He tugged back on the reins and spoke soft words to his steed to calm it. Roble pulled his horse's reins to the right and circled his horse around.

"What are you doing?" Shawndirea asked.

"I want to know if something approaches us from behind," he replied.

From the mist wall a form moved and floated much like the mist itself. Slowly its form slipped closer. The facial features became clearer. The eyes were blacker than onyx. She wore a tattered white gown and hood that hung loosely around her.

"Roble," Lehrling said, pointing. "There."

Roble swung the horse around. The ghostly form drifted toward them, and its horrifying eyes stared at them. No emotion appeared on her face, but her haunted eyes were hollow with sadness, betrayal. She hovered between Roble and Lehrling at the center of the road.

Lehrling's knuckles were white from how tightly he gripped his sword. Although Roble held his knife, he didn't see any reason to use it. There wasn't any way that he could think to defend himself from a spirit, and this one didn't seem hostile.

"What now?" Roble asked.

Lehrling shrugged. "I can guarantee *that's* not Bausch."

"Kind of had that idea myself," Roble said.

"My mistake," Shawndirea said.

"What do you mean?" he asked.

"It's not Bausch's spirit. It's a Banshee," she said. "Someone will die."

A cold chill settled over Roble. His stomach knotted. He wasn't certain what Banshees were like in Aetheaon, but what myths and legends he had heard from his childhood meant that whoever heard the Banshee's cry was the one destined to die. Neither he nor Lehrling had heard the Banshee. However, Shawndirea had.

The spirit floated and slowly retreated into the white mist and snow as if she had never been there. Her interest was not in their party. At least that's what Roble hoped.

Roble looked at Lehrling and said, "How far are we from any type of civilization?"

Lehrling replied, "In this weather, it's hard for me to say. All the trees along the path begin to look similar after a time. And with this growing fog, it gets difficult to predict anything."

"And the Banshee? What do you make of her?"

"I think Shawndirea's right," he replied. "But *whom* will die is the question we don't have the answer for."

Roble swallowed hard and glanced at the faery. "How is it that you heard the Banshee, but we didn't?"

"I'm Fae," she replied. "The Banshee is a form of faery as well. It's not the first Banshee I've heard. Near battlegrounds I tend to tune out their cries as they are many and their stressful laments are burdening. But here, in the depths of this eerie icy forest, I take the utmost precaution. Too many horrible things have happened to those who have ventured here."

"If you're able to hear them, can you ask them whose death they warn is coming?" Roble asked.

Shawndirea shook her head. "No. Their appearance comes mainly to grieve over their lost loved one they can no longer protect."

"I always thought they were heard by the one that was doomed to die."

"They deliver a forewarning," she said, "But they are not Death. They do not deliver the deathblow. If neither of you heard her, that means others roam this forest or that we're getting near the hidden trading post of Glacier Ridge. And she is tied to whomever is nearby."

Lehrling coughed, cleared his throat, and then he said, "We stick to this path."

"We can barely see it," Roble said. "The weather seems to be getting worse, not better."

"Aye," Lehrling replied. "Our pace will be slower, but we must continue on the dark path through the forest. If we get off this road, we'll wander aimlessly through the forest and perhaps die before we find any place to get food and provisions."

*A*n hour passed. Their horses trudged through the heavy snowfall and nightfall settled along Glacier Ridge. The narrow path sloped downward but the forest remained dark and thick on both sides. Owls hooted deeper in the dusky branches. Their golden eyes glowed eerily like strange lanterns. The cold breeze whistled and howled. Other eyes watched them ride past, and every now and then, wings fluttered and birds sought to hide further away from the winding path.

Finally, the snowstorm diminished to flurries, but the sky remained overcast but darker. Lehrling looked up and frowned.

"Nightfall is upon us," he said.

Roble studied the sky and said, "And we've nowhere to stay tonight."

"Without moonlight," Lehrling said, "We'll lose the path. Even the snow will appear black."

More odd sounds came from the dark forest. They rode down a sharp bend of the path. The horse hooves clopped on the hard icy surface. Had the horses been a smaller breed, they probably would have slid or lost footing, but these massive beasts chopped deep enough into the ice to keep traction.

The horses' ears backed, their eyes widened, and they snorted.

Shawndirea's nose crinkled. "I smell smoke, food, and ale."

Roble gave her a surprised glance.

"Well," she said, "I do."

Lehrling pulled back the reins and held his hand out, motioning Roble to stop. Roble did. Lehrling pointed. "Look, light from a lantern."

Roble squinted and looked beyond the last of the forest trail. A glowing lantern hung outside a small cottage. As his eyes adjusted, he noticed more lanterns along both sides of the cobblestone street. A rope hung above the street and was strung between buildings on both sides of the road.

The disturbing thing for Roble was that had the burning lanterns not been there, they would have ridden right into the town before they had even known a town was there.

"If my guess is right, this is Glacier Ridge," Shawndirea said.

"Aye," Lehrling replied.

Roble studied the buildings along both sides of the street. An occasional shadow moved along the edge of the buildings and passed the lanterns. A couple of robed individuals skittered quickly across the rooftops and disappeared into darker shadows. Roble's hand rested on the hilt of Bausch's sword. His fingers tensed. When he noticed his hold on the sword, he was curious why instinct had not drawn him to his knife instead. He was efficient with knife throwing, but the sword was a new weapon he had yet to test.

"What makes you certain this is Glacier Ridge?" Roble asked.

"It is where Bausch and I encountered the bounty hunters," Lehrling replied. "Or perhaps I should say, where they *confronted* and took us into their custody. More may lie in wait."

Shawndirea placed her hand to Roble's cheek and said, "Don't be quick to trust anyone in this place. It is a den of thieves and murderers."

"And you expect to make a fair trade with these horses here?" Roble asked Lehrling.

He shrugged. "We may not get the better deal, but we should be able to make a trade."

"Or lose our lives in the process?" Roble asked.

"Nah," Lehrling replied, shaking his head.

"It is a possibility," Shawndirea said.

"I don't see any horses," Roble said.

Lehrling nodded. "There's a stable master near the center of town. For a price, we can keep them there. Otherwise, thieves would make off with them before you downed your first mug of ale."

"How do you know that he's trustworthy?"

Lehrling laughed. "Like the faery said. You can't trust anyone here. But he's probably the most honorable."

"Why's that?"

"In his type of business, you'd die quickly if you can't keep track of a man's horse."

"So," Roble said, "Did you and Bausch leave your horses there?"

Lehrling grinned. "We did."

"Then he should still have them, shouldn't he?"

"Aye."

"That's good," Roble said. "Let's go."

"A word of warning," Lehrling said, looking to Shawndirea. "It's best that you keep yourself hidden."

"Why?" Roble asked.

Shawndirea nodded. "He's right."

"In this area, a faery is worth our horses' weight in gold," Lehrling said. "For whatever reason, wealth seekers will kill you to get her."

Roble looked at her. "Is this true?"

She nodded.

"Why?"

"Lots of reasons. None are good for the humans, however. Fae don't take kindly to bondage, and we do get our revenge in the most inventive ways."

"Still," Lehrling said. "It's best for you to hide."

She slid beneath Roble's cloak below his left ear and whispered, "Don't forget that I'm here."

"I can't forget about you," he replied.

Shawndirea smiled and pulled the cloak over herself.

Roble and Lehrling gently tapped their horses' flanks, coaxing them to move ahead. The horses walked slowly.

"The place looks deserted," Roble said.

"That's the deception of a town where thieves gather. We're being watched from every tavern and inn on both sides of the street. Even at the top of the hill that overlooks this place, they are watching. No one enters here secretly. Not even the best thief."

"Interesting."

"Spies have spies," Lehrling said. "That's why Bausch and I were taken into custody so quickly. A few pouches of gold coins handed out here and there as reward will make even the most dishonorable thief loyal for a while. Unless you pay them more than the other pays."

"Loyalty to the highest bidder?"

"So to speak."

Midway through the town, the cobblestone street widened into a large circle. The marketplace was deserted. The vendor tables were empty, either due to the frigid air or because it was late in the evening. The surrounding buildings blocked the harsher winds, but the cold hung around them. Several metal fire pits atop tripods blazed. Specks of red embers rose in the heat of the flame and went dark once they escaped the fire's hold. The crackling logs should have been inviting for tired and cold travelers, but few people lingered in the street.

Two men dressed in leather armor stood next to one fire and talked. As Lehrling and Roble rode closer, the men ceased talking, placed their hands on the sword hilts, and glared at them until they rode on past. Secrets were sacred, even among thieves.

Directly ahead, at the far end of the circle, the cobblestone road ended outside the mouth of a massive cavern. No guards were posted, which indicated law and order wasn't something easily enforced. Large burning fires were at each side of the cavern opening, and more fires flickered further down the cave path.

"What's inside the cave?" Roble asked.

"The largest part of this village. Due to the harsh winter climate, the more expensive establishments have been built inside the shelter of the ridge, but that doesn't mean it's any safer. In fact, it's probably more dangerous."

"And why few people linger outside these buildings."

"Exactly."

Lehrling nodded toward a long building that stood outside the circle to the right of the cavern. A half dozen fire pits were spaced along the side of this building. The wall was divided by dozens of doors.

Lehrling said, "That's where we stable our horses overnight."

Roble nodded.

Near the center of the stable houses a forge glowed orange. The clanging racket of a hammer striking metal echoed. Sparks rose from the molten metal as the hammer shaped it. Water hissed and steam rose when the man thrust the crude metal blade into a barrel of cold water.

Roble and Lehrling rode closer. A giant of a man stepped from the open center of the building with a heavy hammer in his hand. He stood seven feet in height, weighed close to four hundred pounds, and other than his oversized gut, he was more muscle than fat. The light from the fires revealed his scarred face and hardened emotionless features. He had suffered from many fights, but apparently also remained the victor. Sweat dripped down his face, and even in the wintry bitter cold, the man wore no sleeves, which revealed his enormous biceps and forearms. The man wasn't a stranger to hard work, and his tempered glare was enough to intimidate the most twisted murderer.

The man looked a lot like the men that held Lehrling captive except he didn't have extra thumbs, and doubting that this man ever smiled, Roble wasn't certain about fangs.

Two smaller young men stood behind him with their hands resting on their swords.

"I am Riese, the stable master," the mountainous man stated in a gravelly deep voice. "*What* do you need?"

Lehrling eyed the massive hammer in Riese's huge muscled hand and then gazed into Riese's cold, unblinking eyes. His eyes were difficult to stare at for a long period of time, simply because they looked like shimmering ice that reflected the souls of those who dared to make eye contact.

"We need," Lehrling said, "A place to house our mounts overnight."

The man stepped to the side of Lehrling's horse. Riese's face was almost even with Lehrling's. "You were here a couple days ago. Were you not?"

"Aye," Lehrling said, swallowing hard.

"You owe me rent for your horses already in my stables."

"I do."

"I thought you had abandoned them," Riese said.

"No," Lehrling said. "Wasn't in a position to retrieve them."

"And these horses," Riese said, studying the brands on their hindquarters. "These belonged to other men as I recall."

Lehrling glanced at Roble and back at Riese.

Before Lehrling replied, Riese said with amusement, "Shall I wager that they won't be coming here looking for these?"

"Not any more," Roble said.

Riese's attention turned to Roble. He gave a solemn nod. "It doesn't surprise me, but do know that others like them are here tonight."

"How many?" Lehrling asked.

"Half dozen," Riese said. "I see more of them lately. Can't say that I like their presence coming into this region."

Roble thought the comment odd because Riese was every bit as massive a man as the ones feeding the ice ravens in the forest. Even though Roble didn't know much about the heritage of different races in Aetheaon, he couldn't help but guess that Riese's lineage could be traced back to the bounty hunters that served Lord Waxxon.

"How about a trade?" Roble said.

Riese frowned. "For these that you ride?"

Roble nodded.

"Name your price."

"He owes you stable fees for the other two horses," Roble said. "The tethered one behind him should be more than enough to pay that debt."

Riese walked to the horse behind Lehrling and checked its hooves. He ran his hand across its sides and then checked the horse's teeth.

"She will do nicely, yes," Riese said with a fangless grin. "And you're wanting to get rid of the two you ride?"

"Aye," Lehrling replied.

"What do you ask for those?"

Roble looked at the hammer in the man's hand. "You're a blacksmith?"

"I am."

"What weapons do you have?" Roble asked.

Riese smiled with great pride. "More than you could carry with a dozen of these colossal horses. Any particular weapon you seek?"

"Knives, daggers, and axes," Roble said.

The stable master walked from horse to horse, inspecting each one carefully.

"And the saddles?" he asked.

Lehrling gave a quick nod. "Those, too."

"Come," Riese said, resting the massive hammer on his shoulder. "My sons will stable these while I show you the weapons."

"You're not worried about their brands being noticed by the other bounty hunters?" Roble asked as he and Lehrling climbed down from their mounts.

Riese laughed heartily. "They won't know they're here. Besides, I can cover their brands with my own. Not difficult for a smith to alter."

"Most horses are smaller," Lehrling said.

Riese shook his head. "Look at me. None of my horses are smaller than these. They would never survive carrying me."

Roble chuckled. "I suppose not."

Riese led them into his smith. The hot temperature was overbearing from the glowing forge. Hanging along the rock wall were numerous swords, daggers, and axes. The steel blades reflected the orange-yellow flames.

Roble found throwing knives atop a thick wooden table. He held one to check its balance in his hand. He liked the way it felt. After testing a few more, he set three knives aside that he liked better than those he had brought with him.

Riese frowned. "That's it?"

"No," Roble replied. "Still looking."

"May I see your blade?" Riese asked.

Roble shrugged and pulled it from its sheath. He handed it to Riese.

The blacksmith was stunned when he held the blade and eyed it for quality. He gave several sharp swings in the air, listening to the blade's delicate song as it sliced. He checked the hilt and shook his head in disbelief.

"Nice," Riese said. "Odd to find one crafted better than my own. Who forged this?"

Roble looked at Lehrling.

Lehrling replied, "Beren Tiwele of Woodnog."

"An elf?"

Lehrling nodded.

Riese handed the sword back to Roble. "Finest quality I've seen. Mind if I test it?"

Concern crossed Roble's brow. "What do you mean?"

Shawndirea whispered, "Watch out."

As she spoke the warning, Riese swung his heavy sword at Roble's head. He ducked and dodged quickly out of Riese's advancement. Riese pivoted, spun, and with all his strength swung again. Roble brought up his sword to parry the blow, and to his surprise, sparks exploded as the blades clashed. A third of Riese's blade broke loose and hit the floor.

The impact of the battling swords knocked Roble backwards. His hand ached from the violent shockwaves that radiated down the sword into his hand. His fingers burned and after a few moments, numbed. Pain radiated up his arm and into his shoulder. Riese brought his broken blade back and over his head, quickly plunging a downward blow. Roble's blade deflected the blow, and suddenly he became concerned about Shawndirea's insistence that he learn how to use a sword effectively. He had no doubt that was *next* on his to-do list.

Roble stared into Riese's eyes. He couldn't read whether this was game or a fight to the death. The man's eyes revealed nothing. No emotion at all. Since Roble had never sparred, he wasn't certain how his reaction should be. Riese seemed bent on drawing blood or dismembering Roble.

Roble braced himself, watching Riese charge forward with a side sweeping slash. Roble dodged to the side, and Riese continued moving past. Roble kicked behind Riese's right knee, which knocked the massive man off balance and sent him face first into the floor. Riese rolled over to get up and found the tip of Lehrling's sword pressed to his throat.

Roble took deep breaths and lowered his blade.

"What is this?" Lehrling asked. His narrowed eyes indicated his anger. "Have you sided with the bounty hunters?"

Riese chuckled, gritted his yellowed teeth, and shook his head. "Never! I wanted to test the metal of his blade. It is truly Elven. That's all I wanted to know."

Lehrling eased back his blade. Riese stood and held out his broken blade. He shook his head and said, "Look at this. The strongest steel I've ever used. So heavy and thick. Yours? Light and thin, but stronger than anything I've made. Actually, stronger than any I've *seen*."

Lehrling sheathed his blade.

Roble took a deep breath. His heart raced in his chest. Riese approached quickly, and he wasn't certain whether to raise his sword in defense or to sheath it like Lehrling. Lehrling gave a slight nod, and tapped his belt. Roble sheathed the blade.

Riese extended his massive hand toward Roble. Roble placed his hand to shake and the blacksmith's hand wrapped around and hid his.

He smiled at Roble and said, "Didn't mean to alarm you."

Roble shook his head. "From the rumors that surround Glacier Ridge, I wasn't certain if you were going to kill me to get the blade."

"No. I live and thrive here, but not from the misdeeds of thieves and bounty men. I would, however, like to one day be introduced to this Beren Tiwele of Woodnog."

Lehrling nodded. "If ever you're in that region, it will be my pleasure to introduce you."

"Very well," he said. "Now. Back to business. Surely you need more than those knives."

"An ax," Roble said.

"A battle ax or one to cut wood?" Riese asked.

"To cut wood."

"I was going to say that if you have a sword like that, you have no need for a battle ax. Most are too bulky and heavy to maneuver unless you're built like me."

Riese looked at his weapons on the wall. He took down an ax and handed it to Roble. "Will that do?" he asked.

"Yes," Roble replied.

On the table where Roble had placed the throwing knives, he noticed smaller daggers that were far too small for a human's hand.

"What are those?" Roble asked.

"The faery blades?" he laughed. "Never had anyone want those."

"I'd like a couple of them."

Riese's thick eyebrows rose. "Really?"

Roble nodded.

"Why?"

"Trinkets."

"Ahh. I could see that. Know an enchanter?"

Roble shook his head. "No, but I'm certain to eventually come across one."

"Hopefully on their good side."

Lehrling laughed. "Hopefully."

"What else?" Riese asked. He looked at Lehrling and back to Roble. They simply shrugged. "I know my weapons are great, but the modest amount you're taking in exchange for the horses isn't sufficient for a trade. You're making me out to be a thief."

"No," Roble said. "We simply don't have need for any more weapons or those horses. More weapons will just weight us down."

"Then I pay the difference in gold," Riese said and nodded firmly. "I will not cheat anyone."

Lehrling said, "Consider it a gift and of course, payment for my other horses' long stay."

Riese shook his head. "Nay. I will not be indebted to another."

"We don't consider it like that at all," Roble said.

"Perhaps not, but I always will. No, there must be something more."

"Drinks!" Lehrling said. "Buy us a round of drinks in the tavern."

A grin spread across Riese's face. "Now *that* I can do, but that still won't compensate the difference in our trade."

Roble gave an even smile. "It's a start."

"Very well," Riese said. "Hobskin's Tavern is where we'll go. While we drink, I'll find a suitable thing to make this trade more even."

"Honestly," Lehrling said, "It's not necessary that you do more."

"I do, or no trade at all."

Roble shrugged. "Then let's get something to drink."

CHAPTER 25

After venturing into the cavern, they stopped at the third building on the right, which was Hobskin's Tavern. The buildings were constructed from roughly hewed logs. Mortar between the logs looked like frozen clay. Oil lanterns burned smoothly; their wicks shielded by beveled glass. A large guard stood at the door of the tavern. He hefted a large ax in his massive hands. The quality matched that of what Riese had hanging on his stable wall. The guard's face was hidden beneath a cloth helm that was painted to resemble a demon skull. More intimidating was that the man's eyes glowed red behind the mask. He wasn't human, and Roble wasn't certain exactly what race this guard was.

Riese stared down at the guard as he approached. The guard took a step away from the door and lowered the ax. Riese grinned and pushed open the heavy wooden door. Lehrling and Roble followed. Stepping inside, they were enveloped by warmth. A large fireplace roared. An iron pot filled with bubbling soup balanced above the flame. Most tavern patrons cowered at the sight of Riese and backed out of his path to let him pass. Others eyed Roble and Lehrling, sizing them up and checking out what they carried.

Hanging oil lanterns and a couple of large candle chandeliers dimly lighted the tavern. About two-dozen tables filled the area away from the bar. Strange animals unlike anything Roble had seen in the Overlands were mounted and displayed on the walls and above the bar. Sitting at the crude tables were mostly humans that drank from large mugs while whispering to their neighbors. Many of these kept their gaze on Roble and spoke in a hushed manner as Riese looked for an empty table.

Roble wondered if they were able to detect that he wasn't birthed and reared in Aetheaon. His uneasiness showed on his face, but to those studying him, he feared they might believe that he was an easy target to rob. He narrowed his gaze and stood tall, knowing that confidence often made people second-guess a man's toughness.

A wooden sign hung on the wall behind the bar. "Hobskin's," was engraved in the wood. A crude rusted sword was fastened to the wall below the sign. A strange green hand still held the hilt of the sword. Like the preserved animals, this hand had been treated to prevent decay.

"Why is that hand there?" Roble whispered.

Riese replied, "As a warning to anyone who befriends any hobgoblins that enter Glacier Ridge from the underground passageways."

"So they have?"

Riese nodded. "That one died by my ax. His head is stuck on a pole above the tavern. Hobskin was that goblin's name. Thus the tavern took his name, and I donated the sword and hand for decoration purposes. Come on, I see a table."

Near a back corner, Riese found an empty table and motioned for them to join him. "Here," he said.

Roble eased his back against the wall while Riese did the same at the adjacent seat. Lehrling sat down with his back to the crowded tavern.

A few tables over, nearer the kitchen, a large round table was surrounded by six creatures that Roble could only describe as half rat and half human. They were large muscular creatures with beady red eyes and pointed noses. Their sharp, yellowed teeth were as dangerous a set of weapons as a dagger would be in a close fight. Their long tails resembled thick ropes and curled behind them and beneath the table.

Their noses twitched as they talked or ate the thick stew from wooden bowls. Their brown fur was bushy where they lacked armor. Leather skull-caps covered their heads in between their large round ears. They wore their silver daggers on the outside of their leather armor, but their medium length swords rested on the table near their bowls and mugs. Their wicked claws were jagged like small knives.

"Don't stare at them too long," Lehrling warned.

"Why not?"

"The Ratkins view it as a threat and won't waste any time confronting you with their paranoid rants."

"Rough place," Roble said, looking away.

When Riese smiled, his wild wooly beard parted. His eyes narrowed as he gazed around the room. If it were just an intimidating glance, it frightened onlookers into quickly looking away. All except one. An elf with long silver hair that flowed like silk down his back didn't flinch. His eyes focused on Roble and no one else.

The elf wore all green. He sipped from a silver mug but never averted his eyes from Roble. His armor looked like large scales and not like the other patrons' armor. Humans wore leather, chainmail, or black robes.

Loud laughter echoed from across the room. A table with four dwarves clanked their mugs together and then they downed their drinks. A large keg sat at the center of their table. Roble watched them momentarily, but his attention turned back to the Elf who continued to watch him.

Roble stared back with boldness and didn't dare break their gaze. He knew the game from the time he had lived in a large city one summer as an intern. Never show weakness or retreat when someone sizes you up. That gave a possible enemy confidence that they were stronger.

Lehrling noticed Roble's determined frown and asked, "What is it?"

"The elf. He's staring at me."

Lehrling looked over his shoulder.

Riese nodded. "So he is? What of it?"

"Just odd."

"Well," Riese said. "You're at *my* table. If he wants to make something of it, he may find he doesn't like how I deal with those who trouble my guests."

"Perhaps he knows you," Lehrling said.

Roble shook his head. "I've never met an elf."

"*Never?*" Lehrling asked in surprise.

"No."

Riese frowned. "From where do you venture?"

"Places you wouldn't know," Roble replied. "Cider Knoll is my home."

Riese nodded. "You're correct. Never heard of it. Is it from another continent or in Aetheaon?"

Roble struggled for a way to explain without letting them know he was from the Overlands. Right as he opened his mouth to speak, Lehrling smiled and nodded.

A busty barmaid brought three large mugs of ale to their table. Roble took a gulp of his ale and the bitter taste tightened his throat. He forced the liquid down. The aroma was stronger than any beer he had drank before and possibly the alcohol content was much higher. He decided one drink was more than enough in this strange land. Best to keep his senses keen, just in case he had to quickly defend himself.

The barmaid smiled at Roble and Lehrling, did a slight curtsy, and left their table. Her face looked familiar, and for a moment, he struggled to think where he had seen her before. The question faded when he glanced at Lehrling's pale face. Lehrling knew her face, too. When their eyes met, they read one another's nervousness. Her face was identical to the female spirit in the forest.

"Honey ale," Shawndirea whispered to him.

Her gentle words shook him unexpectedly. Roble tilted his head to the side and whispered, "What?"

"I thirst. Order some honey ale."

Roble rose from his seat and said, "Excuse me."

"Where are you going?" Lehrling asked.

Roble didn't reply. He walked from the table and deliberately passed the elf on his way to the bar counter. Due to several large seated patrons at the bar, Roble had to go around to the other side of the bar, which was out of view from Lehrling and Riese.

The barkeep turned and frowned at him. "Can I help you?" he asked, placing his hand on his dagger at the front of his belt.

"Honey ale," Roble said.

The barkeep's brow rose. He turned and faced the large mirror on the wall behind the bar. As he poured a glass of honey ale, a strange grin spread across his face.

"A problem?" Roble asked.

"It's a woman's drink," a voice said from behind.

Roble turned to find the elf standing directly behind his right shoulder.

The elf laughed and then he whispered, "But it's not for you, is it? It's for the faery on your shoulder."

"What?" Roble asked.

"Easy," the elf said. "We don't want the others to know she's here."

"What do you want?"

"To talk. Nothing more."

Roble gave a slight nod. "What do you wish to talk about?"

The barkeep returned with a small cup of honey ale and blew a kiss at Roble. Roble frowned and opened his mouth to speak, but the elf tossed a gold coin to that barkeep and quickly said, "Let it go and take the drink."

Feeling uneasy about the situation, and now taking the drink he ordered, he grabbed it anyway and stepped away from the bar.

"Let's find a table more private," the elf said.

Roble followed him through the other side of the tavern. A set of stairs led upward and the elf took them. Roble stood at the bottom for several moments, hesitating. He glanced around to find most of the seated patrons were drunk or had their heads down on the table, unconscious. None were watching him like they had on the other side of the tavern near the entrance.

Roble headed up the stairs. When he reached the top, he found the elf seated at a table in the darkest corner.

Shawndirea peered from beneath the edge of the cloak.

"Should I seat myself or return to the others," Roble asked.

"See what he wants," she replied.

"How did he know you were with me?"

"Possibly detected my magic."

Roble pulled back the rugged chair and sat down. His hand rested on his dagger.

"Bring her out. Let her drink," he said, extending his hand palm up.

"Who are you?" Roble asked.

"Odlon of Eyllisathem," he said, staring at Roble as though the name should hold high relevance. "You are?"

"Roble from Cider Knoll."

Odlon studied Roble while he thought about the information. The elf's complexion was perfection. No scars or blemishes flawed the radiance of his fair skin. His emerald-colored eyes almost matched the color of his armor. The silver necklace he wore had a large emerald in the centerpiece, which was surrounded by six smaller emeralds.

Shawndirea crawled from beneath the hem of the cloak and jumped to the tabletop. She hurried to the honey ale and sipped it from the cup.

"Gods help us," Odlon said. His eyes widened. "Your wings. What happened to your beautiful wings?"

"Not your concern," she replied.

Odlon propped his elbows on the table, crossed his long fingers together, and rested his chin on the finger-bridge. "Odd that you're so far from your homeland, faery."

Shawndirea looked up from the honey ale and said, "Again, not your concern."

Odlon grinned and looked at Roble. He said, "Feisty little thing, isn't she?"

"It's the cold weather," Roble replied.

Odlon chuckled. "Did she tell you that? Or is that your theory?"

She glared at Odlon, rested her balled fists on her hips, and said, "What exactly do you want?"

"To talk to Roble."

"About what?" Roble asked.

"Your reason for crossing the Underworld and coming to Aetheaon," Odlon said evenly. "You don't belong here."

"How did you know?" Roble asked.

A smirk curled Odlon's lips. "You don't have the hardness in your features to survive in this world."

"I've done okay so far."

"There is more fear and uncertainty than strength in your eyes," Odlon said.

Shawndirea's eyes narrowed.

"Easy, faery," Odlon said, raising a finger. "I'm being critical, but I have reasons."

"Which are?" she asked.

"To offer my assistance to wherever he wishes to go."

She took her eyes off the elf and returned to drinking the honey ale.

Roble frowned. "Why?"

"Do I need a reason?"

Roble looked around the tavern and nodded. "Because we are where we are; yes, a valid reason is worth quite a lot. Who has hired you?"

"No one."

"You seem too regal to rub elbows with the dirty thieves that occupy this ridge, and the reputation of this region is either to hire or be hired for thievery or as an assassin."

Odlon smiled. "You learn traditions quickly."

"One must in order to survive."

"I like your wisdom. For an Overlander, you may well make the transition to survive here where others haven't."

Roble sighed. "I have nothing else in the Overlands."

Odlon stared and marveled with curiosity. "Nothing? Nothing at all?"

"No."

"And what do you wish to gain here? Treasures? Become a mercenary? What?"

"Weighing my options."

"The faery plays a big role in whatever you're hoping to gain."

Shawndirea lifted her head from the honey ale. The cup was one-third emptier. "He's mine," she said, slurring her words. She shook her index finger at Odlon. "Just leave him alone. Or else."

Odlon smiled and shook his head. In an elegant tone, he said, "Not quite the answer that I expected. Has she placed any spells upon you?"

Roble shook his head. "No."

"None!" she insisted, staggering and giggling.

"Are you certain?" Odlon asked. "We can get you to a witch and find out."

"I will never cast a spell upon my love," she said before a loud hiccup escaped her mouth. She grinned and clamped her hand over her mouth.

"I volunteered to pass through the Underworld to take her home," Roble said.

"Why?"

"Because the damage to her wings was my fault."

Odlon's brow rose. "I see. And yet, she's in love with you?"

"Seems so, which still shocks me."

"And what do you feel about her?"

"Is it too premature to say that I've fallen in love with her?"

Odlon shook his head. "Not if that's truly how your heart feels."

"I can honestly say that I've never had feelings for another like I do for her. But it's the differences in our height and race."

"Trivial," Odlon said, "Where love matters."

"That's what I keepsh telling him," she said. She plopped down on the table beside the honey ale cup and giggled some more.

"You still haven't answered my question," Roble asked.

"About why I'm here?"

"Yes."

Odlon glanced around the small upstairs room. "Darkness grows in the center of our lands. I believe Waxxon's men are partly behind it, and I look to find Lady Dawn and help return her to power."

"As is Lehrling."

"The man that was seated with you?"

"Yes."

"So he believes she's alive, too?"

Roble nodded. "He believes it strong enough that he ventured here and put his life at risk."

"The Dragon Skull Order?"

"Yes."

"And did they recruit you?" Odlon asked.

"No."

"You wear their pendant and clothes."

Roble explained how Waxxon's men had killed Bausch. He also told about how cold he was after leaving Devils Den and that he cut Bausch down from the tree and took his clothes.

"And Lehrling doesn't protest about you becoming one of their Order?"

"He has not said."

"Their number is few, but there are members of all races that are deter-mined to overthrow Lord Waxxon."

Roble said, "I get that feeling, too. Waxxon's henchmen are not well liked here."

Odlon chuckled. "They're not well liked *anywhere*. However, without the proper heir to the throne, anyone that assumes power there will never be welcome."

"So don't attack until Lady Dawn is found?"

"That's the ideal time. But worse than finding her has occurred."

Roble frowned. "And what would that be?"

"Waxxon is backed by something dark. A force that perhaps grows within Mortel. And if that's true, our battle to reclaim Hoffnung must begin there."

"Why?"

"We must destroy the source of his power to prevent him from getting even stronger."

"That will take an army."

Odlon shrugged. "We will have the numbers. We just don't know *what* we're fighting once we enter."

Roble looked confused. "Why wouldn't you know?"

"Not one human, elf, dwarf, or otherwise, has entered and survived to tell what resides there."

"Why not send a group to examine what's there?" Roble asked.

"In my search for Lady Dawn, I have travelled close to Mortel. Darkness hangs over the area. Some have named the place the Black Chasm, which is appropriate given that it started from the deepest pit of the valley. I stopped atop a ridge that overlooked Mortel. You cannot see through the haze. It's a strange swirling black and purple mist that conceals what's within. Every so often it shimmers like lightning strikes inside."

Shawndirea's head tilted to the side and her eyes closed. Her body slumped against the glass. She lay unconscious.

Odlon smiled.

"That's interesting armor you're wearing," Roble said. "What is it made from?"

"Dragon scales."

"She told me that no dragons existed in the Underworld."

Odlon's eyes glanced from the drunken faery to Roble. "She's correct."

"And yet . . ."

"This was made from the *last* dragon in the Underworld."

Roble admired the armor scale pattern. Seated closer, the detail of the shimmering dragon scale was more vivid than he imagined.

"Who killed it?" Roble asked.

"I did."

"In a sense that's a great victory, but in another, it seems sad that no more exist."

Odlon shook his head. "To the contrary, encountering this dragon almost killed me. It still ended worse for me than I had expected."

"Were you looking for the dragon?"

"No. But any exploration in Aetheaon has its share of unexpected surprises. No doubt you'll encounter some along your journeys as well."

Roble gave a slight nod and sighed. "I have already."

"Oh?"

"Yes. All my life I had heard about the eternal pit of Hell. I simply regarded it as myth. Never thought I'd actually pass through it on foot."

"River Styx?" Odlon asked.

"Yes."

"Incredible."

Roble laughed. "At the time, I didn't find it an appealing place."

"I imagine not." Odlon studied Roble's eyes and his mannerism. "So how long have you been traveling with the faery?"

"Barely half a day."

Odlon eased forward in his seat. "Nice choice of weapon. Elven, is it not?"

Roble nodded. "It is."

"If you carry it, you must know how to use it proficiently. Perhaps you'd like to show me?" Odlon said, rising to his feet and drawing his blade.

CHAPTER 26

Lehrling turned in his seat and glanced around the tavern. "He's been gone for quite some time now."

"You're worried about him?" Riese asked.

"Doesn't seem a safe thing to do."

Riese turned his mug up and downed the contents. He slammed the mug on the wooden table. "He's a man. Not a boy."

Lehrling nervously rubbed his gray beard.

"He's also one of the Dragon Skull Order," Riese said. "That requires a lot of special training."

"Well, not officially he isn't."

Riese frowned and gruffly said, "He wears the pendant and your light armor."

"He does."

"Is he an imposter?" Riese asked.

"No, he seems noble enough."

Lehrling explained how Roble rescued him from Waxxon's men.

"Ahh," Riese said. "So that's why he favors daggers and knives?"

Lehrling nodded. "Yes."

"Few are as good with knife throwing as most are with swords, but if that's where one's talent lies, he can be a deadly man to face."

"I've never seen anyone walk toward three men as fearlessly as Roble did," Lehrling replied.

"Too bad I missed that."

At the corner table to Riese's left sat three men who laughed and drank. The thin man in the center was dark skinned with a black beard and braided hair that hung down his back. Riese eyed the man until the man became uneasy and looked away.

"Friend?" Lehrling asked with a chuckle.

Riese's eyes narrowed. "Hardly."

"Foe?"

"I'd say he's working on it."

"Why?"

"That is Crukas," Riese replied.

"I thought he'd be bigger."

"You know of him?"

Lehrling nodded. "Most kingdoms know his thievery accomplishments, but no one's ever caught him."

"He's the master of thieves, but I've warned him *not* to come here."

"Because of his reputation?"

Riese shrugged. "That, and he's violated the sanctity of Glacier Ridge by not abiding by the rules."

"What did he do?"

"He recruited three murderers into journeying with him to Ironwood, the small town north of Woodnog, for a chance to gain great wealth quickly," Riese said while staring at Crukas. "The only thing he didn't tell them was that the wealth was for himself. He turned them into the magistrate for the rewards. They were hanged in the center of town."

"You think that's why he's returned?" Lehrling asked. "To hire unsuspecting thugs to cash in on their bounties?"

"Could be, but this time, he's the one that will suffer."

"You have to admit, that's a sly way to make money while eliminating his competition."

"He's cunning, but Glacier Ridge is a retreat for otherwise wanted criminals. If they wish to trade wares they've stolen outside the ridge, they are more than welcome. But traitorous behavior will be eliminated."

Lehrling glanced around the tavern again. No sign of Roble.

"Still worried about Roble?" Riese asked.

"Yes."

"He'll turn up."

"It's *how* he might turn up that worries me," Lehrling said with worry showing in his eyes. "If Waxxon's men are here, I fear that Roble could get himself into some real danger."

Riese smacked several gold coins onto the table and stood. "Then we should find him."

~

ODLON CAME from around the table with his sword drawn. Roble was hardly to his feet and struggled to draw the blade. In the split second that Odlon moved, Roble's hand left the hilt and quickly grabbed a sharp dagger and flung it. The blade struck the elf in the center of the chest.

Odlon's eyes widened in surprise. He lowered his sword and gazed down. The dagger didn't penetrate the dragon armor, but lodged itself into between two scales. Odlon took a deep breath and tugged the blade free. Roble had a second blade already drawn.

Odlon sheathed his sword and held his hands upward. "Didn't expect that," he said.

"And here I thought we were having a friendly chat," Roble said.

Odlon smirked. "Understand I was just testing your reflexes. Great with a dagger, but not so with the sword."

"I know. I've thrown knives and metal stars at targets since I was a child. Never had a sword to practice with."

"I can teach you some tactical moves," Odlon said, handing Roble back the knife. "Just hope you don't have to use the sword before then."

"I'd appreciate it," Roble said. "But why do you wish to help me get the faery home?"

Odlon shrugged. "Perhaps you'll return the favor for me. Besides, you need training."

"Lehrling can do that."

"That old fat man?" Odlon said. "He's slow. I'm nimble and quick. You'll progress quicker from my challenges."

"That's probably true."

"Probably true?" Odlon asked with one brow cocked.

"Definitely true."

"Fine. Take your faery and hide her safely before someone sees her. Now is not the time to draw attention to her or yourself."

Roble walked to the table and picked Shawndirea up. He admired her in the dim candlelight. She slept with her mouth slightly open. The shape of her mouth was enticing. He wanted to kiss her perfect lips, but she was so small. He carefully placed her into his front jacket pocket.

"You said that the dragon almost killed you?"

Odlon nodded. "Yes. For the damage and pain he inflicted upon me, I made certain that his hide would always be on my body."

"What did it do?"

Odlon turned his back to Roble and said, "Lift my cloak."

After Roble did, Odlon slid his right arm out of the chest piece, revealing the blistered and burnt flesh that covered seventy percent of his back. When the air touched the wound, Odlon took a deep breath, closed his eyes, and groaned.

"This looks fairly fresh. When did you kill the dragon?" Roble asked.

"Ten years ago."

Roble's eyebrows rose. He shook his head. "Ten years and it still looks like this?"

"Yes," Odlon said, pulling the armor back over his shoulder and tightening it into place. He winced.

Roble pulled out a chair, and Odlon promptly sat down. Roble took the seat on the opposite side of the table.

"Why doesn't it heal?" Roble asked.

"Like I told you earlier, I wasn't looking for this dragon. In fact, I never expected to find one during my lifetime. I ventured into a cave to hunt for a rare herb my sister needed for a potion. I found the herb in plentiful supply and while I harvested more of it, I walked deeper into the narrow passageway that opened into a grand cavern.

"The dragon apparently heard my approach, and perhaps he thought I was there to steal treasure, but I never saw any gold or silver. No treasure at all. Just a large crop of these herbs and other rare plants alchemists use as well."

Roble nodded. "Perhaps the dragon protected the herbs."

"Never thought about that, but I suppose that may have been his treasure."

"Who would need such plants?"

"Wizards, witches, and perhaps healing priests," Odlon replied.

"Would a dragon protect herbs for someone?"

"Possibly. While picking the herbs I never noticed the dragon until I smelled the brimstone. When I turned, it craned its long serpent-like neck around and faced me. Without warning the green drake opened his mouth and tried to snap me with its jagged teeth. I rolled and pulled the lance from off my back. When it lunged for me I threw the lance. The point went directly through its eye. The shaft sank about four feet deep.

"I turned and ran down the corridor. It rose and roared. Glancing back, I watched it thrash its head side to side and struck the side of the cavern, driving the lance even deeper. It growled and hissed. A wall of flames spread from its mouth and followed me down the corridor. The licking fire ignited my leather armor and consumed it. I dropped to the cold hard floor and rolled over, batting the flames with my hand. The dragon dropped forward and pronounced his curse on me moments before it died."

"What curse?"

"That my burns never heal."

Roble said, "There must be a way to reverse it."

"My sister has tried every spell she knows for healing. Nothing has altered it. The only thing that prevents my pain is wearing the dragon's hide and scales."

"Have you returned to that cavern to see what other herbs might grow there?"

Odlon replied, "I have."

"You never know," Roble said. "The cure to his curse may be hidden there."

"Sadly, no. When my sister and I returned to harvest more herbs, they were either all wilted or dead."

Roble frowned. "Dead?"

Odlon nodded.

"I don't know anything about dragons since I'm an Overlander," Roble said, "But could this have been a magical dragon? Did anything like that exist?"

Odlon thought for several moments. A barmaid brought him another mug of wine. He took a long drink. "So much lore is no longer taught. But, to answer your question, dragons have always had some magical abilities. Like any race that practices magic, one is only as good as they research and practice."

"Are you certain yours was the last dragon?" Roble asked.

"No one is ever entirely sure," Odlon replied. "When I brought out this dragon's head with enough hide and scales to craft my armor and shield, the residents of my city were shocked that one had lived so close to us. We changed the name of our city to Eyllisathem, which means "Land of Dragons.""

"To honor the dragon?" Roble asked.

"No," Odlon replied. "To strike fear in travelers that venture to our city. The dragon's head, which is only the skull now, rests atop a tall pole right at the gates."

"Dragon skull," Roble said, rubbing the pendant between two fingers.

Odlon nodded. "That's why I believe the gods have crossed our paths. It is not mere coincidence that you passed through the Underworld, wear the clothes of the Dragon Skull Order, and have teamed with one of their knights."

"This battle isn't mine. The only reason I have came here is to ensure that Shawndirea gets home safely."

"That may be your intention, but trust me, the gods make no mistakes. They may occasionally amuse themselves by drawing people into unusual situations just to see how they squirm when put to ultimate tests."

Roble glanced at Shawndirea in his pocket. "You think this is a test?"

"What do you think?"

"I'm not certain anymore."

Odlon smiled evenly. "I know Fae do occasionally cross into the Overlands merely out of curiosity, but has she ever given you a reason why she did?"

"To find me."

Odlon rose from his chair. "Did she actually phrase it like that?"

"Yes, that's *exactly* how she said it."

"See?"

"But she meant as a husband to end the animosity between the human race and the Fae."

Odlon shook his head. His long silver hair gleamed in the faint candlelight. "And what inspired her for such a quest?"

"Arrogance of male Fae."

Odlon laughed. "I'd have to agree on that point, but still, there are plenty of humans here, and yet, she chose to seek one from the Overlands."

"So?"

"She was struck with a lust to hunt for someone outside the Underworld. The gods, or at least one very mischievous one, decided to sour any thought of her settling for one unless it was in the Overlands."

"I'm hardly one equipped for the conflicts and explorations you and Lehrling keep speaking of," Roble said, placing his hand on the sword. "I'm not a swordsman. I am great at throwing knives but not skilled enough to defend myself with a sword as one who has lived his whole life here can do."

Odlon studied Roble's face for a few moments, and then he slowly walked around Roble and sized him up. "You're framed to be a very agile but yet strong fighter. With the proper training, which I or Lehrling can do, you'd be a feared man on the battlefield."

"I didn't come here to be a warrior or soldier."

Odlon cocked his head to the side and said, "And did you think the Underworld consisted of numerous luxuries of sitting in meadows or lying beside trickling, cascading rivers? These lands are crude, violent, and dangerous. You fight or you die. It's as simple as that. And if you get this faery to her homeland, what do you expect will happen there?"

"I'm not certain."

"Do you expect an open arm welcome?"

"No," Roble said. "She said that her mother wouldn't like her choice to be with me."

"*None* of the Fae will like her choice, no matter how noble and upstanding a human you are. Understand what she sacrifices once you get her home and she announces her decision."

"I know."

Odlon frowned and anger rose in his voice. "You have absolutely no idea what's at stake for her."

"The decision, her choice, remains to be hers," Roble said. "If she chooses to be with me, I'll accept their decision for myself, but believe me, I will try to sway her not to be with me."

"You cannot sway that. She's smitten by you. There's no changing her heart. But understand this."

Roble nodded. "Okay?"

"Even when you get her home and she's safe, her kingdom is not."

"Why?"

"Because the forces controlling Lord Waxxon are a danger to every continent within the entire Underworld and throughout all the kingdoms. The darkness that spawned in Mortel is intensifying. It grows and festers. It will spread and spread until everything falls beneath that black veil. Waxxon is just the beginning. His henchmen roam the lands. Their numbers are immense."

Heavy footsteps thudded up the stairs.

"Roble!" Lehrling said as he and Riese stepped into the small dim room. He glanced at Odlon and back to see the uneasy expression on Roble's face. "Is everything okay?"

"Everything's fine," Roble replied.

"Is this the Elf that kept staring at you?"

Roble nodded and said, "Lehrling, this is Odlon. He is also looking for Lady Dawn."

Lehrling gave a slight nod of recognition but could not suppress his concerned expression. "What interest of yours is Lady Dawn?"

"The same as yours. To see her take back her rightful claim to her family's throne."

"I appreciate your desire to see her seated where she belongs, but why does that matter to you?"

Odlon smiled. "It is not I, or the elves in general. You will find most kingdoms along this continent, regardless of their race, support her being found and Hoffnung back under the proper rule. Lord Waxxon leaves a distaste in the mouth of all."

Riese stood in a stooped position because the ceiling was too low. His hammer was held tight in his muscled fist. He eyed Odlon with suspicion.

Lehrling said, "What does he want?"

"He has offered to travel with us," Roble replied.

Riese said, "Where are you from, Odlon?"

"Eyllisathem."

"The Land of Dragons?" Riese asked. His thick eyebrows rose with interest. He stepped closer and examined Odlon's armor. "Are you the one that killed the dragon?"

"I am."

"And your purpose here?" Riese asked.

"The same as Lehrling," Odlon replied. "To find Lady Dawn and destroy Lord Waxxon's self-appointed reign in Hoffnung."

Riese opened his mouth to speak, but the main entrance door of Hobskin's Tavern swung open and slammed hard against the walls downstairs. Two barmaids screamed. The clamorous drinkers became less noisy. The barkeep shouted an obscenity filled threat but stopped midsentence.

The bartender yelled, "You have no jurisdiction here!"

Riese turned, headed for the stairs, and said, "Seems we have unwelcome company."

Lehrling pulled his sword and followed.

Odlon drew his sword, pushed past Roble, and said, "Keep out of harm's way. I will help you get the faery home, and we'll see what occurs. If I'm correct in my assumption, you will help me inspect Mortel."

Roble followed Odlon down the crude staircase. Five of Waxxon's henchmen stood to block the exit. Their leader held his jagged sword to the barkeep's throat.

Riese stepped forward and held the hammer at his side. "What is it you seek?" he asked.

The leader turned to face Riese and the blade pressed to the barkeep's throat lowered. "Who are you?"

"The one to take your life unless you leave quickly."

The leader stood a couple inches taller than Riese, so he appeared amused by the threat. "At least give your name so I'll know who to haunt in the afterlife."

Riese laughed heartily. "*I'll* haunt you in your afterlife. The thought of my face will be your torture."

Recognition set in the leader's eyes. "You're the stable master? And you dare threaten Baron Tierman?"

"As the barkeep said, 'you have no jurisdiction here.'"

The leader approached Riese and said, "Glacier Ridge has no true laws that I know of. A place where chaos rules over order."

"There are only six of you. Dozens of us," Riese said. "You may strike fear in peasants, townsfolk, and maidens, but you might rethink where you are right now. These are the worst of the worst that fear no one."

Roble glanced around the tavern. Dwarves, humans, and other races stared at the henchmen with narrowed gazes and angered brows. None were happy that their drinking had been disrupted. Their hands went to their weapons. Apparently Riese noticed the same. Friction and tension increased amongst the alcohol-induced patrons.

"Aye!" two dwarves said in agreement. They pounded their ax heads together and hunched forward, ready to charge into the brawl.

The leader of Waxxon's men glanced nervously around the tavern and said, "Don't think I only brought five men. More are searching the ridge for the Dragon Skull Order."

"I checked your horses in," Riese said. "No others came with you."

The five henchmen near the door pulled their swords and braced themselves for attack. Two of the men held leashed beasts that resembled skinless dogs. Their red scaly skin was covered with small thorn-like bones. Grabbing one with bare hands would be impossible without shredding skin and flesh to the bone. Their mouths were filled with rows of sharp, pointed teeth. They growled and gnashed their teeth.

Tierman eyes suddenly widened when he looked past Riese and noticed Lehrling and Roble.

"Release those two men of the Dragon Skull Order into our custody, and we'll leave peacefully," Tierman said, pointing.

Riese glanced back at Roble. Lehrling gave an even grin. He turned toward Tierman and said in a thunderous voice, "You dare infringe upon the patrons of Hobskin's Tavern as if you have authority over us?"

Chairs scooted from tables as the half drunken people rose and stood. Tierman turned and looked around. Uneasiness settled over his face. It was then Roble realized that although there wasn't a set governmental body over Glacier Ridge, Riese was their actual leader and had the ability to set the battle cry whenever the need for action arose.

Riese shook his hammer in the air and looked at the tavern customers and shouted, "Are you going to stand for this kind of interruption?"

"No!" the patrons shouted in near unison.

Lehrling watched Crukas slink back into a corner of the room where the shadows were darker. He slid barbed fist weapons onto his knuckles. Lehrling looked away for a few seconds. When he looked back, Crukas was gone.

Riese roared and said, "Time we show these men their rightful place!"

And with that, Riese rushed Tierman and swung his massive hammer hard before the baron braced himself for the assault. The head of the hammer clanged against Tierman's chest piece and sent him toppling backwards. Tierman hit the floor hard, slid, and winced. He toppled several heavy stools, and they crashed atop him. He lay on his back and hardly moved for several seconds.

The table of dwarves rushed the two men nearest them and yanked them to the ground. They pummeled them with their thick fists and smashed their faces with their silver mugs.

The two hellish beasts broke free of their leashes and sprinted into the frenzied crowd. The Ratkin grabbed their daggers and swords, quickly decapitating the hellhounds. They knelt and lapped at the blood.

Tierman rolled when Riese swung his heavy hammer downward at his head. The hammer cracked the floorboards. A layer of dust puffed into the air. Chairs and tables rattled as the vibrations traveled through the floor.

Tierman spun around with his sword, but Riese moved faster. The head of his hammer caught the sword's blade. Sparks flew as metal struck metal. The hammer blow knocked Tierman's sword arm back and tilted him off balance. Riese shoved his shoulder into Tierman with enough force to knock the man off his feet and into the air. He landed on his back, slid, and stopped several inches from Roble's feet. Roble stared down at the baron and simply shook his head.

Tierman's eyes were filled with pain. He clutched his chest where the shape of the hammer dented his chest piece. Riese rushed forward and brought the hammer up over his head with both hands. Tierman flung his hands over his face and closed his eyes tight, anticipating the deathblow.

"No, wait!" Roble shouted over the raucous brawl.

Riese paused, held the hammer overhead, and frowned. "You want me to spare this dog? Why?"

"Answers," Roble replied.

"He plots to kill you and the others in the Dragon Skull Order."

"That may be what he had hoped to do, but look, he's in no position to do anything," Roble said, pointing to the maddened crowd. The other five henchmen lay on the floor in pools of blood. The crowd fought amongst themselves over the dead henchmen's armor, weapons, and any other valuables they discovered in their pockets.

Riese shrugged. "Then why let him live?"

"He's a baron, which means he knows a lot of information about Lord Waxxon's plans and strategies. Not to mention, he may well know where the sentries are being positioned."

"You cannot trust anything he tells you."

"I wager he's more trustworthy than most of those men and women over there."

Riese lowered the hammer and shook his head with disappointment. "He's yours at your own danger."

Lehrling looked at Roble with uncertainty. "You really want to keep him alive?"

"For now."

Riese turned to leave.

"Wait," Roble said. "I need you to help."

"With what?" Riese asked with a gruff soured voice.

"We need a place to question him. The tavern isn't exactly a good one. If he doesn't talk, do whatever is necessary to *make* him talk."

Riese smiled and his bushy eyebrows rose with interest. He looked at Odlon and said, "Check him for daggers, hidden knives, and escort him back to the stables. I'll get answers for you."

Riese headed out the tavern door. Lehrling helped Roble get Tierman to his feet while the other drunken patrons scuffled and bickered over the loot they had gathered from the dead bounty hunters. Odlon pressed the tip of his sword to the baron's back. Roble stood. Shawndirea awakened and stood in his pocket and looked around.

One of the Ratkin's noticed her. His eyes narrowed when she made eye contact. It tapped its comrade's shoulder and pointed at her. Although very tipsy, she quickly ducked down inside Roble's pocket.

Roble, Odlon, and Lehrling exited the warmth of the tavern and entered the frozen hell of Glacier Ridge with their prisoner.

CHAPTER 27

*R*iese's sons pumped the bellows to increase the forge's temperature. The baron's legs were tied to the legs of a heavy wooden chair. His hands were tied tightly behind his back. He winced and wheezed each time he tried to breath. The shrewd harsh winter wind had not alleviated his hampered breathing and entering the forge room's immense heat added further pain and complications.

Dried blood caked the sides of Teirman's mouth and beneath his nose. As hard as Riese had struck the baron's chest with the hammer, Roble was certain several of the man's ribs were broken, but the man probably suffered worse damage as well. A rib had probably punctured one of his lungs.

In the blazing, roaring fire, Riese turned the end of a branding iron over and over in the flames until the metal dragonhead glowed orange. He held the glowing dragon tip inches from the baron's cheek. Although the baron swallowed hard, his eyes held anger, not fear.

"Since you seem to despise dragons," Riese said, "I chose this one just for you."

"You dare inflict such pain upon one of your own brethren?" Tierman asked.

"You're no brother of mine."

The baron shook his head. "You are every bit one of our brethren."

"If so, from where are you?" Riese asked.

"Hoffnung."

"No, you voyaged there under command of Lord Waxxon. I know my homeland, and I've never ventured to Hoffnung."

Riese moved the searing branding iron closer to Tierman's face. The heat formed a red outline on the man's flesh even though he had not yet touched him. The baron tightened his jaw and braced for the pain.

"Where is your homeland before Lord Waxxon summoned you?"

Baron Tierman's eyes narrowed. He looked from the brand into Riese's eyes. He said, "Go ahead. I won't tell you anything."

Riese lowered the brand and pressed it to the wooden seat between Tierman's legs. Tierman took a sharp breath and held it. Smoke rose as fire singed the wood and the edges of his leather pants that covered his inner thighs.

Tierman released a nervous breath and glanced down to see the burnt impression of the dragonhead in the wood.

Riese took the brand and returned it to Tierman's right cheek. "Last chance to tell me."

Tierman closed his eyes. Sweat beaded his brow. He coughed and fresh blood coated his teeth and spilled out onto his wiry beard. "Do it! There's not much more life in me. You see I'm dying, so I refuse to speak more."

Riese pressed the brand against Tierman's cheek. His jaw clenched. His head shook as flesh blistered and bubbled beneath the dragon brand. When Riese didn't pull the branding iron back, Tierman finally screamed. Blood-spittle frothed from his mouth.

Odlon turned and walked out of view of the fiery interrogation.

Roble winced and looked away. Although it was his idea to make the baron talk, he didn't imagine Riese would go to such lengths of torture, and he certainly didn't believe Riese would enjoy doing it so much.

Riese lowered the brand and placed it back into the fire. He grabbed Tierman's scalp hair and clenched it tightly. He peered into his wide eyes and said, "The next one will be worse. Where's your homeland?"

Sweat covered Tierman's face. He panted for air. The smell of urine drifted from the chair as his whole body quaked. Still holding Tierman's hair, he grabbed the branding iron from the glowing fire. Riese aimed the bright orange dragon at Tierman's right eye.

"The Isles of Welkstone in the Misty Seas of Reus," Tierman said.

Riese released Tierman's hair and gave a slight nod. "Where is that?"

"You don't know?" Tierman asked.

"No."

Tierman frowned in disbelief. The burn on his face puffed and bled. "You should know. It's your lineage, too."

"Never heard of it. Never been there."

Roble seemed surprised at Tierman's insistence and found himself agreeing with the baron. There wasn't any way by physical characteristics that Riese could rightfully deny that he was not related to Waxxon's henchmen.

Tierman coughed and leaned forward, vomiting a pool of blood between his legs. When he finished, Riese grabbed his hair and yanked back his head. Tierman's eyes lulled in their sockets. His tongue hung from his mouth. The baron was no longer breathing.

With disappointment in his voice, Riese said, "He's dead." He shoved the branding iron into a pool of cool water. Steam rose.

"It's late," Lehrling said to Roble.

"I know."

"I have rooms above the stables," Riese said. "If you'd like a safer place to stay the night."

Roble nodded. "That would be great. That will make our trade even."

Riese shook his head. "I don't see that worth horses."

Roble smiled. "You cannot put a decent price on a good night's sleep. And safety in this ridge is priceless."

"Very well. Looks like I have gained six more horses besides yours now," Riese said, smiling.

"Eliminating visitors is a quick way to add to your profits," Roble said, jokingly.

Riese's eyes narrowed. "I do not add to my wealth in such a manner."

"I didn't mean to imply that you did," Roble said.

Riese held a hardened gaze at Roble for a half minute more and burst into roaring laughter. "The occasions do arise from time to time though. And since I'm the only stable master here, their losses are my gains."

Roble looked at Lehrling and Odlon. All were uncertain of whether to laugh along with Riese or not.

Riese pointed and said, "Those stairs to the right lead to the rooms. I have no other tenants tonight, so help yourself to any room you find to your comfort."

Lehrling nodded and smiled, "Thanks for your kindness."

Odlon followed Lehrling's lead and said, "You're too gracious."

Riese crossed his arms and said, "After my sons dispose of the baron's body, they'll lock down the forge and stables for the night. The walls that surround us are thick steel."

"Good to know," Roble said to Lehrling.

"Aye."

Odlon joined them at the foot of the stairs. As they walked upstairs, Riese's sons carried Tierman's body out the front of the forge room. And although the outside temperature was well below zero, the heat from the forge would keep them warm through the night. Perhaps too warm, Roble thought, wiping sweat from his forehead.

Lehrling struck a match against the wall and lighted the lantern in one room with two bunks. The room smelled of stale hay and mildew. Once the lantern light grew, Roble helped Shawndirea from his pocket. She stepped off his hand with slight stagger in her step onto the small table where the lantern set.

The mattresses were thin layers of hay atop a hard wooden slat. A woolen blanket covered the hay. Roble didn't realize how tired he was from the journey through Devils Den to Glacier Ridge. Once he sprawled back on the rough bed, he dozed off.

WHEN ROBLE AWAKENED several hours later, the room was pitch black. Snoring rose abruptly from the cot across the room, which he assumed was Lehrling. He listened for other noises, almost afraid to move while he hoped his eyes would adjust to the darkness, but they never did. The room was much colder than he expected. He wondered how the forge could cool so quickly. The rising heat should have kept them comfortable through the night. He rubbed his hands together.

"Roble?" Shawndirea whispered.

"Yes?"

"Good," she said. "You're awake."

"Is something wrong?"

"Strange sounds awakened me earlier."

"You sure it wasn't Lehrling's boisterous snoring?"

"No," she replied, feeling her way across the bed to him. When she reached him, she curled into a fetal position on the crude pillow near his face. "Definitely not. This was a gnawing sound. Like something was trying to gnaw through the walls or the ceiling."

"I don't hear anything," Roble said.

"It stopped."

"When?"

"A few hours ago."

Roble sighed. "Perhaps it was the wind blowing the wooden shingles."

"Perhaps, but I don't think so."

"You remember the harsh wind that we weathered through the frozen forest."

"Of course, but this was different."

"I didn't realize you liked to drink so much," Roble said.

"Normally, I don't. But honey ale, after our long journey, was something I couldn't resist. I was parched and exhausted. Clearly not in my best frame of mind."

Roble smiled. "I was afraid to drink much. I needed to keep my senses keen."

"I'm sorry," she whispered. She ran her fingers through his short beard.

"For what?"

"I should have done the same. I wasn't in any position to help you when you needed it."

"Odlon, Lehrling, and Riese took care of matters."

"But still," she whispered with disappointment, "You're only here because of me."

"There's no regret in this journey for me. Dangers arise but seeing this new world and even this frozen wilderness with strange races I never imagined existed, I cannot wait to see what I encounter next. I've always loved exploring."

"This room smells odd," she said softly.

"Mildewed hay," he replied.

"Possibly. Or there are vermin nesting in the walls."

"Rats and mice are usually a problem in stables and barns. Anywhere there is feed and hay."

Shawndirea's right fingertips glowed green and seconds later, a ball of green light illuminated on the palm of her hand. She smiled at him in the faint green glow. He stared at her beauty, the gentle curl of her lips, and the brightness in her eyes. In the light of the small orb something else caught his attention. Five sets of silver eyes reflected in the dark corner across the room. Before he could move to grab a knife, a burlap bag covered Shawndirea and her light vanished.

She screamed.

"I have her!" a raspy voice said.

The door flung open and Odlon entered with a lit lantern. He set the lantern down and quickly drew his sword.

Four of the Ratkin beasts rushed Roble while her captor leapt and reached for the extended hand of another Ratkin perched upon the overhead beam. The one pulled the other onto the beam and both scaled out to the rooftop. Nimble footsteps rushed across the roof. Shawndirea's next scream was muffled and further away.

Roble kicked the closest Ratkin in the gut and pivoted it backwards, impaling it with Odlon's drawn blade. Roble tried to rise to his feet, but the other three Ratkins lunged at him, snarling with their jagged teeth bared.

Lehrling rolled over and rubbed his eyes, being awakened by the snarling, growling beasts. He shook his head and his eyes widened.

"What nightmare is this?" Lehrling asked, swinging his feet off the edge of the bed and grabbing his sword.

Odlon placed his foot against the back of the skewered Ratkin and pulled his blade free of its corpse. He hurried across the room to help Roble get free from two of the Ratkins that had climbed on top of him.

Twisted yellow teeth gnashed and bit at Roble. He fought to prevent them from biting him, fearful of what diseases these unusual beasts might carry. He clutched one's throat so tightly its eyes bulged and its tongue stiffened in its wide-open mouth. Their breath smelled of rotten fish and garbage. Roble fought the urge to vomit. He wondered why they wanted Shawndirea, and his thoughts immediately went to finding and rescuing her.

Anger and desperation rose inside him. His grip around the Ratkin's throat magnified, and he squeezed even harder. The choking sound that gurgled in its throat stopped as bones in its neck cracked and snapped. He shoved its dead body off, kicked one Ratkin away, and grabbed the third one with both hands. The creature's wild eyes gleamed and narrowed. It lifted Roble into the air. Its strength was incredible, and given that it was about a foot shorter than he, he didn't think expect such power in its thin arms.

Right when he thought the creature would ram him into the wall, a sudden surprised expression covered its face. Its eyes widened and it gasped. It lowered Roble with shaking arms. Life faded from its gaze, and its long pointed fingers released him. Roble pushed back from the Ratkin to see Lehrling's sword sticking partway through the beast's gut. Lehrling smiled.

"Thanks," Roble said.

"Any time."

The fourth Ratkin's head plopped and rolled across the hardwood floor, followed by its headless body collapsing to the floor. Behind where the beast had stood was Odlon. He gave a smile of triumph.

"These Ratkin were at the tavern," Odlon said.

"I know. I remember," Roble replied. He nodded toward the hole in the ceiling and said, "Help me up there."

"You're going after them?" Odlon asked.

"Yes. They have Shawndirea."

Lehrling gasped. "Gods have mercy."

"When I catch them, I won't," Roble said.

Lehrling cupped his hands together and leaned forward for Roble to place his foot. Once Roble balanced, Lehrling heaved him upward. Roble grabbed the beam and climbed his way to the hole. The opening was narrow, but once he got his shoulders through, he was able to pull himself onto the roof.

CHAPTER 28

The frigid cold wind stung as it blasted its way across the rooftops. More snowflakes and bits of ice flicked off his face. He was amazed how little the cold affected the rest of his body. The dark lightweight armor he had taken from Bausch was better insulated than anything he had owned back in the Overlands.

In the vast darkness, he couldn't see anything along the rooftops. Without a visible moon and the unrelenting dense dark clouds looming overhead, there wasn't enough light to see ten feet away. The howling wind prevented him from hearing movement. He imagined the same was true for those who had taken Shawndirea, but he didn't know if they actually fared better or worse seeing in the darkness than his eyes allowed.

Thinking of her, his heart ached. Where did they go with her? *What* did they *want* her for?

Light rose behind him. He turned to see Odlon pushing the lantern through the opening. Roble grabbed the lantern and then helped Odlon to the roof.

Roble whispered, "They're gone."

"We'll find them."

"Not in this darkness. By dawn, they could be anywhere."

In the lantern's glow, Odlon's piercing eyes peered into Roble's. Determination and confidence rose in the elf's voice as he said, "We'll find her."

Roble shook his head. "I doubt it."

"Don't accept defeat before you begin," he said, clasping Roble's shoulder. "You're definitely new to our kingdoms. For one, the Ratkin *won't* stick to the rooftops. They are like rats. They'll seek to travel through sewers or underground tunnels."

"But, with this town being full of thieves, won't they try to sell her to the highest bidder?"

Odlon shook his head. "No. There are too many others who'd kill to take her. The brawl you witnessed earlier was tame compared to what they would do to get Shawndirea. And only two of these rat beasts survived. They'll want to leave Glacier Ridge unseen."

"How did they know she was with me?"

Odlon knelt and slid partway into the hole in the roof. He looked up at Roble and said, "I don't know. These Ratkins were all black furred, so none are mages. Should there have been one with white or cream colored fur, he might have detected her magic. My guess is somehow they saw her during all the chaos."

"But she was unconscious."

"Not when she was on the table upstairs with us."

"That's true." Roble looked down at the elf. Only his head remained above the hole. Roble pointed across the roof and said, "Where are you going? They went that way."

"They'll seek underground tunnels, which means, we need to get back inside and wake Riese."

"Why?"

"Because he will know how to get us there."

"I hope you're right."

Roble followed Odlon through the roof and dropped down into the room where the four dead Ratkin lay. The room smelled of mildew, sewer stench, and death. He rolled over the largest Ratkin and anger pulsed through Roble. These were dead, but when, or if, he found the two that had escaped with Shawndirea, he'd make them suffer before he killed them.

He glanced at the pillow where she had rested beside him just minutes earlier. His heart ached. A part of him was gone. He longed to hear her sweet whispers in his ears again, to see the radiance of her face, and to ensure she got back to her homeland safely. And yet, as he thought of her, his greater disappointment was in knowing he had failed to keep her safe.

Odlon placed his hand around Roble's elbow and turned him. He said, "Now is not the time to wallow in self-pity or weigh blame upon yourself. None of us expected such a thing to occur. But to find her, we must act quickly before they put too much distance between us."

"Accepting the blame is difficult *not* to do."

"Maybe so, but if you wish to survive a long time in my realm, choose not to display your emotions on your face. At the tavern, your uncertainty made you appear nervous and worried. That's not something you want thieves to see. They thrive on weakness. The meaner you look, the less trouble you'll face."

Roble nodded. "I understand. The same is true where I come from, but I'm not from a place where that's a problem to worry about most of the time."

"You're not in your homeland anymore. The world here is much more different. Few have a conscience, and those that do? They *never* show it."

"I don't know where to start searching for her."

"Take heart," Odlon said. "You don't have to search for her alone. Lehrling and I will accompany you. First, let's see what these filthy beasts have on them. There's always the chance that we'll find information that is helpful in finding where they're headed."

Roble checked the belt of the large Ratkin. He found a rolled map, two small pouches of gold, and another scroll. He took the crooked dagger and a strange spiked weapon similar to brass knuckles in his world. He found another pouch filled with silver trinkets strapped at the back of its belt. Roble found an iron key in its vest pocket. The key was nearly out of view, but must have been jostled loose during their fighting. He glanced quickly around and noticed Odlon and Lehrling busying themselves rummaging through the pockets of the other dead Ratkins. Roble hid the key in his hand, and quickly tucked it into his own pocket.

Odlon stripped two of the other Ratkins of their gold pouches while Lehrling searched the other one.

Odlon stood and counted the oddly shaped gold coins. "We have a decent amount to hire others to help us find the beasts."

"No," Lehrling said. "That puts Shawndirea at greater risk of being taken by whoever finds the Ratkins."

"I agree," Roble said. "Too many fighting over her could easily get her killed."

"Very well," Odlon said. "Then we best find Riese and search any underground tunnels."

Roble exited into the hallway behind them. Once they descended the stairs, Riese stood near the forge sharpening a sword. He glanced up to see them and his thick eyebrows rose. "Up early?" he said, rubbing the whetstone across the edge of the blade.

"Ratkin came through the roof," Odlon said.

Riese set down the blade and stone. His face flushed red. "What?"

Lehrling nodded. "Four of them are dead on the floor of our room."

"Damned rat filth!" he roared. His eyes narrowed and his jaw tightened. "There's nothing here they should want."

"Apparently they gnawed and cut their way through the roof. Then they attacked Roble," Odlon said.

Roble looked at Odlon and shook his head. He didn't believe they should tell Riese about Shawndirea.

"And you killed them all?" Riese asked.

"No," Odlon said. "Two escaped across the roof. We wish to pursue them."

"Why? What did they take?" Riese asked.

Odlon opened his mouth, but Roble stepped forward and cut him off. "What they took from me is something I value greatly but care not to divulge exactly what."

Riese cocked one eye and said, "Why is that?"

"For personal reasons."

Riese studied Roble for a couple minutes and finally said, "I can respect that."

Odlon said, "Are there tunnels beneath the town's taverns where they may have fled?"

"The only tunnel entrance is at Hobskin's Tavern, but it is locked up at this hour," Riese said.

Roble stared intently into his eyes and said, "But you have a key, don't you?"

"What makes you think that?" he asked with a suspicious glint in his eyes.

"Because you are the official authority in Glacier Ridge, whether you post it or not," Roble said. "No one questions you and all hail your commands. That much was evident at the tavern. They charged Waxxon's men at your word. You are the only order in this town."

Riese smiled, crossed his massive arms, and shook his head. "I only rule because I allow thieves into this town without question or judgment, provided they do not attempt to rob my people or the marketplace. This is the only township where thieves and murderers have refuge and delivered bounties are worthless. That's why Waxxon's men were killed so easily. Had they not made demands and simply wished to sit and drink with others at the tavern, their lives were safe."

Lehrling coughed and cleared his throat. He looked at Riese and said, "And what happened with Bausch and myself? He died at the hands of Waxxon's other bounty hunters. They would have killed me had it not been for Roble."

"Tis true," Riese said, nodding. "But where did they capture you? It wasn't in the tavern or here at my stables."

"No," Lehrling said. "We had crossed through the marketplace after we left the stables and were looking for an inn. Bausch insisted we get a room at the inn we passed on our way into town."

"Myrtle's Inn?"

Lehrling nodded. "That's when we encountered Waxxon's men standing outside."

Riese frowned. "I remember them stabling their horses for the night, and one quickly returned to take them. They hadn't been stabled an hour."

"Yes. One was sent after the horses while we were robbed of our weapons by the other two. They held us at blade point until the other returned with the horses."

"And then what?" Riese asked.

"They shackled our hands, tied us to their saddles, and led us out into the icy forest."

Riese shook his head. "I had no idea that was going on. I don't tolerate such activity here."

Roble frowned. "So the Ratkin? Are you prohibiting us from finding them?"

"No. Find them and kill them. Few Ratkin venture this far north. Most live near the sea or wide rivers where they can loot unloading cargo ships or wagons carrying wares. They travel light and don't ride horses, which is why I wasn't even aware of their presence until I entered Hobskin's Tavern. I figured since they were there to drink, they weren't a threat or harm to anyone else. Apparently I was wrong."

Lehrling said, "They did quite a bit of damage to your roof."

"I will send my sons to patch that once the day starts."

Roble studied Riese's hands. He didn't have extra thumbs, nor did the baron or Waxxon's other men.

"Might I ask something?" Roble asked.

Riese nodded.

"The men that had taken Lehrling and killed Bausch had extra thumbs, but so far, none of the other men that serve Waxxon do. Why is that?"

"They are the sons of King Obed and his demon wife, Xaeeria. Some of her physical characteristics are passed to her children. They are powerful except when they are too far for her magic to aid them."

"Like here?" Roble asked.

"Yes."

Odlon stood and admired the weapons along the wall. On the work-table he picked up a crossbow. He held it and checked the sights.

"You like that?" Riese asked.

Odlon nodded.

"Take it. That is, if you're planning to help them kill those worthless Ratkins."

"Thanks," Odlon said with a smile. He grabbed the quiver of arrows off the table and positioned it over his shoulder.

Riese walked to the other side of the forge and into a small side room. He returned with four unlit torches that had soaked in pitch with tied ropes around the top. He handed each of them one torch and kept one for himself. "At this hour," he said, "It's best you light a torch and keep it handy, especially if you plan to search for them in the sewers beneath the cellar."

"Why not a lantern?" Roble asked.

"Torches make good weapons," Lehrling said. "Lanterns tend to gush fire wherever the oil splashes when they burst, so if oil leaks over you, you're engulfed in flames."

Riese placed the tip of his torch to the open forge. It blazed and crack-led. Roble and the others touched their torches to Riese's torch until they flamed and burned brightly.

"Come, let's go," Riese said, heading toward the locked double gate. He turned a steel key in the lock, and then he lifted a heavy metal bar from its hold. He pulled the door inward only enough to allow the others to pass through. Once they were outside, Riese shoved the door shut.

The sharp night wind didn't diminish its harshness. Their torches flick-ered in the breeze, but the coldness overcast any heat the flames may have offered. Their heavy footsteps crunched the icy hard snow. Roble stared past the torch and his mind raced. He worried that Shawndirea may already be dead. And if so, what then?

He pictured the full detail of her face in his mind. Every dimple. Every curve of her face. The radiance in her eyes, and how she had captured his heart with her smile. A lump formed in his throat. He refused to shed a tear. To do so meant he had lost her forever. That wasn't a fate he'd accept unless he found her lifeless body. And then, his life mission would be to kill every Ratkin he encountered, city-by-city, town-by-town. He'd hunt them relentlessly until he wiped their species out.

As heated anger stirred through his soul, a sudden thought stopped him dead in his tracks. His stomach became nauseated. Lehrling stopped as well and asked, "What is it?"

"The banshee," Roble replied.

"Oh, shit," Lehrling said.

Riese stopped, turned, and faced them. "What banshee?"

Roble explained what they had seen in the forest. The ghostly female figure had loomed out from the white fog.

"What are you saying? You heard her?" Riese asked.

"No," Roble replied.

Riese held his torch toward Lehrling, and seeing the nervousness in the round man's face, Riese asked, "Did you?"

"No."

Riese shrugged. "Then what importance is that to you? She didn't come to sing of your death."

"I know," Roble replied softly. "Not for us, but for Shawndirea."

"Who?"

Roble explained and then he said, "She was only one who had heard it."

"Dammit!" Riese said. "You should have mentioned that sooner. Come on."

"What would that matter?" Roble asked.

"No time to explain, but if you hope to find her alive, you cannot waste time out here."

Riese picked up his pace to a near jog while Odlon, Roble, and Lehrling hurried along behind the near giant. They stopped outside Hobskin's Tavern, only to find the door open. Wood had been partially gnawed away near the keyhole. The gnawed wood was just enough to allow them to pry the door open.

"Damn rat-men," Riese said.

Riese pulled the door open and headed around the side of the bar to a door, which opened to the storage room where barrels of ale and hard liquors were stored. He turned and said, "Keep torches held high. Don't burn the tavern down."

At the far end of the storage room was a set of stairs that led downward. At the foot of the stairs the large wooden door stood ajar. The area around the lock was solid steel and not wooden, where any gnawing could have taken place. Cold air drifted from the opening.

"They picked the lock?" Roble asked.

An even grin parted Riese's beard. "No lock is safe in a town that welcomes thieves."

"Perhaps it's time to change those rules," Roble said.

"They're not stealing from *me*," Riese said. "They're trying to escape."

"They have taken from me."

"When you find them, kill them."

"I plan to," Roble replied. As soon as he said the words, he immediately caught the coldness in his voice and his lack of hesitation in stating such a harsh vow. He had never been a violent person, and yet, since his arrival into this realm where strange creatures and races lived, he had already shed blood and taken lives. This primal way of living was unlike how he had been raised. The laws were different here. Survival was different. And whether or not he liked it, he was adapting to the hardness of life in this realm.

Riese placed his huge hand at the side of the door and looked at Odlon. "Elf, when I pull this door open, be ready to fire arrows."

Odlon nodded.

Riese heaved the door toward him. Odlon held the bow ready, but when the door widened, the passageway was empty of Ratkin or anyone else.

Roble stepped around Riese and used the torch to light the narrow tunnel. He didn't see anything stirring. He looked at Riese and said, "Where does this lead?"

"Beneath most of the town. It is where waste is dumped from all the houses, taverns, and inns."

"But does it lead outside Glacier Ridge?" Lehrling asked.

Riese shrugged and replied, "I've never ventured inside them, so I don't know. Someone or something picked the lock, so your best hope to find them is to search it out."

The walls, carved from thick permafrost, were coated with layers of blue ice. Slender icicles hung from the ceiling. The floor was semi-frozen slush formed from discarded water and waste. The further they walked, the worse the stench became.

CHAPTER 29

John McKnight drove his pickup to the dead end road and parked beside Ben's SUV. After he shut off the engine, he stared across the pasture at Devils Den. He found it odd that Ben had not emerged during the night. The officers, who had entered the cave to search for Ben, had not found any trace of him.

John unlocked the gate, got back inside his truck, and started the engine. Although he feared the cave, he worried that Ben might be in trouble. He parked as close to Devils Den as he could. He got out and walked to the cave mouth.

"Ben!" he shouted. His shout echoed several times through the cave, but no answer ever returned.

"What's with him?" John said aloud, placing his hands against the cold cave wall. "Something always makes him want to explore this damn place."

"Don't you think it's about time that you seal this place up?" Deputy Higgins asked.

John turned with a start and said, "I didn't hear you pull up."

"Just came back for another quick inspection of this cave. Still no sign of your brother-in-law, eh?"

"No."

"Well, I hope he comes out soon."

John looked at Higgins and asked, "Why? Is he in some kind of trouble?"

"No. No trouble. Too many in this community believe it's hazardous for you to keep this old cave open. I was out at Old Man Harper's store earlier, and well, most everyone believes that this cave leads directly to the mouth of Hell."

"Do you?" John asked.

Higgins wiped sweat from his brow with his handkerchief and replied, "Doesn't really matter what I believe. It's what's best for the people that matters most."

"What's on my property is mine," John said evenly. "I won't have a bunch of ninnies and wives' tales worriers telling me what to do with this old cave."

"I don't disagree with you, but Mr. Harper told me that you seem uncomfortable with the old cave, too."

John nodded. "There are times the cave has made me uneasy, but Ben has gone inside numerous times. He insists there aren't any dangers inside."

"And yet, he's not resurfaced."

"I know."

"Has that occurred before?"

"Actually, he's stayed a couple days inside before. And as long as he's inside, I certainly won't seal the cave shut."

Higgins replied, "I understand. But Mr. Harper insists that evil exits this cave."

"What does he mean by that?"

"There have been a couple of strange occurrences near your farm."

"Like what?" John asked.

"We're not quite certain, but several of your neighbors have filed reports detailing their sightings of what appears to be a walking corpse."

"Surely you don't believe that?" John asked.

"Certainly I'm not one that would accept that's what they saw. But, they're all nondrinking churchgoers. They've seen something."

"When?"

"Last night."

John wiped sweat from his forehead. "And how is it they tie this back to the cave?"

"Two of them are your neighbors, the Ridgeways, that live on the road that runs on the other side of your property," Higgins said, pointing toward the dark wooded section of John's property. "Whatever they saw entered your pasture, and they watched it by moonlight. It headed to the swampy section of your tree line over there."

John's face paled. He swallowed hard. "Nothing except tall pines and hemlocks grows in that section of my property. No grasses or small trees. Hell, even briars won't grow there."

"You've never seen or heard anything unusual here?" Higgins asked.

"No, sir. That's why I don't view the cave as a problem."

"As a favor, would you mind riding out with me to your neighbors' house so you can tell them that you've not seen anything?"

John glanced at his watch and shrugged. "How long will that take? I need to get to my insurance office in an hour."

"Shouldn't take more than fifteen minutes at the most."

"Sure, if you think it will help."

"I appreciate it. And Dr. Deiko hasn't improved any, either."

"Really? He looked delirious from the heat."

"Premeditated attempts to commit murder aren't usually the result of heat stroke."

"I don't imagine so."

Higgins scratched the back of his neck and said, "The doctors informed me that the only word Deiko keeps saying is, 'Elias.'"

John shook his head. "I don't understand that. I don't know anyone around here by that name."

"I've had others research it, and they cannot find any records of anyone living in this area with that as a first or last name. No one at the university has that name, either. And the university hasn't heard anything from Ben since the other day."

"He only has the SUV," John said. "He's still somewhere in there."

From the dark grove of pines, a flock of crows squawked and burst into flight, which startled John and Higgins.

"Reckon what scared them?" Higgins asked.

"I have no idea. Let's go, if you want me to talk to them before I have to go to work."

John got into his pickup and Higgins followed him out of the pasture in his patrol car. John parked beside Ben's SUV and then got into the passenger side of the patrol car. As they neared John's mailbox, he asked that Higgins stop for a second. John's son, Jack, and his friend, Donnie were carrying their fishing poles and tackle boxes.

"You boys keep an eye out for Ben," John said.

Jack squinted as the morning sun struck him in the face. "He's still not come out of the cave?"

"No, son," John said. "Not yet."

Higgins leaned toward the open window and said, "If you see or hear him, hurry home and call 911. Dispatch will let me know, okay."

"Sure," Jack said.

"Catch a big one," John said.

Jack and Donnie smiled. "We'll try."

"And beware of boogiemen," Higgins said.

"What?" Jack asked.

"Just stay away from the cave, you two," John said.

Donnie snickered and looked at Jack. He said, "We're not afraid of that ol' cave."

"Well," Higgins said, "to be on the safe side, don't go in there right now."

"Nah, we're too interested in catching a lunker," Jack said.

"Be back in a bit," John said.

ELIAS JACKSON STOOD beneath the shadow of a large Canadian hemlock branch. He watched Higgins and John talk outside Devils Den. His aged body ached. He needed to find a pure hearted person to sacrifice before the moon began to wane at midnight.

Deiko had failed him and mind control over another individual had drained Elias even more. Had Deiko been able to capture that faery, there was no end to what possible power Elias would have gained by sacrificing a rare, magical creature.

In his pursuit for immortality he had called upon the dark power of the Loa, and to his surprise, the Dark Chancellor had appeared to him and offered to give him his wish provided Elias, in turn, rose every twenty years and offered a blood sacrifice of an innocent child as homage to his new dark master. But the toughest feat would be to successfully perform this seven times.

Elias wasn't a fool. After his third resurrection, he realized the chancellor was using his sacrifices to gain more power while not giving Elias needed regeneration to his body to prevent further decay.

Time had not fared well for Elias' decomposing body. He was decaying, and to keep that to a minimum, he shunned daylight and tried to lurk during the darkness of night. He knew if anyone witnessed him, they'd speculate that he was a walking corpse. But even though magic had allowed him to live well beyond his years, he was not yet immortal. Weapons could kill him and end his quest for eternal life prematurely. Despite living well over a century, his body was in better condition than he had expected after nearly one hundred twenty years of dormancy. Part of his success to prevent his body from decomposition while sleeping was due to his knowledge of black magic as a Bokor Voodoo priest from Haiti. So instead of offering sole sacrifices to the chancellor, Elias made extra sacrifices strictly for himself that reverted his aging process and turned back the hands of time, allowing his body to rejuvenate while dormant, rather than decay.

The stench of partial decay emitted from his body. He detested smelling rancid during the extreme summer heat, but there wasn't anything to do to alleviate it. The longer he stayed in the sweltering heat, the worse his odor became. Flies and other carrion insects pestered him.

A crow dropped from the top of a dead pine and dug its claws into his shoulder. Elias swatted it with a strong backhand. It squawked in terror and alarmed dozens of perched crows in neighboring trees to burst into the air and add their frightened cries to his. The crows circled and drifted further into the dark swampy forest.

After Higgins and John left the front of the cave and departed in their vehicles, Elias edged along the tree line and quickly ran for the coolness of Devils Den. Once inside, he welcomed the decreased temperature. He pressed his body to the cold, wet cave wall and clung to it. Now that he was inside the cave, where for two days he had painstakingly traveled so he could hide, he needed to wait until nightfall and find a suitable sacrifice.

But he never thought the sacrifice would come to him.

JACK AND DONNIE set their tackle boxes on the bank of Miller's Pond. They cast their lines and reeled in the rooster tail lures quickly. The spinning blades caught the early morning sunlight, and the gleam usually attracted the attention of hungry bass or large bream, but not today.

The overwhelming summer heat, even at the early morning hour, deterred fish from attacking artificial bait or live bait. The frustrating thing for the twelve-year-old boys was that they saw large bass lying near the bottom of the clear water pond. No matter what they used to entice them, the bass refused to strike.

"I can't believe this," Donnie said.

Cicadas hummed in the trees around Devils Den. Dragonflies darted and skimmed above the still pond.

Jack shook his head. "I've not caught anything in days. I was hoping the early morning would be better."

Donnie wiped sweat from his face. Sweat beaded above his upper lip. He ran his tongue across it. "It's already getting hot."

"Another hundred degree day, I bet. Might as well head back to the farm and play a game inside."

"Or we could go inside the cave," Donnie said.

"Nah. You heard my dad and what Deputy Higgins said. We'd better not go inside."

"Why not? Isn't your uncle inside?"

"That's where he went yesterday, but I don't know why he's never come out."

Donnie stared across the pond and squinted against the beaming sun to see the cave. "What if he's in trouble? We might hear him calling for help or something?"

The windless morning made the sun feel even hotter. Jack had been inside the cave a couple of times with his father and once with his uncle Ben. The temperature there was much cooler and definitely would be more pleasant than standing on the bank hoping the fish would bite.

"I guess it wouldn't hurt to go right inside the entrance and see if we hear him," Jack said.

"All right!" Donnie said, placing his fishing pole on the ground beside his tackle box. "You know if we find him, we'll be heroes."

Jack shook his head. "We're not going far into the cave. Just right inside, okay?"

"Why? Are you afraid of the boogieman that Deputy Higgins was teasing about?"

"No, but my father will get mad if we go inside without him being here. Besides I didn't bring a flashlight."

"Me, either."

They left their fishing gear at the pond and walked across the pasture until they got to the trees. As they came closer to the entrance, the cool air blew past. With the wind came the rotten odor of something dead.

"Eww," Donnie said.

Jack pulled the collar of his shirt over his nose and said, "Yeah, I smell it too."

"What is it?"

"Probably something like a raccoon crawled in here and died."

"Cool. Let's find it."

Jack said, "No. We stay where there is light."

"What are you afraid of?"

"Nothing."

"Then, come on, just a little further," Donnie said, taking several more steps.

"Donnie, wait!"

Donnie darted deeper into the cave where Jack couldn't see him. Jack hesitated. Then Donnie screamed. The loud scream frightened Jack, but what scared him most was when Donnie's scream suddenly muffled and went quiet.

A lump rose in Jack's throat. He took a couple of cautious steps deeper into the cave. Donnie kept trying to cry out, but his mouth seemed to be covered. He was in trouble. Jack took another step, and light faded. Two more steps, and he knew he'd be standing where it was pitch black. No light.

"Donnie? You okay?" he asked, hoping his friend answered, hoping this was a mean prank.

Jack stepped further into the cave. The decayed smell became stronger. Heavy breathing caused fear to paralyze him.

Donnie struggled with something in the dark. Apparently he pulled himself partially free of its hold and yelled, "Run, Jack! Go get help!"

Before Jack could move, an arm reached out, grabbed him, and spun Jack around. The arm wrapped around his throat, and Jack pulled forward to run. He had enough adrenaline-filled strength that he dragged their attacker out of the dark shadows and into the faint light.

The black slimy arm tugged him back. Pieces of skin were missing. Still in its hold, he spun enough to see the black man's face. Most of the man's skin was missing and his facial muscles were visible. The man's yellow eyes bulged and for a moment, Jack forgot to breathe. When he came to his senses and realized what was happening, he glanced at Donnie's terrified face. Shock overcame his friend, who stood wide-eyed and silent, and too fearful to help fight this hideous living corpse.

Jack shoved and kicked at the man. "Let him go!" Jack shouted.

The man, who by all reasonable means to Jack should be dead, was powerfully strong. Jack fought to get free, but the man's grip was unbelievable. He finally reached for the man's throat, and in the faint light, he grabbed the man's necklace, which resembled finger bones linked together to encircle his neck. He pulled and the bone necklace dropped from its throat. When the necklace was gone, he noticed a deep scar around the man's throat. He wondered if the man had been strangled or hanged. But how was he still alive?

When the necklace hit the ground, the man's eyes widened. He clutched his throat and gasped for air. His strength decreased enough that Jack broke loose of his hold. Donnie jerked and suddenly tried to try to escape, too.

"Come on, Donnie! Run!"

The corpselike man yanked his necklace off the cave floor and his strength returned. He pulled Donnie close to his chest and pointed his long finger at Jack and said, "You're next!"

Terrified, Jack turned and sprinted out of the cave. He ran all the way home, and once inside the house; his mother tried to console him and kept asking him what was wrong. But Jack was too afraid to speak. Shock consumed him. He shook uncontrollably.

"Where's Donnie?" his mother Lib asked.

"It got him," he finally said.

"What?"

"Some man in the cave. It has him."

Lib hurried to the phone and called 911. They relayed the message to Higgins who said that he was on his way back.

When Higgins and John returned, they rushed inside the cave with flashlights but never found Donnie or any trace that he had been there. When nightfall came, Jack kept his bedroom light on and his hunting knife near his pillow. For some reason he believed the man was going to come back for him, and his inner fears prevented him from closing his eyes until sunrise came.

CHAPTER 30

*B*otis, the Dark Chancellor, sat on his throne of skulls and held his ebony staff in his hand. The large crystal across the room glowed to life. Soon the violet color turned crimson red. A magical line seeped from the crystal, crossed the floor, and crept up the staff. Botis tilted his head back and closed his eyes as the power from Elias' blood sacrifice flowed through the staff. Warmth and energy radiated up his arm and throughout his body.

Botis grinned. Soon Elias would crawl back into his grave and not emerge for another twenty years. By that time, Botis was certain to find a way to prevent Elias from completing his quest for immortality.

Roble held his torch at a forty-five degree angle to keep the flaming tar from dripping onto his hand. He used his torch to light sconces every twenty feet or so while they headed through the rough permafrost tunnel. The floor was littered with broken crates and empty wooden kegs. Dead mice lay all through the debris. Their throats had been slit.

Riese had left them at the door to inspect the tavern and make certain nothing of value had been stolen. Odlon kept the crossbow ready as they sloshed through the half frozen sewer mush. Lehrling coughed a couple times and spit a wad of green phlegm onto the nasty brownish ice. He leaned against the cold wall to catch his breath.

"You okay?" Roble asked him.

He nodded. "Yeah, just trying to adapt to the putrid smell."

"The sooner we check out the tunnel, the quicker we leave," Odlon said, motioning them forward.

Roble lighted another sconce and glanced upward. Overhead, about twelve feet up was another grate, which indicated they were beneath another building. Four sconces blazed behind them. By his estimate, they had probably crossed beneath the street to the other buildings. And if so, he didn't see a set of stairs that led upward. Only Hobskin's Tavern had an exit that led back to the streets.

"It's a dead end," Roble said. His heart sank. He feared Shawndirea was lost to him forever.

"No, it isn't a dead end," Odlon said. He pointed at a busted keg that was tilted against the wall. The sewer sludge dripped and drained beneath it.

Roble pulled the keg from the blocked hole. Warmer air flowed from the opening. Roughly hewn steps descended with a thin layer of sticky sludge oozing over them.

Lehrling gagged as he came closer. "Surely you don't think we should wade into that muck?"

"You two don't have to," Roble said. "I'll go alone. I won't rest until I find her."

Odlon shook his head. "No. I'll come with you."

"I'm not saying I *won't* go," Lehrling said. "I'll go if you believe those Ratkin are in there."

"I honestly don't know, but rats kill mice and there's a lot of dead mice in all this mess. They were killed recently, too." Roble held the torch lower to check the opening. Red beady eyes reflected in the light. Seconds later, they were gone.

"Rats," Odlon said.

"Which means the Ratkin could be in there," Lehrling said. "Rats are loyal to the Ratkin."

Roble lowered himself to his knees and whispered, "I hope this is where they've gone."

Odlon and Roble easily slid through the narrow opening, but Lehrling had a difficult time getting his gut squeezed through. Once through the hole, they stood and walked down the slick stairs.

The sewer tunnel beneath the taverns was narrow, but after they reached the bottom of the stairs, they found themselves standing inside a larger room. Although cool, the air was much warmer than where they had been moments before. The water was deeper without any ice. Large rats swam through the water emitting frightened squeaks. Roble and the others held their torches, trying to get an idea of how large the room was, but they had no idea.

Footsteps sloshed through the water rapidly.

"There!" Odlon said, pointing. He fired an arrow but missed.

Two figures ran quickly and disappeared outside the light radius.

"My guess is that's them," Lehrling said.

"Good," Roble said, pulling his knife. "I will skin two Ratkins."

SHAWNDIREA TOSSED BACK and forth in the burlap sack while the running Ratkin carried her. She didn't know where she was or who had captured her. She wondered what had happened and where Roble was.

His warm smile when she had lain beside him had been wonderful. She knew he was the one she had been destined to find, and as she had grown comfortable beside him, his gaze of love had turned to sudden alarm and panic. Someone else had been in the room, and obviously she had been taken before he had a chance to protect her or himself.

She wondered if he were still alive. Her heart and mind ached, wanting to see him, to be with him, and return to her homeland to renounce her right to the throne in order to wed him. She doubted that she'd experience any of those things now.

The smell of wet vermin was terribly strong, and she gagged. She wanted to use her magic but due to the abrupt jarring around, she couldn't concentrate well enough to focus her drawing of magic. She grabbed fist-fuls of the bag material to steady herself and prevent further bruises.

Water sloshed beneath her. The strong scent of sewer water sickened her worse than the vermin smell. She pressed her nose against the cloth wall surrounding her, and desperately hoped it lessened the odor. It did, but not by much.

"Keep moving!" a harsh voice shouted.

"I am. I am," replied a closer voice, which she guessed to be the one carrying her while running through shallow water.

"They sees us!"

"How much further?"

"Not far. Not far."

"We has her," the one carrying her said. "Great reward for this one, yes?"

"If alive, yes. Not as good if she's dead."

Tears filled Shawndirea's eyes. She whispered, "Where are you, Roble?"

~

THE OPEN ROOM WAS DARK. The only light was the radius surrounding their small circle formed from three torches. Small chunks of earth dropped occasionally from the ceiling, making splashes or plunks where they struck. Roble kept his eyes on the watery path ahead of him. Little groups of brown rats squeaked and ran from where he stepped.

"Where do you think we are?" Roble asked.

"Sewers," Lehrling replied.

"No mistaking that," Roble replied, "But . . . sewers beneath where? The temperature here is much warmer. No ice. And if I gambled a guess, I'd say the overhead ground is about to cave in."

"Could be under the mountain," Odlon replied. "Deep enough and insulated enough to keep the frigid temperature out."

"Maybe," Roble said, taking another step through the ankle deep water.

"Why?" Lehrling asked. "What are you thinking?"

"Passed through Styx to get here. Surely we're not heading back?"

Odlon chuckled. "Doubtful."

The splashing footsteps dashed across the center of the room. The immense darkness prevented them from seeing their exact position.

"This could just be a very large enclosed room with only one way in and out," Odlon said.

"True," Roble said softly.

"In which case," Odlon said, "One of us should probably be positioned near the small doorway."

"I'll gladly go," Lehrling said, gagging.

"If they head toward you, call out to us."

"I will."

Odlon and Roble walked side-by-side, heading toward the splashing footsteps. As they did, the walls seemed to be closer together. The room wasn't as big as Roble had thought. Whispering echoed in the shadows each time the rapid splashing ceased. Then they took to running again.

"I think you're right," Roble said.

"About?"

"There might not being another way out."

Odlon smiled. "Be prepared. They may run swiftly toward us."

Roble moved his torch to his left hand and pulled his dagger.

"I should inform you," Odlon said. "The Ratkin are known to carry many different diseases and plagues. Avoid getting clawed or bitten."

Roble remembered their jagged teeth when they had snarled and tried to bite him. They didn't need steel weapons with those teeth, and if they were plague-carriers as well, that made them that much worse to deal with.

"Why would they take Shawndirea?" Roble asked.

"She possesses magic. She is powerful."

"And if they have her, wouldn't they fear her?"

"Possibly. But they have her where she's not a threat to them," Odlon replied. "A lot of races will drain a faery of her power in order to gain favors for themselves."

"How?"

"A sorcerer can place a spell to tap the faery's magic or some races drain the blood and drink it."

Roble swallowed hard. His stomach became uneasy.

"But with these Ratkins that have her, I don't think that's the situation," Odlon said. "Since they were here in a thief's sanctuary, they wanted to get her somewhere to sell her and make gold off her."

"So you don't think they'll kill her?" Roble asked.

Odlon shook his head. "Not here. They know we're after them and nearby."

"You don't think they'd risk killing her to gain power?"

Odlon chuckled. "They don't have time. Since they are hiding inside this sewer tunnel, and it's obvious they are; they're too panicked to carry out any ritual that we might interrupt. No, they're trying to get out of Glacier Ridge, and as a last desperate move, they might actually offer her in exchange for their own lives being spared."

"They will die."

Roble kept walking forward, holding his torch ahead of them, and watching the brownish water as they sloshed forward.

"Watch out!" Odlon shouted, pushing Roble toward the wall.

In the torchlight, yellow teeth gnashed at them. One of the Ratkin leapt from the side of the wall. Roble's right shoulder hit the wall, and the Ratkin lunged and ripped at Odlon. Odlon turned and pressed his flaming torch against the Ratkin's throat, setting its fur on fire. The beast howled in pain and buried its face into the nasty water to extinguish the flame. The stench of burnt hair rose in the smoke.

"Where did it go?" Roble asked, searching the tunnel with the torch.

"He swam off. He's hurt, but he's not dead."

"Not yet, anyway."

"I don't think he has Shawndirea," Odlon said.

"How could you tell?"

"He didn't have any packs or bags with him. Most likely he is trying to frighten us to let his companion escape with her."

Roble hurried forward, only to find the water was getting deeper.

Odlon grabbed his arm. "Careful. You don't know how deep that water is."

"I can swim."

"Not as good as they can." Odlon held his torch over the water and said, "See?"

Dozens of rats swam through the water toward them.

"So? Those are regular rats, not Ratkin."

"These rats hold allegiance to the Ratkin. Often they do whatever the Ratkin request, which in this case is to attack."

The small swimming rat swarm treaded the water and squeaked. They swam and gnashed their sharp teeth. Roble backed up and positioned the torch between him and the rats. The blazing torch came close enough to singe a couple of the rats. The rats parted and circled further away into the darkness. Only their red eyes glowed, reflecting the torch flame.

"Roble!" Lehrling shouted. "Over here!"

Odlon glanced at Roble and said, "Hurry."

Roble and Odlon sloshed through the water to make their way to the small opening that Lehrling guarded. The water slowed their progress, but two shadowy figures struggled with Lehrling, knocking his torch into the water. The light vanished.

Roble moved faster than he thought possible, but when they reached the door, Lehrling lay on the slimy steps and partially through the door. Frantically, he tugged one Ratkin by the leg.

The hairy ratman snarled and angrily jabbed at Lehrling's gloved hand.

"Let go!" it cried.

Once Roble reached the shallower water, he ran toward the opening. Lehrling gasped and groaned, trying to hold the creature tighter.

"Hurry," Lehrling said, panting for air.

Roble drew the sword, and although not proficient with it, he swung it hard and fast. The blade sliced just an inch above Lehrling's hand and chopped the Ratkin's foot off. The sudden release sent Lehrling forward, and Roble pushed himself around the heavy man, and then he squeezed through the small opening.

The lit sconces flickered enough to brighten the room.

A pool of blood surrounded the severed foot. A heavy trail of dark blood lined across the semi-frozen sludge on the permafrost floor. The

Ratkin hobbled and turned to see Roble approach. Its voice rose in a strange shrill.

"No!" It said. "Let me free!"

Roble rushed across the cold floor, tossed his torch to the frozen floor, and flung a dagger. The knife buried into its right shoulder with enough force to spin the Ratkin forward and off balance. It fell face forward, but turned to the side and spun around enough to land and catch itself with its left elbow.

In terror, its eyes widened. Blood streamed from its footless leg. Roble stood over the Ratkin and placed the tip of the sword to its throat.

"Where's the faery?" Roble asked.

"I not have," It replied. It's long tongue hung from the side of its nasty yellow-toothed mouth.

Roble glanced back for a moment to see Odlon helping pull Lehrling through the small hole. He faced the Ratkin again and pressed the blade harder to its throat. The Ratkin was losing a lot of blood quickly. The other one was nowhere in sight. Roble wasn't certain the beast would live much longer. He needed to know where its partner had gone or where it planned to go.

Roble stepped on its bloody stump with enough force to stop the flowing blood. The abrupt pain forced the Ratkin to scream, but with the sword's tip pressed to its throat, it wasn't able to attack.

"Where is she?" Roble asked.

"Dirf has her."

Odlon and Lehrling stood beside Roble.

Lehrling said, "Both of them ran past me. I could only grab him."

Odlon aimed the crossbow at the Ratkin's good leg and said, "And where is Dirf?"

In a half chuckle, half pain-filled gasp, it said, "Gone. Gone."

"Where is he going?" Roble asked.

The Ratkin snarled. "I not telling."

Roble twisted his foot back and forth on its bloody stump.

It howled out. "That hurts!"

"It's supposed to," Roble said, pressing harder.

"I not tell!"

"You think more of your comrade than he does you," Odlon said.

The Ratkin turned and its rat-like ears twitched. "What you mean?"

"He's not concerned about your pain and suffering. He's not interested in helping you at all. And yet, you're willing to let him escape and reap great wealth without you?"

"So?" it said. "Look at me. I no good to run anymore. Gold not do me good."

Roble pressed the side of the sword blade against the Ratkin's throat, trapping it against the wall. Then he grabbed a loose strand of its sleeve and ripped it off the soiled shirt. He handed it to Lehrling.

"Tie that around his leg tight enough to stop the bleeding," Roble said.

"Why?"

"Because I don't want him bleeding to death."

The Ratkin's eyes brightened with hope. "You save me to find Dirf?"

"No."

Curiosity overcame the Ratkin's expressions as it studied Roble. "You're bandaging my wound."

Roble's eyes narrowed as he looked at the Ratkin. "Oh, you're going to die," he said, smiling. "You need to decide whether it's going to be instant or *painfully* long."

The Ratkin's eyes grew wide with fear. Roble took the sword hilt in his left hand and drew another dagger with his left. The shining steel blade flashed in the glow of Odlon and Lehrling's torches.

Roble slowly moved the dagger toward the Ratkin. Its whiskers twitched and it tried to crawl out of reach, but it was pressed against the wall.

"I doubt rat pelt is worth much," Roble said.

The Ratkin swallowed hard. His breathing increased.

"Where is she?" Roble asked again.

The Ratkin hesitated.

"Remember," Roble said, "Quick death or torture. Your only choices."

"He go to Icevale," he said. "Make it quick, please?"

Roble looked at Odlon questioningly.

Odlon smiled. "The valley north of Glacier Ridge. Not far."

Roble stepped back from the Ratkin.

Odlon said, "Allow me."

The elf fired a quick shot through its heart. Its body sagged as death claimed the rat-man beast.

"Let's go get our horses," Lehrling said. "It's time we get to a better climate. I've had enough of Glacier Ridge for a lifetime."

Odlon nodded.

"How do we know the Ratkin was telling the truth?" Roble asked.

"We don't," Lehrling said. "But it's the best we'd get out of him anyway."

"Why's that?"

"Can you ever truly trust a thief?" Lehrling asked.

"Good point," Roble replied.

Odlon shrugged. "Sometimes you're left without a choice."

They headed back to the steel door to leave. They found Riese lying facedown on the stairwell. Roble hurried to Riese and turned him over. He was breathing regularly but unconscious. He couldn't see how the escaping Ratkin could have possibly beaten Riese in a one-on-one fight. He checked his head for lumps, but he didn't find anything unusual.

"He's out," Roble said.

Odlon pried open Riese's eyes and examined them. "He's been gassed."

Roble shook his head. "I didn't figure the rat beast could have fought him."

"Nor you and I together," Odlon said with a wry smile.

"Help me get him to a table in the tavern."

Odlon and Lehrling braced under Riese's enormous size and helped Roble lay the giant across a tabletop. Riese groaned and his head tilted to the side.

"Look," Lehrling said, pointing.

On the floor was the head of the last Ratkin that possessed Shawndirea.

Roble's heart sank. Riese was unconscious and the Ratkin was dead. Neither had her. Where was she?

At the tavern door stood a man that Lehrling immediately recognized. "Crukas," he said.

"You know him?" Roble asked.

"You've never heard of him?"

"No."

Lehrling's eyebrows rose in surprise. "Indeed you come from a place I don't know."

"I told you," Roble said with an even smile. "Intrigue me."

"Crukas," Odlon said, "is one of the greatest thieves of all times. He's known throughout all regions."

"I have what the Ratkins stole from you," Crukas said. "Do a favor for me, and she's yours."

Odlon brought up the crossbow and aimed. Crukas vanished and appeared on the other side of the bar. "That's a nasty way of making acquaintances," he said.

"How did you know she was with me?" Roble asked.

Crukas tightened the knot that braided his long black hair and smiled. "I followed them out of the tavern after that *lovely* brawl Riese stirred up. I watched them for several hours as those filthy rat beasts worked their way through the rooftop, and then followed the two as they fled away. Of course, I stopped following them once they scampered into the sewer wastes. I do have to draw the line somewhere."

"What is this favor you ask?" Lehrling asked.

"I need protection to get through the forests on the outskirts of Ironwood," Crukas said.

"Where is she?" Roble asked with his hand on his knives.

"She's safe."

"Where?"

Crukas smiled and waved him toward the bar. "Come see."

Roble took a step.

Crukas said, "Hands off the knives."

Roble held his empty hands out before him and walked toward the bar. When he reached the bar, Crukas pointed at the glass bottle where Shawndirea was trapped. She glared at Crukas with fiery indignation.

"Why do you need protection to get around Ironwood," Roble said. "Looks like what you really need is protection from her. She's ready to do you great harm."

Crukas laughed. "Yes. She might, but she's not as mad as some in Ironwood are. I am now a very wanted man there."

Riese rolled to his side and groaned. He squinted and tried to focus, but apparently the drug was strongly affecting his vision. He lowered his head and closed his eyes again.

"And," Roble said, "I'd fear what Riese will do to you once he awakens."

"Yes, that is a greater concern. I need to leave Glacier Ridge immediately."

"Release her, and we'll get you past Ironwood safely," Odlon said.

Crukas looked untrusting.

"It's the best offer you'll get," Odlon said. "You may have some magical abilities, but eventually that weakens your energy. Besides, I don't tire easily when it comes to shooting. Plus, I like a good hunting challenge. Moving targets are nice practice."

Crukas motioned his open hand flamboyantly toward the bottle and stepped away. "She's yours. I just thought getting her back for you was something well worth asking a favor. Nothing more."

Roble opened the wide-mouthed bottle and helped Shawndirea out. She raised her hands and her fingertips glowed. Roble shook his head and said, "No."

"Give me a reason why I shouldn't," she said angrily through clenched teeth.

Roble pointed to the Ratkin's head on the floor. "Because *that* was the one that took you. Crukas decapitated him."

Shawndirea glared and said, "*He placed me in a bottle!*"

"I'm sorry."

"*He* owes me an apology. Not you."

"I understand your anger. I'd be infuriated, too. The good thing is that you're safe and you're with me again," Roble said. "I was afraid I had lost you."

Sadness came to her eyes. "I feared the same for you."

"How close is Ironwood to your homeland?"

She took a deep breath and slowly exhaled. After some of her anger subsided, she replied, "It is on the way. We must pass through it."

"Then we return the favor since he killed the one that took you. Otherwise, the three of us would have had to travel to Icevale to find you."

"Fine," she said.

Crukas gave an apologetic smile to Shawndirea and said, "My apologies for placing you into the bottle. But would you have immediately believed that I was not the one that had captured you?"

"Probably not."

"So will you forgive my transgression?"

Shawndirea crossed her arms and said, "I'll think about it."

Crukas glanced from the faery to Roble and said, "So you'll help me?"

Before Roble could reply, Lehrling tapped his shoulder.

"May I talk to you for a moment, Roble?" Lehrling asked. "In private?"

Roble nodded. He turned and left Shawndirea eying down Crukas. Roble followed Lehrling to a table on the far side of the tavern.

"What is it?" Roble asked.

"Riese."

Roble glanced toward the giant bearded stable master. He was still sprawled across the table, deep in sleep.

"What about him?"

"If we leave here with Crukas, you will lose all favor with Riese."

"Why? What are you talking about?"

Lehrling coughed, beat his chest with his fist, and cleared his throat. His reply came barely above a whisper, "He spoke with me in the tavern while you were talking with Odlon. He dislikes Crukas a *lot*. Perhaps even *hates* him. We cannot aid this man in *any* way."

"He told you that he despises him?" Roble asked.

Lehrling nodded. "In so many words, yes. He's already warned Crukas to stay out of Glacier Ridge but here he is. When the fights started here with Lord Waxxon's men, Crukas vanished."

"Where did he go?"

Lehrling shrugged. "Who knows? He's one of the most famous of all thieves, second only to one other thief. A man named Fraud."

"Fraud? Interesting name for a thief."

"Yes. I agree. But Crukas may have taken the opportunity to pick the locks to the sewers. You saw him vanish and reappear. Who knows what else he may have taken during the distractions."

"You think he worked with the Ratkin?"

"It's possible. His table was beside theirs."

Roble frowned. "Then why not use the Ratkin to get him past Ironwood."

"Those rat vagrants would immediately draw the attention of the town's border guards. He needs a group like ourselves to blend in and not draw suspicion."

"But if he had befriended the Ratkin, why would he kill this one?"

"To keep the blame off himself maybe? Once he got what he needed, there's no reason to keep them. Thieves cannot be trusted, and they certainly don't trust one another."

Roble asked, "So do you think Riese's distaste for Crukas is linked to him needing a way to bypass Ironwood?"

"Most definitely. I'm certain they want his head worse than Riese does. Otherwise he would not have been so bold to allow Riese to see him at the tavern. And then, he gassed Riese with something in order to overpower him? Roble think seriously on this before pledging an oath to assist him."

"So you won't go?"

"I will to aid you getting Shawndirea home," Lehrling said. "I owe you that much, but you may well earn a bounty on our heads from Riese because he will definitely feel betrayed and believe we're aligned with Crukas."

Roble stared at the floor and shook his head. "We can't have that."

"Not a way to build a healthy relationship with townships, especially if you're going to be a member of the Dragon Skull Order."

Roble said, "You're right. I'm not a member of your knights, so it's best I swap for other clothes."

"No," Lehrling said. "Don't be hasty. I never meant to imply that you're an imposter. We need you. You're a man of nobility and that's rare in these lands."

Roble smiled. "I'm not a swordsman. I know which end to hold, but I'm not trained."

"I can train you. I'm certain Odlon would as well."

"And what makes you think I'm worthy to be one of your knights?"

"A lesser man would have left me to die," Lehrling said with a weak smile. His eyes grew misty. "You didn't. You risked your life even though you had no idea what kind of person I am."

"Maybe I just like to go against the odds."

"Aye, I know better than that."

"Okay, so what do I do now?" Roble asked. "I've sort of promised that I would help him."

"We trick him and turn him over to Riese."

"Are you saying a man of nobility should not keep his word?"

"Do you consider lying to a thief a great offense?"

Roble shook his head. "No."

"Nor do I. After all, can you truly trust him?"

"Probably not."

"Well, according to Riese, Crukas comes to Glacier Ridge to find thieves with high bounties, befriends them, and then he turns them over to authorities in neighboring towns and villages for the rewards."

"Really?"

"Aye."

"Never trust a thief," Roble said. "If I must be dishonest with him, I aim to make him believe my lies. Riese has done too much for us. I cannot ever make him think I'd double-cross him."

Lehrling grinned. "Since Crukas needs protection, it will be easier to convince him that he needs us than it is for us to believe anything he says."

"How long do you think Riese will be out?"

"Depends on what Crukas used."

Roble frowned. "Anything that you know that could awaken him?"

"There are things I could try."

"Good. We'll leave you here with Riese and while we head to the stables, see if you get him awakened. Tell him where we are with Crukas."

Lehrling ran his hand through his beard and nodded. "Sure."

"Then I guess we should get started."

"Indeed," Lehrling said.

Roble approached Crukas and said, "What did you use to knock Riese unconscious?"

"Just a mild vapor I've learned to concoct from a wizard."

"How long does its effect last?"

Crukas shrugged. "Not long, which is why we should hurry."

"Do you have an antidote?" Roble asked as Odlon moved closer with the crossbow trained on the small thief.

"Sure, but if you give it to him, he'll kill me."

"Leave the antidote with Lehrling while we go to the stables."

Crukas looked startled. "Why should I do that?"

"Do you want our assistance or not?" Roble asked.

"Yes."

"Then leave the antidote with him. I'll explain on the way."

Crukas lifted a small corked vial filled with a pale yellow liquid from inside his inner coat pocket. He hesitated before he finally handed it to Lehrling.

CHAPTER 31

Outside Hobskin's Tavern, Odlon and Roble walked alongside Crukas as they headed to the stables. Shawndirea rested in Roble's shirt pocket where she was shielded from the harsh wind. The sky was lighter, but still a dark gray. Roble wondered if the sun was ever visible here. But it was no longer night.

Roble kept his torch. Odlon carried another one. The wind flickered the flames.

"That's the deal," Roble said.

Crukas shook his head and said, "So you want me to *pretend* that you're shackling me to turn me over to the officials at Ironwood?"

"Yes."

"Why should I do something so foolish? No one has ever had me in cuffs."

"Riese has been very hospitable to us while we've been here. I want to leave Glacier Ridge in good favor with him, especially after you drugged him."

"He won't know any better," Crukas said. "He didn't see me use it."

"His sons have our horses. They will tell him, and when they do, he'll send people after us. Possibly to kill us. I gather he's not fond of you anyway."

Crukas laughed. "No town leader ever is."

"Thieves' reputations aren't stellar, and since you're known border to border," Odlon said, "what do you expect?"

"I'm used to it. Trust is not something I expect any to offer, which is why I scoff at your request to shackle me."

"Let's put it this way," Roble said. "If you don't, by the time our horses are saddled and ready to go, Lehrling will be here with Riese. I'm certain that his view of you will be less hostile if he believes we have you in custody and returning you to Ironwood than if you're not shackled."

Crukas remained silent for a few moments, pondering the information. His dark eyes glanced around while he thought. Finally, he surrendered a sigh and asked, "And once we're always from here, you'll remove them?"

Roble nodded.

Crukas stared shrewdly into Roble's eyes, trying to read his thoughts. "Either you're a very good liar," he said, "or you're the most honest person I've met."

"I realize you're taking a risk to trust me," Roble said.

"You have no idea. I seldom have trust in anyone, including myself."

They reached the stables. Roble hammered the closed door several times with his fist. After several minutes, one of Riese's sons unlatched the inner lock bar and pulled it ajar.

"We're back for our horses," Odlon said.

The young man widened the door and looked out. He asked, "Where's my father?"

"With Lehrling at Hobskin's Tavern. They're on their way."

The young man nodded and opened the door wider. After everyone was indoors, he shut the door again but didn't place the steel lock bar back into place.

"Do you have a set of shackles we can use?" Roble asked.

Riese's son looked questionably.

Odlon stood slightly behind Crukas with the crossbow aimed at the thief's back.

Crukas played along and in rich proper accent, he said, "They're taking me to Ironwood to collect my bounty."

"He has some over there," he replied, pointing at the wall where other odd and end tools rested.

Roble looked at the different sets of shackles and located one that would hold Crukas securely. He took these and returned to where the thief stood. Crukas reluctantly held out his hands, staring intently into Roble's eyes. Roble gave a slight nod, and then he looked down at the shackles. He placed them around Crukas' wrists, tightened them into place, and locked them. The metal was heavy enough to force Crukas' arms down before him.

Crukas checked the strength of the shackles and became apprehensive.

"You vow to remove these once we get out of Glacier Ridge?" Crukas asked.

Roble looked into Crukas' eyes and nodded. "I do."

The stable door opened and a gush of bitter cold wind flowed through. Riese staggered through the door with Lehrling trying to support the near giant's weight. Roble shoved the door closed after they entered.

Riese's eyes were bloodshot and his face was beet red. Roble didn't have to guess the man's anger had shaded his face more than the harsh winter wind.

"Where is he?" Riese said, looking around. When his eyes located Crukas, he stormed across the stable floor and towered over the small thief. Riese's muscled hands wrapped around Crukas' throat, and he lifted him three feet into the air.

"Easy, Riese," Roble said. "We have him shackled. He will pay for his crimes and trespasses against you."

"And how is that?" Riese asked.

"Lehrling didn't tell you?"

"Oh, he mumbled a lot of things I couldn't understand due to the wind and my throbbing head."

"We're taking Crukas to Ironwood and turning him in for the reward."

Riese chuckled and slowly lowered Crukas back down to the floor. "I'll do you one better than that. I'll escort you to Ironwood myself."

Roble shook his head. "That's not necessary."

"I insist," Riese said. "I want to see him dangle from the tree branch when they hang him."

"There's really no need for you to leave," Roble said.

"Either I watch him hang or I gut him right here and now," Riese said in a low, angry voice.

Chills ran down Roble's back and arms. The darkness in Riese's eyes revealed how intent he was to ensure Crukas died one way or the other. There was no mercy in his voice, no compassion in his eyes.

Riese leveled his glare at Roble and asked, "Which shall it be?"

"Ironwood," Roble said, hoping that buying time might allow him to find a way to make good on his promise to Crukas. Roble turned and walked away.

Roble glanced at Lehrling in passing and whispered, "Well, shit."

Riese turned to his sons and said, "Marc! Jez! Hook up the wagon and lower the iron cage onto the back."

"Yes, father."

Riese eyed Crukas and said, "I warned you never to return. Did I not?"

Crukas looked to the floor. "You did."

"And you defied that command."

"Yes."

"Any regrets?" Riese asked.

Crukas looked at Riese and then he glanced at Roble. "More by the minute."

A half hour passed while Riese's sons saddled the horses for Odlon, Roble, and Lehrling. Then they rolled out an old black wagon and hitched two of Waxxon's massive horses to it. Riese carried a crate of smoked meat and jerky and slid it beneath the wagon seat. He placed a small keg of ale next to the crate.

He turned, smiled at Roble, and said, "It's a long trip."

Marc and Jez lowered a large iron cage into the back of the wagon. The cage was a long cylinder that was barely tall and wide enough to place Crukas inside. The iron bands were far enough apart that left him vulnerable to the freezing cold temperatures and assaulting winds. The bands were too close together to allow someone as thin and agile as Crukas to squeeze through in order to escape. Odd symbols were welded onto the iron bands.

"Don't you think this is a bit extreme for transport?" Roble asked.

"Not at all," Riese replied. "Exactly how did you plan to transport him to Ironwood?"

"Place him in shackles and tether his horse behind one of us."

Riese chuckled. "For a thief who can vanish into thin air? That would never have worked. You would have lost him once you reached the ice forest above Glacier Ridge."

"But isn't the cage excessive?"

"No, it is simply taking precautions," Riese said. He placed his massive hand on Crukas' shoulder and forced the thief into the narrow cage.

"How?" Roble asked.

Riese slammed the iron cage door shut and locked it. He said, "Iron neutralizes Crukas' magic. And these runic symbols are an added assurance that he cannot somehow bypass the metal cage with any spells. They counteract his incantations."

Crukas looked disgruntled and a bit worried. Not only was he caged, his hands remained shackled.

"Riese," Roble said. "There's no reason you should have to trouble yourself by accompanying us to Ironwood."

Riese frowned harsh and long at Roble, almost daring him to question his motives one more time. Roble nodded and stepped away. Riese climbed onto the driver seat and grabbed the reins. "We leave for Ironwood now."

Marc opened the stable doors. Riese snapped the whip and the pair of horses pulled the wagon from the heated stable and outside into the blowing snow. Crukas stared at Roble with pleading eyes. Roble could only reply with a shrug.

Lehrling brought a bay gelding to Roble. He handed the reins to Roble and said, "This was Bausch's horse. He's young and strong. Should make a great riding companion for you. Even if you decide not to help us find Lady Dawn later, keep the horse. His name is Bleys."

"Thanks," Roble said.

Lehrling looked as though he might reply, but his eyes moistened with tears. He quickly turned and got on his pale mare.

"Bleys," Roble said, looking into the horse's dark eyes. Shawndirea stretched her hands out and rubbed the white star patch on the horse's forehead. She giggled and kissed Bleys. The horse replied with a soft snort.

"Best hurry, Roble," Odlon said. "Riese isn't waiting on us."

Roble swung upon Bleys and glanced at Lehrling. He said, "Lehrling, I didn't expect Riese to accompany us."

Lehrling laughed and shrugged. "Nor did I, but you will find hard justice comes in strange ways. I warned you about the distaste Riese has for Crukas."

Roble nodded. "You did."

Odlon rode to the stable door and stopped. Strapped to the side of his saddle was an emerald green shield, which was made from a large dragon scale. Fastened on the outer side of the scale were spikes that must have been small dragon teeth. Roble was intrigued, if not totally impressed, by how Odlon fashioned his armor and shield from the dragon that had inflicted him with a never healing blistered back. The scaled armor and shield seemed more a reminder that even though the dragon had taken its best attempt to kill Odlon, the elf was the victor of their battle, and he wore dragon plate to display his triumph.

Odlon said to Lehrling and Roble, "What happens to a thief that should concern us except that he can no longer rob another man if the noose is his end?"

"True, elf," Lehrling said. "But more dangers lurk in the dark forests. Especially if Crukas has partners lying in wait."

"Why would he?" Roble asked.

"Do you really believe that he alone could bring several other thieves to collect bounties by himself?" Lehrling asked.

"I never really thought about it."

"Neither has Riese. It is best that we all keep our senses keen."

Odlon nodded. "You are right.

The three rode their horses into the frigid wind while heavy snow swirled. Jez and Marc pulled the heavy stable doors closed. The overhead sky was dark gray. Heading up the slope that led out of Glacier Ridge, Riese cracked his whip. The two horses' hooves crunched through the layers of hard icy snow as they gained traction to climb while pulling the heavy wagon.

Shawndirea rested her folded arms on the rim of Roble's shirt pocket. With her hood pulled over her head, she seemed content watching the windblown snow filter through the leafless trees and evergreen shrubs. Her eyes sparkled. Her smile never faded.

Roble chuckled. "You act as though you've never seen snow before."

She looked up at him and replied, "That's because I haven't. Not like this."

"So what do you think?"

"Beautiful and deadly."

"Deadly?" he asked.

She nodded. "Winter is death."

"I think of winter merely as a postponement until the spring thaw."

"Not here," she said softly. "This place knows no spring. Death lingers over this ridge."

"So what do you make of the spirit we saw on our way into Glacier Ridge? Ghost or banshee? No one died."

"No one we know," she replied. "Someone in the forest may have died. We just didn't witness it."

"Should we be concerned?"

"You didn't hear her, so her cry wasn't for you."

Roble nodded. "I know. But something at the tavern still bothers me."

"What?" she asked.

"The barmaid that served our table. She looked exactly like the female ghost."

"You noticed, too?" Lehrling said, riding up beside him.

"Yes."

Lehrling coughed violently and pounded his chest with his fist.

"Are you okay?" Roble asked. "Perhaps we should find a physician and have you checked."

Lehrling shook his head while coughing. Once he cleared the phlegm, he spat onto the frozen ground. "It's the winter air. Makes it hard to breathe."

"It sounds worse than that," Roble replied.

"I'll be fine. Just an old man who cannot handle extreme weather elements anymore."

"So you noticed the barmaid resembled the ghost?" Roble asked.

"Yes. Worrisome, but she was still alive after the raucous fight," Lehrling replied. "I saw her huddled behind the bar with the nervous barkeep."

Shawndirea's brow furrowed. "Then her death has yet to come, but it will occur soon. I feel uneasy."

"Why?"

"The forest seems stranger this morning than when we first arrived."

"You indicated that others may be in the forest," Roble said.

She nodded. "Travellers, mainly thieves and bondsmen, use the frozen path quite often. Waxxon's men did. And now so are we."

Roble glanced toward the wagon as he, Lehrling, and Odlon rode closer. Crukas stood in the tight cage. His dark eyes bore into Roble's with an expression that declared he had been betrayed. Even if Roble rode closer, Riese was too close for Roble to explain to Crukas that this had never been his plan. He doubted that Crukas would believe any explanation he offered.

Roble leaned closer to Lehrling and Odlon and said, "I gave him my word. I should find a way to keep it."

"Crukas is a con artist," Odlon said. "No matter what you promised him, you need to understand that if the situation was reversed, he wouldn't bat an eye to betray you or us for better gain."

Roble clenched his jaw. "What do you think, Shawndirea?"

"They speak the truth. A master thief is almost incapable of telling the truth. Their promises often are worthless."

"And Crukas'?"

"You cannot be a master of thieves and be an honest person."

"You're right about that. But what if Odlon is correct?" Roble asked. "Crukas may have a group hiding in the forest and attack us as we cross through."

She pursed her lips. "Be prepared to fight. Should any of his friends be waiting for us, it will be difficult to hear their movement over the horses and wagon wheels. At least it isn't totally dark."

"The clouds still make the forest darker."

"Yes, so watch for moving shadows."

The metal wagon wheels creaked as they rolled and crunched the frozen road. The wind whistled, whipping through the icy-bark trees. The treetops were dark against the gray sky, and the white fog billowed with frozen ice crystals, making it more difficult to locate any shadows. Roble shivered, more from nervousness than the cold. What hid within the fog and behind the trees?

Shawndirea's uneasiness had become his own. She was right. Hearing slight noises of movement off the frozen path was impossible. The wagon was loud and gave away their presence to anyone or anything that might be lying in wait.

They rounded the bend, and the road became more difficult to see. A heavy white veil of fog hung across their path. Roble looked from person to person. Odlon and Lehrling frowned while they searched the area. They appeared edgy, too.

The horses backed their ears and their eyes widened. The two horses pulling the wagon whinnied and reared slightly. Riese cracked the whip overhead, and they pulled forward. Their eyes remained wide. They flared their nostrils. Although scared, they seemed more afraid of Riese than what was in the fog.

Riese stood at the front of the wagon and pulled back the reins quickly. The horses stopped. They restlessly stepped side-to-side, bucked and reared.

"Easy!" Riese commanded. He turned and motioned with his left hand for Roble and the others to stop. They all pulled their reins and halted on the frozen road.

Other than the horses panting and their nervous snorting, they didn't hear anything. At first. The wind abruptly calmed. In the swollen veil of fog a large shadow appeared. Vague and shapeless. A constant creaking like moving ungreased hinges squeaked closer. The nearer the dark object came, the less obscured the fog made it.

Ahead on the frozen road a black carriage approached. Riese sat on his wagon seat, gripped his large hammer, and waited. Once the fog peeled away, they could see it. The blackest horses Roble had ever seen were pulling the black carriage. Their dark eyes were odd with a fiery red glow encircling them. The driver wore tattered black robes with a hood that drooped slightly over his brow. He had no facial hair, not even where his eyebrows should be.

The carriage slowed when it reached the side of Riese's wagon. The driver pulled back the reins and glanced at Riese. Shawndirea ducked deeper into Roble's pocket and hid. The sight of the man made Roble hold his breath and his hands tightened around the reins.

The driver was stooped forward. He tightened the reins and then tied them to the side of his seat. When he straightened, the hood eased back and revealed his face. The old man had paper-thin skin, dark large eyes, and narrow lips. His pale complexion held a slight blue tint, and he resembled that of a corpse.

"Ah, travellers," he said with a feeble voice. His thin lips barely moved while he spoke. "Where might the nearest town be?"

"Who are you?" Riese asked. His jaw tightened while he studied the old man. His brow creased from his intent frown.

"I'm a weary old man in need of some food, strong drinks, and a warm place to stay for several days," he replied. Puffs of frosty breath drifted from his mouth. His withered, boney hands shook from the cold.

Riese rose and glanced toward the back of the carriage. The windows were black with tattered cloth rolled down the outside of the glass.

"How many ride with you?" Riese asked with his eyes narrowed.

"Only I."

Riese climbed down from the wagon with his hammer held tight. "And who are you? *What* is your name?"

"Mors," he replied.

"And where is your homeland?" Riese asked, holding the hammer with both hands.

"I drift from town to town and have my entire life."

"Mind if I check the carriage?" Riese asked.

"Help yourself," Mors replied with a crooked grin. Most of his teeth were missing, but the remaining ones were black and broken.

Roble slid his hand onto his dagger, and Odlon's hands tightened on his crossbow. Riese walked to the side of the carriage and pulled the passenger door open. He leaned his head into the compartment and looked around. A few seconds later, he slammed the carriage door shut. He stepped back around to the driver.

"See?" Mors said in a raspy, tired tone. He hugged himself and shivered. "No one inside."

Riese nodded. "Follow the road. It dead-ends in Glacier Ridge. There are taverns, inns, and a stable. I'm sure you'll find whatever you need."

Mors smiled. "Oh, I'm certain I will. Thank you. I was beginning to believe that I'd die my death of cold out here. You've been most helpful."

Riese gave a slight nod and climbed back onto his wagon. Crukas looked at Roble and lifted his shackled hands while pleading with his eyes. All Roble could do was nod.

"Hope your journey is a prosperous one," Mors said to Riese. He untied the reins and snapped them across the black horses' backs. They jerked forward quickly.

Roble watched Mors' face as he rode past. His eyes bulged and an eerie smile crept across his lips. A chill shot through Roble.

The carriage rocked and creaked and headed on down the frozen road. When Roble glanced back, the carriage vanished into the foggy mist. Its sound silenced.

"Onward," Riese said, snapping the whip.

Odlon slid the crossbow into a compartment on the side of his saddle.

Lehrling shook his head and said, "That's about the strangest sight ever."

"Why's that?" Roble asked.

"Why have a carriage and not have passengers?"

Roble shrugged. "It is odd, but not the strangest thing I've seen."

Lehrling chuckled. "And what would that be?"

"You wouldn't believe me if I told you," Roble replied.

CHAPTER 32

An hour passed and no one had attacked them. So Crukas did not have a team. He was alone. And now, Crukas seemed destined to hang. Roble struggled with the thought because, even though Crukas wasn't an honest man, Roble had promised to help him. Instead, he was escorting the man to his death. Perhaps it was justice, but Roble didn't like the idea that Crukas would die, feeling complete betrayal when the thief had actually rescued Shawndirea from her abductors. He also believed that had Crukas not intervened, Shawndirea would have been lost to him forever.

They rode further down the road, which now had occasional slushy places and sticky mud, indicating they were nearing a warmer climate. However, the fog here was thicker. At least it had looked like fog. But figures moved within the white haze, and Roble recognized them to be ghosts.

One spirit drifted to the side of the wagon and hovered alongside Riese. He yanked the reins and shouted, "Damn be the gods!"

The ghost said in a panicked voice, "Father! Help us!"

Riese jumped from the wagon, unharnessed one of the massive horses, and climbed onto it bareback. He tossed keys to Roble, kicked the horse's flanks, and galloped back toward Glacier Ridge. As they sat on their horses, watching Riese ride furiously toward his town, dozens of ghosts appeared from the fog. Stunned, Roble recognized a lot of them. The barkeep, Riese's son Jez, and the barmaid that the banshee had come to warn, were all drifting spirits. All dead.

"Should we go help him?" Roble asked.

Odlon turned and was ready to head after Riese, but Crukas said, "No. There's no need."

Odlon frowned and looked at Crukas. He asked, "Why not?"

"The man on the carriage," Crukas said. "He's the plague-bringer. Where he rides, death follows."

"And you didn't warn us?" Roble said.

Crukas shrugged and lifted his shackled hands. "Why should I? Riese was delivering me to my death. I figure that's justice served."

Angered, Roble said, "But Riese's sons were innocent. You're a known thief!"

Crukas laughed. "They're not as innocent as you might think. The entire town was filled with deceptive people."

Lehrling dismounted and marched to the wagon. His hands were balled into fists. "Seems you're only trying to eliminate your competition any way possible."

Crukas grinned. "Such things are trivial. Besides, I didn't call the plague-bringer here. He came on his own."

"But you knew who he was," Roble said.

"Their deaths are not my fault. The plague-bringer chooses his victims. Not all die when he appears."

"As badly as you wanted to flee Glacier Ridge," Roble said, "I believe you had forewarning that he *was* coming."

Crukas looked away. He shook his head back and forth to adjust his long black ponytail.

"Do you deny that?" Odlon asked Crukas.

"No. But you being here with me as your prisoner is perhaps what has spared your lives as well. Now, as was our deal, release me from these shackles," Crukas said.

Roble climbed off his horse and led it to the front of the wagon.

"What are you doing?" Crukas asked. "He gave you keys. Surely one of them unlocks the cage so you can free me."

Roble shook his head. "Thievery I can handle, so long as it isn't me that's being robbed. However, the fact that you allowed Glacier Ridge's townspeople to die and not give Riese a chance to defend his own, you will face whatever punishment Ironwood orders."

Crukas' tanned face seemed to pale. "Please. I beg that you reconsider."

"I imagine you do. But no, justice will be served, and I will drive the wagon to Ironwood to make certain your death is carried out."

Roble backed his horse up to the wagon hitch. Lehrling helped fasten Bleys to the hitch. Shawndirea climbed on Bleys' back and lay down. She rubbed his back with her hands. Once they had the horse fastened alongside the larger horse, she stepped onto Roble's shoulder.

Roble climbed into the driver seat and glanced down at Lehrling. Roble asked, "Do you believe it's useless to help Riese?"

Lehrling nodded. "There's nothing we can do now."

"I'd almost rather take Crukas back to Glacier Ridge and let Riese get his revenge."

Odlon shook his head. "No. Going there will only expose us to whatever killed the townspeople. We must head to Ironwood."

"Agreed," Lehrling said.

Roble nodded, turned, and cracked the whip. The horses tugged forward and headed down the thawing road. At the bottom of the steep decline, sunlight brightened the path. The glare was almost blinding. Once their eyes adjusted, the meadows came into view. The grass was brown, and the earth was muddy.

RIESE HELD a handful of the horse's mane as he rode the large beast down the frozen path that led into Glacier Ridge. He gripped the heavy hammer in his right and looked for the wagon and the rider. He didn't see them, but he did see the carnage that the withered pale man had left behind.

Several bodies lay on the street. Some slumped over rock fence rails. Others were lifeless on the frozen marketplace cobblestone. He kicked the horse's flanks and rode to the stable. His heart raced as much as the horse beneath him. His was from fear of what he would find in what used to be his homestead.

He had recognized Jez's spectral face and voice. What had happened? Where did the old man go?

One of the stable doors was partway open. Riese swung off the panting horse. He hurried to the door and peered through the crack. He saw no movement or bodies. Pulling the heavy door open, he entered and glanced around the room.

Although he knew it was useless to call out for them, he did anyway. "Jez! Marc!"

His voice echoed throughout the forge room. No verbal answer replied. A metal object clanged on the floor from the other side of the heated forge. Riese's eyes narrowed, and he cautiously stepped closer. He eased around the side of the forge and caught the movement of a shadow cross from the tool bench toward the anvil. Riese readied his hammer and brought it back to swing.

The figure stepped into the glow of the burning coals. He turned and faced Riese. In surprise, he lowered the hammer. His jaws tightened. He tried to swallow the lump rising in his throat.

"Jez?" Riese said, shaking his head.

Jez's eyes set upon him with a hollow unblinking stare. His face was disfigured with swollen pocks of green pus. Buzzing flies swarmed around his son's head.

"No," Riese said. "The gods be cursed! No!"

Jez hobbled toward him. His mouth moved in biting movements. Strange groaning sounds escaped his lips, but no hint of words or recognition set in his eyes. Patches of skin flaked and peeled from Jez's face, arms, and hands. Black spots mottled along any exposed flesh.

Riese brought the hammer back, reluctant to swing a deathblow, but at the same time, he realized his son was already dead. This was his body controlled by another source or a curse. He had heard his son's voice in the frozen forest above Glacier Ridge. As Jez's living corpse stepped closer, Riese back away, struggling with the thought of striking him.

"Forgive me, Jez," Riese said with tears forming in his angered eyes.

Riese brought the hammer back, closed his eyes, and swung with all his strength. The blow crushed the left side of the corpse's face, pivoting the undead Jez backward. His lifeless body dropped to the floor.

With hot tears in Riese's eyes, anger flushed through him. He took Jez by the boots and dragged his body to the front of the forge. Careful not to touch any exposed, diseased skin, he tossed his son's corpse through the fiery forge door.

Riese dropped to his knees and wailed. He shook his muscular fists toward the ceiling and cursed. Furious, he rose to his feet, grabbed the hammer, and marched back into the marketplace.

After he expelled his pent up anger and remorse, he stood and immediately wondered where Marc was. He searched all the rooms surrounding the forge. When he didn't see any sign of Marc, he went to the upstairs rooms and checked each one. Still nothing indicating that his other son was alive.

He ran downstairs, opened the stable door, and rushed to the center of the marketplace.

"Where are you, old man?" Riese shouted. The question echoed throughout Glacier Ridge but no reply came.

Pellets of ice and large flakes of snow swirled around Riese. Steam rose from his body. He gripped the hammer tightly and went door to door looking for the wagon rider.

When he opened Hobskin's Tavern, the mass movement inside the bar shocked him. All the patrons looked similar to his son Jez. Walking diseased corpses. They headed toward the door, so he quickly yanked the door shut. He didn't wait to see if they could open the door. He ran back through the cavern mouth and back to the marketplace. He searched the ground for the carriage's tracks, but none were found.

A small dark creature darted from the side of the building across the path from Hobskin's Tavern. It moved swiftly. Its eyes glowed yellow. In seconds it sought the dark shadowed areas behind the buildings, and Riese hurried after it. He had never seen anything like it before, but he believed that it was a product of the strange old man on the black carriage. Perhaps by following it, he might find the man that infested his town with disease and death.

When Riese crossed the icy path and stepped to the side of the building, the creature wasn't there. Old wooden crates and a couple of empty wine barrels was all he found. He moved crates aside, looking for the small creature. Instead he found a small hole into the building's cellar. Dropping to his knees, he peered into the hole, but without a torch or lantern, he couldn't see what was inside. And even with a source of light, the hole was too small to put his head through. He started to turn and leave when he heard a muffled voice of someone trying to cry out. Someone was fighting to break free or shout.

"Help," the strained voice finally said.

"Who is it?" Riese asked.

Then the voice returned to being nothing more wordless stifled grunts and moans as someone or something bound the victim's mouth.

Riese looked at the dark crevice in the cellar wall. The opening was large enough that the little creature could have easily passed through. There wasn't enough time to find a torch and return. With whatever disease that was consuming his town, he needed to save the person in the cellar.

He took the hammer and swung it against the rock foundation. The rock chipped and crumbled. He struck again and again, knocking away more of the stone, making the opening larger. The whipping wind spiraled down the narrow alleyway and whistled into the cellar hole, stirring to life the creatures that hid there.

Hisses and wild chattering noises echoed in the dark cellar. His attention focused on discovering what was in there that held one of his townspeople hostage. Riese hammered away more rock and mortar from the foundation until a large section of the wall collapsed inward. The sounds in the cellars grew more agitated, so Riese took a step backward.

A black imp rushed through the large hole and lunged at Riese. Its high-pitched squeal rose into a fevered howl. It chattered, revealing its yellow teeth and fangs as it charged fearlessly at Riese. Sharp claws lined its small fingers and it slashed at Riese's legs as he moved back and to the side.

Riese brought the hammer down to strike, but the nimble imp leaped backwards. The hammer struck the icy cobblestone, blasting chunks of rock and ice into the air like tiny pellets, which showered down around the hammerhead.

The imp ran forward bearing its sharp rows of teeth with froth bubbling from the sides of its mouth. It hobbled side to side with its hands raised above its head. Its rapid movement made it difficult for Riese to use his hammer to smash it. And before he could lift the hammer, two more of these black imps emerged from the cellar opening.

"Father!" the voice in the cellar cried.

"Marc?"

"Help!"

Determination to save his surviving son surged through him. The town was doomed to whatever pestilence the old man had released, and perhaps he had summoned the imps as well. Whatever grip Death held over Glacier Ridge was more than Riese could fight alone. At least if he rescued his son, he wouldn't leave his town empty-handed and alone.

The three imps separated and sought to encircle Riese. Once he noticed their intention, he edged his back against the wall of the building across the alleyway. The imps leapt at him. He kicked the closest one. His boot caught its midsection and slung it into the air. As it soared across the alley and struck the wall, he grabbed the next imp around the throat and squeezed until its eyes bulged and bones cracked in its neck. He tossed its lifeless body on the cobblestone and brought his hammer back.

The third imp snarled and green spittle dripped from its mouth. Eying the hammer in Riese's hands, it backed out of his range. The imp that had struck the wall staggered toward Riese but remained cautious in its approach.

"Come on!" Riese said, swinging the hammer side to side in front of himself.

The imps narrowed their eyes and hissed.

"You filthy beasts! I'll kill all of you!"

Riese charged with his hammer and struck the weaker one in the head.

It reeled in pain, spiraled around in the air, and landed facedown on the cold cobblestone. Riese jumped and planted his feet into the center of its back. Bones cracked and its insides squished.

He kept the dead imp pinned beneath his feet and swung the hammer around. The imp dodged the blow, kicked off the wall, and sprang into the air. It landed on Riese's chest and scrambled up to bite his throat. Riese grabbed its feet and slammed its head against the street, cracking its skull.

After the three were dead, he hurried to find Marc. Before he reached the hole in the cellar wall, an imp's head rolled out onto the cobblestone. Its eyes were wide in death, and it's black tongue hung to the side. Seconds later, Marc pulled himself through the hole and rose to stand in the alleyway. He had bite marks on his hands and forearms. Other than looking haggard, he seemed to be okay.

Riese asked, "Was that all of them?"

Marc nodded.

Riese embraced his son tightly.

"Jez didn't make it," Marc said softly, pulling away from his father's hold. "Whatever broke out here overcame him."

"I know," Riese replied. "Did you see the old man in a black carriage?"

Marc nodded.

"Where did he go?"

"I'm not certain. He parked in the marketplace. Jez noticed his arrival and went to see if he needed to stable his horses," Marc said. He looked at the ground and wiped his eyes.

"What happened?"

Marc took a deep breath, closed his eyes, and when he opened them, Riese noticed his son was no longer a young man. What he had witnessed had taken any innocence he had and forced him to be a man.

"It's okay," Riese said. "You need to tell me. We'll find this man and kill him."

"That won't be easy."

"Why?"

"He and the carriage vanished not long after he handed Jez the burlap sack."

"What was in the bag?" Riese asked.

Marc swallowed hard, and then he said, "The old man asked Jez if what was in the bag was payment enough. Jez opened the bag and a swarm of strange buzzing insects flew out. Some were dark flies that flew in a greenish dust-like cloud. Others were beetles. Jez tried to close the bag, but the flies covered his face. He dropped the bag and while he swatted at the attacking flies, scuttling beetles covered the ground by the hundreds. They must have had come from magic. There's no way that small bag could hold that many insects. Even the flies on his face continued to increase in number."

"Did you not help your brother?"

"I tried, but by the time I reached him, he turned and his face was covered with hideous sores with yellow pus running from them. He didn't respond to me. I pulled my sword and tried to get to the carriage driver, but he and the black carriage vanished."

Tears moistened Riese's eyes. He asked, "How did you escape the swarm?"

"I ran back to the stables. The flies came for me, but I reached the forge and pumped the bellows until the heat increased. When the flies neared, I stood as close to the flames as possible. The heat was too much for them. Hundreds of them dropped dead on the floor. The remainder of the swarm retreated from the stables. I don't know where they went."

"Hobskin's Tavern is filled with walking corpses."

Marc nodded. "I discovered that, too, which is how I ended up in the cellar. I went inside the main door around front. I barricaded it, but some of the townspeople beat against the door, so I headed to the cellar hoping that I was safe. But, those imps were waiting down there.

"At first I didn't see them. When I heard you calling out, I tried to go back upstairs, but they attacked me."

Riese placed his hand on Marc's shoulder and squeezed. "You're safe now."

Marc looked from the alley back toward Hobskin's Tavern.

"You said that some of the townspeople tried to get through the front of this building?" Riese asked.

Marc gave a slight nod while still watching the front of Hobskin's Tavern.

"Where did they go?" Riese asked.

Marc's face paled. He slowly raised his right hand and pointed. Riese turned to see at least a dozen disease-ridden corpses staggering toward them. There wasn't any way to get around them. Riese only had his hammer. Marc held his dagger. The undead townspeople marched forward, blocking Riese and his son in between the two buildings and cornering them against the ridge wall.

Riese looked at his son and said, "Be brave, even until the end."

Queen Istrell summoned her crystals by placing her weary hands upon them. A faint glow emitted from the stones, momentarily, but she was unable to draw their full power. Her mirror remained dark. No matter how much she focused, it gave her no clear picture to let her see where Shawndirea was. All she knew was that her child had been in a very frigid climate, and the closest region with such icy temperatures was Glacier Ridge.

"Why?" she asked aloud. "Why would you venture there? No faery can withstand such frozen conditions."

And after the human clothed her in the black cloth, she seemed to have gone stealth by a different kind of magic.

"What has the human done to you?" she asked, holding the crystals tighter, hoping to make a connection that might clue her to where Shawndirea was now. But the crystals grew cold and refused to respond to her touch.

Frustrated, Istrell said, "I've warned you about humans, and yet, you always have to stubbornly ignore my counsels."

Istrell left the small room where she kept the crystals and hovered along the downward winding path until she reached the throne room. When she reached her throne, she plopped down and released a long sigh. She covered her eyes with her right hand, trying hard not to cry.

"Your Highness," a dainty faery servant whispered.

Istrell opened weary eyes and replied, "Yes, Feather?"

"I have brought you some honey wine," Feather said.

"You are always a dear one," Istrell said with a tired smile.

Feather's hair was long, curled, and black. Her eyes were a bright blue that sparkled like rare jewels. She wore a pink flowing gown to match the pinkish tint in her delicate wings.

Feather handed the large golden goblet of wine to the queen and curtseyed, gliding backwards in respect of the throne. She smiled and said, "What is troubling my queen?"

Istrell downed the strong wine in one quick gulp. She set the goblet down and replied, "Shawndirea."

Feather's eyes widened. While refilling the goblet, she asked, "Is she missing again?"

"Has such news roamed my kingdom?"

Istrell drank half the wine, licked her lips, and narrowed her eyes when she focused her attention on Feather.

Feather tucked her chin to her chest, looked at the floor, and shook her head quickly. "No, Your Highness."

Istrell finished the second goblet of wine, set down the goblet, and rose to her feet. She held the throne arm tightly and swayed back and forth. She took a staggering step forward and said, "Not that it should be any surprise at all. One builds hope in her heir to be the greatest queen this kingdom has ever had, and she disregards her destined responsibilities."

Feather extended her hand for Queen Istrell to grab. Istrell didn't hesitate to cling to it.

"Your Grace," Feather said softly. "Have you eaten?"

Istrell shook her head.

"When did you last eat?"

"I don't recall. Probably a couple days."

Feather extended her right arm and Queen Istrell looped her arm around Feather's. The dainty faery braced the queen and said, "Allow me to walk with you to the Great Hall so you can eat."

The strong wine had taken effect quicker than normal. Istrell slurred her words and continued rambling, "And then she foolishly allows a human to capture her."

"A human?" Feather gasped.

Istrell nodded and said, "Yes. Destroyed her magnificent wings."

"Oh my, not her glorious wings?"

Istrell closed her eyes and shook her head in disappointment. "Shredded. Absolutely shredded."

"Here, My Grace," Feather said, helping Istrell sit at the head of the long banquet table. "I will see what the cook has prepared."

Istrell nodded sleepily. "Thank you, my dear one."

Seconds later, Istrell folded her arms on the table and rested her head. Her heavy eyelids slowly blinked closed. She snored.

Feather shook her head. "My poor Queen Istrell."

"Has my aunt become such a lush?" the male faery said with laughter in his voice. He drifted along the top of the long table and hovered over Queen Istrell's head while she was lost in drunken slumber.

"Dirk?" Feather asked. "You've been eavesdropping?"

Dirk chuckled and flicked his long golden hair back. It shook like fine threads of silk. He said, "Knowledge is what I seek in order to claim the throne."

"Shawndirea is destined for the throne."

He shrugged. "She does not have the qualities of a true Queen. She's too busy pursuing idle fantasies and not disciplined enough to reign over our kingdom."

"So you'll be our King?" Feather asked.

"I will."

Dirk took her hand and pulled her close. He kissed her passionately and embraced her tightly. He backed away and looked into her eyes. He said, "And you, my love, will be my Queen."

Feather smiled and squealed with delight.

"Just keep milking her for information," Dirk said. "I need to know where Shawndirea is and prevent her from returning."

"As you wish," Feather replied.

"Istrell is in no state of mind to rule our kingdom. Especially not in her current condition."

CHAPTER 34

*R*iese heaved Marc upward at the side of the building. Marc grabbed the edge of the roof and held tightly. Riese placed his hands beneath his son's feet and shoved with enough power to get Marc securely onto the roof.

Marc reached down his hand. Riese shook his head. "I'm too heavy for you to lift."

"I can try!"

"No. Stay there. Don't move."

Riese swung the hammer back and forth, smashing the steel head through several of the walking corpses' heads, which parted the way enough that he rushed through and got to the other side of the icy path.

"Father!" Marc shouted.

"Stay put!" Riese replied.

Two of the undead lay motionless on the cobblestone path. Blood oozed from the large dents in their skulls. The remaining undead corpses staggered toward him. Pustules burst on their skin. Little green vapor clouds puffed from the lesions while yellow ooze leaked. Riese understood he must avoid touching any of the leaking bodily fluids and the drifting green vapor. Otherwise the disease that took their lives would infect him as well.

Their hollow dead eyes chilled him, but at least Marc was safe being on the roof. All Riese needed to do was destroy these creatures that had once been friends and townspeople he held dear without exposing himself to the plague. Once they were really dead, he and Marc could get to the stables and get out of Glacier Ridge.

The one advantage Riese held was that the undead townspeople were slow. They didn't recognize him, but they seemed to be following orders to kill from another source. And should that be the case, Riese believed the old man who had infected them with the disease was also summoning them to kill any living survivors in the town.

Riese tightened his grip on the hammer, shook his head with partial regret, and one by one, he brought the undead men and women to the last peace they'd ever know. And like those dead on the street, Glacier Ridge was dead also.

Tears heated his eyes as he gazed at the broken bodies on the icy cobblestone. Small green clouds of plague hung over their pus-filled sores. He eased clear of the disease clouds and set the hammer against the side of the building and helped his son get down.

Marc embraced his father and said, "What about those inside Hobskin's Tavern?"

"Leave them be," Riese said. "I doubt I have enough stomach to eliminate more."

"What do we do?"

"We pack up and leave this godless town."

"Where will we go?"

Riese shrugged. "I have to catch up with those that stayed last night."

"The ones with the thief?"

Riese nodded. "Yes. But first, we need to see if we can find the black carriage's tracks. I want to find that old man. He will suffer for what he did to Glacier Ridge. He will suffer dearly."

Marc and Riese studied the marketplace cobblestone. Only one place seemed to have a short path of where the carriage wheels had pressed down on the ice. Riese reasoned it must have been where he had stopped the longest and handed to bag to Jez. After that, the tracks disappear.

"I see nothing else, father," Marc said, making his way from the trading lot toward the stable.

"I know, son. I don't see any marks other than these."

The oddest part was that Riese had never found any along the icy road after the old man had asked for directions and driven away. It seemed the man had magically disappeared.

Riese ran to catch his son. "Let's hurry, Marc. We pack up some weapons and food and leave."

"Can we ever return?"

Riese's jaw tightened. "I hope to someday. For now, we concentrate on staying alive. You're all I have left in this world that is dear."

Marc didn't reply. He wiped tears away as he thought of Jez.

Riese placed a hand on his son's shoulder and said, "It will be okay. I was foolish to have left the town."

He and Marc returned to his stables, packed up their best weapons, and slung the double-sided pack across the massive horse. He slid bags of gold and silver into several bags. The rest of his gold wealth he hid beneath floorboards in the back of his forge room and slid heavy crates on top of it. He would not leave Glacier Ridge forever. With what gold he carried with him, he could hire others to come back to eradicate the undead townspeople and reclaim his small township.

Riese saddled the horse and fastened a bridle into place. Marc did the same with his horse.

Riese was at the stable doors and pushed them open. Cold rushing snow and wind dropped the forge room temperature quickly. When he turned around, Marc was pulling his horse and Jez's horse behind him.

"What are you doing?" Riese asked.

"I can't leave Jez's mare behind, father. Jez would haunt me forever. And what about all the horses we've housed for the . . . our former patrons?"

Riese nodded. "We need to release them. Perhaps we can get them to follow us out of the ridge. They can graze in the grasslands below Glacier Ridge."

They tethered Jez's mare behind Marc's horse and weighed the mare with weapons, food, and more supplies.

Riese and Marc opened dozens of stalls and led the horses out to the marketplace. Then they climbed upon their horses and headed up the icy path. Eventually, the freed horses would follow them up the hill, along the frozen mountain path, and down the next ridgeline where fields of green grass bent with warmer breezes.

Marc was silent during the long cold ride. The loss of his brother weighed upon him. They were close. The best of friends. Coldness set in Marc's eyes. Firmness hardened his jaw. Seeing his son become a man should have been a blessing, a moment of celebration, but how Marc reached that plateau was more costly than Riese wished to dwell upon.

Riese's small town inside Glacier Ridge was dead. He had nothing left there. His heart ached. Where the icy path thawed, he found wagon wheel tracks and hoof prints. If he hurried, he could join Roble and the others as well as take delight in watching Crukas hang.

CHAPTER 35

Marshall Jackson, an FBI agent in his mid-forties, sat across the table from Deiko in a mental hospital in Somerset, Kentucky. Marshall was a massive black man with broad shoulders, huge arms, and massive hands. On the table in front of Marshall was an odd leather covered book, a yellow notepad, and a black ink pen. Marshall folded his hands together while he studied Deiko's demeanor.

Deiko's hands shook. His lips quivered and when he glanced at Marshall, he quickly avoided eye contact and mumbled softly to himself.

"Mr. Deiko," Marshall said in a very deep voice.

Deiko shuddered when Marshall spoke.

Marshall sat back in his chair, making notes on his yellow notepad. "Mr. Deiko, what did you see inside the cave?"

The blonde nurse's aid shook her head. "He won't speak. We can't get him to say anything."

Marshall's eyes narrowed as they flicked from Deiko directly to her. "Ma'am, I wasn't speaking to *you*."

"I know," she replied nervously. "I was just trying to be helpful."

"Well, *don't!*" he said, slamming his fists on the table. "I'm a federal investigator and if I *need* your opinion, trust me I'll *ask* you for it. Do you understand?"

"Yes, sir. I'm very sorry."

Marshall shook his head, pointed toward the door, and said, "Why don't you busy yourself with some of your other chores. I need to speak to Dr. Deiko. *Alone.*"

She nodded and hurried out of the room.

Marshall waited for the door to swing shut. When it closed, he smiled at Deiko.

"Mr. Deiko. Would you kindly tell me what you saw in the cave?"

Deiko's nervous eyes braved enough to look into Marshall's.

"It's okay, Mr. Deiko. I'm not here to hurt you. I'm here to help. I want to know about this Elias that you saw in the cave."

"El-El- Elias?" Deiko said, biting his fingernails.

"Yes. Elias. Do you happen to know if his last name was Jackson?"

Deiko's haunted eyes looked away. He visibly shook.

"Mr. Deiko, I know you're frightened. I know. But believe me, I want to stop this Elias from hurting anyone else. I know that you understand what I'm saying. Tell me what I need to know, and I won't let the doctors and nurses know that you're sane. You can stay in here as long as you're where you think you'll be safe."

Deiko snapped to attention and looked around the room. Seeing no one other than Marshall, his nervousness vanished. In a calm collective voice he asked, "How did you know?"

Marshall shrugged. "A hunch. Sometimes when people see something that frightens them and they have no rational way to explain it, they simply want to hide in a place where security is higher than home."

"What I saw? Was it real?" Deiko asked.

"What *did* you see?"

"A man that looked like a walking corpse. He was old and rotten, but he was walking, moving."

"In the cave?" Marshall asked.

"No. In my mind."

Marshall frowned. "I don't understand."

"He had mental control of me. How is that possible?"

"Anything is possible when you're dealing with the paranormal."

Deiko shook his head. He glanced around the room again, checking to see if any doctors or nurses were secretly watching him.

Marshall smiled and said, "We're alone."

Paranoia gripped Deiko. In a sense he knew he'd be relieved to tell someone else about what had happened, but he also feared that Elias might also hear and return to kill him. He wondered how this agent knew about Elias, too.

"Are you certain?"

Marshall nodded. "You said that he took control of your mind. Any idea how long that occurred?"

"Not really. I believe it happened after I found my friend and colleague while he was butterfly hunting. I was watching him with binoculars and saw him catch a faery."

"A faery?" Marshall's eyebrows rose, and he looked at Deiko with such speculation that Deiko knew the statement made him sound even crazier. "What medications do they have you on?"

"Yes. I know you don't believe that, but after seeing the faery, that's when I found myself determined to kill Ben to get her."

Marshall frowned and wrote on the yellow notepad. "Ben?"

"Dr. Ben Whytten. He's a zoologist at the campus and a friend."

"He's your friend?"

Deiko nodded. "Yes. Well, probably not any more."

"So you tried to kill him to get the faery?"

"Something dark possessed me to get her at any cost. I remember looking in the mirror and my eyes were different."

"How so?" Marshall asked, jotting down notes.

"My eyes were black. Even where the white should be."

"Okay," Marshall said, "When did Elias release you and do you know why?"

"I entered that cave. I followed it for a ways, looking for Ben. I had my gun with me and knew if I saw him that I'd kill him. When I couldn't find him, Elias turned on me. He battered me and forced me to leave the cave."

Deiko showed Marshall the scars on his arms and face. He lifted the back of his shirt and showed him more.

Marshall stood and walked around the table. He took Deiko's wrist and studied the marks carefully.

"Well, the good thing is," Marshall said, releasing Deiko. "That he didn't carve any symbols in your flesh."

Deiko stared at the marks and then looked at Marshall. He said, "What does that mean?"

"He has no more purpose for you. If he had cut symbols on your arms or back, I'd be worried. But he's done with you."

Deiko looked relieved. "So he won't be back?"

"Not for you."

"So I can leave the hospital?"

Marshall shrugged. "If that's what you wish to do, sure."

Deiko glanced around nervously. His eyes were timid like a frightened rabbit. His breathing increased. He shook his head and said, "No, I think I should wait a few more days. Okay?"

"Whatever you wish to do," Marshall said in his deep voice.

"You won't tell them?"

Marshall took his notepad, shook his head, and headed to the door. He walked down the hall and stopped at the nurse's station and said, "I need the list of medications that you have Isaac Deiko on ASAP."

The nurse looked up from her notes, unimpressed.

Marshall slammed his badge on the countertop, frowned, leaned over her and said, "That means *now!*"

His thunderous voice made the woman shake. She searched through all the clipboards on the desk until she found Deiko's file. "One second, sir," she said. "I'll run off a copy for you."

WHEN MARSHALL RETURNED to his car, he picked up the newspaper off the seat and read the headline: "Strange Occurrences at Cider Knoll Cave." After talking to Deiko, he didn't believe he had enough information to help him find Elias.

He grabbed his radio receiver and contacted his secretary. "Ms. Banks, any new information?"

"We do have something," she replied.

"Well, do tell," Marshall said impatiently.

"We tapped into a radio call from Sheriff Douglas to Deputy Higgins near the area where you are at."

"What information did you get?"

"Sheriff Douglas called Higgins about a possible three homicide in a small mobile home at ten fourteen Maple Ridge Road in Cider Knoll. That's approximately a quarter mile from the cave where the boy was last seen."

"Thanks. Keep me posted if anything else comes up, Ms. Banks."

"I will, Agent Jackson."

Marshall drove from the mental hospital and headed to the rural area of Cider Knoll. So a boy was missing. His friend was too much in shock to tell authorities what had happened. But it occurred in the same cave where Deiko reported Elias had attacked him. Now three more people were dead nearby. He needed to get to the crime scene before local authorities contaminated possible evidence or they accidentally stumbled upon Elias. The officers had no idea how much jeopardy their lives were in should they encounter Elias.

SHERIFF DOUGLAS WAS LEANING against the front of his patrol car when Deputy Higgins turned into the short driveway. Douglas was a stocky man about five foot seven. His burred silver hair didn't cover his sunburned scalp. He crossed his arms and nodded at Higgins.

The old mobile home was tan, silver, and coated with rust.

Higgins parked his car and got out. "What happened?" he asked.

"I don't know how to explain it," Douglas said.

"How bad is it?"

"The worst thing I've ever seen."

Sheriff Douglas pulled his gloves on and opened the trailer door. He stepped aside and allowed Higgins to go up the stairs first. He entered the small living room with drab green carpet, a green sofa, and a glass-topped coffee table. He stepped back when he saw the blood and the three bodies. Their bodies were positioned in odd forms, as if they were meant to represent symbols. Strange marks were carved in their skin, too.

A horrible odor permeated the air.

Higgins looked from the three bodies to Douglas. "How do you even begin to write up a crime scene like this?"

"It won't follow proper protocol."

"And what kind of sick person would do something like this?"

Douglas shook his head. "Hell, I don't know. Cult? Devil worshippers? I'm open to suggestions."

"I have none. Someone cut them up pretty badly. And those bloody sketches on the wall. What kind of language is that?"

"Nothing I'd know."

Higgins covered his nose and mouth with his handkerchief. "That smell. Is it meth?"

Douglas nodded.

"So how do you want to write this up?" Higgins asked.

"I don't."

"What?"

"We write this report up as what it is, and we'll have Feds in here thinking we're too incompetent to work as police officers. It won't make sense and might actually cost us our jobs."

Higgins frowned. "Then what do we do?"

"We rig this place to burn and blame the meth lab in the back room as the reason the trailer burned to the ground. The bloody paintings on the wall, the bizarre murders, everything—goes up in smoke," Douglas said with a devious smile.

"Sir, I really don't think that's a good idea. We need to know who is behind such a hideous crime, don't we?"

Douglas nodded. "We do. We'll keep looking, but we cannot let our community know that something this sick lurks in our midst. Think of how much panic that will cause. Hell, the old men that sit and talk at Harper's Grocery have already sent most of the county into an uproar over Donnie disappearing. This area is already too superstitious for something of this nature and magnitude to hit their rumor mill. We need to put an end to this before it gets further out of hand."

Higgins rested his hands on his hips and scanned the trailer. Two dead men and a woman lay in such a sick, twisted display that he was sickened at his stomach. From his viewpoint he couldn't figure out how they had been killed. Two handguns, a knife, stacks of money and small bags of white powder were only a couple feet from their bodies. Whoever killed them wasn't interested in money or drugs. Just wanted them dead. This wasn't a typical murder, either. Far from it. Higgins felt certain they *should* have the FBI involved in this case.

"Before you got here," Douglas said, "I drove out to the gas station and bought several gallons of gasoline. It's in the trunk. Help me go get it and we'll prevent the county from going into hysterics."

"Sheriff," Higgins said. "Don't you think we should get CSU out here to gather clues to discover who's behind this?"

Douglas turned and pushed Higgins against the trailer wall. He pressed his forearm against Higgins' throat. "Do you *want* to keep your job?"

Higgins nodded. "Of course."

"Then let's dispose of what happened here. We can investigate what happened without getting our county folk constantly calling our office, talking to the media, and seeking to do their own investigations. You have no idea how crazy things will be if word of what happened here leaks out."

Douglas released the pressure from Higgins' throat, freed him, and slowly backed up. He allowed Higgins to walk to the door. Higgins rubbed his throat and took a deep breath.

Higgins pushed the screen door open and said, "Aren't you a bit frightened by what happened here?"

"I'm scared shitless," Douglas said. The veins in his throat and forehead were swollen. He wiped sweat from his brow. "We're dealing with a maniac at best, but a crime scene this bad means we're facing something much worse. CSU can't make *that* any clearer."

"That's true, but . . ."

Sheriff Douglas frowned and then he pointed a firm finger at him. "Don't say anything else. Let's get the gasoline and torch the place."

~

MARSHALL DROVE around a sharp curve in the narrow two-lane road. Where the road straightened, two sheriff patrol cars headed toward him. They passed at what seemed an incredibly odd high rate of speed for such a rural area. The patrol car lights were *not* on.

Once he found the small trailer at the edge of the road, he pulled his sedan into the drive. The edge of the driveway had grooves dug in the gravel where two different vehicles pulled out quickly. It didn't require a lot of deductive reasoning to know that the cars were the patrol cars he had just passed. He wondered why they fled so quickly when the sheriff had called about a possible three homicides at this exact residence.

Marshall got out of his car and left the door open. He walked across the driveway and peered through the living room window. The Venetian blinds were down, but a small section was crumpled and didn't prevent anyone from seeing in or out. He saw the bodies and the bloody ritualistic murder scene, which was something he expected to find. Why had they left without doing a more thorough investigation?

He stepped up the rickety trailer steps and pulled open the screen door. He almost grabbed the doorknob when he stopped. He smelled gasoline and propane. He peered through the small window on the door and noticed the gas-stove door was all the way open.

"Shit!" Marshall said, leaping from the steps and running for his car.

He was halfway across the drive when the trailer exploded into a giant ball of fire. The pressure of the explosion sent him into the air. He hit the gravel, rolled, and hurried behind the back of his car. He wiped dirt and grass from his suit jacket and watched the blazing fire through the windows of his car.

"Sons of bitches!" Marshall said, his jaws tightened.

He marched around the side of his car, got in, and slammed the door shut. He started the engine, backed up, and slung gravels as he exited the drive and headed down the county road. He glanced at the leather-bound book in the passenger seat, and sadly, he shook his head. Although the two officers needed to lose their jobs and be tried in court for destroying valuable crime scene evidence, doing so wouldn't help his cause. He wanted to find Elias, but if he had made these ritual sacrifices and had the boy, Elias wouldn't be back for another twenty years.

"Dammit!" Marshall said, slapping the steering wheel. He placed his right hand on the leather journal. "I was so damn close to stopping you, Elias."

The next opportunity to destroy Elias and prevent the man from achieving immortality returned in twenty years. Wherever Elias hid in dormancy was a place Marshall might seek to find, but periodically, Marshall had hired several archaeologists to hunt for the man's tomb. No one had found where he lay hidden.

The leather-bound journal had once belonged to Elias, which vividly explained all the wicked spells, rituals, and symbols to gain immortality but nothing in it detailed where he hid during each dormant twenty year period. Marshall wanted to find Elias and destroy him because Elias was his great-great grandfather, a voodoo Bokor, and a vicious murderer that had, in Marshall's opinion, tarnished the Jackson name. In twenty years, Marshall knew he had to be ready.

So there was no reason for Marshall to stick around and hunt for Elias. Elias was done for the next twenty years, so Marshall didn't need to make his presence known. At least not yet. However, he planned to have investigators remove Sheriff Douglas from office for destroying evidence and for not having enough backbone to do his job to protect his county.

CHAPTER 36

Roble and the others stopped the wagon and horses at an open field at the foot of Glacier Ridge. The air was much warmer. Sunlight not only brightened the horizon, it brightened their spirits with Crukas being the exception.

Roble had always been one to stand up for the underdog, to help those who were in need, but he also never backed down from a fight if the cause was worthy. Being in this realm, he felt that he was changing, becoming harder and less affable. But the rules were different and sometimes unclear, as he had seen with the three demon-men that had held Lehrling prisoner.

Crukas looked up, closed his eyes, and let the sunlight warm his face. He mouthed words without a sound. He raised his shackled hands toward the sky and smiled.

Roble pulled out the food crate from beneath the driver's seat. When he opened the crate, he found dried meat, cheese, and stale bread loaves. Odlon and Lehrling took knives and cut off portions for themselves while Roble offered Crukas food.

"Why trouble yourself with me?" Crukas asked. "You're simply wasting what food you and the others need since I am going to be hanged."

"You're not dead yet," Roble replied.

"I'd rather starve than hang."

Roble smiled and shook his head. "Perhaps you should have sought a different occupation."

Crukas' eyes narrowed.

"Don't taunt him," Shawndirea said.

"Does the faery harbor pity for me?" Crukas asked.

"Hardly," she replied. "I just don't like seeing caged animals picked on."

Lehrling and Odlon laughed.

Crukas' face reddened. He placed his hands on the iron bars and said, "Well, I see the stable master knew *how* to contain me. He even went to the trouble of neutralizing my magical abilities with the metal and engraved counter spells. Seems he knows quite a bit of magic himself."

Roble handed a large chunk of meat, cheese, and bread to Crukas and said, "Eat it or toss it. I don't care. At no time will I allow myself to let another suffer hunger."

"But you'd see me hang?"

"For justice."

"Justice?" Crukas said with a wide smile. "What world do you live in? You're a bit deranged if you believe such a concept exists. At best, fate sets things into motion, and at times, people pay their dues, but justice? Justice seldom prevails. People simply remove whatever they deem a thorn in their sides. Hangings aren't justice. They're entertainment. Nothing more. Adults and children flock to the square to watch hangings."

Roble shrugged. "Perhaps from your perspective it is entertainment. Not from mine. Especially when it pertains to you."

"And what injustice have I bestowed upon you?" Crukas asked, taking a huge bite of food.

"You allowed many in Glacier Ridge to die when you could have prevented it."

Crukas chewed the wad of food in his mouth and said, "The Plague-bringer would have struck us all down with disease and continued to the next town if we had attempted to stop him."

"You don't know that," Roble said.

Shawndirea nodded. "He's right."

"You agree with him?" Roble asked.

"In that point he is correct," she said. "Confrontation with the Plague-bringer is death."

Odlon walked to the rear of the wagon. "No one has ever stopped the Plague-bringer. He's a worse sight to behold than one's own banshee spirit. Death follows him. Something else summons him."

"So do you believe Riese is dead?" Roble asked.

"It's hard to say," Shawndirea replied. "Depends upon whether the Plague-bringer was finished and gone by the time Riese got back to Glacier Ridge."

"If you know so much about him, why didn't any of you say anything?" Roble asked.

Lehrling swallowed a bite of hard cheese and said, "Because he comes in many forms. No one knows for certain what form he may present. He was an old feeble looking man today. Might be a rich knight tomorrow, or a female bard singing songs for money. One never knows. Once he came as an elder priest and cursed the Temple of Bridgebarrow. Half the town was dead within a day. So no one can know what he looks like."

"But Crukas knew," Roble replied. "How is that?"

Crukas gave a firm nod and then a slight shrug. He said, "He wore a golden ring on his right hand. The stone is a skull-shaped emerald with inserted ruby eyes."

Roble frowned. "And how does this ring indicate who he is?"

"To be truthful, I wasn't certain it was he. However, I have heard the tale from another survivor when the Plague-bringer arrived in a village wearing such a ring. The man survived the plague but his body and mind are forever scarred."

Lehrling looked at Roble and Odlon and said, "It's best that we head southward. We're out in the open and need to get to Ironwood as soon as possible."

"Indeed," Odlon said, nodding and then he glanced across the meadow. "We're easy targets here."

"More bandits and thieves?" Roble asked.

Shawndirea said, "We travel the path that leaves Glacier Ridge. Outside travelers don't know what has occurred there. News spreads slowly. It may be weeks before thieves know not to venture here."

"That's true." Lehrling smiled and said, "We take advantage of the sunlight. That gives us a good five hours to travel. It's not midmorning yet."

"What awaits us between here and Ironwood?" Roble asked.

Odlon mounted his horse and looked back at Roble. "Several small towns, trading posts, forests, and wilderness. Woodcrest is the first place we must pass through."

"Friendly town?" Roble asked.

Lehrling shrugged. "Sometimes. Sometimes not. Depends upon what they lack in wares."

"Any trading posts along the way?"

"On occasion you pass those. However, there are also small huts where people are disguised as traders. But they lure travellers in to rob them and take what they want," Lehrling said. "I'm guessing you don't travel much."

"Not in this region," Roble replied. "Sounds like folks here are more hostile than friendly."

Shawndirea whispered. "Dangers are everywhere in Aetheaon. Never let down your guard."

Roble nodded. "You keep saying that."

"Only because it is true, and you don't seem to take my warnings seriously."

"I've yet to see anything I view as exceedingly dangerous."

"Doesn't mean you won't encounter such."

"You're right. I should be more cautious, especially after nearly losing you and what the Plague-bringer probably did in Glacier Ridge."

Roble saw the concern in her eyes, which vaguely hinted of her inner fears. He followed her gaze and looked beyond the grassy meadows to the woods that were shrouded within more shadows, more mists, and more mysteries.

Suddenly he took her warnings more seriously. The abrupt pang in his stomach made him realize that he had been more nervous all along their journey. Every odd situation from the moment he was almost dropped into the Styx River until the intense sight of encountering all the ghosts of Glacier Ridge had slowly built more anxiety inside him. Stomach acid was burning a huge ulcer.

Although Roble loved exploration and seeing species and races he never knew existed, he understood that carelessness definitely would make him extinct.

Shadows crept along the edge of the woods. All the horses' ears backed. They snorted.

Odlon stared back at Roble and Lehrling. "We need to head into the shelter of the trees," he said, "Quickly."

CHAPTER 37

The Dark Chancellor stood before the violet crystal and focused until the crystal shimmered. He held his staff with the Sages of Vylan trapped inside.

"Botis," a low voice said as a dark image materialized in the glowing crystal. "What reason do you have to contact me?"

"Lord Tyrann," Botis said, offering a bow. "Glacier Ridge has been stricken with the plague. The occupants now serve your dark commands. Other towns will follow."

"And Vylan? What news have you?"

Botis held up the ebony staff. The red eyes blinked. "The Sages of Vylan are now in my grasp. Their power is mine."

"That leaves Vylan to fall under my control then," Tyrann said. Dark misty shadows swirled around Tyrann, preventing Botis from ever seeing Tyrann's face.

"Yes. And the neighboring fowl-kin occupied forests will be yours as well."

"Good."

Botis smiled, "My Lord, the Black Chasm grows as does your power."

"Indeed," Tyrann said, "And my faithful servants, such as yourself, will reap blessings and power as well."

"You are most gracious, my Lord."

"And Elias? Have you struck him down?" Tyrann asked.

Botis stared at the cavern floor.

"He lives?" Tyrann said angrily.

"He will not succeed in gaining immortality. You have my word."

Through the swirling mists in the hanging crystal, Tyrann's eyes glowed crimson red. "That promise you made years ago. One more cycle after this one, and an Overlander becomes immortal. Why have you not stopped him? How has he eluded you all this time?"

"Elias is much more resourceful than I expected. He has made certain to never step into my magical circles."

"He detects the power of your magic?"

Botis replied, "Unfortunately, yes."

"Which is why magic should never be granted to those on the other side of the Underworld. They are beyond our grasp. We cannot control them. Any sorcerer should understand that danger."

Botis bowed to Tyrann's harangue. "It was a mistake that I deeply regret. He has grown dormant once more."

"And will rise in twenty Overlands years?"

Botis nodded. "Yes."

"How has his mortal body remained intact for so long without rotting and turning to dust?"

"He has powers of his own from the Overlanders' magic."

"What?"

Botis took a step back, bowed, and said, "He is a master of black magic from his realm."

Tyrann raised his hands. Bluish fire shot from his hands through the crystal and propelled Botis into the air. Botis landed on his back, and the ebony staff clacked and rolled across the floor. A light chuckling echoed from the staff. The glowing eyes of the Vylan Sages glared at Botis.

"I should destroy you right now," Tyrann said in a frightening low tone. "You have allowed a wizard from the Overlands access to our power? Should he succeed in gaining immortality, everything we possess here is subject to chaos and ruin. There is no stopping him, you fool!"

"Apologies, my Lord. Thousands upon thousands of apologies. I had no idea when he first solicited my power until after the first sacrifice was made."

"Destroy him when he resurrects for the final time or I will imprison you worse than you have the Sages of Vylan."

Botis kneeled and bowed his head to the cold cavern floor. "Yes, my Lord. He will die."

Tyrann broke their connection. The shimmering crystal went cold, dark. Botis waited several minutes before finally rising to his feet and grabbing the ebony staff. Fear weighted his soul.

"You were warned," Staven hissed from the staff. "Is the sacrifice you made for the ebony staff still acceptable?"

Botis gripped the staff tightly and walked out of the crystal chamber. He shook his head.

"Well?" Staven asked.

"Debatable," Botis replied.

"Your allegiance to Tyrann was a costly mistake. Not only will he destroy Vylan, he will consume *you*. You may contain us within your staff, but you do *not* control our power. We will resist your commands."

"Perhaps, for now," Botis said with amusement. "But soon, I will feast off your power. You will do my bidding."

"Even after Tyrann's chastising, you're willing to obey him? You're much weaker than I imagined."

"It has nothing to do with weakness. It has everything to do with position."

Staven cackled. "There isn't another throne within the Black Chasm that houses the City of Mortel. Only Tyrann's. He will not share his power. His plan is to conquer the entire continent of Aetheaon beneath his dark power."

"I have my throne. I have no need to be seated within the Black Chasm."

"The Black Chasm will spread and devour your cavern, your throne, and your soul."

Botis turned down a winding dark path. In the darkness a waterfall cascaded from an unseen ledge and splashed against the rocks. A mist saturated the cold cavern, and without light, Botis continued his walk unworried about stepping off the path.

"Your warning is more vengeful desire than a concern for my well-being," Botis said.

All ten sages laughed.

After climbing a crude set of stairs in the dark cavern, Botis turned another sharp corner and flickering sconces lighted a large room. Small prison cages housed different races—elves, dwarves, Ratkins, humans. They cringed, closed their eyes, and shielded their faces when they saw the Dark Chancellor approach.

Each prisoner was missing appendages. Some more than others, but none were whole-bodied. A small altar stood in the center of the cages. A silver bowl and dagger lay upon the altar.

"What is this?" Staven asked.

"Where I make my sacrifices," Botis replied. "Dark magic requires sacrifices. The darker the magic, the more blood and flesh I must offer, which is why I have taken these to use in my stead."

"And what spell do you seek?"

"To silence you and merge your wills to obey my commands. From this day forward, your voices are silenced but your magic is mine to direct."

CHAPTER 38

The shadowy forest held an eerie atmosphere. The thick canopy blocked most of the sunlight, but at least the temperature was slightly warmer. The path that was formerly solid ice had become hard compacted black soil from years of horse-pulled wagons traveling through. The forest floor, however, was deeply layered with leaves, briars, and thick underbrush. Straying off the path would be challenging if the need ever arose.

Within the forest were broken marble columns and moss-covered headless statues of a fallen kingdom long forgotten.

Deeper in the shadows strange sounds echoed. Branches on the forest floor snapped and crackled. Roble wondered what the shadows moving along the outskirts of the forest had been. Now he kept more alert than ever. At least out in the open they could see attackers when they approached. In the dense forest they'd never know until the moment they were attacked.

The rugged wagon moved slowly down the black road. Shawndirea almost didn't breathe while she studied the narrow ditches. Crukas looked grim. He no longer stood but slouched down into the base of the iron cage and hugged his knees. Occasional bursts of wind whistled through the woods, and quite often, Roble was certain he heard voices.

Midway through the dark forest, Roble said to Shawndirea, "How far until we get to your homeland?"

"Still several days."

Her soft voice soothed him. He wanted to do anything to take his mind off what the trees hid from their view. The deeper into the forest they rode, the more frightening the area became. Thick leafy vines clung to the highest branches and connected throughout the canopy. Occasionally branches overhead shook. Leaves swirled and drifted downward.

"No shortcuts?" he asked.

Her frightened eyes scanned the treetops. She said, "What do you think this is?"

"I was hoping *this* was the long way."

"No."

A strange anguished cry echoed off the trail from something hiding in shadows.

"Ride!" Odlon said, raising his crossbow and firing into the dark forest.

Roble cracked the whip over the horses, alarming them enough to yank the wagon forward and increase their speed. Odlon fired another arrow. Roble kept glancing back to get a glimpse of what was pursuing them, but he didn't see anything.

"Look out!" Crukas shouted. He crouched tightly into a ball at the bottom of the iron cage and closed his eyes.

Lehrling pulled his blade in almost the same exact moment the creature lunged from the tree branches and knocked him off his horse. His sword struck the road with a clang. Lehrling groaned in pain, rolling over and over on the harsh road, stopping short of the thick briary underbrush. The black furred cat-faced humanoid bared its teeth and sprang into the thicket before Odlon got a clear shot.

Though in obvious pain, Lehrling crawled several feet and reached for his sword. He grabbed the hilt of the blade, but when he pulled the short sword closer, he realized the blade was not his. His blade lay several feet away.

Odlon kept his eye trained through the crossbow sight while he scanned the forest, but the creature seemed to have vanished. None of the underbrush rustled from its fleeing movement.

"What the hell was that?" Roble asked, pulling back the reins to stop the horses. Once they stopped, he tied the reins to the wagon seat.

Shawndirea shook her head. "It's not a natural creature."

"Meaning?"

"A product of sorcery, possibly dark magic."

Odlon moved his horse closer to the front of the wagon. Eying the forest, and quickly glancing at Shawndirea, he said, "You sensed it too?"

"Yes," she said, nodding.

"It's more than that, faery," Crukas said.

Shawndirea looked at the thief with worried eyes. "What do you mean?"

"It's sorcery, but the sorcerer behind the magic seeks to stop someone within our party."

Lehrling slowly sat up, coughing and wheezing, and hardly able to get his breath. His face paled and due to his age and weight, he had a difficult time trying to pull himself to his feet. Although he held the strange blade, his eyes searched the road for his own weapon. Concern creased his brow. He seemed concerned that the creature might return and finish him before he stood and defended himself.

Roble stepped down from the wagon. Shawndirea sat on his shoulder, holding tightly to his collar.

"Keep going," Crukas said. "That beast will return."

"No, Lehrling needs our help," Roble said. "I won't leave him behind for the beast to attack and kill. Besides you're not one to give me orders."

"By being locked in this cage, I'm vulnerable," Crukas pleaded. Still sitting on the hay, he gripped the bars and tugged.

"Which is only due to your decisions. Should it return and kill you, your death leaves us with one less problem to deal with," Roble said.

Crukas feigned a hurt expression and said, "You'd allow a helpless prisoner to be ripped to shreds?"

Roble shook his head, refusing to entertain Crukas with trivial banter, and jogged back fifteen yards until he reached Lehrling. The old man coughed, beat his chest several times with his fist, and spat bloody sputum onto the ground. After Lehrling inhaled deeply and finished wheezing long enough to catch his breath, Roble extended his hand and helped Lehrling stand.

"We need to get you to a physician," Roble said.

Lehrling shook his head. "No, I'm fine."

"No," Roble replied, "you're not. I think you have pneumonia. If you don't get medicine, you're going to die."

Odlon sat on his horse and watched the dark area of the forest floor where the strange creature had disappeared. Wearing the green dragon scale armor, the elf looked more than regal. Faint light shimmered off the armor as if the dragon's magic still clung to its scales. The glory shrouding the armor made Roble wish the dragon still lived, so he could see its true power.

The large shield hung across Odlon's back. His fierce eyes were alert and his finger rested against the crossbow trigger. It seemed that more than his eyes watched the dark trees, and it was almost like he had the ability to see through shadows and detect what hid in those dark crevices. In that moment, Roble wondered if Odlon had inherited more than just the armor and somehow had taken a part of the dragon's spirit into his own.

"Do you see the creature?" Roble asked, helping Lehrling balance against him.

"No," Odlon shook his head. "Whatever it was, it's damn fast."

"Or it can turn invisible," Crukas said, slowly rising to his feet.

Roble brushed away mud and dead leaf matter from Lehrling's back. He asked, "Other than your difficulty breathing, does everything else feel okay? No broken bones?"

A weak smile widened Lehrling's tired face. He clasped Roble's shoulder and then slapped it. Lehrling scratched his white beard and in a hoarse voice replied, "I'm certain, being an old man, that my bruises and lumps will bother me soon enough. Nothing hurts worse than age sometimes."

Roble smiled.

Lehrling held the blade out for Roble to examine and said, "This isn't my sword. Mine is over there."

"Then where did this come from?" Roble turned and picked up Lehrling's sword.

Lehrling shook his head and turned toward the edge of the road. He pointed at the edge of the thick briary underbrush and said, "There's your answer."

In the crude ditch, almost hidden beneath the thorny branches, were two dead bodies. Their coat of arms was the same as the men that Roble had to kill in the icy forest to free Lehrling.

"More of Waxxon's demon-men," Roble said. He knelt beside them and examined their wounds. The blood on their scratched faces was fresh. "They haven't been dead long."

"What killed them?" Odlon asked, riding closer.

"Apparently that creature," Shawndirea said, "because the marks on their faces and throats are from large cat claws."

"It never even attempted to claw me," Lehrling said.

"It could have easily killed you if it wanted," Roble said. "It definitely had the advantage."

"I know." Lehrling sheathed his sword and brushed debris from his pants. He and Roble headed toward the wagon.

"We need to keep moving," Odlon said to Roble.

Crukas nodded and said, "Yes. The sooner the better."

Roble watched the trees, expecting to see the catlike creature again. When the total calm of the trees and underbrush convinced him the creature wasn't near, he said, "How far until we reach Woodcrest?"

"Shouldn't be much longer," Lehrling said. "Over the next rise."

"Can you ride?"

Lehrling smiled and said, "I told you that I'm fine."

"I'm convinced otherwise," Roble said, bracing Lehrling's shoulder to steady the old man. "You've had difficulty breathing since we met. We need to find a physician in Woodcrest."

"Good luck with that," Crukas said.

"Why?"

"At best you might find an herbalist there," Crukas said.

Odlon shrugged. "That's good enough."

"Not in his present health," Roble said.

Shawndirea pursed her lips and then she whispered into his ear, "You cannot be too picky here, Roble. The luxuries of your world are scarce in ours. We accept what assistance we can, whether it's good or not, it's all we have."

Roble climbed back onto the wagon seat, untied the reins, and said, "The sooner we get to Woodcrest, the better. For Lehrling's sake."

Odlon nodded. "You see anything moving along the edge of the path, or elsewhere, let me know."

"I will," Roble said. He looked back and watched Lehrling struggle to mount his horse. Even though he didn't know Lehrling that well, he felt close to the man in the same manner as he would an uncle. The old man was sick and that concerned Roble.

As they rode, Roble whispered to Shawndirea, who sat upon his shoulder, "Why would a sorcerer create a beast like that one? Is it the same wizard that had the beast awaiting us in Devils Den?"

She shook her head. "No. That one was placed there to protect the rift, possibly to prevent me from crossing back to this realm."

"Why?"

"I honestly don't know. That catlike creature went for Lehrling though. Not me. However, its attack was not to kill him, or it would have."

"So it seems, since it had apparently killed two of Waxxon's riders." Roble glanced back at Lehrling again.

Shawndirea placed her hand to his cheek and said, "You're worried about him, aren't you?"

Roble nodded and smiled. "Of course."

"And yet you barely know him."

"So?"

"Never lose that," she said softly.

"What?"

"Your compassion for others. Circumstances in my realm tend to harden men's hearts. No matter what you encounter here, please never allow it to kill your compassion. That's what I love about you the most."

"Does my desire to see Crukas pay for his crimes alter how you view me?" Roble asked.

"Not at all, my love," she replied. "None in the least. He's guilty of many things, but not warning Riese about the Plague-bringer was sheer spite. He thought only of himself and not the toll that was about to be struck on Glacier Ridge. Crukas is not a man with great qualities, and I, like you, believe justice does exist. Crukas spoke some truth. Justice is very limited here. Perhaps you can change that now that you're one of the Dragon Skull Order."

"Only in attire," Roble said.

Shawndirea shook her head. "Also in virtue, kindness, and loyalty. You probably possess more high qualities than any other member of the Dragon Skull Order."

"Lehrling seems to possess those qualities."

"I agree, but he is also older and not tarnished by greed like most men your age and younger. That's why I sought to find you. Darkness is possessing our lands. That creature, the Plague-bringer, and Waxxon's henchmen forewarn of worse things to come."

Roble watched the road and the right edge of the forest while Odlon kept his focus on the left side. The road grew steeper and curved to the right.

Roble continued to whisper and said, "Odlon mentioned the Black Chasm. What do you know of it?"

Her eyes widened slightly with fear. "Dark things grow there. The growing mists hide what was once there."

"Which was?"

"The City of Mortel is beneath the growing darkness."

Roble frowned. "Who dwelt in the city?"

"Mainly humans. A few elves."

"I wonder why this black mist has overshadowed the place."

"We don't know," she replied. "The mystery is almost as unknown as the Plague-bringer."

"Do you think there's a connection between it and what has been happening since I came here?" he asked.

"It's possible. Evil is sweeping the kingdoms. The fact that Lady Dawn is alive and Waxxon seeks to find and kill her shows how evil seeks to strangle good. Queen Taube was the most honorable ruler in the kingdoms of Aetheaon. Her radiance brought so much hope."

Odlon rode up beside Roble and pointed. "Woodcrest is up ahead," he said.

"I wouldn't advance any nearer to Woodcrest if you wish to remain alive, elf," a man said, stepping from around a dark tree near the path ahead of them.

CHAPTER 39

Odlon turned and aimed his crossbow at the man. The man wore long bluish-gray robes. His long flowing, black beard was peppered with strands of silver. His unusual piercing eyes narrowed as he stared at the tip of the arrow. His pupils were black dots inside silver irises. To gaze into those eyes brought chills down Roble's back. He had never seen any human feature so eerie.

Zauber calmly leaned upon his long staff. He wore a ruby ring on his right hand and a blood quartz ring on his left.

The tall bearded man shook his head. "Odlon, I'm not here to harm you. I'm here to keep all of you alive."

Odlon frowned and lowered the crossbow. "How do you know me? Who are you?"

"I am Zauber, Wizard of the Misty Bogs." Zauber offered a slight bow. "I'm familiar with all of you."

"The Misty Bogs?" Roble said, looking to Odlon.

Zauber nodded. "Yes, it's well south of here."

"I thought it was a desolate swamp," Lehrling said hoarsely.

"Appearances can be deceiving," Zauber said with an even smile.

Odlon tapped the flanks of his horse and eased closer. He hung the crossbow on his saddle horn. Looking down at the wizard, he asked, "Why is Woodcrest dangerous for us to enter?"

"You found the two dead men over at the edge of the road, I presume. Lord Waxxon, who should never hold such a title, has more men in Woodcrest. He now controls it."

Shawndirea stood on Roble's shoulder. She said, "Are you the one who has slain them?"

"Not directly, my dear faery. But my pet creation took them down."

"The cat beast?" Crukas asked. "He's yours?"

"Yes, he's my pet and familiar. And my apologies, Lehrling, for the near attack. He mistook your party as another of Waxxon's group of plunderers. He's young, so if you'll pardon him."

Lehrling offered a weak smile and nodded. His pale face was covered with dripping sweat. He coughed and said, "Just a few more bruises is all."

"He's harmless until he encounters those under Waxxon's orders," Zauber said. "Those two just passed no more than an hour ago."

"I detected magic surrounding your pet," Shawndirea said, "But I thought it was something much darker."

"That was my intention. I veiled him with a deceptive aura. I wanted him disguised so it was less likely for anyone to know I'm here."

"Why is that?" Roble asked.

"I seldom leave my tower in the Misty Bogs. My power is stronger there," Zauber said.

"Most wizards tend to be solitary," Shawndirea said.

Zauber smiled. Wisdom reflected in his light silvery eyes. He said, "And Shawndirea, you have quite worried your mother. She has sent search parties to find you."

Shawndirea gave an agitated sigh and frowned. "*That* doesn't surprise me in the least."

Zauber chuckled. "And it's not the first time you've aged her with worry."

"The way she frets, it won't be the last, either. My arrival home will be much worse on her than my absence."

Zauber nodded and his eyes glanced toward Roble. He said, "Roble won't likely earn her blessings. Not at first."

"How do you know about us?" Roble asked.

"Ah, Overlander, there's much more important tasks for us to attend to at the moment," the wizard said, glancing back at Shawndirea. "For some odd reason, little faery, she is unable to see you. Where did you get your dark clothes?"

"Roble cut a piece of cloth from his cloak for me to wrap around my body so I didn't freeze to death," she replied.

Zauber studied her garments, boots, and the hood. Then he walked over to Roble and inspected his clothing. "Where did you get these clothes?"

"From my friend and comrade," Lehrling said. "Bausch had been hanged. Roble—"

Roble said softly, "I had need of them."

Lehrling studied Roble for a moment. "Ah, it's starting to make sense to me why you are unfamiliar with so many things. The wizard addressed you as an Overlander. Is that true?"

Roble nodded. "It is."

"An Overlander dares to pronounce his judgment on me?" Crukas asked, shaking the cage bars. "You have no right . . ."

"Silence!" Zauber said, waving his hand toward the thief.

Crukas glared at the wizard, and when he tried to speak, no sound came from his mouth. A horrified expression claimed his face. He motioned for Zauber to come closer and even pointed at his mouth in pleading hand signs, hoping the wizard reversed the spell.

Zauber gave a slight shrug and grinned. "That's much better."

"Roble, how did you get to Glacier Ridge?" Lehrling asked.

"He can tell you about it later," Zauber said. "Lehrling, who crafted the Dragon Skull Order's armor?"

"No particular armorer. Mine were fashioned in Hoffnung. Bausch had his made in Woodnog."

Zauber held his right hand before Roble's chest and moved it right to left. He frowned. "Seems these have been enchanted. Any odd occurrences, Roble, since you've been wearing them?"

Roble shrugged. "They seem to adjust to the temperature. When I was freezing cold in the forest overlooking Glacier Ridge, they immediately made me warmer and immune to the cold. After we left that climate, they've acclimated to keep me cooler."

"Same for me," Shawndirea said.

Lehrling rubbed his beard and smoothed it. He glanced at Roble and said, "Now I understand why you've never been trained with swords. But, when you confronted Waxxon's three henchmen you showed no fear of them whatsoever. Why is that?"

"I honestly don't know. I don't remember what happened."

"Interesting," Zauber said.

"What?" Lehrling asked.

"Were the three men who held you prisoner the same men that hanged Bausch?"

Lehrling nodded. "Yes."

"Perhaps Bausch was the one that enchanted his own clothes," Zauber said.

"No," Lehrling replied, "He's not capable."

"Maybe not magically. But perhaps he placed a curse before he died that whoever took the clothes would kill the men that killed him."

"A vengeance spell," Shawndirea said. "That makes sense. Roble went into some kind of trance when the three men attacked. He showed no fear and killed them quickly."

"Like I said," Roble said, "I don't remember what I did."

"So, Overlander," Zauber said, "Have you been initiated into the Dragon Skull Order?"

"No."

Lehrling cleared his throat and said, "Not yet."

Zauber rubbed his hands together and smiled. "So much for you two to discuss."

"He's noble enough to join the order," Lehrling said. "But never has an Overlander been initiated. Certainly not someone untrained with a sword. And what brought you to the Underworld?"

"She did," Roble said, nodding toward Shawndirea. "I promised to get her back to her homeland."

Lehrling looked at the faery and said, "You went to the Overlands?"

"I've been several times."

Zauber shook his head. "Much to your mother's disapproval. And look at your wings."

"I know," she said sadly.

"That's my fault," Roble said. "And why I insist on getting her home."

Zauber studied Roble. After a couple minutes, he said, "Again, Queen Istrell *won't* be receptive of your arrival."

"I expect not, but how do you know this?" Roble asked. "And why is our situation important to you?"

"We tend to other matters first, but let's just say, I'm here to help. When my duty is done, finding me will be like one of those mysteries you enjoy solving. Waxxon's soldiers are our concern at the present. The simple people of Woodcrest need our help."

"So you've been hiding in the forest and picking them off one by one?" Roble asked.

Zauber smiled. "I'm not a warrior, so crashing the gates isn't quite the option I'd choose."

"I suppose not," Lehrling said, adjusting his weight in the saddle. He bent forward and kept one hand pressed against his chest. "Any idea how many of Waxxon's men occupy Woodcrest?"

"Last count, before these two died, no less than a dozen more."

Stunned, Roble looked at Zauber and asked, "Only a dozen soldiers took Woodcrest?"

"Woodcrest is a small town of mostly unarmed villagers," Zauber said. "Fear is what controls the town more than Waxxon's men."

"But still, even a small town should be able to prevent a dozen soldiers from taking over," Roble said.

"They are farmers with modest walls to protect them from wolves and bears during the night. Waxxon's men attacked when they were working their fields on the outside of Woodcrest's walls. Their gates were wide open. And even if they stood to fight, hoes and rakes are no match against swords and axes."

Odlon angered at the thought of Waxxon's men plundering a defenseless township. His emerald eyes narrowed. He aimed the bow, trying to get a glimpse of a guard. He said, "Tis true."

Roble studied the wizard's strange silvery eyes. "And how do you know that only a dozen men or so still occupy the town?"

Zauber pulled a glowing orb from inside his robe. It held an odd vibrant silver luminescence, similar to the wizard's eyes. Beneath the dense dark forest canopy, the orb shimmered brightly

"Look for yourselves," he replied with a broad grin. "I've watched where they wait, which is why my patience has enabled me to eliminate them when they exit the gates."

Odlon, Roble, Lehrling, and Shawndirea peered into the glowing ball. The orb revealed the corner wall towers where several of Waxxon's archers stood guard. Swordsmen guarded both city gates. The poor townsfolk were dressed in tattered fur clothes. Their faces were dirty and their hair unkempt. Although they worked their normal menial tasks, their fearful eyes kept side-glances toward their captors.

In the center of the town two bodies hung from a tall tree. These unfortunate souls were better dressed than the survivors in Woodcrest, which meant they had probably been members of the town council. Other dead bodies lay side-by-side in the street while flies and other insects swarmed their decaying bodies.

Waxxon had wanted to drive fear into the hearts of these farmers and hunters, and from their defeated facial expressions, he had succeeded.

Tall crudely cut timber walls fortified the small town. The thick surrounding forest added an additional deterrent that Waxxon's men now oversaw, which averted any hope that neighboring farming villages might come to Woodcrest's aid.

While Roble and the others stared into the glowing orb, brittle dead leaves crunched softly on the forest floor, moving closer and closer to their vicinity. The small chorus of insects suddenly silenced. Several small sparrows chirped and flew deeper into the trees. The approaching steps were light, but not so soft that the leaves didn't emit a whisper from their breaking sounds. Their stalking movements crept closer, pausing briefly at the edge of the thick brush.

Roble looked to the forest and pulled a throwing knife.

Zauber raised a hand and slowly shook his head. "Easy, Overlander," the wizard said. "It's only my pet."

From the thick bramble and thorns a black cat slinked onto the dark road with its tail raised. A white star patch of fur splotched the center of its chest. Its emerald eyes studied the group before walking to Zauber and rubbing its head and body around the hem of his long robes.

"Surely this isn't the . . .?" Roble began.

"The beast that killed Waxxon's men?" Zauber gave a firm nod and smiled while twirling a strand of his black beard with his finger. "Indeed it is."

The black cat purred and leapt into Zauber's arms.

"The magic has worn off, so Phantom won't be stopping more of Waxxon's men for a while." Zauber scratched between the cat's ears. Phantom closed his eyes and purred louder.

"If Woodcrest is occupied," Lehrling asked weakly, "How can we get around it? As best I remember there are no other roads to bypass it."

Zauber smiled. "There are ways."

Odlon shook his head. "The forest growth is too thick to cut our way through. Heading back to Glacier Ridge isn't good either."

Zauber approached the iron cage and said, "And what of your loud-mouthed prisoner? What is his crime and where are you taking him?"

Roble explained about the Plague-bringer, what other crimes Crukas had committed, and that they were delivering him to Ironwood.

Thunderous hooves beat the road behind them. Roble turned to see Riese and Marc galloping toward them at full speed. Riese's eyes were full of horror, hatred, and vengeance. Such a combination was deadly for foes or friends. As they neared the wagon, Riese pulled back so hard on the reins that his horse's eyes bulged. Its front hooves dug into the black road and slid across the hard surface. Before the horse fully stopped, Riese swung off the steed and ran along beside the horse. Froth dripped from its mouth. It panted hard. Marc stopped his horse but didn't dismount. Instead his eyes focused on Zauber.

Riese held his hammer clenched tightly in his massive right hand. He bore his teeth and headed toward the wagon. Crukas noticed the boiling hatred in Riese's eyes and not certain what the giant blacksmith might do; the thief lowered his head and held his hands over his head. Crukas mumbled odd bits of poetry that Roble thought could be a prayer, incantation, or a vile curse. Whichever it was, none would aid Crukas once Riese got to him.

"Riese," Roble said, stepping into the smith's path. "Is everything—?"

Riese's huge left hand grabbed Roble's vest and heaved him aside much like a straw scarecrow. "Outta my way!"

Crukas opened his eyes just enough to see where Riese was, and then, just as quickly, he shut them tightly again. The phrases the thief mumbled became louder and spoken more rapidly. Riese walked past the iron cage and climbed back onto the wagon seat. "Everyone, we ride!"

"Wait!" Roble said.

Riese turned and glared coldly at Roble.

Roble never broke their gaze in spite of the smith's massive size.

"Wait? For what?" Riese said, spittle flying from his mouth as he spoke. "My son Jez is dead. The whole town is dead. I want to find the wagon rider who killed them. He will die for his pestilence!"

"We cannot head through Woodcrest," Roble said. "At least, not yet."

"And why not?"

"Waxxon's men now control it," Odlon said.

A mad grin spread across Riese's face. His voice deepened when he said, "Then we shall take it from them."

"How?" Roble asked.

"Crash the gates."

Zauber shook his head and said, "We need a more subtle approach."

Riese frowned and his glare focused on the wizard. "Who are you?"

In a soothing, almost hypnotic voice that trickled like an invisible stream, Shawndirea said, "He is the one who can get us through Woodcrest alive so we can find the Plague-bringer that killed your son and the inhabitants of Glacier Ridge. No justice can be carried out if we're all dead."

Riese shook his head slightly. The lure of her voice sliced through his anger and found its way into where he hid his pain, unlocking the sadness that he longed to keep buried. The hardness of his brow softened. Tears brimmed in his eyes. A couple tears escaped and slid down his cheeks.

Riese wiped his face with the back of his left sleeve and looked at Zauber, quite angry with himself for shedding tears in public, and especially in front of Crukas. But even the tough smith couldn't hide agony of loss.

Riese asked, "How?"

"We wait," Zauber replied.

"How long?"

"Until nightfall," Zauber said. "And then Waxxon's men will fall."

CHAPTER 40

After the Plague-bringer had entered the tavern and tossed his bag of disease carriers onto the floor inside Hobskin's Tavern, Drucis—a dark-skinned dwarf—hid in a half empty barrel of dried nuts behind the bar. Having been a master explosive technician who worked deep in the Mines of Gordurth, Drucis had, at first, thought the bag contained a miner's bomb, so he scrambled across the tavern, leapt and rolled over the top of the bar, and plunged into the barrel of unshelled nuts. Minutes later, when no raging explosion rocked the tavern, he peered through a knothole in the side of the barrel. What he saw paralyzed this normally otherwise fearless dwarf with quaking horror.

The small bag vibrated on the floor and tipped over to its side. There were strange ticking sounds but unlike the crude mechanisms he used for countdown pieces. Through the bag's opening, a maddening swarm of black beetles scuttled across the floor and immediately attacked whoever was closest. He watched his two comrades stomp and crush dozens of the insects into puddles of green goo, but the numbers continued increasing at a magical rate. The bag seemed to hold a never-ending supply. Moments later, he was stunned to see the beetles climbing the dwarves' legs and covering their bodies. Though they screamed for help, dozens of the other thieves and rebellious rogues fought similar losing battles of their own. Drucis watched in terror as the biting insects overtook the half drunken patrons inside Hobskin's Tavern.

Shame overtook Drucis for his moments of cowardice. He struggled to find the courage to leap out of the barrel and help his comrades, but he realized there wasn't anything he could do. Draken and Sorgen, his thieving partners and fellow travelers, dropped to the floor, madly slapping and raking the beetles from their faces, their beards and long hair, but the expanding swarm soon covered them. Draken and Sorgen's hands slowly stopped fighting and dropped motionless onto the floor beside their paralyzed bodies.

Drucis ducked deeper into the barrel, but he suddenly worried that staying inside the barrel might seal his fate in death as well. However, after waiting an hour, which seemed more like days, he braved enough to rise up, peer out, and look around the tavern. Instead of finding his friends and patrons lying dead on the dirty floor, he found them staggering aimlessly around. They were like the undead villagers he had seen in the Ruins of Sturn, where he and Draken and Sorgen, had taken sport shooting the staggering undead with arrows while standing atop the ledges of crumbling pillars. That had been fine entertainment on an otherwise boring day, until they discovered a wraith had summoned the undead for her use. Their sporting shots had almost brought her wrath upon them. Never had his short stubby legs ran so fast to escape anyone's fury.

Wraiths weren't the source behind the sickening transformations inside the tavern, but he still faced the dilemma of escaping with his life. He wondered why the scuttling insects had not entered the barrel and diseased him as well. He didn't know where they had disappeared, but none skittered across the floor, which partially relieved him, but he refused to let down his guard.

Twice the tavern door had opened, and twice it had been slammed shut. This had attracted the attention of the undead and kept them lingering near the door. He took the opportunity to pull himself out of the barrel and quietly set his heavy boots onto the floor. As quietly as possible, Drucis shook the shelled nuts from his long white, braided beard and picked pieces of hulls and skins from his thick white ponytail.

Drucis looked for his jewel-studded battleax and noticed it still lay atop the table where he and his comrades had finished off two kegs without succumbing to the slightest tipsiness. Even with his ax in hand, he didn't think he could get to the door without being surrounded and taken down by the mass of undead. Of course, he would have to *get* to the ax first. He didn't see any possibility of doing so without drawing the attention of the undead patrons.

He edged around the side of the bar, grabbed a half-filled mug of ale, downed it, and then he noticed the almost hidden door that led down to the cellar storage room where more kegs of ale and strong liquors were kept. Needless to say, he didn't set the mug down. He kept it, a smile parted his thick snowy white beard, and his eyes widened at the intoxicating paradise that now surrounded him. To a dwarf this treasure was almost as valuable as gold.

Seeing the mouth-watering delights, he soured at the idea that came to him, which was the only way that allowed him to escape the tavern alive. Searching through the storage shelves near the wooden kegs, he found a small mallet. He hurried to the kegs and smashed off the spigots of the aged whiskies, brandies, and rum. Before the kegs were completely emptied, he grabbed a small keg of ale and tucked it under his arm.

He took a lit oil lantern and smashed it against the wall. The leaking oil burst into flames and ran down the wall, igniting the inch-deep liquor. Drucis ran further into the icy cellar before the scorching flames swooshed and hissed into a towering wall of fire, quickly engulfing the barrels, the storage shelves, the side of the wall, and the bottom of the floor above. The heat filled the room and the wooden kegs crackled as the fire's intensity roared.

Drucis pulled the metal door closed, opened the small keg of ale, and sat down to drink while the flames licked upward and started burning the floorboards of the tavern above. He filled his mug with the ale and smiled. The earthen ceiling overhead assured him that when the tavern burned and collapsed to the ground, the flaming embers would not bury and consume him as well.

He filled the first mug, raised it before him, and said, "Aye, Sorgen and Draken, to your memories. We fought many battles and looted many treasures. I will miss ya both. Nothin' worse than drinking alone."

Drucis sat with his back pressed against the metal door. The inferno on the other side gradually heated the door until he finally had to move to the colder side of the room. Several explosions quaked, which had been sealed barrels of liquor treasures now forever lost. The raging fire had apparently burned through the floor overhead. Burning tavern tables and chairs plummeted through the weakened floor and crashed into the cellar. Horrendous wails and screams shrilled from the burning undead right outside the metal door.

He shook his head and poured another mug. The metal door rattled as more flaming debris stacked against it. He wondered now if what he had done was only barricade himself into his own tomb. The gray metal door brightened, turning yellow, orange, and red. The metal was far too hot to touch, but worse was the hinges were giving way and would soon collapse. The temperature inside the room where he sat was already toasty warm.

While he doubted any of the undead had survived the fiery destruction, he worried about how long he'd have to wait for the heat to dissipate enough for him to trudge through the charred rubble and smoldering embers so he could leave Glacier Ridge forever.

Several hours passed. The buckled metal door cooled and activity on the other side diminished. He impatiently sighed and his breath was a visible puff of white. He set down the mug and walked to the door. With his gloved hands he tugged at the warped edge of the door. It stubbornly resisted. He pulled harder until the weakened rivets and bolts popped loose and the door widened.

A gush of smoke filtered into the room. He listened for a half minute before he peered out. Little of the tavern's remains were recognizable. Part of the bar still had licking flames but most everything else was charred black with white ash running along the outer edges. An occasional burst of wind awakened red glowing embers, but he didn't see any of the undead moving. A lot of brittle skeletons smoldered in the rubble.

"At least you're at peace now," Drucis said, kicking his way through the mess.

He kept his attention on the floor until he found his battleax. It was covered with soot, but the flames had not affected its soundness. The heat of the consuming blaze that destroyed the tavern was pale in comparison to what a Dwarven forge produced. Even the welded runes and jewels along the edge of the blade and down the reinforced handle had not lost their polish. The runes didn't glow, which was a good sign. Otherwise a sorcerer remained nearby.

Drucis picked up his ax and brushed away the soot with his thick fire-proof gloves. Feeling his confidence grow now that he possessed his favorite weapon, he marched through the black smoldering remains of Hobskin's Tavern. The icy wind whipped through the narrow passageway that led back out to the marketplace. He bowed his head into the wind and stepped out onto the cobblestone street.

The square and the streets were eerily silent, other than the wailing of the sharp cutting wind and pellets of sleet plinking off the icy rooftops. The stable doors were wide open, and some smoke exited the chimney, but he assumed those inside were probably cursed with the same disease as those in Hobskin's Tavern.

Hooves clopped along the cobblestone behind Drucis, and he turned quickly with his battleax gripped in both hands. He lowered the ax and his small gray horse, Grey, walked toward him. He rubbed its nose and patted the side of its face.

"Wouldn't leave me, eh?" Drucis said, smiling. "Let's find our saddle and get out of this frosty hellhole."

He walked to the open stable and searched until he found his saddle, the bridle, and a couple of saddlebags.

"Taint no one be needing these," he said to Grey. He looked through the tools and weapons, grabbing different things he felt might be necessary now that he was forced to travel alone.

Before he bridled Grey, he led her to a trough and let her fill her belly with oats and sweet grains.

"Be a long journey back to Gordurth, so eat up!"

Grey eagerly ate while Drucis watched the wide open doors and released a long sigh. He missed his comrades and wasn't certain if more of the undead villagers wandered the streets. Perhaps more survivors like himself were still trapped inside other buildings, their homes, or some might have been fortunate enough to get out of Glacier Ridge before the pestilence overtook the exposed townspeople. He considered for a moment of searching for survivors, but in doing so, he might actually open doors to more masses of undead.

"Nah," he said, shaking his head. "Best be moving on."

Drucis patted Grey's side and moved to her head. Gently he slid the bridle into place and turned her toward the door. That's when movement from the corner of his eye caught his attention. A half dozen undead hobbled his direction.

Drucis spat on the floor and cursed under his breath. He didn't know whether to mount Grey and gallop out or use the battleax to dismember the strange undead men and women headed toward him. He only had seconds to make such a decision. His life and Grey's depended upon him making the right one.

CHAPTER 41

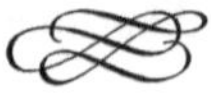

Smoke rose over the horizon. Lehrling pointed.

"That's over Glacier Ridge, isn't it?" Roble asked.

Riese and Marc turned and looked. Both nodded without saying a word.

"What's burning?" Odlon asked.

Riese shook his head. "I don't know. We never set anything afire before we left."

"Could someone have survived?"

"Maybe," Riese replied. "We didn't search through all the shops and homes."

"Why not?" Roble asked.

Riese swallowed hard. "After seeing what had happened to Jez and all the patrons inside Hobskin's Tavern, I didn't see the point. I figured everyone else had been diseased."

"That makes sense," Lehrling said in a hoarse voice. He coughed until he couldn't catch his breath and his face flushed crimson red. He beat his chest with his fist several times. Finally after the severe coughing fit passed, he spat a bloody wad onto the black road. Sweat covered his brow, his eyes rolled back, and he dropped off his horse, collapsing unconscious on the road.

Roble, Zauber, and Odlon rushed to him.

"He's in bad shape," Roble said.

"Riese," Odlon said, "Could you please get him to the wagon?"

Riese tied the reins to the seat and jumped off the wagon. He marched to where the rest of their party encircled Lehrling. Riese grabbed Lehrling, and effortlessly slung the rotund man over his shoulder. Riese carried him to the rear of the wagon and set Lehrling onto the hay that surrounded Crukas' iron cage.

Roble whispered to Shawndirea, "Can you heal him?"

"I can try, but it's hard to say," she replied.

Zauber shook his head and said, "No, he needs some herbs and rest. We can issue a spell to ease his pain and allow him to rest, but we must also provide him medicine."

"But you're a wizard," Roble said almost agitated.

Zauber nodded. "Yes, but magic *isn't* a cure all. Powers are attained differently for every caster. Mine are not aligned to restore health but to ward off evil."

Roble glanced at Shawndirea. She shook her head.

"But what you did," Roble said to her, "At my house. The dead butterflies and moths."

"Yes, dear. I know. I understand your frustration, but remember I'm the Butterfly Queen. My energy and magic are connected to the earth, and I bestow blessings and healing for them. Not humans."

Odlon glanced at Roble and said, "If we were nearer to Eyllisathem, my sister has potions and salves that would cure him. I'm sorry."

Roble looked at Lehrling. The man lay unconscious on the bed of the wagon. His irregular breathing was something Roble had seen with people suffering from serious pneumonia. He swallowed hard.

"So he's going to die?" Roble asked.

Zauber frowned. "We'll do everything we can, but this matter isn't something we have power over."

Shawndirea placed a hand to Roble's cheek and then she kissed him. "I'm sorry," she said.

Even though Roble didn't know Lehrling more than a day, he really liked the man. He hated that Lehrling had survived the henchmen and possibly dozens of other dangerous situations, and now would die due to pneumonia. He didn't like it. It angered him.

"What about inside the walls of Woodcrest? Do you think there's someone there that could help?" he asked.

"It's possible," Zauber replied. "However, other than finding medicine to treat his sickness, we need a priest. Priests are the ones who have better effects with healing."

Frustrated, Roble said, "Any priests in Woodcrest?"

"Only if one has traveled to the city before it was occupied by Waxxon's soldiers. Woodcrest holds no allegiance to any deity."

Roble turned and walked away. "Damn luck couldn't be any worse."

"Don't give up hope," Shawndirea said.

"But look at him. He's dying."

"I'm sorry."

"There has to be something more we can do," Roble said, forming tight fists.

Zauber stepped beside him and placed a hand on Roble's shoulder. Warmth rushed through Roble. His anger and frustration eased.

Zauber said, "Patience, Overlander. Nightfall is but a few hours away. When we get through the gates of Woodcrest, we will find what we need. They may not have priests or healers, but they are farmers and gatherers, so herbs are things they collect and store."

"And how will we get past the gates?" Roble asked.

"Still working on that," Zauber replied. "But approaching before darkness falls will automatically identify you and Lehrling as members of the Dragon Skull Order. At night it will be more difficult for them to see your armor."

Roble ran his hands through his brown hair and sighed. He glanced at the dark forest surrounding them. The blue-tinted broken statues and pillars were the brightest objects amongst the thick vine and moss-covered trees. The dark forest seemed determined to subdue their brightness and hide them forever.

"What was this place?" Roble asked.

"The Ruins of Sturn?" Zauber glanced back at the ruins and said, "Once a great temple and monastery stood and thrived here before dark elves attacked and slaughtered the monks within."

"And Woodcrest?"

"Not settled and established for many years after this slaughter."

Roble walked toward the edge of the road and studied the marble statues. All the heads and hands were broken away. The statement the dark elves detailed with such vandalism was that any follower of light in this forest became an enemy no one would remember. Or perhaps the dark elves issued a greater warning. They didn't fear followers of the light and the darker path held more power.

Zauber slipped further away from where Roble stood. Alone with Shawndirea, Roble asked, "Do you trust him?"

"Zauber?" she asked.

"Yes," Roble whispered while watching Zauber.

"He is not a stranger. My mother has sought his council many times after my father died."

"So you trust him?"

"Of course."

Roble glanced toward the wagon where Lehrling lay unconscious. The old man's chest rose and fell slowly. His eyes remained closed. Zauber placed his left hand on Lehrling's chest and raised the staff with the right. After speaking some words, the blood quartz ring glowed and dimmed. Lehrling's body jerked, but his eyes didn't open. He did, however, roll to his side into what looked like a more comfortable position.

Roble looked into Shawndirea's beautiful eyes. She smiled and blushed at him. "And if he tells your mother where you are? And about me . . . us?"

She shook her head slightly. "No, he won't do that."

"How can you be certain?"

"He'd rather I make my approach to her and not have her patrols bind me and return me to Elvendale."

"They'd actually do that? Bind you?"

"Yes, if her anger toward me has grown that severe. It's never happened before, but she has . . . *her moods*. She's insistent that I take the throne, and soon. I don't want that responsibility. I have always been adamant with her about me *never* assuming the throne."

"Zauber believes your mother will not accept me."

Shawndirea nodded. "That's true. I expect that she won't."

"You seeking me and choosing me, that isn't out of spite toward her, is it?"

Her eyes widened with hurt. Tears formed and welled up. "Surely you don't believe that?"

"I'm sorry. I shouldn't have said that. I'm just thinking out loud."

Shawndirea wiped tears from her eyes. Her shoulders drooped. "So your mind still questions *us*?"

"I'm sorry. No, I—"

She looked away. "I thought I had made my intentions clear. Do you not believe I love you?"

Looking in her tearful eyes, reading her body gestures, and hearing the hurt in her voice, he grieved inside for bringing hurt to this beautiful faery. Very gently, he put his finger beneath her chin and looked into the most beautiful green eyes ever. He said, "I believe you do. I just wanted to be certain that I'm not the only reason you won't assume the throne. No sense adding more animosity from the Fae than what I will probably face."

"No, you're not the reason. I've never wanted to be Queen of Elvendale. I will always remain the Butterfly Queen because that's where my heart is, and it is also my birthright. But I refuse to take the throne of Elvendale and marry whomever they believe is the best choice for our next king. And what about you? Do you love me? I know you're human and most humans think love develops over time, but what are your true feelings toward me?"

"If I had not gotten you back after the Ratkins took you, I'd never stopped hunting until I found you. I do love you. I knew that when we first began this journey. Actually I knew it before then, when you had brought my collection back to life.

"But when you were taken from me—my heart was torn in half. Emptiness consumed me and determination pushed me to find you. I've never felt such an inner ache as I did at the thought of losing you, or finding you dead. The second I saw you in the bottle, mixed emotions rushed through me. I was ecstatic that you were near but angered that you had been placed inside the bottle."

"So you'll stay with me?" she asked, looking into his eyes, studying them intently.

"Of course."

Her eyes never left his gaze. Worry and hurt still overshadowed her as she asked, "You don't miss the Overlands?"

"No. I'm tired of dealing with all the problems there. Too much technology has infected the people. I'd prefer living a simpler life."

"I won't say that life here will be easier."

"I expect it won't be," Roble replied. "I'm also tired of dealing with so much politics."

Shawndirea smiled. "You won't escape that here. Politics abound wherever populations exist. There's no getting away from it."

"I suppose not. But I've discovered more beauty here than where I grew up."

"It's far more dangerous than you imagine. But will you ever go back to the Overlands?" she asked.

"I have things I need to do there for closure. I don't want my sister to worry for the rest of her life about how I might have died. It's best I let her know I'm alive but moving around a lot."

"That's probably the best thing to do. Will you tell her of the Underworld?"

Roble shook his head. "No. I don't want her thinking I've gone insane either."

"I understand."

"Although I may want to visit there, I don't know that I'd like to go back the way we exited. A bigger problem is that I'm not certain I can find my way back to my home."

"There are rifts throughout the plane, mostly caves, but other landmarks as well. Zauber may be able to give you an enchanted object that allows you to find your way back," she said.

"If I go to the Overlands, I will always return quickly to you. That's a promise you can rely upon."

$\sim$

NIGHTFALL CAME. Darkness settled over the forest outside Woodcrest. Glowing eyes peered at them from all the trees. It was the most eerie sensation Roble had ever experienced. Strange bird and insect sounds echoed. The broken statues shimmered a murky bluish tint in spite of the surrounding blackness. Roble wondered what else lurked in the shadowy trees.

Odlon stood beside Roble and said, "Are you ready to fight?"

"As I'll ever be."

"We've not had the opportunity for me to train you with a sword, but once we can get settled in somewhere safely, I will."

"I appreciate that."

Odlon smiled. "For what it's worth, your skill with knives is excellent."

"Thanks."

Roble followed Odlon to the rear of the wagon. Lehrling was still unconscious but buried beneath straw and a couple of sweaty horse blankets. Sweat drops beaded on his forehead. His breathing was staggered and hampered by thick phlegm.

Shawndirea sat on the side of the wagon watching Lehrling.

"He's getting worse," Roble said to her.

"I know."

Crukas sat on the floor of his cage and hugged his knees. His eyes revealed how defeated he was. Still with the silence spell over him, he was unable to voice his disdain for being caged like an animal.

Roble looked at the wizard and said, "How do we enter Woodcrest?"

"You're not going to like my suggestion," Zauber replied.

Roble folded his arms across his chest and said, "At this point, I'm almost willing to try anything if it gives Lehrling a better chance to survive."

"We need to release the thief," he said.

"What?" Roble and Odlon asked.

Riese raised his massive fists and rushed toward Zauber. The wizard tightened his hand around his staff. The crystal atop the staff glowed crimson. The sudden burst of light made Riese reconsider his approach. He lowered his hands and stopped his advancement.

Through clenched teeth, Riese hissed, "He remains caged until we get to Ironwood."

"Very well," Zauber said, "But know that we have no hope of passing through the forest tonight or tomorrow for that matter. Woodcrest is the only path that gets us to the other side. Unless you wish to leave your wagon, horses, and supplies here while you attempt to cut your way through the ruins."

The mention of freeing Crukas jolted the thief from his depression, and he rose to his feet. He gently rattled the cage door, hoping to gain their attention and sympathy with his pleading eyes. Purposely, none of the party regarded him. Crukas sighed and stared at his feet.

"What do you have in mind?" Roble asked.

"Crukas stays with you, me, Odlon, and the faery," Zauber said. "Riese will drive the wagon to the gate."

Riese shook his head. "Crukas is a thief capable of vanishing and reappearing somewhere else. You release him, and we'll never see him again."

"Should he attempt to escape without aiding us," Zauber said, "He won't be able speak again. Only I can reverse my spell of silence upon him."

"I still say that it's too risky," Riese replied. "He could panhandle as a mute beggar in Hoffnung or any other grand city. People pity folks like that. He'd probably earn more gold begging than he does as a thief."

Crukas glared.

Zauber looked at Crukas. "Are you willing to help us in order to gain back your voice?"

Crukas nodded.

"Of course he's going to agree," Riese said.

Roble asked, "What exactly do we need him to do?"

"Unlock the gate."

Odlon shook his head. "They'll kill him before he gets to the gate."

Riese smiled broadly. Crukas' hopeful smile faded.

"Riese will be our distraction," Zauber said.

Riese's smile vanished. Confusion tightened his brow. "What?"

Zauber said, "Since you're of the same bloodline as most of Waxxon's henchmen, you can ride the wagon to the gate without fear of them killing you."

"I am *not* one of them."

"I won't argue your heritage," Zauber said, "But you can distract them long enough for us to kill the men at the gate towers. Once we do that, Crukas unlocks the gate and you move the wagon inside."

Riese looked at Crukas. Crukas smiled sheepishly.

"I still don't like this idea," Riese said.

"Noted, "Odlon said, "But there's always the chance that Crukas dies."

Crukas stopped smiling.

"Can you guarantee that?" Riese asked.

Roble shook his head. "What has Crukas done that demands that he die?"

"Thievery from my supplies in Hobskin's Tavern. Turning on fellow thieves and collecting the bounty rewards on them, which is in direct violation of Glacier Ridge. All bounty hunters I turn away. Once I discovered what he was doing, I forbade him to ever return."

"And none of us ever will," Roble said. "Glacier Ridge is gone."

Fury rushed through Riese. "For now. But I will reclaim it."

"Here," Zauber said, handing Riese the leather armor from one of the dead soldiers from the side of the road. "Wear these. It will lessen the chance that they think you're *not* one of them."

Riese took the armor and opened his mouth to speak but the wizard cut him off. "No argument," Zauber said, "Unless you want to spend the night in this darkened forest. The less time we spend here, the less chance we need to worry about the roaming angry spirits of the fallen monks and priests."

Riese's eyes widened slightly. He nervously glanced at the forest trees. When it came to fighting physical beings, he was beyond brave, but spirits were something only those who possessed arcane abilities could battle effectively. And apparently, Roble reasoned to himself, this giant of a man was also fearful of magic casters.

"Now," Zauber said, "unlock his cage."

Riese took his key ring from Roble and searched through the keys until he found the one that opened the cage door. Before he turned the key, he looked at Zauber and said, "I still say trusting him is a mistake. I know what he's capable of. He can vanish and reappear elsewhere."

Roble nodded. "I've seen him do it."

"He may flee," Riese said, turning the key.

The lock clicked loudly.

Zauber smiled. "If he flees, he won't get far. Another spell hangs over him. Should he run, he goes blind. Permanently."

"Ah, well," Riese said with a broad smile. He swung open the whining cage door. "In that case, by all means thief, step on out."

Crukas hesitated. His nervous eyes glanced from Riese to Roble and quickly to Zauber before he finally took a step forward. He held his cuffed hands out to Riese. Riese gave a grunt and found the key to unlock the cuffs.

Once the cuffs dropped to the hay beside Lehrling, Crukas rubbed his wrists and gave a humble bow of thanks to Riese and then to Zauber. Riese grabbed the leather armor, turned, and headed to the front of the wagon to change.

After Riese put on the armor, he climbed back onto the wagon and untied the reins. "Are we ready?" he asked.

"Not quite yet," Zauber replied.

Zauber motioned for Odlon, Roble, and Crukas to stand in the center of the road with him. Shawndirea stood on Roble's shoulder.

Zauber looked at Odlon and said, "Be ready to use your crossbow immediately. Just in case."

Odlon gave a firm nod.

"Faery," Zauber said, "Draw upon your power while I utilize my own."

Shawndirea closed her eyes, raised her hands, and her fingertips glowed. Zauber stood in the center of them and drove the tip of his staff firmly into the road. Red swirls of light formed a large glowing red circle that wrapped around them. Wind whistled and in an instant they were gone.

Seconds later they stood in the center square of Woodcrest near a well.

"What the hell?" Roble whispered, looking around and grabbing a wooden post to keep from falling over. "How?"

"Translocation spell," Odlon said with a wide grin.

"We're in Woodcrest?"

Odlon place his forefinger to his lips and nodded. He motioned Roble to move away from the center of the square and stand behind a wagon filled with cut wheat stalks. Roble quickly obliged while the elf moved into the shadows of the town hall and disappeared. Zauber headed the opposite direction, and he too, vanished.

Crukas was already gone before Roble had thought to look for him. Roble understood why Crukas was renowned for his thievery skills, but he suddenly realized *why* Riese feared the thief would leave the party without aiding them.

"What do I do?" Roble asked Shawndirea.

"Keep your eyes open and watch for any patrols."

"The town is too quiet," he said.

She nodded. "Waxxon's men hold it under their control. The townspeople are probably too afraid to move about."

"A curfew . . ." Roble whispered.

Roble glanced around and noticed two townspeople's bodies still hanging in crude nooses on a tree near the center of Woodcrest.

"What does Waxxon gain by occupying this little town? The buildings are poorly constructed. They can't possibly gain riches from these people."

Shawndirea shrugged her tiny shoulders. "Woodcrest sets in the direct crossroads that leads to Glacier Ridge. Many thieves travel this direction, and some, as you've well seen, are willing to kidnap for ransom."

"So I just hide in the shadows?" Roble asked. "That seems quite cowardly."

She shook her head. "Odlon will take out the men on the towers, Crukas will pick the lock to the gate, and Riese should be heading to the gate. You simply are an extra preventative should any guard pass this direction."

Roble placed his hands on the daggers tucked inside his belt and waited. The quiet town slept, but soon, he feared, it would awaken to the tragedies of unexpected living nightmares.

CHAPTER 42

Riese had his teenage son crawl up beneath the seat of the wagon before he headed to Woodcrest's gates. He packed hay around his son to make certain he could not be seen. While they might accept Riese as being one of their brethren, which was true, but not something he openly confessed, his son did not favor his bloodline. He was like his mother, who was not of Vyking descent.

Dressed as one of Waxxon's soldiers, Riese's conscience struggled with momentarily pretending to still be one of the bloodthirsty bastards. He detested his race that much.

Riese's appearance alone was as foreboding as any of them, and perhaps, his anger and hatred ran deeper because of what his bloodline had done, which was also why he had separated himself from them and why he now despised them.

Jez and Marc were twins, born to Riese from Odrissus—a half elf—and the love of his life. Her heritage was why his sons were nowhere near his size and appearance. They favored her in size and gentle mannerisms. His heart ached at losing her, and her death was why he hated the Vyking Lords that served Waxxon.

Before he renounced his allegiance to the Vykings, he had served King Obed on the Isles of Welkstone, and paid homage to their God, Reus. While pillaging and plundering a small port, he had found Odrissus frightened and pleading for her life from three of his comrades. They sought to do great harm to her in unspeakable ways *before* they killed her. No amount of begging and pleading would have dissuaded their minds. They had her surrounded in her bedroom and their lust prevented them from seeing Riese slip up behind them with his battleax.

They had ripped her blouse open, laughing at her helplessness. She clutched her long braided red hair across her bare breasts, trying to cover herself while scooting across the hardwood floor and crouching into a corner. Her wide blue eyes pleaded with fear, but the three men circled her with broad grins. They, like him, stood nearly seven feet tall, with dark skin and long, thick beards. Tattooed runes covered the arms and bare chests. They roared with deep laughter as she squirmed on the floor. The more she fretted, the more pleasure they took in her fearful pleas.

Two of his comrades were beheaded before the third could even reach for his sword. He turned to face Riese and said, "Brother, what have you done? You know we always take what we want during our raids, even the women. Especially the women."

"Not her, Tryke," Riese said.

"The king will have your head for this," Tryke said, "for killing two of your brethren."

Riese spat on the floor and said, "To the abyss with King Obed!"

"Traitor!" Tryke said.

Tryke's eyes narrowed, and he gnashed his teeth with fury, but it was the last living act Tryke did. The sharp battleax blade separated his head from his shoulders, and he dropped in death like his two comrades had done minutes before.

Riese turned to the redheaded maiden and extended his hand. She flinched and covered her face. Moments later she peered through her fingers and said, "Please, don't hurt me."

"I won't hurt you. Take my hand."

Timidly, she slowly reached for his hand. When she placed her tiny hand into his, he pulled her to her feet.

"What is your name?" he asked.

"Odrissus. And yours?"

"Riese."

Her soft blue eyes stared into his. She read that she was safe with him, that she could trust him. Her fear slowly faded and her breathing returned to normal.

"Quick," Riese said, "Find clothes and get dressed. Others will be along soon enough."

Odrissus found another blouse and quickly pulled it over her head. "Why are you helping me?"

"Hurry," he whispered. Outside horses galloped past. He pulled open the door slightly and watched more Vyking soldiers ride past. Smoke billowed from the burning huts. Swords clashed and people screamed in anguish.

She hurried to the door and stood beside him. She stood a little over half his height. Her ears were pointed, similar to an elf's but slightly different.

"My horse is over by the fence," he said. "Most of my people are too busy to notice us, but we still must be quick and not draw attention to ourselves. Understand?"

Odrissus looked up at him and nodded. "I run fast," she said.

"Good."

Riese pulled open the door, and they bolted across the compacted dirt field until they reached the horse. He swung upon the horse in one smooth movement and extended his hand down to her. She grabbed it, and she pulled herself behind him on the saddle. He pulled the reins to the right and kicked the horse's flanks.

"Riese!"

Riese glanced over his shoulder as another rider's horse galloped forward. His general sat atop a magnificent steed and glared at him. Two soldiers exited Odrissus' hut with their swords drawn and reported what they had found.

"Don't let him escape!" General Yerdrick shouted.

The two men with drawn swords rushed across the path while three horsemen circled back and headed toward Riese and Odrissus.

"Hang on," Riese told her.

The two swordsmen moved quickly, and Riese believed he had a better chance rushing them than being circled by the three horsemen. His horse thundered across the barren field. Riese brought his battleax around and caught one man in the gut with the ax blade. The ax sliced through the man's armor, his midsection, and protruded out the man's back. The momentum propelled the man upward, and Riese viciously yanked the blade free. The man rolled over in the dirt several times, and once he stopped, he never moved again.

The second swordsman rushed and was kicked in the face by Riese, which knocked the man off balance enough. Riese's horse charged past without injury. Once the horse got to full gait, there was no way the man on foot could catch him. Riese tapped the horse's flanks harder, glancing back only long enough to see the three approaching horsemen.

Although the Vykings were seamen at heart, they were also experienced horsemen, and Riese had to be crafty to lose them. As good as he was with his ax, even he realized fighting three of his brethren at once wasn't great odds.

Waves of smoke drifted in dark sheets across the small village. Thatched roofs blazed. Huts engulfed with raging fire crackled. Other than the three men pursuing him, the rest of the pillagers were too busy looting to notice his betrayal to King Obed and his fellow comrades.

Riese rode up a side path that led away from the port village and up the side of the mountain. The three horsemen pursued.

Once Riese reached the top of ridge, they rode into a dense forest. It was here that Riese hoped he'd lose the men or, he hoped, they'd turn back. They didn't. Their determination to capture him was as dedicated as his was to escape.

Odrissus wrapped her arms tightly around his waist and pressed the side of her face against his shirtless back. As the horse galloped through the darkening forest, he held the battleax firmly in his right hand. Drying blood dripped from the silver ax blade.

The one thing that was to Riese's advantage was that none of his brethren were archers. All preferred heavy axes or swords because such meant strength and power. Plus, they loved hand-to-hand combat simply because they could watch the life drain from their enemies' eyes when they ran swords straight through them.

Riese glanced back to see his three pursuers slow their approach. Their horses were as tired as his, but he wondered why they had slowed suddenly. When he directed his attention ahead of him, he noticed why, and he pulled back the reins to slow his mount as well.

Ahead, on the narrow path, were over fifty men, wearing modest fur jackets and ragged leather pants. They carried various crude weapons, mostly farming tools and hatchets, and when they noticed Riese, they set to a running charge like raging fools.

"What is this?" Riese asked.

"A neighboring village."

Riese shook his head. "What do they plan to do?"

"Help protect us. When your ships docked, our leader sent a rider into the neighboring town for help. So you can leave me with them, if you truly wish to rescue me."

"No, I can't leave you here. They are not contenders against my people, in spite of their foolish bravery. These men will be slaughtered, and if you remain with them, so will you."

Riese turned the horse, tapped its sides, and headed through the forest. Rather than pursue him, the three horsemen turned and headed back to the port village. He figured they would tell the other warriors of the approaching villagers. They would kill these simple men in less than an hour. It was what the Vykings thrived on. Lust for loot and bloodshed.

He halfway expected her to protest, but she held tightly to him as the horse galloped around trees, down rugged rocky slopes, and further away from the easier path. Not familiar with this terrain, he really had no idea where he was headed, nor did he actually care. The seaman life he had always known was over, and he would find a place far inland where he could live, perhaps raise a family, and never deal with his people again. Or so he hoped. But in spite of wherever he chose to settle down, he knew there was always a mark on him. King Obed would never rest until someone brought back Riese's head.

After several days of riding and camping at night, Riese found a small quiet place nestled in a wooded area near a clear spring and a wide creek where he could fish for food. They stayed sheltered beneath a rocky shelf against the ridge while he built a small hut with a thatch roof.

The second morning he awoke, he found Odrissus sitting at the edge of the creek watching darting minnows along the water's edge. Her bright blue eyes glanced up into his brown eyes. He smiled at her, and she returned the simple greeting.

"Odrissus," Riese said. "You may take the horse and head back to your people if you choose. I don't want to keep you against your will. You're free to go."

"I do not wish to leave," she replied. "Even if I could find my way, it is doubtful my village has many survivors. Isn't that what you told me?"

Riese looked away and nodded. "Aye. It is."

"Would you mind if I live here with you?"

His eyes immediately returned to hers. The warmth inside her eyes and voice let him know that he was more than a plundering murderer that ransacked any harbor town they happened upon. She smiled at him and stood.

"I would like that very much," he said softly.

Odrissus pulled back her hair, revealing her elven ears, and said, "As you can see, the village was not my true home. I was a servant traded to them when I was only a little girl. I can be your servant, if you'd like."

Riese shook his head. "Nonsense. You'll be no such thing. I would have you be my wife, if that pleases you?"

The statement made her eyes widen with surprise. "You would wish that of me?"

"I would like that very much."

"I've known nothing except being a servant. Never had I thought I'd be a wife."

Riese smiled. "From today forward, you serve no one."

Tears moistened her eyes, and she rushed to him, embracing him tightly. When she glanced up at him, he gently put his finger beneath her chin and tilted her face upward. He leaned down and kissed her lips. When he placed his arms around her, she leapt up and wrapped her legs around his waist. He carried her back to where they had slept and lay beside her, holding her close, and kissing her for hours.

CHAPTER 43

*R*iese had worked hard for several weeks to build a hut large and secure enough so they could live comfortably. From sunrise to dusk, he cut down trees, shaped the logs into square planks for lumber, and toiled endlessly until their home was built.

Nine months passed and her stomach was swollen with their child, which when she went into labor, they discovered, to their surprise, that she carried twins—Jez and Marc.

The twins were so small that Riese feared his huge hands would crush them. Odrissus laughed when he expressed such fears and finally coaxed him into holding his boys, one in each hand.

"You'll make the greatest father," she said with a smile.

Riese had never known such pride—a beautiful dainty wife and two sons—and what he felt inside outweighed any sensation he had ever experienced before then. The boys favored her, and they grew quickly. Before he realized it, they had lived at the edge of the wooded creek for nearly six years. He marveled at how quickly time passed. His boys were fast, rambunctious, and quick learners. They learned to fish, track game animals, and climbed trees as swiftly as squirrels.

Few people traveled along the creek, so seeing strangers that Riese could trade with was impossible. From time to time he loaded up dried fish, animal furs, and other items and carried them two days to the closest town he knew. He traded his supplies for weapons, so he could train his boys how to effectively use them if ever the occasion occurred. Eventually it did.

Riese brought more furs to the town and after trading for new weapons;

he noticed a faded sign at the corner of a tavern. It was written in his native language, and a large reward was offered for him, dead or alive. The crudely drawn poster didn't rightly resemble him, as it could be almost any bearded, dark-haired man. However, the words, should any others in town be able to decipher, detailed Riese greatly.

None of the townspeople apparently could read the wanted poster, as they paid him no attention, no more than they would any ordinary trader. But fear nipped at his soul. His brethren had been the ones that tacked the poster in the town and that meant they had been within two days of his homestead. His wife and two sons were home without him. He packed his swords and battleax over his shoulder and hurried through the trading square, down a short cobblestone street that exited the town and headed back into the wilderness. Once he was out of sight of the town, he ran away from the path and through the fields and forests, cutting his journey's time by almost a full day.

Out of breath and weak from overexerting himself, Riese stopped only long enough to eat berries, dried jerky, and drink water. He took to running again. When he reached his home, he hurried across the creek, splashing and sloshing his giant boots as he ran.

The rear door of their hut was wide open. A large dead man lay face-down in the dirt. A sword protruded from the man's back. He immediately recognized the blade belonged to Jez.

Riese turned the man over, noticed the man's tattoos and King Obed's coat of arms sewn to his leather chest piece. His brethren had come for him.

"Odrissus!" Riese shouted frantically. "Jez! Marc!"

No answer.

His heart thundered in his ears. Sickness turned his stomach, and for a moment, drawing his next breath seemed impossible.

"Odrissus!" he shouted again, following footprints that led away from the hut.

Two sets of prints were too large to be any of his family and very similar to his own. The twins were too light to leave impressions in the soil. But he did make out Odrissus' barefoot outlines where her toes had dug into the ground while she fled.

While Riese ran from his home toward the thick brambles, he came upon the slain body of another of his brethren. The man's throat had been sliced so deeply that Riese was surprised the man's head had not been removed from the body completely.

"Jez! Odrissus! Marc!"

He didn't care that shouting gave away his whereabouts, and he actually *hoped* the remaining man would come for him. Riese needed to know that his family was safe, and he really wanted to kill the man himself.

Deeper in the trees, Odrissus screamed.

Riese sprinted through the trees and saw her. Her long red hair flowed behind her as she fled from the large man chasing her.

Where were his sons? He wondered, rushing through the forest.

The man grabbed Odrissus' red locks and yanked her to him. She struggled and kicked. Her tiny hands clawed at the man's face as he lifted her off the ground and growled.

"Odrissus!" Riese shouted, hurrying toward her. He was a matter of ten yards from where she and this man fought.

Breathing heavily, running with everything he had, he came at the man but before Riese reached him, he watched the man's dagger thrust into Odrissus' side. He yanked back the bloody blade and shoved her to the ground. She clutched her ribs and curled into a fetal position.

"You bastard!" Riese shouted, coming straight at the man.

Before the man brought the dagger around to defend Riese's attack, Riese thrust the palm of his hand against the man's leather chest piece. The devastating blow brought the man off his feet and flung him backwards. The man's sternum cracked and the sound echoed through the forest. His dagger dropped into the loose leaves. The man's eyes widened with pain and surprise. He hit the ground and all the air in his lungs expelled.

The man writhed on the ground and placed his hands on the center of his chest. Riese stood over him and immediately recognized the man to be General Yerdrick.

Yerdrick blinked in surprise, more from the strength Riese possessed than from recognition. Blood coated the general's teeth. He coughed and blood bubbled from his lips. He forced a smile.

"Ah," Yerdrick said. "You spoiled the surprise."

Riese's eyes narrowed. He tossed his sword aside, reached down, and grabbed the general by the throat with one hand. He squeezed until Yerdrick's eyes bulged, his face purpled, and seconds before the man lost consciousness, he loosened his hold.

Riese released the general's throat. Yerdrick could barely hold himself upright. With a huge open hand, Riese smacked the side of Yerdrick's face so hard that the man spun all the way around and dropped to his knees.

Though weak, Yerdrick laughed and said, "I have to admit you picked a feisty one. She was full of spirit like yourself."

"You'll die slowly for this," Riese said. "Painfully slow."

"Kill me, Riese. End me now. But know this, my brother Quenid knows I seek you. He will continue the search, as will others. You'll never find peace in this world."

"Then he will meet you at the River Styx!"

Riese glared down with a murderous stare. A purple handprint pulsed on the general's cheek where Riese had struck him. Blood leaked from Yerdrick's nose and mouth. He chuckled. "Good thing she only had two swords. She'd probably have killed me, too."

Anger and rage rushed through Riese. His huge fist struck Yerdrick in the face—cracking his nose and shattering his teeth. After the general collapsed on the ground, Riese bent over him and continued pounding his face until the man didn't move. Most of the man's facial bones were sunken, crushed. He was no longer recognizable and no longer breathing. Even though his former general was dead, the only regret Riese had was that it had been too quick.

Riese spat on the man and slowly stood, wiping blood from his bruised fist. He hurried to Odrissus and dropped to the ground beside her. He rolled her slightly and rested her head on his lap. Her blue eyes stared at him. A weak smile formed on her lips. She panted to breathe.

"Odrissus," Riese said. Tears formed in his eyes, and he brushed her long red hair with his fingers. "Don't die, my love and my lady."

She looked at him with sad eyes. She said, "I love you. Take care of our boys."

"Where are they?"

"In the cellar. They are safe."

Riese's voice shook as he said, "I'm sorry I was not here."

"It's not your fault. I almost stopped them all."

"You did well, my wife."

Her breathing slowed. He brushed her red hair from her face. Her cheeks were getting colder. He leaned over and kissed her lips. She smiled again and her eyes went distant. Her breathing stopped.

Riese wailed. His voice echoed through the forest. Birds and animals fled deeper into the forest. He clenched his fists and shook them at the heavens. Veins popped up on his arms and forehead as he flexed muscles throughout his entire body in rage. At that moment, his fury was enough that he could kill a bear with his bare hands. He continued growling like a mad animal until his vision darkened, and he collapsed beside Odrissus.

When he awakened, he closed her eyes, leaned over, and pressed his cheek against hers. Tears flowed, wetting her hair, and he wrapped his arms around her lifeless body and held her. His heart was torn. He felt empty inside.

Riese walked through the forest until he found his blade and returned to Yerdrick's body. He swung the blade up over his head and quickly hacked downward, decapitating the general that he hated.

Riese returned to Odrissus, picked her up, and marched through the forest until he came to his house. Before he went to get his sons, he placed Odrissus on their bed, gently fixing her hair and crossing her arms across her chest. He wrapped the blanket she had made over her body, and one last time, he kissed her cheek, which now was colder than marble. He left her, went down into the cellar, and found his boys sitting in the corner playing with the wooden animals he had carved them.

"Come Jez and Marc," Riese said, trying not to let his voice waver. "It's time to go."

Riese saddled his old horse, which he had retired from long trips and only used to plow their small garden. He placed the twins upon the saddle, returned to the house and gathered the best weapons and tools they had. After he placed these into the saddlebags, he went to the cellar, took several oil lanterns, lit them, and then tossed them down the stairs where they shattered. The flames ignited the oil. He hurried back to his horse and his sons, and led the horse by the bridle reins.

Before he went down the next ridge, he turned to see the small hut engulfed in flames. Although he no longer claimed the traditions of his brethren and ancestors, he did want to guarantee that Odrissus entered the heavenly afterlife. The general and his two soldiers, on the other hand, were left for the crows and wolves where he hoped their unburned bodies awakened and suffered their rightful torment in the depths of the hottest hell.

CHAPTER 44

The memories caused rage to burn through Riese as he drove the wagon to the gates. Remembering the loss of his wife, and now Jez, angered him. He had no problem taking out any of Waxxon's henchmen. He already despised them, but due to keeping his sons safe, he never openly engaged in attacks against them in Glacier Ridge. But secretly, when they stabled their horses with him, he sabotaged their riding equipment by weakening saddle straps, bridle bits, and embedding sharp burrs in their saddle blankets. While such small things weren't actual assaults toward the former brethren he now despised, it was a small thorn in their side that he considered a subtle forewarning of the stormy attack he'd eventually pursue.

Whenever any of the Vykings entered Glacier Ridge, they simply thought he was being a cordial stable master, but what they didn't know was that he cursed them beneath his breath and awaited the day when he could slaughter them like they had his fair Odrissus, and now that day had come.

Torches blazed on the stone pillars at each side of the gate. Massive oaks towered inside the gates near the watchtowers. The massive trees allowed the guards shade during the daylight and camouflaged hiding places after sunset. Watchmen above stood near more torches while others moved higher in the tree branches, invisible only if they did not move.

When the horse was within a few yards of Woodcrest's gate, a deep raspy voice beckoned from the tower. "That's close enough! Come no closer."

Riese pulled back on the reins.

The watchman shouted, "Who goes there?"

"You not recognize one of your own brothers?" Riese shouted back. He held up a lit lantern near his bearded face.

The man above leaned near the edge and looked down.

"What brings you out in the dead of night?"

"Delivery for Lord Waxxon," Riese replied.

"Oh? And what might that be?"

"Quite the trophy," Riese said. "I deliver to him one of the Dragon Skull Order."

Suddenly more curious guards surrounded the man in the tower, and although surprised, Riese never expressed it. However, he counted over a dozen men between the two gate towers, which meant that Zauber either underestimated the true number of Waxxon's guards or he had deceived them.

To make matters worse, several of the men that stepped into the glowing light of the blazing tower torches turned out to be archers. The Vykings didn't have archers. But these archers' armor and helms were something Riese immediately recognized. He had, on occasion, repaired some exactly like these in his smith shop. These archers were dark elves, which meant his party was in a more serious situation than the wizard had been led them to believe.

"Where is this man you speak of?" the guard asked.

"In the wagon bed."

"Dead?"

Riese shook his head. "Not quite yet. He's alive, but not in good health."

"So he could be interrogated?"

"If he awakens, yes."

A long rope ladder rolled down from the watchtower. Seconds later, one of Waxxon's guards climbed down while archers guarded him. He approached the driver's seat, took Riese's torch, and walked to the rear of the wagon. Riese's gaze went to the towers. The archers aimed their arrows at him.

The guard brought the torch over Lehrling's face. He felt for a pulse and gave a slight nod. He ran his finger over the Dragon Skull pendant.

He raised the torch with a broad grin and shouted, "He speaks the truth!"

The man held the torch and looked around the wagon. He stopped beside Riese again and asked, "What's the cage for?"

"The prisoner, of course."

"Then why taint he in it?" the guard asked.

Riese smiled evenly. "He's a bit large for that cage, don't you think? After he lost consciousness, I took him out to ensure he stayed alive. After all, dead men don't talk."

The Waxxon guard grinned and said, "They don't, do they? What exactly is wrong with him?"

Riese chuckled. "I'm not a physician. I just seek my compensation in gold from Lord Waxxon for finding him."

"Compensation, you say?" the man asked curiously.

Riese nodded.

"No one asks Lord Waxxon for compensation for our sworn duties."

"What?" Riese said angrily. He pointed at the golden button on the guard's shoulder pad. "What do you call that?"

"It's a medal of honor," the man replied.

"And isn't that compensation enough?" Riese asked with a harsh frown.

"My apologies, brother. I thought you meant gold *pieces*. Of course, there be medals for such trophy finds like yours."

Riese nodded. "That's all I ask."

Waxxon's soldier peered closer to Riese and his eyes widened with recognition. "Say, don't I know you?"

Riese studied the man's face. He shook his head. "You don't look familiar to me."

"Which of Waxxon's bands are you with?"

Riese replied, "I am the last of mine."

The man studied Riese's eyes suspiciously. Riese never flinched or looked away. He handed the torch back to Riese and motioned for the gate to be opened.

Where is Crukas? Riese wondered.

The gears of the wooden gate cranked and slowly opened inward. Something wasn't right, but Riese now had no choice but to go forward. Outnumbered possibly ten to one, whatever more resided on the other side of those walls might well be their demise.

Light poles lighted Woodcrest's modest intersecting streets. Atop the poles, housed in glass, were yellow glowing crystals that prevented the town from being completely shrouded in darkness during the night. On occasion, lighted candles flickered where nervous townspeople dared a peek outside their windows.

Roble hid in the shadows behind a trader's wagon that contained tanned hides tied in bundles. Shawndirea stood on the metal wagon wheel near him. The market square was divided by the intersection of two compacted roads. Although Woodcrest was small, it was a hardy trading town. Stringed dried fish dangled from the sloped roofs of small wagons. Small traders' huts lined the corners of the intersection but were boarded up for the night. Loaded wagons of grains, produce, and dried fish lined the streets. Apparently since Waxxon's men had taken over, they had shut down their trading routes, prohibiting Woodcrest from sending out their goods to neighboring towns and villages.

Woodcrest supplied Glacier Ridge with breads, flours, and ale they made from their farmed grains.

The smell of fresh bread and beer lingered in the still night air. Roble's stomach growled, but he forced himself to ignore his hunger.

Riese's loud voice soon drown the sound of Roble's growling stomach. They listened intently to the gate guard questioning the stable master's arrival.

A white marble statue of a new nude maiden gleamed beneath the closest light pole. At the base of the statue was a marble altar. A water dish rested atop the altar. Shawndirea noticed it and gasped.

"What is it?" he asked.

She replied, "The statue. It's in tribute to Aerlene."

"Who?"

"One of my mother's sisters long believed dead. It seems they worship her as a guardian to bless their crops and harvests."

Heavy iron clanked and groaned. Chain links clattered from the far end of the street to their left.

"The gates are opening," Roble said. "But did you hear what Riese said?"

She nodded.

"He offered Lehrling up. That wasn't part of the plan."

"Riese had to give reason why he was at the gate," she said. "Otherwise the guards might kill him. Few people, except bandits and rogues, travel the roads late at night."

"You don't think he'd really give Lehrling up?"

"Why would he?" she asked. "You don't trust many people."

"That was your advice."

"I know."

"Besides," Roble nodded. "I'm skeptical by nature. It's how you survive."

"Has Riese given you any reason not to trust him?" she asked.

"No, but we've given him reason to turn on us. As much as he hates

Crukas, we freed the thief. If Riese chose to exact revenge, now's the best time to get even."

"I doubt that's his choice, but the offer *did* get the gates open."

Roble nodded. "And I thought *that* was what Crukas agreed to do. So where is he?"

Shawndirea's brow furrowed. "That's a good question."

ODLON FOLLOWED the edge of the shadowed buildings along the wooden town wall until he neared the two guard towers at the gate. He favored the darkest crevices of the buildings well out of the arc of the yellow lanterns that brightened the main roadways.

Crouching low, he edged to the side wooden wall and slowly rose. He placed an arrow on the crossbow and drew back. Scanning the guards along the tower wall, he realized there were far more men guarding the gate than what Zauber had told them. And worse, posted with Waxxon's guards, there were dark elves, which were mortal enemies to his bloodline.

He quickly counted four dark elf archers and eight Waxxon Guards. He eased the tension on the crossbow and placed the arrow back in the quiver. At the gates stood four more guards at ground level.

"Dammit," Odlon whispered.

Why were dark elves in league with Waxxon?

Odlon was fast with any type of bow, and if there were only swordsmen to deal with, he could overpower these men in a matter of minutes. But four dark elf archers weighted the scale in their favor, not his.

And while it was true the green dragon armor Odlon wore could possibly thwart any arrows the dark elves possessed, they were the most accurate archers he might ever encounter on the war fields. He didn't wear a helm, and one quick headshot from a dark elf marksman would be his demise. Their eyesight was keen, and more so after the sun set.

He slinked further into the shadows and headed back to find Roble. He turned quickly when he heard Riese offer Lehrling to Waxxon's guards. He paused and listened to the ongoing conversation until the guards began winding the wheel to open the gate. Odlon sprinted through the dark town, looking for Roble, and hoping they had a better plan that enabled them to save Lehrling and set Woodcrest free. Since they had entered the center of Woodcrest by the wizard's spell, they were now trapped inside and by his estimate, greatly outnumbered.

~

CRUKAS TRIED to use his invisibility spell but couldn't since he was unable to verbally cast the incantation. He did not have to power to mentally will himself invisible. After all, he was only a novice in the realms of magic. The best he could do was hide behind a covered wagon where the townspeople had hung their herbs to dry.

His resentment toward being ordered to open the gate made him simply want to retreat and find another way out of Woodcrest. However, doing so meant losing his sight, and what good was a blind and mute thief? Besides, not helping Roble and the others possibly meant his own death by Waxxon's men for trespassing in their newly acquired town.

Crukas squatted lower and when he noticed movement along the top of the gate wall, he rolled beneath the wagon and crawled between the front metal wheels where he peered out to see the wall, but where he hoped they couldn't see him.

CHAPTER 45

*L*iving the life of a thief had enabled Crukas to have luxuries he'd never had otherwise. The notoriety for his fame had become his honor. He enjoyed hearing people whisper his name in taverns, towns, and in the bards' tales. There were disadvantages, too. Being a famous thief warned all vendors and wealthy travelers to keep a constant watch on him whenever he entered a town or city, which was why he hired knowledgeable sorcerers and apprentice wizards to teach him spells that allowed him to vanish in a crowd to escape quickly.

Crukas' childhood in Hoffnung was one filled with poverty and hunger. He learned to steal food in order to stay alive. He explored the sewers and other hidden passageways beneath the otherwise glorious city of Hoffnung, and once he learned the ease of slipping in and out of grates, through smelly drains, and dark trashy tunnels, he picked more expensive items to loot.

News soon caught the attention of guards about the young thief that no one could catch. His wanted poster intrigued someone else, too. Agretor, the leader of the thief guild in Hoffnung, found him in the sewers after Crukas had stolen rare jewelry from the wife of a city magistrate.

Crukas tried to escape, but instead, six other thieves appeared out of the shadows and surrounded him. Frightened like any teenage boy might be when confronted by a group of scarred, weapon-carrying thieves dressed in black hooded robes, Crukas cowered into a corner.

"What do you want?" Crukas asked, looking around at the cloaked figures. They tightened their circle around him, preventing him from fleeing.

Agretor lowered the hood on his tight-fitted robe. He was a gray-haired man, thin and muscular. Although an elderly man, he appeared agile and quick for his age. His bright blue eyes studied Crukas for several moments before offering a slight smile. "You have not gone unnoticed, boy."

"For what? What have I done?"

Agretor laughed heartily and the rest of his guild members did as well.

"Your thievery," Agretor said. "Although you're quite resourceful, you've drawn the attention of the city guards, which has in turn made it even harder for us to do our labors. You're good, but you need improvement. A great thief never allows himself to be seen."

The critique offended Crukas. Unable to contain his anger, he held up the ruby and diamond jeweled necklace. The large jewels glinted great radiance even in the dim torchlight. "How can you improve upon *this*? Have any of *you* ever stolen anything this valuable?"

Crukas studied the thieves' eyes, and he immediately realized that his revelation had been a horrible mistake. They couldn't hide their lust for the necklace. Several minutes passed before Agretor could reply. Finally, he said, "A great thief steals without immediate notice, often creating distractions that leave the victim to look at the misdirection and not upon the one that has stolen from them."

"I am getting better," Crukas replied.

"How long before a guard nabs you? They know what you look like." Agretor unrolled a tattered wanted poster with Crukas' image. He said, "It is a spitting image of you in every detail. So much so it makes me wonder if you stopped and *posed* for the artist to draw you?"

The other thieves chuckled, but their attention remained on the necklace clutched tightly in the young man's filthy fingers.

Crukas frowned at the bitter ridicule and their laughter.

But in a soothing tone, much like a father might offer corrective advice to a son, Agretor said, "Eventually, they will catch you. A rat-infested prison isn't a place you'd want to live your life, is it?"

Crukas shook his head.

Agretor smiled and said, "We can teach you how to be one of the best, only quicker and without stumbling through all the trial and error."

Crukas frowned and studied the men. "Why would you do that for me?"

Another within the thief party lowered her hood. Crukas was stunned to see a young female elven thief with coal black hair as one of their members. She sighed and shook her head. "Agretor is inviting you to join our guild. We can help you polish your skills."

Crukas smiled and looked from the girl back to Agretor. The old man nodded and said, "Darrath speaks the truth. Accept our invitation."

"And if I don't?"

Agretor shrugged. "We'll turn you over to the authorities. Where you have continually escaped them, you won't us. We cannot allow an unruly thief to tarnish our reputations. Rumors spread, and we truly don't want such an inexperienced thief like you to be falsely accused of being one of our own. Imagine the shame that would bring on us."

The thieves drew their daggers. Their eyes and intent focused upon him.

The blood drained from Crukas' face. He still recalled that moment of decision, and although he had not been given much choice but to join them, he never regretted siding with the guild. After all, no one is his or her own master.

Darrath smiled at Crukas and said, "I was about your age when they invited me. We never hunger or thirst. We have the finest of all things, but we don't announce our presence when we steal treasures. We strive to become invisible."

"She's right," Agretor said. "Our reputation is so well known that knights and noblemen have hired us to steal for them."

"Okay," Crukas said, nodding. Trying to mimic the importance of their guild, he replied, "I'd be honored to become a member of your society."

"Good," Agretor said, extending his hand to Crukas.

Crukas offered his small hand to shake, but Agretor shook his head.

"The necklace," Agretor said. "That's your contribution to join us."

Crukas was stunned. His stomach sickened at the thought of parting with his most recent prize, but the lust and greed in the rogues' eyes was alarming. None had sheathed their daggers even after he had accepted their invitation. They stepped closer to keep him pressed into the corner to prevent any attempt to escape. Their gazes made him fearful that if he didn't hand the necklace over, they'd kill him and toss his body into the rat-infested sewers. No one would ever miss him or look for him. He'd be forgotten. Forever.

Reluctantly, he handed to necklace to Agretor.

"Now," Agretor said, "Your training begins."

Crukas spent seven years in their guild, learning their tactics and secrets that eventually made him better at thievery than they were. After Agretor's death due to his old age, the guild disbanded to join rival guilds in various cities, but not before Crukas stole back the necklace from the treasure vault and fled from Hoffnung. Knowing they would pursue him for robbing the guild, Crukas moved through forests and from village to village, town to town, and city to city. Ever on the move, he kept them guessing where he was. Of course, he kept adding more stolen trophies to his list as well. That is, until he ventured to Glacier Ridge for the first time and stumbled into Darrath outside Hobskin's Tavern.

Her fury set harsh in her elven green eyes. She wanted the necklace and had Crukas actually had the necklace with him, she'd have slit his throat in an alley and taken it, regardless of the Glacier Ridge mantra. But after she patted him down and discovered he didn't have it, he convinced her that if she released him unharmed, he'd take her to where he had stashed the necklace.

Darrath lowered the blade and agreed. But instead, when they arrived at Ironwood, he turned her over to authorities, collected the bounty, and rode away a hero. He did this with each ex-guild member he came across. Glacier Ridge was the best place to wait because eventually the most successful thieves showed up to boast about their greatest thefts. The only disadvantage was Crukas didn't realize Riese had been watching and studying his ill-gotten deeds in a town where thieves roamed freely and without fear of being apprehended.

Thinking back on his actions, Crukas didn't feel much remorse. Without the former guild members he had lived with in the dank sewers of Hoffnung, Crukas could go to any town without fear of being revealed to guards or competing thieves who he was. The last thing he expected was becoming an enemy to Riese and being handed over to the Ironwood's town council to be hanged for the exact deeds he had turned in his former thieving guild members. And even more unexpected was being forced to *help* Riese, the very man that wanted Crukas to swing at the bottom of a rope.

Fate was funny like that sometimes.

*R*oble scanned the town. Footsteps steadily marched along the path. Due to how the wagons were lined along the crude intersecting streets, he was unable to see who walked closer. His hands rested on the hilts of two throwing knives.

A lantern swayed. The Waxxon guard walked past.

"Patrols," Shawndirea whispered.

Roble's heart hammered in his chest. His hands relaxed on his knives. He glanced at Shawndirea. She gave a half smile and a slight shrug, but her eyes revealed her nervousness as well.

Seconds passed and Odlon slipped up beside them.

Roble almost jumped in surprise at how silently Odlon moved.

Odlon whispered, "Zauber lied to us."

Roble turned with a harsh glare, frowning at the disturbing news. "What?"

Odlon nodded.

"What has he lied about?" Shawndirea asked.

"There are far more than a dozen of Waxxon's men here."

Stunned, Roble asked, "Are you certain?"

"Yes. More than that number are at the gate where Riese is entering," Odlon said. "And to make matters worse, dark elves are here as well."

Shawndirea gasped.

Roble glanced at her. He said, "I take it that that's bad?"

"Worse than you might imagine," she replied.

Odlon looked around, still in a whisper, he said, "Where did the wizard go? We have to get out of here."

Roble shook his head. "You went that direction, and he quickly went the other way. What about Crukas? Did you see him near the gate?"

"No. Not any sign of him."

"I thought you said that Zauber is trustworthy," Roble said.

Shawndirea nodded. "Yes, he is."

"Looks more like he has set us up."

"And why would he do that?" she asked with her fists planted on her hips.

"You tell me."

"Shh," Odlon said. "We don't have time for arguments."

Roble nodded. "I agree."

A flash of blue light caught Roble's attention. As fast as it gleamed, it disappeared. Then it shone brightly again for several seconds, then faded.

"Did you see it?" Roble asked.

Both Shawndirea and Odlon shook their heads.

"See what?" she asked.

"Come with me," Roble said.

Roble let her climb upon his shoulder. He slipped further away from the lighted intersection and into an area of the town shaded by thick, leafy trees. An old hut with a hay thatched roof almost blended in completely with the trees and strange vines that surrounded it. The blue light flashed again as fast as lightning bugs blink.

Odlon drew an arrow as they crept from the side of the road toward the dark building. Roble kept his hands near his knives, but when they came closer, the light gleamed again, but what attracted him to this building turned out to be a reflection off the building's crude window.

Roble turned. The light emitted from near the base of another building on the other side of the intersection.

"What do you think it is?" Roble asked.

Odlon shook his head. "No idea."

"You?" Roble asked Shawndirea.

"Not certain."

Roble pulled his throwing knives and said, "Let's find out."

They slowed near the intersection, and Odlon did a quick glance down the streets. When he was certain the guard wasn't heading their direction, they sprinted across to the building.

The blue light glinted again from a cellar door window. Roble and Shawndirea descended the steps and started to peer through the window when the door slowly creaked open.

"Careful," Odlon said, loading his bow and slipping past Roble.

"No weapons," an old woman said with a harsh, raspy voice. "We're peace-seekers here."

Roble sheathed his knives, and then he slowly placed his hand on Odlon's forearm and lowered the crossbow. Odlon looked at Roble with a confused glance.

"Our enemies are along the gates and the wall," Roble said. "We need assistance from anyone in Woodcrest that may help us."

Odlon nodded and placed the arrow into its quiver.

"Come inside," the old woman said, "before the damn bastard patrols head this way and see you."

Roble stepped inside with Shawndirea. Odlon followed and quietly pushed the door shut. Once the door closed, they were engulfed in near darkness. The only light in the small cellar room was the faint, crackling fire in her fireplace. The dim cellar was dank and smelled of various herbs, earth, incense, and oddly, the pleasantry of homemade stew—reminding Roble of his grandmother's house on family weekends.

Near where her voice spoke, something rustled in the corner, rasping and feathery in sound.

"That's better," the woman said. A bluish light shimmered, and it was then they could see her.

She sat in a wooden rocker that was constructed from dried thin saplings, possibly willow, judging by the bark's texture. In her lap was a lantern that held a blue glowing crystal, which made her features even more eerie to look upon. At first glance she appeared every bit like the evil crone images most people in the Overlands associated with a witch. Gazing at her sent chills up Roble's back. Her eyes were wide, bulging.

Her wrinkled thin face and long flowing hair seemed strange in the light of the blue crystal. She struck a match on the side of her rocker's armrest and lit a candle, next to her black crystal ball. Tapping the glass box on her lap, the blue crystal dimmed and went cold. The candle flame rose and revealed shelves filled with bottles of herbs, potions, and various animal skulls, claws, and bones. More shelves were lined with thick, aged books. Scrolls were tucked above and around various books as well.

On a perch behind her rocker was a white crow with deep blue eyes; exactly like those he had seen near Bausch's hanging body. On the floor a midsized gray kitten played with a dehydrated crimson newt.

Once the candlelight grew to full flame, they could see the old woman more clearly. Absent the blue light, her appearance was far less frightening. Her wrinkles weren't nearly as etched, her hair was smooth silver, but her aura remained mysterious. She was blind in her left eye, and her right eye was a milky white. Her few teeth and chin were soiled brown from snuff, and when she breathed, her nose whistled slightly.

Wanting to avoid offending her, Roble asked, "What is your name, my lady?"

She cackled wildly and waved her hands in the air. "Dispense with such nonsensical words and manners, Roble."

Astounded, Roble started to speak, but she held up a boney finger and shook her head. She studied him carefully. Brown drool leaked from the side of her mouth. He found it difficult to maintain eye contact but forced himself to be polite.

"Tis no need for questions, Overlander. You are not of the Dragon Skull Order, but yet, you wear their emblem and armor."

Roble tilted his head slightly to favor a bow as well as a nod. "While true, do know that we are here to restore order to Woodcrest."

She spat brown juice on the floor near other similar, drying stains. The little gray cat wrinkled its nose and smacked the dried newt away from the rocker and across the room, quickly scampering after it, quite possibly seeking refuge outside her spitting range.

Across the room a small fire crackled beneath a large black iron kettle. The stew in the kettle bubbled, and if Roble had his guess, it smelled very similar to vegetable soup. It was then that he realized how hungry he truly was. He had worried about so many other things that he had given little thought to eating, and what little they had eaten from Riese's rations had been hours earlier.

"Ah, nice gesture you offer, but you should know, Woodcrest's invaders hanged two of your order in the center of town when the sun was high in the sky yesterday. They also killed some of the town council members, too."

"Ma'am," Roble said softly.

"Haigla," she replied.

"Two of the Dragon Skull were killed?"

"Aye."

Roble shook his head. Although he didn't know any of the order other than Lehrling, he grieved. Their numbers dwindled on the side of order while Waxxon's number and chaos grew. If others within the Dragon Skull Order were as noble and caring as Lehrling seemed to be, they somehow needed to be preserved.

"And the dark elves?" Shawndirea asked. "Why have they come?"

"In time, little faery."

"Haigla," Roble said, "We were summoned into Woodcrest by a wizard."

Odlon stepped beside Roble and said, "Yes. Do you know where he might be?"

She smiled, revealing a mouth with few brown-stained teeth. "I suspect he's nearby."

"But—"

"By listening you learn much more than by speaking," she said. "You see, Woodcrest is a simple town of farmers, hunters, and gatherers. We're neither servers of the Light or the Darkness, but we pledge our devotion and allegiance to the one that blesses our harvest, Aerlene. While you say that you're here to aid us and possibly set us free, you must know why the greedy bastards are here in the first place."

"To find Lady Dawn," Roble said.

Haigla waved her index finger back and forth and placed it to her lips. "Now," she said, in a rough voice that creaked painfully as she spoke, "You overstep your thoughts, and doing so distorts the true nature of events, making you blind to understand the truth. There is more to this maddening occupation than Lady Dawn. They overtook this town, not in hopes of gaining her, but in expectation of finding another."

"Who?" Shawndirea asked.

"One of your very party, my dear."

Odlon and Roble exchanged glances.

"Who?"

"Crukas," Haigla said.

"Why do they want him?" Roble asked with sudden surprise.

"That you must find out from him. Why else would Waxxon's bastards overtake the only town that trades with Glacier Ridge, a town that houses and entertains despicable thieves? It's a far impossibility that Lady Dawn would ever pass this direction. There is, or shall I say, *was* no hope or harbor for innocents in Glacier Ridge. They do *not* seek her here."

"Perhaps there is reason why Riese wanted to deliver Crukas to Ironwood himself," Roble thought aloud.

"Ironwood?" Haigla asked.

Roble nodded. "They want him hanged for his crimes. Riese assumes it is because Crukas betrays his own by tricking other thieves into joining him to steal treasures, only he turned them in for rewards."

"Thieves are cunning," she said. "Difficult to trust."

Odlon nodded and said, "He never reached the gates like he was supposed to do."

"Could be the dark elves," Shawndirea said.

"You defend him?" Odlon asked.

"No," she said, "But *what* turned you back?"

The elf's jaw tightened, but he gave no reply. He looked back at Haigla.

Roble squeezed Odlon's shoulder. "You know, she is probably right. But worse is that Riese is entering the gate with Lehrling ailing. They are no match for the guard or the dark elves."

"Those defiled, unholy dark elves," she said with rage rising in her voice. "Despicable excuse for wasted air breathed."

Odlon gave Roble a quick side-glance and whispered, "That's how I'd define them as well."

"Why are they here?" Shawndirea asked; her eyes were filled with worry.

"The dark elves are here for reasons different than the plundering Vyking bastards. They attempted to take the area soon after they destroyed the monastery, but another intervened. They have only joined the Vyking cause, but I assume their loyalty to the Vykings is only temporary. Once they have aided them in their quest, they hope to gain Woodcrest as their own."

"So they are indirectly after Crukas as well?" she whispered.

"Aye," Haigla said, "And the one true disadvantage Woodcrest has is that we do not have a Holy Priest or wizard. Otherwise, the dark elves would never dare set their attention on us. What say you, Odlon, Dragon-slayer of Eyllisathem?"

"I am nothing more than an archer."

Shawndirea frowned and said to Haigla, "You practice magic and healing, why have the dark elves *not* set their attention on you?"

She cackled and replied, "Because they think me daft and harmless."

The daft Roble could envision but harmless? Hardly. The woman had more power than what she wished to reveal, even to them.

Haigla kept her attention on Odlon for a moment longer. She said, "You wear the armor of a dragon once contained in magic of its own. Surely there is some power the armor offers you for protection."

He nodded. "Yes, but for my own health. Nothing more."

Haigla shrugged. She studied Roble and tilted her head to the side. She pointed at him and said, "You are touched by magic, Overlander, and not that of your faery. There is something odd about it, and not a power I've sensed before. Who has enchanted something for you?"

Roble shrugged. "I've seen no one, but Zauber believes this armor was blessed by an enchanter."

"Or cursed," she said in a near mumble. Her lower jaw trembled. Taking her twisted cane, she rose from her chair and hobbled in a stooped position, moving toward him. The ice crow stretched its white wings, flapped, and quickly flew to perch upon her shoulder. Its blue piercing eyes watched Roble and Shawndirea with keen interest.

She hobbled past them toward the bubbling pot of stew, and Roble asked, "Are you a healer?"

Haigla stopped walking. Without turning, she said, "I have learned the ways of old remedies, if that's what you ask."

"Lehrling suffers from an infection deep in his chest," Roble said. "Do you have something that can cure him?"

"Lehrling is of the Dragon Skull Order, is he not?"

"Yes."

"And he's on the wagon with Riese that enters the gates as we speak?"

"Yes."

"His dangers are not with the infection, Overlander," she said, "But with surviving the hands of Waxxon's bastards."

Haigla made her way to the boiling pot, reached above the mantle, and took down a stack of clay bowls. "Come, come," she said. "Fill your bellies."

"But we must help Riese and Lehrling," Roble protested, but his stomach sided with her offer. The food looked appetizing and warm.

"Hunger is a distraction, Overlander. Eat. Time is still on our side. Besides, I'm an old woman. Feeding visitors is deeply-rooted within me."

She handed Odlon and Roble a clay bowl, and then she took a wooden dipper and poured steamy soup into their bowls. She pointed to a small table in the corner of the room well out of sight of the door's window. As they seated themselves, she brought a wooden thimble full of soup for Shawndirea.

"Sit, eat, and wait. The night's truly about to become very interesting, if not quite troublesome."

CHAPTER 47

*R*iese stepped down from the wagon. His heavy boots thudded along the street while he walked. He held his hammer tightly in his hand. Without making obvious surveillance of the wall guards, he counted four dark elves, a race that he loathed simply because they often lived in dark caverns and ransacked villages during the night. These elves trained their bows on him, and he knew if he made any sudden movements, they'd fire without hesitation.

In Glacier Ridge he had encountered a few dark elves, but most didn't like exploring the colder regions like he and his Vyking race thrived within. But other than that, the only other thing he knew about them was how they thirsted to shed blood and kill more than his Vyking brethren did.

Two large guards wound the gears to close the gates while two more headed to the rear of the wagon to get Lehrling. Ever mindful of the dark elves, Riese placed his heavy hammer into the loop on his belt. They eased back on their bowstrings.

Lehrling coughed when the men brought him into a seated position on the back of the wagon. His eyes parted slightly, but then his head lulled back again. He remained unconscious.

"What's wrong with him?" One guard asked.

"Not sure," Riese replied. "He's been that way for most of the trip. I wouldn't get too close to his face if I were you. You might catch whatever he has."

Lehrling coughed again and both guards cringed.

Riese watched the two men loop their arms around Lehrling and carry his dead weight. "Where are you taking him?" Riese asked.

"The old town council where our general awaits. You should come. I'm sure he'll want to speak with you personally."

I'm sure, too. Riese thought. *But there has to be a way out of it.*

Another Waxxon guard circled from behind Riese. His greedy eyes stared at the wagon bed. "Any other wares you have stored in there?"

"Just weapons I've crafted," Riese replied.

"Ooh, may I?" the man asked. Although of Vyking blood, he seemed different, or perhaps something was wrong with him. Excitement was not an emotion his race seldom expressed, and any passion Riese ever possessed was forever gone after the death of Odrissus.

The older Vyking searched through the many blades, axes, and swords Riese had setting in the wagon bed. "You made these?"

Riese's eyes narrowed, and he gave a nod.

"You're a masterful smith, that you are."

"Thanks."

The old man brushed his gray beard with his muscled fingers. He looked at a short sword, lifted it, admired the blade, and quickly set it back down. Then he grabbed another and repeated the process.

"Oh, so nice. Such quality. What be your name?" the man asked.

"Riese," he replied without thinking. "And you?"

"Nordell."

Returning to his trader mentality he exhibited so well in Glacier Ridge, Riese smiled at the old man and said, "Great to make your acquaintance."

"Aye, same to you." Again the man turned his attention to the blades. His mind raced while he touched each one. He shook his head. "Such admirable quality."

Riese crossed his arms and studied the old man. In many ways the man acted like a small child searching through toys in a shop but didn't have enough gold to purchase any one of them.

"Nordell?" Riese asked.

Nordell's timid eyes glanced from the weapons to Riese. He wrung his nervous fingers together. "Yes?"

"Pick any weapon. Any one at all, and it's yours."

"Free?" he asked with wide eyes. "No gold?"

Riese nodded. "Free. A gift to you."

Nordell nervously shook his head. "Ah, no. No, no, no. Can't. Wouldn't be right."

"Go on," Riese said. "Otherwise, you'll hurt my feelings."

The old man straightened his beard with his hands, over and over, looking at the weapons and then glancing up at Riese. "Any one?"

"Any one," Riese agreed.

"I like this one," Nordell said, picking up a short sword. A few seconds later, he put it down and grabbed another. "No, this one. This one's better."

"Are you satisfied with that one?" Riese asked.

Nordell studied the broad blade of the Vyking sword. He nodded.

Riese smiled and said, "It's yours."

Tears moistened the old man's eyes.

Riese said heartily in his deep voice, "Nordell, you're a strong warrior and the blade will carry out much justice in your care."

The old man smiled with satisfaction and pride.

"What are you doing?" another of Waxxon's guards said to Nordell. He took the blade and set it back down on the wagon. "Leave it be!"

Angered, Riese stepped toward the man.

"You keep out of this," the man said to Riese.

"I gave Nordell the sword. It is his."

"Nordell cannot have a sword," the man said.

"And who are you to make that decision?" Riese asked.

"Name's Verlon, and everyone knows Nordell is *touched*. He cannot be trusted with a blade."

Sadness filled Nordell's eyes. His shoulders slumped, and he looked down at his feet.

"And why is that?" Riese asked.

"Are ye deaf?" Verlon asked, tapping the side of his own head. "He's touched. Not stable."

"Has he ever hurt anyone with a blade?"

Verlon nodded. "Once. Long ago."

While Riese kept Verlon's attention, Nordell held up a short dagger for Riese to see. Nordell grinned and nodded. He pointed at the dagger and then toward himself, asking if he could have it instead. Riese gave a quick nod. Nordell slid the dagger behind his belt and adjusted his vest to cover the dagger's hilt.

Once the old man hid the dagger, Riese waved his hands in feigned surrender and said to Verlon, "I'm sorry, brother. I didn't realize. But if he's unstable, why does he journey with you?"

Verlon's nose crinkled with disgust. "He's King Obed's nephew. Keeping him with us prevents him from weighing upon Lord Waxxon's nerves."

"I see," Riese said.

"Come Nordell," Verlon said, "We go watch the Dragon Skull's interrogation. As will you, smith."

The man looked back at Riese and the blacksmith nodded. He allowed the two men to get a few yards beyond the wagon, and he paused near the wagon seat. To Marc, he whispered, "Stay still. Sorry for having you stay hidden, but if you move, those archers will kill you. I'll be back soon."

He waited for his son to reply, but no words came; only light snoring.

Riese hurried to catch the others. The last thing he wanted was for them to start interrogating Lehrling. He knew what his people did to make men speak. The overweight old man would die for certain, if whatever disease he had didn't kill him first.

CHAPTER 48

*R*oble and Odlon each ate three bowls of the tasty warm stew. Revived energy vibrated through them, releasing their tensions and fatigue. Shawndirea drank half the thimble of soup but declined more when Haigla brought her a thimble filled with honey ale. She drank it merrily. While they ate and drank, the old woman busied herself by placing herbs into another boiling pot, reading various scrolls, and chanting in a language unfamiliar to Roble.

The old lady didn't offer much more information while they ate; her attention and devotion lay elsewhere. Roble thought it odd that she hadn't questioned why a wingless faery was accompanying the elf and he. Although she did insinuate the faery was his, and this time, Shawndirea didn't protest such a directed conclusion. Perhaps Haigla had already spoken with Zauber and learned of their arrival and quest, or it could well be the news of their journey had already spread throughout the land.

Although Crukas had killed two ratmen to free Shawndirea, it was possible dozens more of the Ratkin had escaped Glacier Ridge well before the Plague-bringer arrived. For what reasons he didn't truly understand, he believed the ratmen thrived in large groups. Perhaps it was due to his knowledge of rats and their social inclinations, and he simply concluded the ratmen were similarly society minded.

A couple more thoughts came to Roble. Why had the ratmen so desperately sought to take Shawndirea? What was their purpose for getting her? And rats had been a big part in spreading diseases and plagues. Could there be a direct correlation between the ratmen being in Glacier Ridge and the Plague-bringer following soon after?

The gray kitten leapt to an empty chair and watched Shawndirea drink from the tiny thimble. Crouching low, the kitten rested its chin on its forepaws, shook its hindquarters, and sprang into the air to capture her. The kitten jumped, its protruded claws in its forepaws lengthened, ready to slash into her.

Shawndirea rolled to the side and shot a ball of green energy from her fingertips, which knocked the kitten off balance and frazzled it. When it landed on the floor, its tail fur was frizzled and puffed. The wide-eyed gray kitten hissed and ran across the room, hiding under the rocking chair.

The white crow squawked with what seemed amused approval.

The sound of a horn blared in the center of Woodcrest's intersection. Odlon rose from his chair and marched to the window. The horn sounded three more times.

Near the intersecting streets he watched a crowd of Vykings gather, Riese standing amongst them. Lehrling, still limp and motionless, was draped between two of the large men. Other men came and placed Lehrling's wrists inside metal cuffs welded to long iron chains. After securing Lehrling's wrists, two more men pulled the chains, raising his arms up above his head. The chains hoisted him upward, but his head remained slumped and faced the ground.

Riese simply stood there with no emotion on his face.

The horn sounded again.

Odlon reached for the doorknob.

"Not yet," Haigla said. "Not . . . yet."

Roble hurried to look out the window. Seeing Lehrling standing helplessly, the urge to help overcame him. A man walked toward Lehrling with a thick leather whip in hand.

Roble grabbed the doorknob and twisted. The door came ajar for a brief second, and then something similar to a harsh wind, only more powerful, slammed it shut.

"I said, '*not yet!*'"

Roble and Odlon turned to face her. Strange electrical energy flowed from her hands. She touched her black crystal ball. Colors swirled within the dark globe.

"Come watch and learn," she said.

Roble tried the door again. He tugged furiously with both hands, but the door didn't budge. They were sealed inside.

In spite of their frustration, Roble and Odlon walked to the crystal ball. Images of the intersection where Lehrling hung came into view. The muscled man with the whip drew back, ready to strike. Sadly, all Roble and Odlon could do was watch.

~

THE MAN BROUGHT BACK the whip. Bloodlust gleamed in his comrades' eyes.

"Wait!" Riese shouted, stepping forward.

Verlon frowned with fury. "How dare *you* interrupt the interrogation? You brought him here!"

Verlon stepped toward Riese with his sword drawn.

Riese said, "He's in no condition for such torture, especially if it's answers that you seek."

"One lash should spring 'em awake," Verlon said, pacing before Riese.

Riese shook his head. "One lash will probably kill him."

From the darkness of the street, another voice called, "What's the ruckus? Carry on, Verlon!"

"Sorry, General Quenid," Verlon said. Spittle frothed the sides of his mouth, and he pointed at Riese. "He delays the interrogation."

The name made Riese's stomach tightened. He recalled Yerdrick's threat that his brother would seek vengeance for his death. However, recalling Odrissus' murder allowed Riese's fury to quickly overtake his nerves and readied Riese to seek vengeance of his own.

General Quenid came into view, and all the other Vykings behind Riese dropped to one knee and bowed. Even Verlon dropped and bowed, but Riese turned and faced the man, standing with evident spite.

"You should know your place," General Quenid said. He was heavily armored and wore his metal helm with pride. His long sandy brown hair spilled out from beneath the helm. He was muscled, stood a good six inches taller than Riese, and was probably fifty pounds heavier. He carried a large round shield in his left hand and in his right was a great sword, which was nicked and scarred from his many battles. And if Riese accurately guessed, based on a general's reputation, the sword had been used to behead many prisoners.

The man's long beard hung past his belt but was deftly braided every ten inches. His piercing eyes narrowed as he stared down at Riese. "What? You *still* won't bow? You will learn the price for defying me, dog."

Riese spat at the man's feet. Quenid's eyes widened and then narrowed from his sudden fury. The other Vykings gasped and became strangely quiet.

"What is your name so that we may announce to the world when I send you to the River Styx?"

"Guess," Riese replied.

The general huffed. His nose flared. He eyed Riese with a murderous glare. "You're not of my band of warriors, but your face is very familiar. I can't place you, but defiance is not something I tolerate. Your traitorous words have announced your death sentence. I will cut your tongue from your head."

Riese grinned. "I'd like to see that."

Quenid glanced around at all his men while he paced back and forth, sizing Riese up. Perhaps he wondered why a man like Riese, who was dressed in simple leather armor and carried a heavy blacksmith hammer, dared to challenge a general dressed in his warrior armor. He glanced at Riese, who continued his defiant smug-filled glare, and then he looked to his men. None of them dared a glance upward. "Who knows this fool?"

"Riese," Verlon said without glancing up.

"Come again?"

Verlon dared to look up and said with a stronger voice, "When he entered the gates, he said that his name is Riese."

The name rocked Quenid. His eyes widened with immediate recognition. He turned to face Riese yet again.

"Now, I know you," he hissed and spittle flew from his mouth. "You killed my brother." Quenid's eyes grew darker than coal.

"You shall join him soon,' Riese said.

Quenid laughed heartily and then spoke to his squadron. "You see how this defiant traitor speaks to your General? Here stands the man who murdered my brother, General Yerdrick."

"He's dead because he slaughtered my wife in cold blood," Riese said.

The kneeling Vykings shifted and some stood, grabbing their blades. Verlon rose, too, and he drew his blade as well.

"Your wife? She was the harlot from the bay where you killed three of your blood brothers to win her? That's what their deaths were for?" Quenid's face flushed red. Veins in his forehead and throat bulged like thick vines. "Today vengeance for Yerdrick's death and your brothers comes with your blood!"

"No," Riese replied, "Today, you meet your brother in death, and if the fires of the eternal abyss exist, it heartens me to hope you suffer forever."

Riese yanked his heavy hammer from the belt loop and caught the edge of Quenid's blade just inches from his face. Metal clashed and sparks flew. The general's strength matched the man's muscular size. He was a strong opponent, and that clearly gave him the upper hand over Riese. Both sought vengeance and that desire increased their strength, however, Riese had the added measure of love lost, which gave him more reason to kill than Quenid's brotherly oath. Riese had held Odrissus, saw the fleeting love and life vanish in her eyes, felt her body grow cold, and listened to her last breath before she left him forever. That weighed more in Riese's favor than the report of Yerdrick's death had to Quenid.

Quenid tapped his sword against the side of his round shield to set the challenge for Riese to take his best shot. Riese grinned. All he was equipped with was his hammer. Was the general that worried that Riese might actually overtake the man? Clearly, even Quenid's men could see the unbalanced nature of the fight, which at best proved Riese's bravery far exceeded their own general's.

Riese had not actually fought combat style since his days under Yerdrick's command, other than having to kill Yerdrick himself. But Riese thrived on challenges and had often fought several men at once during his raiding days. He wondered how rusty his skills might prove now, but armor-wise, he knew he was at a disadvantage. There was only one thing he could do to increase the odds. Sharp wit.

Riese rushed Quenid with his hammer raised high, which was the needed distraction he wanted. As Quenid brought the shield around to block the attack, Riese leapt upward and kicked Quenid's round shield full force with both feet. The weighted impact knocked the general backwards. Using the momentum of the kickback, Riese spun and quickly brought the hammer around, striking Verlon in the side of the head. The hammer made Verlon's helmet ring. Verlon groaned and toppled, landing hard on the road on his back. The jarring pain rattled the sword from his hand. Verlon winced and clutched the sides of his head with his hands.

Riese tossed his hammer to his left hand, rolled, grabbed Verlon's loose sword, and quickly found footing on the other side of the road beneath one of the light poles. Quenid, although huge, moved swiftly. He rushed Riese, striking hard and fast, but Riese parried the blows with the sword, and then battered Quenid's round shield with his smith hammer.

Back and forth, they swung at one another, rage burning in their eyes. They sought to draw blood, but the other quickly blocked each attempt. The surrounding Vykings cheered at the vicious battle, but Riese ignored their shouts, jeers, and praise.

Being a sword-maker, Riese identified the weaknesses in the general's blade. Several deep grooves were in great need of repair, but those notches often were considered marks of triumph in battles where the blade had drawn life's blood. Those nicks Riese kept his attention on.

Quenid brought his sword overhead and downward into a harsh side-swipe, hoping to catch Riese off-guard, but Riese countered and easily deflected the blade. Perhaps the general's heavy armor weighed him down because the huge man was losing stamina fast. His breathing was labored, heavy. Sweat beaded from beneath his helm and dripped down his face.

Riese remained agile and his light armor allowed him to dodge side to side with ease. Using his quickness, Riese infuriated Quenid. Where Quenid expected Riese to be when he lunged, Riese was not. The more he missed his mark, the more Riese taunted the general, and Riese discovered the lighter broad sword Verlon had dropped was more effective for quicker assaults than most Riese had carried on the battlefields before.

Riese's newfound blade was more solid with fewer dents, which indicated that Verlon had not fought with a sword very often. Or, he had just had the blade crafted for him. Whichever was the case, Riese chose to capitalize on the weak points in Quenid's blade.

Quenid huffed a deep breath and brought the sword downward. Riese noticed a wide notch in the blade, spun around to add momentum, and connected a direct strike at the weakest point in the general's blade. The blade shattered. Quenid's eyes widened. The rattling sensation jarred the hilt from his hand. He winced ever so slightly but enough that Riese predicted their battle to end soon.

Normally, an automatic defeat landed to the man whose weapon broke as this meant the man was defenseless, but this wasn't a duel, it was a match to the death. Honor meant a lot to his brethren, so Riese wasn't too worried about another warrior interceding. From the disappointed looks on their faces, he assumed they felt ashamed of Quenid's performance.

Riese came at the general, swinging the sword hard, connecting against the round metal-framed wooden shield, and when he brought back the sword, he countered with the hammer, battering the shield. Over and over, he smashed with everything he had. Fear overcame the general, and he backed his way to the intersection in retreat. His act of cowardice brought jeers from his own followers.

Riese didn't let up, but at the same time, he also didn't see Verlon rise to his feet behind him. Verlon shook his head and blinked several times. When he no longer staggered, he pulled a long dagger from a sheath on his belt and crept slowly toward Riese from behind.

CHAPTER 49

Odlon, Roble, and Shawndirea peered into the crystal ball. Nosiness got the best of the gray kitten and it watched the activity within the tiny globe of light but remained ever leery of getting too close to the faery.

When the man came at Lehrling with the whip, Shawndirea cringed. Roble and Odlon turned toward the door, hands ready on their weapons.

"Wait," Haigla said.

Roble turned and in frustration, he said, "They're going to kill him."

The old woman shook her head. "Look," she said.

Inside the ball, they watched Riese stepped in between the man and Lehrling.

"See?" Shawndirea told Roble, "I told you that he was only telling the guards what he did in order to get inside the gates."

Roble smiled with a bit of momentary relief.

When Quenid stepped into the town crossroads, Roble and Odlon exchanged worried glances.

"We have to get out there," Roble said.

Odlon nodded.

Haigla shook her head. "If you go out there, they will kill you without hesitation. Riese is one of their race. The other Vykings give him respect, but you, an elf and human? No. They will take pleasure in cleaving you to bits with their axes. Let's see what your comrade is capable of."

～

RIESE LUNGED FORWARD with the sword, hoping to bring the hammer in low when Quenid blocked, but the general seemed to guess Riese's strategy and flung the shield up hard into Riese's chin. Blood flew from his busted lips and the impact of the blow spun Riese around. Bright lights that resembled shots of lightning danced behind his closed eyes. He hit the ground, narrowly missing Verlon's blade, and rolled quickly to rise to his feet.

Dazed, Riese blinked and shook his head. The world seemed black for several moments. His vision blurred. He staggered and wobbled but managed to keep his balance. While Riese tried to compose himself and kept enough restraint to prevent passing out, Verlon circled around behind Riese again, seeking to stab him before Riese noticed his presence.

Quenid grinned, roared, and rushed at Riese, lifting the round shield high over his head in order to batter Riese senseless. Riese spun and brought the hammer into Quenid's metal breastplate, denting the plate and knocking the breath out of the man. The shield slid along the hard road while Quenid bent forward and clutched his ribs. He wheezed.

Riese braced himself against his hammer to catch his breath. He wiped blood from his mouth and chin. The taste of iron coated his tongue. His ears rang and his vision came and went. Gazing around the other men, none offered to intervene. Disappointment and disapproval reigned in their eyes. He wondered if it was because their general had retreated rather than stand and fight or face death bravely.

Verlon eased up behind him, preparing to stab Riese in the right kidney. He drew back to shove the blade, and suddenly Verlon screamed in pain and cursed. His dagger dropped from his hand. Verlon fell face first on the road, writhing and trying to pull the steel dagger from his own back. In a matter of minutes blood pooled in a large circle beneath him. His fingers twitched slightly.

Alarmed, Riese glanced back to see Nordell standing over Verlon. Nordell frowned and spat on Verlon. Nordell's crazed eyes met Riese's, and Nordell grinned a broad smile. Riese smiled back and gave a nod of gratitude. Nordell placed his foot against Verlon's back and yanked his dagger free. He wiped away the blood with his tunic and held the blade up, admiring it with an odd hypnotic grin on his lips.

Verlon's backstabbing attempt had gotten him exactly what he deserved. Riese had never fought alongside another Vyking that lacked enough fortitude to attack an enemy head on. Verlon had proven he was more cowardly than Quenid.

Riese took a deep breath, stood, and arched his back. Quenid turned, picked up the shield, and took several steps to stand in the intersection with Riese. Although Quenid stood there, the confidence in his eyes had faded. Perhaps he had overestimated Riese, and now, he no longer believed he was superior to the blacksmith, but the challenge to the death remained. He slipped his arm through the loop and secured his grip on the shield. He nodded.

Riese took his hammer and swung. The blow splintered the front of the shield and the *thwack* echoed throughout Woodcrest. He drew back again, and Quenid squinted his eyes shut. The hammer cracked the shield with enough force that the wood planks broke free of the iron bands and dropped to the ground.

Quenid flung the metal frame down on the road. He placed his hands to his sides and gave a nod for Riese to finish him. Before Riese moved, another Vyking tossed Quenid a dagger, hilt first. Quenid caught and readied it. He grinned.

Riese looked at the blade and immediately his mind carried him to Odrissus' final moments. The dagger looked exactly like the one Yerdrick had stabbed her with. Rage surged through Riese.

He no longer saw Quenid before him. Yerdrick's face carved out in Quenid's features. The accurate resemblance left no doubt they had been blood brothers, but to Riese, the two men were one in the same. He saw the blade thrust into Odrissus as though the horrid event was taking place all over again. In his fury, rage, and loss, Riese charged at Quenid full force.

Riese swung the sword, but Quenid deflected it with the dagger, which proved the general's skill, but without a shield, Quenid was not fast enough to stop the hammer. The hammer clanged harshly against the general's right pauldron. The strike crushed his shoulder, breaking bones and several ribs.

General Quenid gnashed his teeth and released a seething growl of pain. Before the man opened his eyes, Riese slashed Quenid's throat with the blade. The general's eyes widened again. He clutched his throat with bloody hands and dropped to his knees.

Riese whispered into Quenid's ear, "Never forget my name and tell your brother who sent you to him."

He spat in the general's face and then he drove the killing blow through the dented breastplate and into the man's heart. He yanked the blade free and allowed Quenid's lifeless body to drop. The leaves in the trees suddenly rustled. A harsh wind blew through Woodcrest.

Riese lowered his weapons. Heat rose off his tired, aching muscles. A sensation of momentary victory rushed through him. He gazed around the crowd of what he once considered his brethren. Even now, if they welcomed him, he knew that he'd never want to rejoin their plundering ways. His life had changed. He had changed into what he hoped was for the better.

The Vykings drew their weapons and shields and circled around him.

CHAPTER 50

*I*n the darkest area of Woodcrest behind the herbalist's storage shed, Zauber took his staff and outlined a large circle in the soft earth. Within the circle, he used his finger and carefully etched out symbols and runic letters.

He pulled his wizard dagger, Meoriki, from its sheath and pricked the tip of his left index finger, allowing two drops of blood to fall in the dead center of the circle while he softly chanted a spell long rehearsed, but seldom used.

The wind grew stronger, rustling tree branches in mad swirling motions, and blowing his long black beard into twirls. His robes ruffled. With his eyes closed, he didn't notice these changes. In his right hand he rotated his black wand in a counter-circular motion. The wind intensified, so he took the orb from his robe pocket. It glowed brightly, giving his face a yellow tint.

Thick leafy branches whirled in the oak canopy, which wasn't any distraction. His focus of power kept his attention on the bright orb. Seconds later, the orb changed, and through the crystal he saw the furrowed face of Queen Istrell. Sorrow, heartache, and a tinge of fading rage weighted her expressions.

Softly, he sent a message through the orb in a quiet whisper.

"Istrell," he said, "Shawndirea is safe. She's journeying back home to you. Be at peace. She will return."

Although Istrell couldn't see Zauber through the crystal orb, her mind, soul, and heart jumped at the words. She peered around at the colorful crystals she consulted in her palace tree when she sought answers concerning Shawndirea's safety and whereabouts. Her eyes brightened. A slight smile curled her aged lips. She suddenly glowed and her facial muscles eased. She didn't look as aged. Youth softened her lines of worry.

"Hope," Zauber whispered with a smile, "can turn back time."

RIESE HELD his weapons and studied the crowd around him. With only ten or so warriors standing by with their weapons in hand, he calculated his attacks and how quickly he could drop several before they overpowered and killed him. Sacrificing himself, however, offered no reward for his son or Lehrling, for that matter.

Then his eyes were drawn to the buildings and huts further behind where the Vykings stood circled. He saw citizens of Woodcrest had stepped outside their homes to watch the battle. Their frightened eyes held little hope. Riese captured the gazes of the angered circle of Vykings, as they pressed closer. The closer they came, the less room he had to counter their attacks. Besides, he was exhausted. He tossed his weapons to the ground.

The thought occurred to him that his former brethren had not killed all of the townspeople like they often did in plundering raids, which meant they didn't want to maintain Woodcrest for a post. They were here for something else. *What exactly*, he wondered.

"You fought more noble than either of them," the eldest Vyking said, pointing at Quenid and Verlon. He motioned for the others to lower their axes and swords. They did without question or protest. "You have no fear of death, but a haunting rage to contend with."

"General Yerdrick killed my wife. We had two small boys at the time. My rage will never end."

The old man nodded. His eyes testified to losses of his own. He said, "That is understandable."

His saddened blue eyes looked into Riese's. The rugged old man wore scars of battle on his wrinkled face, his arms, and several of his fingers were missing. His long gray hair was pulled back in a ponytail. His beard was frazzled but clean.

"I did this," Riese said, "for her."

"I heard," the old man said. "It is why we won't kill you unless forced. But there's still a bounty on your head. King Obed will want us to bring you back after our mission here is complete. You could argue your case before him. Will you come peacefully?"

"I will, but under one condition," Riese said.

"And what is that?"

Riese pointed at Lehrling and said, "That you spare him."

The old man frowned. "Are you in allegiance with the Dragon Skull Order?"

Riese shook his head. "No," he replied.

"Then tell me why his life is important to you?"

"He's a noble man. He has done no crime."

"He is an enemy of Lord Waxxon and an enemy of Waxxon is an enemy of our king."

"You are?" Riese asked.

"Hordus."

"So answer this for me. What has the Dragon Skull Order done to deserve being tracked down and killed like wild dogs?"

Hordus said, "Lord Waxxon's orders."

"And the cause?"

Hordus shrugged. "Didn't give one."

Angered, Riese said, "Since when have our brethren laid down our allegiance for another man? How is Lord Waxxon tied to King Obed?"

"That is an answer only the king can give. But be forewarned, asking such questions will get your head removed well before you can plead your case."

Riese eyed his weapons on the ground. He could easily get the hammer before Hordus or any other Vyking attacked. But these men weren't his real enemies. They were like he had once been. Men followed the orders of a king that they believed in. Riese no longer possess such allegiance anymore.

The old man took a set of iron shackles and locked them around Riese's wrists.

Hordus said, "It pains me to do this, but only the king can pardon you."

Riese didn't resist. As a prisoner, he stood a much better chance getting close enough to kill King Obed than leading a raid against his throne.

"I will not offer a fight if you release him," Riese said, nodding toward Lehrling.

"Might I consider your request overnight?"

"Do you assume Quenid's position?"

Hordus nodded. "For now, we have no assigned frontrunner. I'm the eldest of our group, so until King Obed appoints a new leader, the decisions fall to me."

"If your wisdom is as great as your years, I believe you have enough knowledge to know that Lehrling of the Dragon Skull Order is not your enemy."

An aged smile creased Hordus' face. "When the sun rises, I will give you an answer."

Hordus led Riese to another set of posts near Lehrling. They hooked chains to Riese's shackles and hoisted them up tightly, placing Riese's hands high over his head until Riese was forced to stand on tiptoes.

Once they locked the chains tightly, Hordus tugged the chains with all his strength. They didn't give.

"Even in the might of your rage, Riese," Hordus said, "These restraints will not yield. Again, I wish I didn't have to resort to chaining you like an animal. Perhaps I, in your very situation, would have done the same. May King Obed have mercy on your soul."

The entire band of Vykings separated and returned to the gates or wherever else they had chosen to house themselves overnight.

Riese gazed at Lehrling. The round old man still had not awakened. His attention turned to his former brethren fading into the shadows of the trees and buildings. He thought of Hordus' last words.

Obed had no more mercy for Riese than Riese did for the king. Death would come, but it would not be his. Then he thought of his hidden son sleeping in the wagon. He still had something to worry about. He yanked at the chains. Hordus was right. The chains were secured. He had to find a way to get to Marc before the guards found him. He wasn't certain how much mercy Hordus had if he discovered Marc.

"Now?" Roble asked Haigla, heading for the door with Shawndirea on his shoulder.

"Yes."

The door unlatched and swung inward. A strong breeze flowed through the cellar and blew several tattered scrolls from the table. Leaves, dirt, and small twig debris swirled at the door of her cellar. She mumbled curses under her breath, and Roble swore that he heard Zauber's name mentioned in the middle of the obscenities.

Odlon, Roble, and Shawndirea crept from the cellar and moved along the shadows lining the buildings but stopped suddenly when a pair of patrols walked the street near where they hid.

Odlon fired two quick headshots, dropping the Vyking plunderers on the road. Roble was stunned at his cold, calculated assassinations.

"Remember," Odlon said, seeing the horror in Roble's eyes, "these are murdering raiders. They killed the leaders in Woodcrest and might kill Riese and Lehrling if we don't free them from their restraints."

Roble helped Odlon drag the large men off the trail and hide their bodies behind thorny shrubs.

"*Kill or be killed*," Roble reminded himself. A worrisome change for his conscience in a world filled with different rules, laws, and power struggles. And while he sought peace about what lay ahead and what he must do to get Shawndirea home, he couldn't ignore the truth that reigned deep inside his soul. Life was life, precious to anyone good or evil. To rid any world of evil through murder tainted oneself with evil as well, didn't it?

Shawndirea caught the troubled look on his face. She said, "Should you stay in our world, you'll see far worse as time passes."

"I will adjust, but it won't be easy."

"To survive, your wits must react before you think your actions through. Sometimes your decisions will be in error, but never underestimate an enemy. Many won't give you time to weigh the odds. Most don't care."

Roble nodded. He wondered how to determine who was actually a friend or foe. In the Overlands he wanted to trust everyone, but Deiko had tainted that ambition. The only ones he truly connected with were his students simply because he had the passion to teach them. Here? He found *himself* the student searching for the correct answers that allowed him to keep his head on his shoulders. The best thing in his favor was that he was quick to learn.

CHAPTER 51

Crukas had watched the majority of the combat between Riese and the Vyking leader. He was surprised at how Riese had taken out a man much larger than himself. The bravery and combat skills Riese had displayed were something that he now admired about the man he had come to despise. But from what he had heard, the entire ordeal occurred because Riese defended Lehrling. And now Riese hung in chains beside him with no real promise that Lehrling would be released when the sun rose.

After the guards passed to return to their posts at the gate, Crukas crawled beneath the wagon and scurried on his stomach toward the intersection. He hurried from wagon to wagon, staying low and in the shadows.

He lay on his stomach, watched, and listened. No footsteps approached from any direction. The dead of night had settled over Woodcrest, and any activity probably remained at the gates of the city. Believing the path to Riese was clear and without opposition, Crukas crawled from his hiding place and sprinted through the intersection until he reached Riese and Lehrling.

RIESE LOOKED SURPRISED to see Crukas show himself out in the open. He knew all thieves sought to remain hidden. They worked their best in the shadows. But what purpose did Crukas have coming to them? To mock him? Riese realized the thief had every reason to begrudge him simply because Riese wanted the thief to pay for his crimes of betrayal and breaking the simple law in Glacier Ridge for thieves to come and go freely as long as they didn't steal from one another or the traders in Glacier Ridge.

Riese narrowed his eyes at Crukas and through clenched teeth, he said, "I guess our tables have turned, thief. Here to find your amusement?"

Crukas shook his head and placed his finger to his lips. He reached into his pocket and removed his lock-picking tools. He grinned and his eyebrows rose.

Perhaps *redemption?* Riese wondered.

"I had thought you had abandoned us," Riese said, "or you had made a run for it?"

Crukas shook his head.

"Oh, that's right. You cannot speak."

With a shrug and sad face, Crukas studied the cuffs, but due to Riese being almost twice the height of Crukas, the thief had no way to reach the locks over Riese's head.

Riese's eyes widened and he shouted, "Crukas, look out!"

Crukas turned to see a crazed Vyking rushing him with a bloody dagger.

"Nordell, no!" Riese said.

Crukas tried to move, but Nordell raised the dagger overhead and growled, swiftly bringing down the blade. Crukas' mouth opened to scream, but no sound came.

ODLON FIRED an arrow from the crossbow seconds before Nordell would have killed Crukas. The arrow tip went through Nordell's back and lodged in his heart. He arched backwards for a moment and then fell forward on the road.

Crukas sat on the ground beneath Riese, trembling. His pale face revealed his evident fear.

Odlon, Roble, and Shawndirea hurried to the shackled Riese and Lehrling. Roble patted Lehrling's face, but the old man still didn't awaken. He placed his head to Lehrling's chest. The man's breathing was hampered. Hoisted into this position wasn't favorable and perhaps was making his possible pneumonia even worse.

"We have to get him down," Roble said.

"Help Crukas free me first. I can get Lehrling down," Riese said.

Odlon and Roble cupped their hands together to give Crukas foot supports to hold him high enough to pick the locks. In seconds, the thief used his picks, and to Roble's surprise, Riese lowered his hands and rubbed his wrists.

Riese walked behind Lehrling. After Crukas unlocked those cuffs, Lehrling dropped back into Riese's arms to prevent the heavy man from collapsing and injuring himself by falling to the ground.

While Riese supported Lehrling's weight, Zauber walked over to join them.

"Good to find you all together," he said.

"Where have you been?" Roble asked. "You brought us all in here and abandoned us. Why did you deceive us?"

Zauber raised his hand and said, "Careful. Our enemies still abound. We must remain discreet."

Roble ignored his answer and again said, "You deserted us once we got into the center of town. Why?"

Riese carried Lehrling to the nearest wagon and laid him gently in the bed.

Zauber looked at Roble and then he gazed around to each of the others. He said, "There has to be unity in your party. Do you understand?"

Roble crossed his arms but didn't reply. Odlon seemed as upset as Roble, especially at the underestimated numbers of the Vykings and the surprise of the dark elves. Shawndirea watched with slight amusement, indicating she knew Zauber's ways.

Zauber focused his attention on Crukas. He said, "Crukas, you have a voice. Your voice *needs* to be heard and respected by Riese."

Riese rested his hands on his hips and nodded. "It is now. He put his life in jeopardy to free me."

Zauber smiled, looked at Crukas, and waved his hand. The thief's eyes widened. He cleared his throat and discovered his voice had returned.

"Thanks," Crukas said.

"Riese," Zauber said, "your inner rage will burn forever after your loss of Odrissus, but know that is *not* Crukas' fault. It's those your bloodline is drawn from. Crukas has secrets of his own that quite possibly in time he'll reveal to you. But he is *not* your enemy."

"I know," Riese replied.

"He is, however," Zauber said, "a very resourceful key to your group's success."

"So you won't hand me over to Ironwood's guards?" Crukas asked Riese.

"No."

A great ease settled over Crukas' face. He gave a slight bow toward Riese and said, "Thank you."

Odlon said, "But to get Shawndirea to Elvendale we must pass through Ironwood. There's no other way."

"First," Riese said, "We have to rid Woodcrest of the tyrants imprisoning them."

"What about the dark elves?" Shawndirea asked.

Odlon's nervous eyes glanced from person to person, which made Roble wonder what power the dark elves held over him. Why did he fear them as much as he did?

Haigla walked past them with a bottle of orange potion. "Leave the dark elves to me," she said, heading to the alabaster faery statue.

Zauber stared at Shawndirea questioningly. Shawndirea shrugged and shook her head.

Riese watched the old woman with curiosity.

Roble looked at Riese and asked, "What are your plans?"

"You're placing *me* in charge?"

Roble shrugged. "You're the largest in our party. You've fought with them before, correct?"

"Yes, long ago."

"Then you know their tactics and how best to approach them. Besides, as huge as you are I'd never consider giving you orders. With our current situation, I trust your decisions."

"We kill them all," Riese said, "except for the old man, Hordus. I want him kept alive. But the dark elves are the biggest problem right now. Archers at a high position have the advantage over us. I want to know how the old lady plans to take care of the dark elves before we approach the gates. And remember, my son Marc is still in my wagon. I want him protected at all costs."

"You got it," Roble replied.

Odlon nodded.

Riese followed Haigla to the statue. When he got there, the rest of the group stood behind him. The old woman knelt before the statue with her eyes closed. She poured the concoction on the feet of the faery statue while chanting.

Glittering little lights like a swarm of lightning bugs flickered in the oak branches. From the trees near the gates, anguished screams wailed only to stop suddenly seconds later.

"The dark elves are no more," Haigla said with a near toothless smile. "Take out the Vykings and our town is free once more."

～

THE DARK ELVES stood watch in the branches of trees along the gateways. Four per gate and each favored a tree of their own. One by one a slight giggle echoed from the tree branches where the dark elves positioned themselves. While searching for what produced the luring laughter, the dark elves climbed the branches and followed. Seeing nothing at first, and then, without warning, dryads that had camouflaged themselves within the trees' patterns, reached out from their hiding places and yanked the dark elves into the bark, which solidified around them, paralyzing and quickly killing them.

The high-pitched screams of the dark elves as the dryads overtook them caused the Vykings to look to the trees, witnessing several of the dark elves' demise.

"What strange magic is this?" a Vyking guard asked, drawing his blade.

"Spirits of those we slaughtered here," another suggested. "They've come for vengeance, Dougan."

They eyed one another and stood back to back, to keep watch around them while they slowly moved away from the gate.

"Dreygurs?" Dougan whispered.

"Possibly."

"Or the trees are enchanted, Wylis," Dougan said.

Wylis gripped his sword tighter. His eyes widened. He turned toward Dougan and said, "The Dragon Skull Order soldiers we killed?"

Dougan shared his worry. He nodded. "And another has entered town. Their spirits have come to protect him."

Their eyes searched near the light poles and into the faint lighted areas beneath the trees. They sought the eyeless ghosts of the town council members they had killed earlier in the day. Nothing slinked within the shadows, but they couldn't shake the possibility that vengeful spirits stalked them.

"Make our way to the center of the town," Dougan whispered, "where there are fewer trees."

Before the two headed for the center of Woodcrest, two arrows from Odlon's crossbow dropped the men quickly.

CHAPTER 52

*D*rucis rode Ol' Grey along the dark forest path outside Woodcrest. His eyes shifted every time he heard a twig snap, a strange bird cry, or rustling overhead. Normally such things didn't disturb him, but after riding away from the undead of Glacier Ridge and through a band of drifting ghosts, he was certain the entire region around him was changing. What else had the Plague-bringer left behind?

The luminous bluish broken and decapitated statues didn't bother him. But his eyes searched around them, for darker moving objects. His hand rested on the handle of his battle-axe, but quickly pulled the ax when the strange screams echoed through the trees. He recognized the cries.

Dark elves.

Grey's ears backed and the horse whinnied slightly as Drucis tugged back the reins. Drucis' eyes again searched through the ruins and statues because he knew the history of the area and how the dark elves had slaughtered all the monks and priests in the towering temples that no longer existed.

Had they returned?

Several more anguished screams rose and silenced in sudden death.

"No," Drucis whispered, looking around the forest. "They're not here. Come now, Grey, let's get on to Woodcrest. Seems they may be needing me ax to aid them."

THE DYING SHRIEKS of the dark elves wreaked havoc upon the Vykings'

336

superstitious nature and frightened them from the trees that stood near the gates. With haunted expressions on their faces, they headed toward the center of Woodcrest where Odlon waited with his readied crossbow. He dropped most before they had turned to even notice he was there.

Hordus shook his head and dropped his weapons and shield.

Riese brought the wristband shackles and locked them around the old man's wrists.

"Why spare me?" Hordus asked. "I'm old and of little use in battles anymore. Is it because I spared your life?"

Riese gave a slight nod and then shrugged. "That's part of it, but it is also because I have a mission for you."

Hordus gave a slight chuckle. "A mission? For me?"

Riese nodded. "Yes. Once we reach the other side of Ironwood, I'm releasing you. I want you to return to the Isles of Welkstone. Tell Obed I'm still alive and I seek to remove his head for joining with the likes of Lord Waxxon."

"You're a fool. Why not release me, and I'll tell him that you're dead? Live the rest of your years in peace. He doesn't need to know you're alive."

"I will never know peace again, Hordus. What was taken from me can never be replaced. There is no redemption for my pain. Nothing can fix what is broken within my heart and mind."

A sad expression crossed Hordus' face. When he looked at Riese, tears brimmed his eyes. "I understand. I do. I lost my wife after many years together but not as you did. She died from sickness. Had what happened to your dear wife happened to mine; I indeed would share your fury. In some ways, I do."

Riese clasped his huge hand on Hordus' shoulder. "In better times, we'd have a lot of stories to share. As long as you ride with us, I promise no harm will come to you."

Hordus smiled. "I never saw you fight on the battlefield, but the stories are often told around the nightly campfires of your courage and how many fell to your blades before you *lost your way*, as they say. I see that you did not, but that you became a better man who had found love, which is a far rarer thing than most consider in this life. And as far as telling stories, it's still quite a journey we must take. Plenty of time to tell tales."

While Riese engaged Hordus in conversation, Odlon circled around Woodcrest and dropped any other remaining Vykings.

The townspeople left their homes and hiding places to help drag the dead bodies to the edge of the intersecting roads at the center of town. Like scavengers, the men, women, and children pilfered whatever caught their eyes. Most though only took gold, silver, or copper coins they found in small pouches and pockets.

When the townspeople lined the bodies up, Riese walked alongside Hordus, and they counted the number of the dead.

"Twenty-two," Riese said. "Would that be all of your band?"

"Yes," Hordus replied.

"Good," Riese said. Then looking to Odlon and Roble, he said, "Woodcrest is free!"

Haigla did a little dance while singing in a strange language. Her brown stained mouth grinned with glee as she jigged.

Still trying to wipe the sleep from his eyes, Marc staggered across the street and stood near his father.

"It's over," Roble said to Shawndirea. "We can head to Ironwood and then to Elvendale."

Shawndirea kissed Roble's cheek.

"Shawndirea?" a female voice asked. The voice was sweet, soft, and almost seductive. A voice any man would love to hear call his name.

Shawndirea turned and was startled by what she saw. Hovering behind her was another faery with strawberry blonde hair and bright blue eyes. "Aerlene?" Shawndirea asked with wide eyes.

"Yes! Child, it *is* you?" Aerlene said.

"Yes."

She took Shawndirea's hands and whisked her away. Shawndirea saw fright widen Roble's eyes, so she blew him a kiss, hoping the action let him know that she was safe and not being snatched away from him again.

Aerlene landed on a high branch near the top of a massive oak. She held Shawndirea's hands tightly. The setting moon on the horizon was spectacular. Stars glittered the darkening sky. She suddenly realized exactly how much she missed her wings and her ability to fly. From the towering height of the treetop she could see lights from small bonfires, dotting the landscape and detailing where all neighboring farmsteads were. The air was cool, fragrant, and almost magical.

Aerlene gasped and her eyes widened. "Your precious wings. My dear, what has happened to you?"

Shawndirea shook her head. "It's a terribly long story. One that would most certainly bore you."

"Don't be silly, child. There's so much we should catch up on."

Shawndirea smiled and hugged her aunt. "Another time, maybe, about my wings. But seeing you is such a grand relief. I thought you were dead."

Aerlene shook her head and giggled. She said, "No. I'm very much alive.

So that's the story circulating Elvendale? If so, your mother has been very busy spreading misinformation again."

"The rumor is one my mother has insisted is the truth," she replied. "She had me and pretty much everyone else convinced."

Shaking her head, Aerlene said, "Tsk tsk. That mother of yours is truly too bullheaded for her own good. I'm surprised we came from the same parents. If you offer even the slightest difference of opinion, she goes to no end with her bitterness and hateful harangues, trying to change what you believe, and if she cannot, she'll carry the grudge until the end of hell. So I told her I'd had enough of her nonsense, and I left Elvendale for good."

"So that's what happened? You didn't die at the hands of a goblin?"

"Only in her *maddest* dream, my dear. Certainly, she's *hoped* that."

Shawndirea hugged Aerlene again. She smiled and said, "I'm so thankful that you are living and well."

"Just before I darted off with you, did I see you kiss that human on the cheek?" Aerlene asked.

"Yes, that's Roble."

"Why are you with him?"

"I've fallen in love with him," Shawndirea said with a bright smile. Her eyes lit up and she squeezed her aunt's hand. "And he loves me."

"Does Istrell know?"

"Not yet. He's taking me to Elvendale so I can get my wings healed."

"So she doesn't know that you're bringing him with you?"

"No."

Aerlene beamed. "You *have* to let me be there when you tell her."

"You'd like that, wouldn't you?"

"Every second of it."

"The truth is that I don't really look forward to going home, but you taking me up here makes me want my power of flight back more than ever. I *have* to go back."

Aerlene nodded. "I'd die without my ability to fly. There's so much liberation when you soar with the wind and fly with the songbirds."

"It is frightening not having my wings. If not for Roble's help, I'd have died by now," she said, trying to protect his reputation instead of revealing he was the reason they were shredded.

"You know bringing Roble to the High Court will no doubt send your mother into a horrible tirade," Aerlene said.

"I expect it will."

"She'll threaten your right to the throne."

Shawndirea smiled. "It's fine if she does because I don't want the responsibility. I hope she denies my right to the throne."

"And does she know this?"

"I've told her often."

Shawndirea watched the fleeting moonlight. Soon darkness would sweep over the night for a couple hours before the sunrise, giving the stars their full magnificence.

"Which kingdom does your Roble call home?" Aerlene asked.

Shawndirea smiled. "The Overlands."

Aerlene feigned a gasp and burst into a fit of laughter. "I've always known there was a rebellious streak in you, my dear. Regardless of what your mother has wanted you to do, you always seek a different path."

Shawndirea gave a sneaky smile.

"Oh I'd so love to see her expression when you tell her this! From the Overlands? Wow, you're going for the kill, eh?"

"No. I'm certain she'll take it that way, but honestly, what I feel toward Roble is genuine. I would never choose a human within our realm, or a faery either, for that matter."

"I'm afraid there are few noble choices here, so I cannot blame you for being resourceful and exploring better options."

Shawndirea curtsied.

Aerlene shook her head at her niece's playful gesture. "In spite of your choice, Istrell will still do everything she can to persuade you to assume the throne."

Shawndirea nodded modestly. "I know. If I don't take it, I will solicit her to let Dirk reign in my stead."

Aerlene shook her head. "No. I love Dirk, but he isn't suited to sit on *any* throne."

"You wouldn't want to see your own son reign over Elvendale?"

"No."

"Why not?" Shawndirea asked.

"He's a tyrant. He's ruthless, self-centered, and cold-blooded. He's the last person I or anyone should want on the throne."

Shawndirea was stunned.

"That surprises you?" Aerlene asked.

She nodded.

"It shouldn't," Aerlene said. "When you two were children, I cannot count the times that you complained about how unfair he played *any* game. He cheated no matter what you played."

"We were children."

"Well, my dear, he's never outgrown it. In fact, he's matured into something far worse. Power is his wealth."

"He thinks you're dead, too," Shawndirea said.

"Good," she said bluntly. "I intend to keep it that way."

Changing the subject, Shawndirea asked, "How did you end up in Woodcrest?"

"Opportunity arose. I accepted it."

"The people here worship you?"

"Some do."

"They've built a statue and altar in your honor. Some I've heard pray to you. Why?"

Aerlene smiled. "I protect them. They rely on the earth to survive, and I help bless their crops and watch over them."

"But the Vykings killed their leaders, and you didn't stop them."

She shrugged her shoulders slightly. "They weren't believers."

"You mean you could have prevented their deaths?"

Aerlene nodded. "Yes."

"Then *why* didn't you?"

"Several reasons actually. It wasn't because they didn't believe in me, but it helps that others in Woodcrest view their nonbelief as the reason I didn't rise to defend them. It will increase their faith and allegiance. However, the biggest issue was how many dark elves might come here. They wish to control this area of the forests, believing some dark relic is still hidden where the old monastery and temple was. They've not found it, nor will they. Once they sided with the Vykings, I allowed ample time to see if more dark elf reinforcements came. They didn't, so I decided to act."

Shawndirea looked at Aerlene with deep concern.

"What is it, child?" her aunt asked.

"You're *not* a goddess. They owe you no allegiance."

"I know, but they don't."

Shawndirea shook her head. "That's not the point. What if Haigla discovers that you're only a faery with limited powers?"

Aerlene smiled. "That old woman? Ah, she's a dear. Her devotion to me is greater than all of Woodcrest combined."

"That's the danger, aunt," Shawndirea replied. "If she discovers you're not as powerful as she, she may bind you and place you in restraints. Or much worse, use your blood in potions to increase *her* power."

"She's merely an herbalist that has learned a few spells here and there," Aerlene said without worry.

"You're mistaken," Shawndirea said. "Have you not watched her? Have you not seen what she can do?"

The questions drained the confidence from Aerlene's face. Her troubled eyes searched Woodcrest, trying to find the old woman. She pursed her lips and asked, "What have you seen?"

Shawndirea mentioned some of the things she, Roble, and Odlon had watched in her dark cellar. The small library of spell books and scrolls indicated she performed magic, and she did have the power to move objects like the door.

Aerlene grew more concerned.

"She used a potion when she summoned you at the statue," Shawndirea said.

"I had not noticed."

Shawndirea nodded. "Whatever spell she used, the dark elves died soon after."

"Yes, the dryads killed them."

"They have sided with you?"

"Not directly. They want only to protect the trees they are attached to. The dark elves were seen as a threat, so they snared and killed them."

Shawndirea shook her head, and gently placed her hand on her Aunt's arm. "No. Haigla made a potion, she chanted her spell, and seconds later the dryads did her bidding. She is the one that controls them, not you."

Aerlene swallowed hard. "That *is* alarming."

"Did you communicate with the dryads near the gates right before they attacked the dark elves?"

"No."

"Then she has control over them. Perhaps she has a control spell on you as well?"

Aerlene shook her head. "No. I detect nothing magical holding me here."

"You're still here within Woodcrest. Fly beyond the town walls and see."

Nervousness claimed Aerlene's eyes. She hesitated to attempt Shawndirea's challenge.

"You fear that she has, don't you?" Shawndirea asked.

Aerlene didn't reply. She shot into the air quickly and flew toward the nearest gate. Right as she reached the guard tower, a flashing yellow light radiated like lightning. Aerlene shrieked, lost her flight balance, and spun helplessly to the ground.

Shawndirea gasped and said, "Aerlene?"

Without her wings, Shawndirea was stuck at the top of the tree. There wasn't any way she could help her aunt, and getting down to Roble and the others was almost as troubling.

CHAPTER 53

$\mathcal{D}$rucis listened to the sudden ghastly shrieks that quickly silenced near the gates of Woodcrest. Grey remained restless with his ears back, his eyes wide with terror.

"Easy, boy," Drucis said. "Don't be thinking we're next, cause we ain't."

Drucis held the battleax handle tightly. His eyes narrowed and his thick eyebrows almost made it seem that he had actually closed his eyes. However, they were deceptively alert with keener vision than a hawk with the sun directly overhead.

After the pain-filled cries silenced, the forest on both sides of the road became oddly quiet. The only sounds were his and Grey's breathing.

Drucis looked to the faint blue statue outlines again, expecting to see more spirits glide past, but nothing stirred. The night birds and insects hushed as though the death of winter had claimed them.

An occasional wind gust slightly rustled leaves high in the treetops.

Grey whinnied.

"Easy, now. We be getting out of these blasted woods soon enough."

He tapped Grey's flanks and coaxed the horse to steadily move toward Woodcrest. As they approached the gates, Grey became more uncomfortable and set his hooves solidly on the paved road. An odd smell hung in the air, and this reminded the dwarf of the deathly decay he had seen in Glacier Ridge when the undead creatures came for him.

But it was more than that. The acrid smell that loomed resulted from painful sudden deaths dealt by magical beings. The exact kind of magical creatures he didn't know, but he was more leery than before. He had sensitivity to magic, and since this had occurred just recently, the power lingered with the night breeze. The runic markings on his ax glowed and dimmed, which indicated his suspicion of magic being used was correct.

The hairs on his arms stiffened. Chills ran down his back. He shuddered even though he wasn't cold. He missed his Dwarven comrades, Sorgen and Draken. They, like him, thrived with delight whenever they happened upon possible skirmishes, especially against those who wielded magical powers because it made such fights more challenging.

The flickering torches that burned atop the Woodcrest gates lighted the top section of the walls. When Drucis noticed a dark elf's mangled armor burrowed partway into the side of a massive oak, he pulled back the reins and directed the horse to the side of the road near the trees. He hefted up the ax and swung off Grey, half expecting an arrow to slice through the night air and strike him or his old horse. When the elf still had not moved, Drucis was more curious than concerned. Had the townsfolk of Woodcrest made some type of scarecrow from dark elf armor to frighten away night travellers? Doubtful, but a possibility nonetheless.

"Stay steady now," Drucis said to Grey.

Hiding in the dark shadows at the edge of the grove, Drucis watched for the slightest movement along the wall. Other than the dancing sconce flames, nothing else moved. He wondered why the dark elf didn't move and why it was there in the first place. When he had passed through Woodcrest with his two companions, the gates were open and the only guards along the wall were a couple of townsfolk. Nothing more.

"What's a goin' on 'ere?" Drucis asked softly.

Then he noticed the rope ladder that was hanging down the side of the wall on the other side of the path. He smiled with amusement. "What fool be leaving dat hanging o'er the wall?"

His stubby legs ran quickly as he headed for the ladder. He was almost to it when he heard the growl behind him. Drucis turned to see a giant of a man running at him with his two-handed sword drawn.

"What the—?"

The Vyking guard gnashed his teeth and said, "Little man, you did this?"

Drucis brought up his ax a second before the sword would have made him a head shorter. Sparks flashed.

"Did what, you ol' filthy ogre?"

"You killed the dark elves," the Vyking said evenly, readying his next attack. He brought the sword overhead with both hands and came at Drucis with a downward slash. Drucis swung his ax and caught the blade with the curve of the handle and blade, twisted and yanked, almost pulling the blade from the near giant's hand.

"If only I would 'ave," Drucis said with a grin, "My day would have ended on so much better a note. However, killing you will most likely amend what I've lacked on such an otherwise sorrowful day."

"Bring your best, little toadstool."

Drucis' eyes narrowed. "I always *do*, you oaf!"

The Vyking was nearly three times Drucis' height, but the size difference didn't deter the dwarf. He loved challenges and the bigger, the better.

He eyed the giant Vyking and said, "Wouldn't you have been so much safer on the *other* side of the wall? It be a bit dangerous out here for the likes of ya."

The angry Vyking swung his sword. Drucis parried the strike with ease, quickly spun, and slashed the giant's thigh. Blood spilled from the gash. The Vyking groaned, growled, and spat on the ground.

"I can kill gutter rats like you all the day long," the Vyking replied.

"You be a bit outmatched this day."

The Vyking growled and rushed toward Drucis. The dwarf stepped side-to-side and then darted between his opponent's legs. He easily could have hacked through one of the Vyking's legs, but he wanted to toy with him a bit longer. He had encountered several of Waxxon's recruits over the past few weeks and watched how they bullied townspeople in different villages. Now he had an opportunity to humiliate one and let him know his race wasn't as strong and tough as they so frequently boasted.

Right after Drucis turned and stood behind the giant, he smacked the Vyking's backside with the flat side of his ax blade, which angered the man even more. The Vyking turned, leaned forward, and rushed again. Drucis flipped his ax and used the handle to strike the man's left shin. He roared in pain and dropped to the ground. Drucis took his ax by the handle and swung to decapitate his newfound enemy, but the blade dug into the dirt.

The Vyking rolled, still holding his knee, and quickly shoved himself up and hobbled on his good leg. Blood seeped from the gash, and the bleeding seemed to be slowing. Drucis pried the ax from the ground, but before he could ready it to swing again, the giant man's fist caught Drucis' jaw and sent him sprawling backwards.

He held fast to the ax, but the man pursued with his sword.

"Aye," Drucis laughed. "If it be fists you wish to exchange?"

"Nay, lil' imp!" The man brought back his sword again, high and overhead.

Drucis took the opportunity for his pre-emptive strike and used the ax head to block the downward blow, pivoted it to the side, and then kicked the man's right shin. Before the man could reach for his injured shin,

Drucis ducked low and caught the man around the knees, lifted him off the ground, and pushed him backwards. With both shins aching and his balance toppling off-center, the Vyking dropped hard and landed on his back.

Drucis didn't allow him time to struggle and get back to his feet. He straddled the man's chest and pummeled the man's face with stubby thick fists. He hit and hit, not easing his blows or slowing down until the Vyking lay unconscious.

Sweat beaded from beneath Drucis' helm. He huffed for air. The only thing he regretted about the battle was there had been no other witnesses than Grey, and his old horse wasn't expounding praise for anyone.

Drucis returned to Grey, grabbed some rope from his saddlebag, and then he led the horse back to where the Vyking lay. The dwarf tied the man's hands and feet in tight knots, and once he was certain the man wouldn't be able to get free when he awakened, Drucis climbed the rope ladder.

At the top of the wall, he examined the dark elf. He was stunned. The tree bark had engulfed the elf's head down to the neck. He tapped the side of the tree near the elf's chest. Solid. The bark wasn't splintered, but the elf was cold to the touch.

"How?" Drucis wondered aloud.

Little chuckles grew into hysterical laughter on the higher branches. He huffed and pointed the tip of his ax to where the laughter faded.

"Aye. Show yourselves. Your laughter will cease."

With a fast swing of the ax, he removed the dead elf's body from the tree. The limp headless corpse landed on the rampart at Drucis' feet. He rolled the body over, removed the elf's daggers, his boots, and two small pouches filled with silver coins.

"Ya won't be needing these," he said with a broad smile.

Drucis hoisted the ladder back up to the platform and then he found the crude stairs that led down to the grounds of Woodcrest. Before he'd open the gates to get Grey, he figured it best to scout around and make certain no other Vyking guards were waiting for him.

Hurrying down the ladder on the inside wall, he slowed when commotion stirred further inside the town. He leapt off the ladder and landed solid on the ground. With his ax held tightly in his grasp, he smiled.

"Aye, a skirmish. Just what I be needing!"

Drucis sprinted away from the wall and toward the bickering voices.

CHAPTER 54

*R*oble searched the dark tree branches trying to see where the other faery had taken Shawndirea. The thick leafy canopy was impossible to see through. He didn't want to think she was in danger, but he couldn't be certain.

"What happened?" Odlon asked. "Where did Shawndirea go?"

"I don't know. Another faery took her."

Riese walked over to them and said, "I think it best that we sleep here today and once the sun rises the day after, we'll head out. Roble, I will get you, the elf, and your faery past Ironwood, but once we pass that township, I have other endeavors to attend to."

"Fair enough," Roble said. He glanced once more to the tree limbs, hoping he could see Shawndirea.

Odlon said, "Get some sleep, and later I can teach you some basic swordsmanship skills. It won't be a lot though for what little time we'll have."

"Every bit will help. Whatever you teach me, I'll practice at great lengths every chance I get."

"After you and Shawndirea get to Elvendale, and she gets her wings repaired, meet up with me in Woodnog for more training. I may even have some trainees that you can spar with."

"Sounds good."

Roble and Odlon followed Riese back to the wagon to where Lehrling still lay unconscious. Haigla placed her wrinkled hand to Lehrling's sweaty forehead, checked his eyes, and then placed her head to his chest and listened. Her good eye widened with intent interest. Seconds later, she rose and shook her head.

"How bad is he?" Roble asked.

"Too bad for him to be travelling. You must leave him here with me," she replied. "He's very weak."

"You have a remedy?"

She cocked her head and gave a faint, snuff-coated grin. "I have lots of things that may work. But if you leave this town with him, he'll die. He's too sick to journey."

Roble glanced to Odlon. Odlon shrugged slightly and nodded in agreement.

"We'll leave his horse and belongings in your care," Roble said to Haigla. "I hope to meet up with him in the near future."

Odlon nodded. "As do I. But, Roble, after I help you get past Ironwood, my journey must detour to the Woodnog swamps."

Roble worried about being left on his own with Shawndirea. He had grown comfortable with this group of new friends in an unfamiliar world. A part of him grieved, but another part looked forward to walking alone with Shawndirea and learning more about her. Too much had happened and prevented them from having intimate time to talk. He wanted to learn more about what she envisioned their future together to be.

Odlon clasped Roble's shoulder and said, "That only leaves you a day's journey. Of course there's always Crukas. I don't believe he will want to stay anywhere near Ironwood. He may well be persuaded to follow you."

Roble shook his head. "Crukas is a thief, not a warrior. He'd rather move in the shadows than take up a sword to fight."

Odlon smiled. "You learn quickly. That skill above all others may be to your benefit. But he will follow you for part of the journey I'm quite certain."

"Why?"

"Roads are the paths to travel between the towns. He won't venture off the path unless it is absolutely necessary, which is advice I suggest you take to heart."

Roble nodded.

"Roble!" Shawndirea shouted from the tree canopy.

He looked up, and still not being able to see her, he said, "Where are you?"

"I'm stuck in the tree," she replied.

"She left you up there?"

"Not intentionally, but I need to get down."

"How?"

"Catch me!" she yelled.

"Wait. Don't jump!"

SHAWNDIREA DOVE from the tree branch. Her light weight prevented her from dropping too quickly. As she neared a lower branch, she grabbed a thick leaf, snapped it loose from its hold and used it to glide between the branches. She moved slowly enough that she didn't have to worry about bruising herself should she collide with twigs or branches.

Roble lifted his hands when she came into view, and Odlon did the same. She pulled both sides of the leaf tighter and bowed the shape enough to catch the wind and change her direction. A gentle breeze caught her leaf sail and spiraled her around toward Roble. When she drifted directly over his hands, she released the leaf and dropped.

"What happened?" Roble said, holding his hands steady so she could stand. "Why did she leave you?"

"It's not what you think. Now hurry," she said, pointing in the direction Aerlene had flown. "My aunt needs our help."

Roble carried Shawndirea and Odlon followed.

"Is she okay?"

"I don't know," Shawndirea replied. The fear in her voice beckoned Roble to move faster. "Be careful. She's on the ground. *Don't* step on her."

A faint pink glow emitted in a thick patch of grass beneath an oak tree. Aerlene lay on her back and squinted up at them while they looked down.

Shawndirea leapt from Roble's hand and ran to her aunt.

"Are you okay, Aerlene?" she asked.

Aerlene shook her head and blinked hard several times. She frowned as her vision slowly cleared. She said, "A bit taken off guard is all."

"So she did cast a spell upon you," Shawndirea said.

"Yes, that nasty witch," Aerlene seethed. Her tiny hands balled into fists. She started to rise.

"Stay still, auntie."

Roble frowned. "Whom is she talking about?"

"Haigla," Shawndirea said. "She has bound Aerlene to Woodcrest, preventing her from leaving."

"Why would she do that?" he asked.

"Control and power," Aerlene said, rubbing her temples. "Perhaps a bit of revenge as well."

Odlon knelt near Aerlene and said, "She just helped us get control of Woodcrest."

"No," Shawndirea said. "She used a potion to get the dark elves killed. The potion controlled the dryads and right after she used it, they had no choice to follow her command."

"But that's what rid us of the dark elf archers," Odlon said. "Without their assistance, we'd still be trying to figure out how to stop them."

"True," Shawndirea said, "But that's no reason for her to have control over my aunt."

"Of course not," Roble said.

"And you don't understand," Aerlene said. "If she already had that power over the dryads, she could have used it at any time. Instead she allowed the town council leaders to be killed by the Vykings and the dark elves. She could have summoned them to kill the dark elves without the leaders dying."

Shawndirea nodded. "Now, the townsfolk believe she's their savior and will probably allow her to rule over them."

"I don't think they're that blind," Roble said. "We just need to let them know what happened."

"No," Aerlene said. "You have to understand that these people are simple folks. They are workers that abhor any means of violence. They refuse to take up arms against others. Partly because they are brought up with the monk virtues that existed within the monastery before dark elves destroyed it. They learned the virtues from old scrolls."

Roble said, "They would simply remain under the dark elves control even though they know these elves were the ones that destroyed some of their ancestors? I find that difficult to believe. Why would they subject themselves to dark elf control?"

Aerlene groaned and pulled herself up into a seated position. "Fate."

"What?" Roble asked.

"They simply attribute it to fate, thinking the gods were punishing them for some ill deed."

"If they assume the gods have a hand in their bondage, why would they suddenly follow Haigla and do her biddings?" Odlon asked. "That contradicts any means of faith."

Aerlene smiled. "You underestimate the power of magic. The townsfolk in Woodcrest fear magicians, sorcerers, and Haigla for being a witch. Now their fear of her gives her prominence. She'll do whatever she wants, and none will oppose her."

"So she's a tyrant?" Roble asked.

"Yes," Aerlene replied. "I believe her goal is to overtake the town."

"Nothing less," Shawndirea quickly added.

Roble looked directly into Aerlene's eyes. "So why did they build a monument to you? Aren't you somewhat to blame for what is going on here?"

Aerlene looked away. She swallowed hard, brushed herself off, and slowly stood. "I made an innocent mistake."

"I don't think I'd call it 'innocent,'" Roble said. "Perhaps more vain than anything."

Aerlene's eyes narrowed. Her jaw tightened.

"He's right, auntie," Shawndirea said. "You know he is."

Aerlene huffed. "Perhaps. But the truth's hard to hear sometimes. She tricked me into believing that she and the others were worshiping me by building the statue as a shrine to me. But what I think she did was magically bind me to the statue and now she controls my magic."

"I never thought of that," Shawndirea said. "That makes perfect sense."

"However, due to my lack of judgment, I don't think it's right that I'm tied to Woodcrest."

"Nor do I," Odlon said.

"There must be a way to free you," Roble said. "Zauber may know a way."

"He may," Shawndirea said, "but that's only if he's still here."

"You think he'd leave?"

"He has no reason to stay here now. The Vykings and dark elves no longer control Woodcrest. Besides, he and Haigla are *not* friends."

Odlon whispered, "I doubt she has friends."

"She's definitely an outcast of any social circle," Aerlene said. "And that may explain why she has bound me here. Using my power of charisma, she could subtly get others to like her."

"So how can we break the spell?" Roble asked Shawndirea. "Especially if your aunt no longer has magical powers."

"I have magic," Aerlene insisted. "But it's limited."

"Destroy the statue," Shawndirea said. Her face beamed. "That's where she has bound you. Destroying it should break her control over you."

"That might work," Aerlene replied. "But only if she isn't anywhere near it."

Roble glanced around the trees and buildings. Seeing no sign of Haigla, he said, "What would that matter?"

"Again, *the magic*," Aerlene said, rolling her eyes. She sighed and then shot Shawndirea a glance and said, "Tell me again *why* you chose *this* human?"

"Now, don't," Shawndirea said. "Remember that where he came from, he doesn't have much knowledge about magic and its properties. He's learning though."

"Sorry," Aerlene said, looking at Roble and waving her hands in slight surrender. "My head's still spinning over that abrupt shot of static that dropped me. And not to mention, my growing anger of things I'd like to *do* to that old hag."

Odlon extended his hand for Aerlene to step upon. He said, "My lady."

Aerlene glowed a radiant flattered smile and stepped upon his palm.

"Find Riese," Shawndirea said.

"Why?" Roble asked.

She smiled. "He has a big enough hammer to destroy the statue. With his powerful strength, I don't think he'll fail."

Roble and Odlon carried the faeries and headed toward the intersecting streets in the center of town. Riese stood talking with his son and Hordus. Although only Hordus' hands were restrained, the elder Vyking didn't attempt to flee. He seemed to respect Riese's authority.

"Riese," Roble said, "We need your help."

Riese frowned. "What is it?"

Roble explained their situation, how Aerlene was being held in Wood-crest against her will, but the mention of Haigla's power made Riese uncomfortable. "You want me to break the statue?" he asked.

Roble nodded.

"And what prevents her from attacking me after I've done so?" Riese said, his eyes hinted fear and uncertainty.

"For one thing," Aerlene said, "Her power will be greatly weakened if the statue is destroyed. Shawndirea and I should be strong enough to counter any vengeful attacks she might make."

"The dryads will also help once they discover her spell over them," Shawndirea said.

Riese headed for the statue, gripping his heavy hammer tightly in his muscled hand.

"Stop!" Haigla commanded. She stepped out from behind the water trough near the town council building.

Riese met her wicked gaze. He swallowed hard and his eyes narrowed.

"I'm warning you, Vyking," she said, raising her hand and pointing her wand in his direction. "Don't go near my statue."

Odlon set Aerlene at his feet and swiftly pulled his crossbow and loaded it. He aimed at the old woman. Shawndirea got on Roble's shoulder, and he pulled two weighted throwing knives from his belt.

Haigla waved her hands. A strong breeze flowed past. Seconds later, the doors to houses, huts, and even the town hall opened. People stepped out into the street and crowded the statue of Aerlene.

Roble wondered if she controlled these people or if they simply were curious as to what was about to happen. The odd gaze in their eyes indicated the former.

"Elf," she said. "Put down the bow."

Odlon chuckled. "No. You may have power, but you cannot stop all of us."

"I won't have to," she replied, nodding toward the gathering crowd. "They'll do it for me."

Riese glanced back at Odlon. The elf nodded and smiled. Odlon boldly took a step forward and aimed the bow right at Haigla's head. She readied her wand and faced him. When she did, Riese flung his hammer hard. Before the hammer struck the statue, one of the townsmen jumped and flung himself into the hammer's path. The hammer struck the man's head, and he dropped to the ground, lifeless.

The rest of the people faced Riese, Roble, and Odlon. Their expressionless faces let Roble understand how much power Haigla had over them. They didn't worship her. She controlled them with such force that they'd die before they allowed any harm to come to the statue.

"Put your weapons away," Haigla said.

Odlon's jaw tightened. He closed his left eye, aimed, and placed his finger on the trigger.

"Wait," Roble said, placing his hand on the elf's elbow.

"Why?" Odlon asked. "I have her in sight. I can kill her."

"I know."

"Then what's the problem?"

"What if her control is still over them after she dies? We'll still have to kill our way out of Woodcrest. These people aren't acting on their own free will. She's forcing them to obey."

Odlon eased the tension on the string and glanced at the increasing mob. The men and women stepped closer, their girth tightening as they approached. With slight agitation, Odlon lowered the bow. His shared sympathy was for the crowd, not Haigla.

"That's better. I showed you folks hospitality. Nice hot soup to fill your bellies," she said in her raspy voice, "and then you turn on me."

"What you're doing isn't right," Roble said.

"Nothing usually is," Haigla replied. "All the years I've lived here with such scrutiny and being shunned like a plague by those I've helped. Anytime someone became ill, they sought me and asked for my help. Never once did I turn them away. When all is well, they want me to remain hidden like an outcast because they don't want to look at me. There's never been any real appreciation."

She held her wand toward Roble and Odlon. The tip of her wand glowed. Riese's face tightened with anger. He stood weaponless. Shawndirea and Aerlene aimed their glowing fingers toward Haigla, ready to counter any spell she might cast.

From the middle of the crowd, Drucis shouted, "Aye! I believe you dropped this!"

The dwarf tossed the hammer over the townsfolk heads. Riese caught it and smiled. Without a hesitation, he threw the hammer at the statue again with all his might.

The hammer struck the head of Aerlene's statue, smashing the marble face. The entire head shattered. Marble fragments exploded and showered over the hypnotized crowded.

Haigla wailed and dropped to her knees. Rage changed her facial features into that of a hideous demon. Her voice deepened.

Aerlene and Shawndirea combined their powers and directed their magic at the old woman. Haigla shuddered, covered her face, and bowed face down on the ground, weeping loudly.

The townspeople shook their heads, as if suddenly awakened from their strange trances. Roble suspected that Haigla was more aligned with the dark elves than she had let on. She only destroyed them after they had ensured the town council members of Woodcrest were dead.

Aerlene flew to her headless statue and looked down at the townsfolk.

"You are free now," Aerlene said. "Haigla is the one responsible for the deaths of your leaders. She tricked me and used my powers to entice you into believing that she was the one to save you. Not only did she charm you, she was about to use her control over you so you'd kill the ones that got rid of the Vykings. She must be punished."

"How should she be punished?" one woman asked from the crowd.

"Yes," a man said, "what can we do?"

"Drive her from your town," Aerlene said. "And make certain she never returns."

Haigla lay prostrate on the ground, sobbing, but no pity came from those standing around. Apparently Aerlene's magic was ripped from the old woman. Haigla fell and flung her withered wand. The wand was far outside her reach.

Crukas appeared from the shadows, grabbed the wand, and hurried back to where Roble and the others were. A young girl ran to Crukas and extended her hand for the wand. He studied her eyes for a moment before handing it to her. She smiled, waving the wand and prancing around. Two men went to Haigla and helped the old woman to her feet. Once she stood, they bound her hands behind her back and led her toward the intersection of Woodcrest.

Tears streamed from her good eye. Her milky white eye increased in darkness until it finally became blacker than obsidian.

"Please take her far from here," the one man said, looking at Riese.

Riese gave a simple nod. "We can do that."

"No," Haigla said. "I cannot survive outside Woodcrest."

"What about Lehrling?" Roble asked.

"Yes!" Haigla said, her face suddenly brightening with hope. "I *must* stay to get him well. Don't send me out, or he will surely die."

A middle-aged woman approached with a smile and said, "I can tend to him until he has recovered."

"You know how to treat his illness?" Shawndirea asked.

The woman nodded.

"Good." Roble smiled. "Thanks. I hate to part ways with him, but he'll die if he travels on with us."

"I will make certain he is well taken care of."

"There are no words to express my gratitude," Roble said.

"None are needed," she replied.

The sun peaked over the horizon and the shades within Woodcrest began to lighten and fade. Men and women gathered their wagons, garden tools, harnessed mules to the plows, and headed along the roads and toward the opening gates for the first time since Waxxon's guards took the town.

While Riese checked his horse, several women came to the wagon with cloth-covered goods—cheese, bread, honey, and skins filled with wine.

"In our appreciation," one lady said when she placed the food on his wagon seat. Marc nodded and gently placed the goods beneath the seat.

Two men brought large sacks of oats and grains for them to feed their horses on the journey. After they set the bags in the wagon bed, Drucis rode up on Grey.

"Be room for one more along your journey, ye old ogre?" he asked Riese.

Riese turned and smiled. He replied, "Drucis, I must have *overlooked* your arrival."

The dwarf's eyes narrowed. "Don't be *overstepping* your boundaries!"

Riese chuckled. "Can always use you along the way. The first stop is Ironwood. After that, we part ways. I don't quite know where we'll be going."

"Anywhere is fine with me. Sorry about Hobskin's Tavern," Drucis said.

Riese's eyes widened. "No others survived?"

Sadness claimed Drucis' eyes and his facial expressions. "No."

"How did *you*?"

"Twernt easy."

The dwarf explained how the Plague-bringer came into the bar and everything that transpired soon thereafter. When he mentioned the loss of his two comrades, his voice weakened and his eyes softened while he spoke.

"Again," he said, "I'm sorry about the tavern. Setting it ablaze was the only way I could survive."

Riese shook his head. "To have you alive, old friend, burning the entire town down would have been worth it."

"Aww, don't be getting all misty on me now. Tears rust your weapons and armor."

"Look who's talking?"

A half hour passed and everyone was set to depart Woodcrest. Roble glanced back at the gates one last time as they rode around the bend. He hoped it would not be the last time he saw Lehrling.

rukas walked alongside the wagon. Amusement curled his lips when he stared at the old iron cage in the wagon bed that now housed Haigla. The bitter old woman stood stooped and held the bars tightly in her wrinkled hands. She studied the bars, the welded runic symbols, and sighed. Hordus sat on the back of the wagon bed with his feet dangling a couple inches above the road as the wagon moved. His cuffed hands were tethered to a lower bar on the cage.

"Who constructed this little cell?" she asked.

"Riese," Crukas said.

Haigla turned in the cell and looked at Riese. She said, "Who taught you these symbols? Most Vykings shun any sort of magic. You've hung a spell to neutralize the powers of the occupant. How did you know to do this?"

Without glancing back, Riese replied, "My wife."

"Not a Vyking, I'm guessing."

"No."

"Then how?"

"Enough about her," he said, bluntly.

Haigla's eyes glanced from Riese to his son. She studied his freckled complexion, his red hair, and how much smaller his body frame was than his father's.

"Part elf?" she said.

Riese handed the reins to Marc, turned, and pointed his hammer at her. His eyes were mean, cold, and determined. "One more word."

The old woman's face paled. There was no questioning the harsh gaze that Riese possessed. Any further word and Roble had no doubt the blacksmith would kill her inside the cage. Rather than reply further, Haigla turned and faced the road behind them. Apparently, she wanted to live even if it were outside of Woodcrest.

Crukas grinned and seemed relieved that Riese's anger was directed elsewhere. Roble sensed a direct change in the thief. However, he never would fully trust the thief. How could he?

A CRUDE WOODEN sign with a carved arrow pointed the direction to Ironwood. Crukas became more apprehensive after they passed it. The road nestled along the side of a steep ridge on the right hand side. On the left, the drop off was dangerously deep and filled with large rocks and trees. Water from a narrow stream splashed off the rocks below. A foggy mist drifted in the cool morning air. What should have been a pleasant morning for walking and meditating was anything except. Despair and anxiety settled over Crukas like a black miserable cloud. The last thing he wanted was to keep moving forward, but he couldn't retreat. Otherwise, he feared, Odlon or Roble might kill him.

Moving forward was a death sentence anyway. Although Roble and the others promised to keep him safe, he didn't think they'd ever get past Ironwood. They might, but he knew the town council of Ironwood wanted him dead at all costs. The thing that puzzled him the most was why.

Each time Crukas had escorted a thief to Ironwood to collect the bounty; the town's council threw a large banquet and celebration. The tables were covered with roasted pork, venison, game fowls, fish, and more breads and desserts than he had seen at most royal gatherings in Hoffnung. The townsfolk ate and drank heartily. Most danced while quartets played their stringed instruments. Bards told tales. Magicians performed fascinating tricks. There were numerous games where skilled men and women entered competitions with axes, bows, and knives. And during all of this, people approached Crukas with gifts or hand shakes. Beautiful women danced with him. Others offered more, and after a day of celebration, he left the town as a hero.

That all changed upon his last venture to pass through Ironwood. He had not brought another wanted thief or burglar. He simply was passing through. Crukas had entered the gate right as the sun was rising and before too many townspeople had aroused to begin their morning tasks. One guard recognized him and shouted for him to surrender.

The request seemed more a practical joke at first. When he turned and smiled to the guard, his smile retreated with sudden fear. The guard had his sword drawn and rushed him. Crukas ran.

Midway through town, the guard blew his horn to get the attention of other guards patrolling the cobblestone streets. Clattering swords and creaking leather clued Crukas to their quick pursuit to find him.

Crukas, a master at vanishing into his surroundings, quickly hid behind a barrel of dried fish. While he crouched low, the light morning breeze rustled the edges of a yellowed, tattered piece of parchment nailed to the corner post of the trader's tent. His eyes widened as he read the wanted poster that had his image sketched on it.

Two guards rushed past his position. He rose, yanked the poster, folded it, and tucked it inside his tunic. More horns sounded. A shrill from a whistle stirred more townsfolk awake.

Crukas ducked down, crawled from the barrel, and slid beneath a trader table. He watched the street for more approaching patrols. Across the narrow cobblestone street several tanned hides hung on a thin rope between two poles. The vendor wasn't anywhere nearby. Crukas looked both directions and scurried quickly to conceal himself behind the vendor's curtain of hides. Once there, the distinct rattling of chainmail chattered his direction. Armored guards sprinted down the street.

He hurried down a side alley, further from the market square, and found a small opening in the wall. The acrid scent that drifted from the hole was one too familiar. The sewers. It had been years since he had to endure such squalor. He had dined with wealthy magistrates, knights, and lords ever since his guild had disbanded. Never had he believed or even dared to think that he'd crawl through the sewers like a wet rat again.

Not certain why he was wanted or what alternative he might have if he surrendered, he squeezed his skinny body through the opening. The small round enclosure was similar to a water well except nothing was drawn from the hole. Waste and garbage were tossed inside, left to rot.

The horrid smell made him gag, but he balanced himself between the grimy, ooze-covered rocks. The roaring guards sounding alerts near the market square left Crukas no choice. He had to go deeper into the sewers and hope that he found the flow that led outside Ironwood. The filth smudged his face, his hands and arms, and his silken shirt was ruined.

Pressing his fingers into the narrow grooves between the blocks for leverage, he climbed downward, going deeper into the darkness and discovering that he now choked to breathe. The gaseous methane smell not only nauseated him, but he neared unconsciousness. If he didn't find a source of fresh air, he'd pass out and die.

His slick filthy fingertips clung to the blocks. His head spun. He coughed and lost his grip. His back struck the opposite wall, and he flung his arms helplessly as he dropped to the bottom of the garbage shaft. His fall ended with a tremendous splash into a deep pool of cold stinking water. The frigid water sharply awakened him. He swam upward and broke through the water's surface. A thick layer of floating waste prevented him from going back under. The smell was terrible but at least the gaseous layer hovered above him.

Water dripped from the walls. His heavy breathing escaped in choking gasps. Surrounded by filth and darkness, he had no idea where to go. There were no torches to light the passage, and he guessed that had been a blessing. A torch would have ignited the gas and fried him. This gutter lacked any system of proper management. Unlike the elegant sewers in Hoffnung, which he thought odd to think in such terms, but it was true. The City of Hoffnung had been well kept with properly dug sewer channels that dipped at the appropriate angle to ensure the waste flowed out of the city and didn't stagnant into one huge pile of rotting dung. The channels were also lined with torches so the city maintenance crews could follow easily to prevent any waste from getting blocked up.

Crukas used a pillow of solid waste to keep afloat while kicking his feet until he rounded a few twists and turns in the long sewer tunnel. At the far end of the channel light brightened the path slightly. Water trickled and cascaded through a metal grate with enough force that an undertow tugged slightly, pulling him toward the grate.

He kicked his feet harder, pushing his way through the garbage until he reached the iron bars of the grate. He clung to the bars and glanced out. The sewer waste spilled through the opening and splattered on rocks a hundred feet below. From his viewpoint he watched the trees and immediately knew that he was on the southeastern part of Ironwood. Being thin, he squeezed through the grate bars with great ease. He'd never known a fat thief, and on that day he understood why. To survive the life as a thief, one had to be quick, nimble, and able to fit through tight places.

It had taken him half the day to get down that side of the rock ledge to the flowing river below. Instead of heading southward, Crukas chose to head back to Glacier Ridge. That decision had led to him joining Roble's party without any way to bypass Ironwood. Crukas shook his head. He wished now that he had headed south, perhaps even to the Woodnog swamps on the outskirts of the City of Woodnog. Should he survive passing through Ironwood this time, he planned to never head north again.

Crukas glanced at Haigla. Her good eye was trained on him. Her blind eye still resembled a shiny orb of black obsidian. Her near toothless mouth hung partly open.

"You do know you will die on this journey, don't you?" Haigla said. The words weren't audible but echoed inside his head.

His eyes widened when he looked at her.

She smiled. "You want to know how I speak to you, eh?"

Laughter rang in his head. He nodded.

"Go on," she said, "Reply in your mind. I can hear you. We can talk."

Crukas thought, "The cage stops magic. How can you speak into my head?"

She cackled. "That's not magic, thief. It's something I have always been able to do."

"Can you read others' thoughts?"

"At times. But getting inside your head to *steal* your thoughts is more amusing than any of the others."

"Why?"

"You're a thief unable to lock the treasures inside your own mind. You worry about what happens when you return to Ironwood, but do know, you will be betrayed when you reach that town."

"By whom?"

"The only way you'll be safe is to get me out of this cage. We can flee together."

Crukas' eyes narrowed. He turned his attention back to the road ahead. Although he refused to look at her, she didn't cease speaking to his mind. He trained his thoughts to other activities like lock picking, boring things, anything to ignore her words. But he wanted to keep mundane thoughts so she'd get tired of reading his mind. In fifteen minutes, it must have worked because she sat down in the cage and closed her eye.

He now worried about who would betray him. He didn't doubt what she had said because if she could read his mind, it was very probable that she had read the betrayal from another's mind in the group. Only when he reached Ironwood would he discover the truth and hope that he might escape with his life.

CHAPTER 56

Drucis rode Grey up beside Bleys. The dwarf looked at Roble and gave a quick nod. He said, "Roble, is it?"

Roble nodded. "Yes."

"Drucis," he replied. "Nice to meet ya."

"Likewise."

He studied Roble for several minutes, looking him over as if sizing him up for a duel. Finally, he shook his head and said, "I don't recall seeing ya in these parts."

"That's probably because it's my first time travelling here."

Drucis frowned with keen interest. "How can that be? The only way to Glacier Ridge is through this pass unless, of course you be from the frost plains and the highlands, but they have more fair skin and white hair. No, you're not from there."

Roble shook his head. "No, I'm not."

"You don't favor the folks from the south kingdoms, either."

With a slight smile, Roble said, "I imagine not."

"Well, lad there be no other roads to lead ya to Glacier Ridge."

"There is a pass through the mountain on the other side of Glacier Ridge."

"Don't be kiddin' wit me, lad. There be no other way."

Roble laughed.

"Something funny?" Drucis said with a harsh glare. Aggravation set in his stern tone, matching the frustration that narrowed his eyes.

"Nothing that concerns you."

"Aye. Well then, tell me why there be a faery riding along with you?"

"I promised to get her back to her homeland so she can get her wings repaired."

Drucis frowned and said, "They do that, lad?"

"We're hopeful."

"Well, lad. You be in good company should we 'appen upon any unruly rogues or bandits. Be swinging me ax, I will."

"Where are we heading?" Roble asked.

Drucis studied Roble for a few moments. A thin grin parted his bushy white beard. "You really don't know the area, do you?"

Roble shook his head. "No."

"Well, this pass will cut into Corwin's Pass, which is far more treacherous. Makes it difficult for armies to invade any towns out this way. The road be too narrow to march in large groups."

Ahead, down the sloping road, two figures approached. The one in the front walked on foot. The second rode on horseback. He wore the armor of Waxxon's men.

"What we be having here?" Drucis asked with excitement growing in his voice. His hand quickly slid to his ax. "The day may not be a total loss."

Riese pulled back the reins and stopped the wagon. He glanced over his shoulder at Odlon, Roble, and Drucis. Crukas slinked in between the wagon and the ridge wall to become inconspicuous.

"Be ready, lad," Drucis said to Roble.

The man on the horse had long braided blonde hair and brilliant blue eyes. His shoulders were broad, his chest thick, and he possessed a steel shield and a sheathed long sword. His armor was tightly fitted and almost looked a size too small for him.

The boy in front wore ragged clothes. His hair was cropped short and his face was covered with grime. The rider raised both hands above his head as he and the walking teen approached.

"We want no trouble," he said.

"Who are you?" Riese asked, standing on the wagon with his hammer in hand.

"Caen."

"You wear the armor of Waxxon's men," Riese stated. "But you aren't of Welkstone blood."

Caen studied each of Roble's group before finally returning his gaze to Riese's eyes and acquiescing a nod. He said, "You're right in your observations."

"You travel alone?" Odlon asked, raising his crossbow.

"Just me and this squire," Caen replied. "We're heading to the next town for supplies, nothing more. If you'll just let us pass without incident, all is well."

"An odd request for someone under Waxxon's command," Odlon said.

"Not all of us revere Waxxon," he replied with an even grin.

The squire's brow narrowed with anger at the mention of Waxxon's name. His hands tightened on his halberd. Although a teen, the young squire kept an intimidating posture that made Roble wonder how difficult it would be to disarm him.

"Again," Caen said, "let us pass and there will be no bloodshed."

Riese shook his head and said, "You dare make a boastful challenge before us?"

"Let me at him," Drucis said, dismounting.

"Apologies," Caen said. "Perhaps I should have phrased that differently. There's no need for attack from either side. You hold the advantage over us, but I'm not seeking any violent skirmish between us."

Riese lowered his hammer and said, "Very well. Pass in peace."

Drucis grumbled and said, "Dammit." Reluctantly, he climbed onto Grey.

"In exchange," Caen said, looking at Roble. "I offer you this. Ironwood has more guards like myself. They will not be as kind to you as I have been. In fact, seeing you are a member of the Dragon Skull Order, they will not hesitate in trying to kill you."

Goosebumps ran up Roble's arms. The hairs on the back of his neck stiffened.

Caen gave a slight nod to Roble as he and the squire passed slowly. Roble glanced into the icy blue gaze of this guard, and Roble didn't see the hardness and hatred that he had in all the others that wore Waxxon's armor.

"Are you fleeing Waxxon's service?" Roble asked.

Caen's tugged the reins of his horse tight enough that the horse stopped. Without looking back, Caen asked, "And what makes you draw such a conclusion?"

"Several reasons, actually," Roble replied. "Your armor doesn't fit. It's too small around your chest, but your leggings are much too long. Another, as Riese mentioned, is that you aren't of Welkstone blood. And I've yet to ever see Waxxon send one guard out alone. Usually in pairs, but sometimes much more."

"All I will say is that more of Waxxon's guard await at Ironwood. A half dozen, and they are well armed. You have been warned."

Drucis laughed heartily.

Caen did turn then. His gaze narrowed. "And what about that is funny?"

"Almost sounds like you're inviting us to join ya by having us turn around. This pass leads directly to Ironwood. There's no alternative route where we be heading."

"At least you have the knowledge that they are there," Caen said, turning away, and tapping his horse's flanks.

"That we 'ave," Drucis said with a broad grin. "By sundown there be a few less of your comrades roaming the lands."

Caen didn't reply, nor did he bother looking back.

"Peace be to you then, soldier," Drucis said in a mocking tone.

Caen looked back over his shoulder and said, "And the witch that you have prisoner, it would serve you best if you kill her before you decide to release her from that cage."

Riese looked at Haigla and then to Caen. He asked, "Why?"

"There's a greater darkness about her than you may think," Caen replied. "The power she holds is much like what reigns in the Black Chasm. The closer you carry her to that place, the greater the power you'll grant her. Best to lighten your load now for the sake of your group."

Roble and Crukas stared at the old witch. Her face tightened with scorn. Worry claimed her good eye and she warily glanced around at each of her captors. Roble, Odlon, and the others all gazed at her with suspicion.

"He prattles nonsense," Haigla said.

Shawndirea said, "He tells the truth. Otherwise you'd have no fear of his words."

"It's not his words that I fear," Haigla said. "It's your *belief* in his words that I fear."

Caen and the squire continued moving further down the road. Riese jumped off the wagon and headed to the rear where Odlon, Drucis, and Roble remained on their horses. "Do you believe what he said?" Riese asked.

"Oh, he speaks the truth," Shawndirea said.

"How do you know?" Roble asked.

"I sense it in her aura. It darkens. The cage may neutralize her powers while she's in it, but somehow she's absorbing power from another source, just like Caen said."

"Not true," Haigla insisted. Her hands gripped the iron bars fiercely. Veins swelled up her thin arms like snaky ribbons. Smoke streamed from between her fingers and the iron. She reeled back and screamed. Blisters puffed on her hands where she had held the bars.

Odlon raised the bow and aimed at her head.

"No!" Roble said.

"Now is not the time for mercy," Riese said to Roble. "You see what she becomes."

"He's right," Shawndirea said.

"How can she become stronger if the runes in the iron bars prevent her from using her power?" Roble asked.

Drucis shook his head. "You've a lot to learn, lad. It's not her magic that grows. Something has entered her."

Odlon nodded. "A demon."

Froth foamed from Haigla's mouth. Her dead eye turned from opaque to fiery red. Strange guttural sounds rumbled inside her throat. Claws sprouted on her fingers.

"We have to kill her," Riese said.

"Why not turn her over at Ironwood?" Roble asked.

"The bars won't contain what possesses her," Shawndirea said. "Her strength or what's inside her will allow her to rip through the cage door long before we get to Ironwood."

Remorse coursed through Roble. He had hoped to spare the old woman because she had seemed kind to them when they had arrived in Woodcrest. Indeed, when they had entered her cellar, she had acted grandmotherly and decent. However, the more things that were revealed about her lust for power and authority over Woodcrest, the nastier her countenance had become. But Roble hoped they could simply remove her from that town and take her somewhere else to lessen the possible dangers she might unleash. Now, seeing this odd transformation, he understood that was no longer an option.

Odlon aimed the bow, fired, and the arrow sunk deep into Haigla's forehead. She dropped hard in a bent position to the floor of the cage, but her breathing didn't stop. She panted like someone that had sprinted for miles. The claws in her hands tore through the ends of her fingers. Her skin split up her arms. Beneath the human flesh was crimson colored reptilian-like skin. She wasn't human, or had she ever been?

Odlon fired another arrow into the Haigla's heart, and whatever moved inside her ceased breathing. He swung off his horse and pulled a blade from his belt. Riese opened the cage door, and Odlon slit the creature's throat. Black oozing blood leaked from the cut.

"What is that?" Roble asked.

Odlon glanced back, still partway kneeing over the creature. He replied, "I'm not certain, but it's not Haigla. Perhaps she was already dead when this thing captured her image so it could snare us?"

Shawndirea nodded. "That's very possible. Or she is still hiding somewhere in Woodcrest. It appears to be a form-taker type of demon. It has taken her appearance."

Drucis and Odlon exchanged worried expressions.

Drucis dropped off the side of his horse with his ax in hand. "That Black Chasm causes chaos throughout Aetheaon. Since its formation, there be odd creatures popping up all over. Pull that beast out onto the ground."

Riese and Odlon each grabbed a leg and yanked the odd creature off the wagon and onto the dark road. A dark trail of blood leaked as they moved it. Drucis took his ax blade and tapped at the creature's skull. More of the human flesh peeled away like brittle plaster, exposing its hideous lizard-like face.

Roble moved closer and said, "Remarkable."

Odlon shot him a perplexed glance.

Roble gave a slight shrug. "It is since I've *never* seen anything like it."

Drucis laughed. "Only say that when it's a dead one. Never marvel over a live one or it be the last thing you witness before death."

"No doubt," Roble said. "So what is it?"

"Ain't seen anything like it before, so I don't rightly know," Drucis replied. He heaved his ax above his head, and in one swift downward swing, he decapitated it.

"And how did Caen *know*?" Roble asked.

"That's a good question," Shawndirea replied.

A horrid stench lifted into the air from the beast's black blood. Drucis glanced at the others and asked, "What do we do with it?"

Riese said, "Leave it for the crows."

Caen and the squire had disappeared out of view down the narrow road.

Roble said, "How does this change our plans?"

"What do you mean?" Drucis asked.

"The townsfolk of Ironwood want Crukas. Not sure if that is dead *or* alive, but now before we can even try to negotiate for his freedom, we'll have to rid the town of Waxxon's men."

"Only a half dozen," Drucis said. "Nothing to be alarmed over."

Odlon nodded. "I agree."

"Perhaps so," Roble said, "But we have this creature that has been with us the entire journey from Woodcrest. If it has any connection to Waxxon's men, they will know that we're headed that direction."

"Aye, that will be a better challenge," Drucis said.

Roble looked at Odlon and said, "And Zauber had misinformed us of the numbers at Woodcrest."

Odlon replied, "That's true."

"It may not have been purposely," Shawndirea said.

"What do you mean?"

She said, "Perhaps some of them were cloaked with invisibility."

Drucis rubbed his thick white beard. "Aye, that could well be."

Crukas stepped closer. His nervous eyes darted from one to each of the others. "We can always turn back," he said.

Roble looked at Crukas and shook his head, "No. That's not an option. So what's the bounty on your head?"

"More than my life is worth," the thief replied. He brushed the jet-black hair from his dark eyes.

"Don't short sale yourself," Odlon said. Drucis frowned at the remark.

"What's that supposed to mean?" Crukas asked.

Odlon replied, "You're known throughout Aetheaon as a master thief. You're probably worth far more than they offer alive."

Drucis' eyebrows rose when he recognized Crukas. "Aye, he's right lad. You're much more valuable alive and to us. We be protecting ya with all we got."

Crukas gave a slight smile of relief.

"What are the chances that this reptilian demon-like creature might have connections with Waxxon's men?" Roble asked.

Odlon frowned. "Do you mean like a spy and magically links his information to them?"

"Yes. Exactly like that."

"We will approach Woodcrest more cautiously now," Drucis said, returning to his horse. "But I have my doubts that Waxxon's men would have anything to do with the likes of a creature like that."

Odlon nodded. "I have to agree with you."

"That is rarer than most treasures I seek," Drucis said with a broad grin.

Odlon laughed. "Indeed."

An hour of riding passed before they came upon a long wooden bridge that crossed Icethaw River. Fog mists drifted above the water that flowed several hundred feet below. The temperature dropped thirty degrees as they rode onto the bridge. The horse hoofs thudded and rattled the bridge. Their moving weight sagged the aged beams and planks.

Roble peered over the side of the bridge but wasn't able to see the rushing river for all the white fog. When he exhaled, his breath formed little clouds.

"It's beautiful," Shawndirea said softly.

Roble nodded his agreement.

"Won't be much longer to Ironwood," Drucis said. "About three hours or less."

"Not bad," Roble replied.

"And still over two days journey to Elvendale," Shawndirea said. "No telling how long we will be hindered in Ironwood."

Drucis smiled. "Not long if I have my way about it."

The temperature plummeted even more when they neared the center of the bridge. Roble enjoyed the sudden coolness, and the rushing river splashing was also soothing. The gap between the two ridges was about a quarter mile, but due to the rising fog, visibility wasn't more than fifteen yards. He worried what they might encounter in crossing the bridge. Occasionally he glanced back to see if Caen had circled back to attack from the rear, but he hadn't. Roble believed the man's warning revealed his sincerity. However, he was not exactly certain what the man's intention truly was. An air of mystery shrouded the man, and the further south Roble and his group travelled, the more he doubted their paths would cross again.

Riding into the thick fog made Roble also wonder if perhaps Caen was a leading decoy and behind him, hidden on the shrouded bridge, were more of Waxxon's riders waiting with their weapons drawn.

Sounds echoed above the rushing waters below. The cries were odd, not human, and if they came from beasts, the deep volume of their voices brought chills to Roble. The loudness reminded him of a lion's roar mixed with an angered ape. They sounded like very large beasts speaking sentences only they understood.

Drucis noticed the worried expression on Roble's face and said, "That be bothering ya?"

"Not sure. Should it?"

Drucis released a hearty chuckle. "Nothin' to be alarmed about from way up 'ere."

"Okay . . . then what is it?" Roble asked.

"That be ice trolls, lad. They're big, burly, and stupid but they never leave the caves and edges of the Ice Thaw River. They probably be spearing fish along the banks. That's about all the smarts they 'ave."

Roble stared over the edge of the bridge, hoping to see them, but the thick mist prevented such luck. "You ever see one?"

Drucis winced. "No sane person travels Ice Thaw."

"Which is why I asked *you*," Roble said with a smile.

"Oh, jest now, will ya?"

"Sorry, couldn't resist."

Drucis chuckled. "No problem, lad. At least your remark can't be taken as a *low* blow or cheap shot about me height. Now, had the *ogre* driving the wagon up ahead said that, well, then we be having different problems."

"Pipe down back there, Drucis," Riese said without glancing back.

Drucis faced Roble and placed his hand partway over his mouth as he whispered, "He hears a bit too good for his old age."

"And you tend to ramble endlessly with your remarks," Riese replied.

"*See?*" Drucis said with a broad grin and his eyebrows raised.

As they neared the end of the bridge, Drucis' hand tightened on his ax handle, which alerted Roble to take precaution. Roble placed his hands near his throwing daggers hidden on his belt. Drucis tapped his horse's flanks and moved ahead of Roble.

Shawndirea shivered slightly on Roble's shoulder. She hugged herself for a moment and rubbed her hands along her arms. She leaned close to his ear and whispered, "The dwarf seems entertained by you."

"That's good I suppose," Roble said.

"It is. You make friends quite easily, which is also a good thing. However, other than those in this party, I must warn you to be more wary. You cannot be over trusting."

"I know. I understand. It's been fortunate for me thus far."

She nodded. "It has. But once we get to Ironwood, be prepared. The townspeople there are from various races, half-breeds, renegades, and tyrants."

Roble frowned. "I wonder why they've turned on Crukas?"

"We may never know."

"He doesn't seem to know, either."

"I know, and the closer we get to Ironwood, the more nervous he has become."

Roble nodded. "I noticed that, too. But they apparently had welcomed and rewarded him for turning over other thieves and now they have a bounty out for him?"

"I guess we'll see once we get there."

They encountered no other riders or travellers crossing the bridge, which was to Roble's relief. He continued thinking about Caen and the mystery that veiled him. The man knew more than what he wished them to know, but Roble had the gut feeling that this man had never been one of Waxxon's guards.

Giant images appeared on both sides at the end of the bridge. When the fog thinned, Roble recognized them to be carved statues. The one on the left was an armored dwarf, and the one on the right was a regal elf with her sword drawn and shield raised.

Roble's tension lessened, and so did Drucis'. Once they were a few yards away from the bridge, the fog vanished and the temperature returned to the post-spring warmth. The road ahead remained narrow and dark. The black forest branches were webbed with white silky mesh, which was inviting in one aspect, but very forbidding in others. The biggest concern for Roble was what had knitted the expansive web.

Little sunlight seeped through the thick branches. The deep long shadows loomed. The wind whispered through the forest while various insects hummed and chirped from their hiding places. Tacked to a tree was a sign indicating the distance to Ironwood.

Drucis smiled and said, "Not much further." His muscled hand wrapped around the ax handle.

CHAPTER 57

The town of Ironwood was centered within a massive grove of giant trees. The trees' bark was smooth and rusty-colored like aged iron. Carved stone blocks were stacked into impressive walls between thick tree trunks that stood as corner posts.

At various places near the road, large trees had been felled, leaving their massive stumps behind. Higher in the trees were platforms and plank bridges that connected from tree to tree. Intersecting roadways that led to shops, inns, and houses for the elite. No one entered Ironwood's gates unseen, and perhaps even now, Roble reasoned, they were being watched.

He couldn't explain it, but he felt eyes upon them, watching, waiting.

Near the gates several riders entered and disappeared from view. Roble and the others watched the activity near the walls of this trading town. They didn't see any of Waxxon's men, but that didn't mean Caen's warning was false. These henchmen might well be on the inside or somewhere up above at a keen vantage point. It did not seem that they had overtaken this town like the others had Woodcrest, which made Roble question the bravery of the men. Woodcrest was a town of farmers who sought to live peaceably and modestly. Ironwood, from what he had been told, was filled with various classes and ruled by at least partially corrupt council members. With Crukas' fear of returning, that seemed evident. For a town to pay many bounties for wanted thieves he had handed over to them, only to become wanted for crimes as well, meant the council did what favored themselves more so than others. No authority that acted in this manner could be trusted. Of course, trusting a thief wasn't any better.

"What's the best way to enter?" Roble asked Crukas.

"I'd say we go around, skip the town altogether, but the forest isn't any safer," he replied.

"Why isn't it safe?"

"Poisonous vines, dark elves, and the traps Ironwood has set for bear and other wild game as well as poachers." Crukas pointed at wooden signs posted on trees that lined both sides of the road. "Their warnings can't be clearer."

"And they held you prisoner?"

Crukas. "No. They tried to take me into custody."

"How did you escape?" Roble asked.

"The sewers."

Drucis shook his head with disgust. "I say we barge in headfirst! I'm not taking the sewers like some ol' damned rat."

Riese smiled. "Only three of us cannot enter for obvious reasons."

Shawndirea frowned.

He continued, "Odlon, Drucis, and I don't have to worry about entering Ironwood. Crukas is the one wanted, and Roble will only draw the resentment of Waxxon's men since he wears the armor of the Dragon Skull Order. We three can actually go inside and scout. Of course, my son can accompany us, but Hordus must stay here."

"I won't betray you," Hordus said.

"Perhaps not," Riese said, "But the others may recognize you and begin to ask questions."

"Very well," Hordus said with a tinge of disappointment in his voice. His eyes reflected his hurt that Riese lacked trust in the old man's words.

"Your idea is not a bad one, Riese," Odlon said, nodding. "We could enter and look around."

"Won't it be a bit odd? What will they think if they see a dwarf and a pale elf travelling around with a big ol' ogre?" Drucis asked. His tone was serious and didn't imply any jest.

Riese towered over Drucis and said, "We don't have to enter at the same time, shoe-scum."

"Easy there," Drucis replied. "Didn't mean anything bad by it. Just an observation *they* might assume. Dwarves and elves ain't exactly chummy friends, ya know? Not even after one or the other is half drunk."

Riese shook his head and chuckled.

Crukas brushed his dark hair from his nervous eyes. He didn't like being right outside Ironwood at all.

Riese pointed his long finger at Drucis and Odlon and then he said, "Saddle up. We three ride in together. If it draws attention, all the better.

The sooner we find where Waxxon's men are, the quicker we can move past Ironwood."

"It may not be Waxxon's men that we need to fear the most," Roble said.

Riese turned sharply with a frown. "What then?"

"Crukas was befriended by the people here for turning over thieves. Then suddenly their attention focused on taking him into custody. Someone else, possibly a council member or merchant discovered who Crukas really is," Roble said. He looked at Crukas and asked, "Did you steal from any merchants in Ironwood while turning in thieves?"

Crukas shook his head. "No. With the high reward they paid, I had no reason."

"Ah, be honest now," Drucis said with scorn. "A thief is a thief, through and through. Always be a temptation to see what one can take without getting caught. Isn't that type of excitement worth more than gold?"

"I admit that is true," Crukas said. "But I never took anything while I was in Ironwood, in spite of obvious treasures I could have taken so easily at any of the banquets they hosted."

Drucis and Riese stared into the thief's eyes. He didn't flinch or look away.

"Aye, he be telling the truth," Drucis said. "And I don't say that lightly, 'cause I don't trust a thief."

Riese nodded. "I agree."

Roble studied Crukas' eyes and his gestures. Nothing about him revealed that he was lying. "Can you think of *any* reason they'd turn on you?" he asked.

Crukas shook his head. "Nothing, I swear."

"You stay here with them," Riese said to Roble. "Let us scout around."

CHAPTER 58

"Where am I?" Haigla asked, peering through the open doorway into the grand alchemy room where the wizard glanced up from his studies.

"Spellhaven," Zauber replied.

"How did I get here?"

"It was necessary."

Her brow furrowed. Her one good eye studied the dark bearded wizard with interest. "*Why* am I here?"

"Let's just say," Zauber said, twisting a long strand of his beard, "If I did not take you from Woodcrest, you'd be dead."

"What alerted you to my danger?" she asked.

"Whispers in the wind, the swaying grasses, and the dryads inside Woodcrest called to me. Strange things keep arising ever since the Black Chasm formed."

"I know, but why does that require me taken from my home?" she asked warily.

Zauber stared out his tower window. Haigla rose from the wooden chair in his alchemist lab and met him at the window. Looking out from the top floor, she studied the marshy terrain below. The tower stood in a thick cypress grove. The river that flowed from the north branched into two smaller rivers that provided a water barrier on each side of his tower, which was a great deterrent to unwanted visitors and allowed him complete privacy.

He had also placed a spell that kept a constant misty haze above the two rapidly flowing rivers to conceal his tower from adventurers. Seldom did he have an unfortunate explorer cross into his peninsula.

Black crows perched on the thick-needled pine branches. Their attention focused on Zauber's rock-walled tower. Their caws were harsh and echoed along with the sound of the two rushing rivers.

"I don't *recall* leaving Woodcrest. What happened? Why am I here?"

Zauber smiled. His eyes sparkled with energy. "You remember your guests that you fed?"

"The elf, and the human with the faery?" she asked.

"Yes."

"Of course. What about them?"

"The man, Roble. Did you detect anything different about him?"

Haigla thought for a moment. As she reflected on the night, she nodded. "He did seem different."

"You realize he's from the Overlands?" Zauber asked.

"Of course. There's no denying that. He's unlike most humans on our side of the rift."

"But there's more to him than I understand. Something different."

Haigla thought for a moment, and then she said, "Perhaps he came because of the Black Chasm?"

"No," Zauber replied. "Nothing like that. But what concerns me is how Shawndirea travels through the rift that joins our realms. What she does is dangerous. She might one day allow something worse to enter our realm or his."

Haigla chuckled, hacked at bit, and then wiped brown snuff juice from her chin. "I don't think she will. She seems content with her human. Now that she has him, I don't think she'll consider crossing to the Overlands again."

Zauber pulled the glowing yellow orb from his robe pocket and watched it flicker. He nodded. "She does have an obsession with Roble."

"Almost a deep love and devotion."

"That may be so. But he's not the one that will stop whatever the Black Chasm is. Although, I believe he will be a factor in destroying the powers that brought the chasm alive."

"How so?"

Zauber stared intently into the orb. He frowned as shapes and shadows twisted and turned inside the small globe. He winced and said, "That, my dear witch, I don't know. At least not yet, but time will tell."

"How long must I endure your hospitality?" she asked, looking out the window.

Zauber laughed softly. "My accommodations aren't to your liking?"

"Are anyone's ever enough for those who practice magic?"

"No, dear lady. No, they are never the same as the home we hold sacred."

Haigla smiled a near toothless smile. "Our powers are always the most powerful where our center of energy flows."

"You can root yourself elsewhere."

Her brow furrowed. "You're not letting me go back to Woodcrest?"

"I won't stop you, if that's your choice, but you need to know the town is no longer safe for you."

"Why?"

Zauber sighed. "Perhaps it's best that I show you. Come with me."

Haigla turned from the open window and followed him across the polished marble floor to his crude work table with various bubbling potions, open spell books, and dried herbs.

The wizard lifted a black cloth off a covered object and revealed his black crystal ball. It glistened in the glowing candlelight. With a gentle wave of his hand, the ball came to life, revealing swirling shadows that soon materialized into an overhead view of Woodcrest. The night sky hung filled with a twinkling array of stars. Soon, an ice crow cawed, and they witnessed the inside of Haigla's shack from the bird's point of view.

Haigla shivered with concern and partial rage. "How long have you been witness to what I've done?"

"Only when necessary," he replied.

"And how was this night necessary?" she asked.

"Don't view me as your enemy, Haigla. As you will see, had I not seen what was to occur that night, you'd be dead."

"What warning did you have? What right have you to enter my house and spy on me?"

Zauber waved his weary hand and calmly shook his head. "Spying is a bit harsh."

She pointed at the crystal ball. "What do you call *that*?"

"Saving your life."

She scowled.

"Now wait, dear witch," he said softly, "And watch."

Haigla leaned closer. Zauber pointed his bony long finger.

Something moved in the shadows behind her spell library. It moved so subtly that had she not looked when he pointed, she'd have missed it entirely. Neither her cat nor the snow raven had noticed its presence.

"What is it?"

"An imp."

The witch glanced from the crystal ball to him. Startled concern creased her brow. "An imp? In my cellar? What was it doing there?"

"Making certain to alert its master when the opportunity arose."

"Opportunity for what?"

"A shape-shifting demon lurked outside your home that night. Its intent was to kill you and replace you, thus taking over the town. But after you fed Roble, Odlon, and Shawndirea, I intervened."

Inside the ball, the little imp leapt from the bookshelf. It stretched its scrawny arms and flailed long fingernails that resembled razor-edged knives. A second before the imp struck, Haigla disappeared. The imp's mouth opened to shriek, but hit the small boiling cauldron where Haigla had been mixing her concoction. The bubbling liquid flamed orange for a brief moment before the imp melted into the soupy mixture.

"That's when I took you," Zauber said.

"I gathered *that* much. Why don't I remember it?"

Zauber shrugged. "Body transportation spells sometimes render a daze effect when one is snatched so quickly without the participant's foreknowledge. On the plus side, you slept well for the past few days."

"Days?"

"Unfortunately, yes. But at least you're alive."

"True," she said, shaking her head. Her good eye darted back and forth as her mind struggled with what all had occurred. Her dead eye remained glazed over with a milky-white film. "But what about my belongings? My spell books and ingredients? My pets?"

"You rambunctious kitten and obnoxious snow raven are on the floor below. As for the rest of your essentials, we can make arrangements to have them brought here."

She shook her head. "No. I don't want to live in your tower."

"I didn't mean *here* exactly. But choose another town or forest grove or wherever, and I will make certain your belongings get to you."

"My wand!" she gasped. "You didn't take it from me, did you?"

"No," Zauber said.

"It must still be in Woodcrest then. I must return and retrieve it."

"I'm afraid that isn't possible."

Haigla shook her head and in a pitiful, whining voice, she said, "Why can't I go back to Woodcrest?"

Zauber had her watch the rest of the events in the crystal ball. When the townsfolk turned on her doppelganger and took it into custody, she cringed.

"I'd never have betrayed those people like that."

"While that may be true, there are no words you can use to convince them otherwise."

"What about—"

"I'm afraid they won't be persuaded by me, either."

She sulked.

"There are many good places within Aetheaon that you could make into a new homestead. Somewhere with more privacy, if that's what you'd like."

Haigla wiped brown drool from her chin and nodded. "That sounds good to me. More isolation. Less people. Woodcrest was nice, but the folk there didn't exactly welcome me with hospitality."

"Simple folk fear the works of magic. Most people fear what they don't understand, so I wouldn't take it personal."

"Wouldn't you?"

"No."

"So why are you out in the middle of the wilderness where there aren't any people around?"

Zauber ignored her question and unrolled a yellowed parchment and used bottles to weigh down the edges. "Here's a map. Study it, and seek wisdom. I'm certain a place will beckon you to move to it. When you know where you wish to reside, I'll send someone to get your wares."

"I need my wand," Haigla insisted.

"Choose a place in Aetheaon to call your new home. You can make a new wand from a tree, which will give you a higher affinity and attunement with nature's power there. Draw off the power where you settle because your surroundings will accept you as part of it. That's why I reside here in Spellhaven where magical mists protect me and my tower."

"I guess a new home isn't all that bad."

"Home is where your magic is strongest. Woodcrest was sapping you. So find a new home. You'll be stronger."

CHAPTER 59

*R*iese rode into Ironwood on the massive stallion that had been pulling the wagon. Odlon and Drucis rode slightly behind him. Contrary to what Drucis feared, none of the townsfolk paid them much attention. Instead, desperate traders and vendors shouted their specials, trying to get the riding trio to stop and buy wares. The three held serious gazes straight ahead, ignoring the vendors' pleas for them to stop.

The path was named Cheapskate's Way because most of the vendors that set up here had poorly made items or peddled wilted produce, soured milk, and moldy cheeses. Others tried to sell deformed chickens, ducks, or runt piglets. The better goods were further into town, nearer the taverns and brothels within the Redlamp Borough, where travellers spent more gold than they had god-given sense.

"Buy this?" a toothless old man shouted, holding up a stained silk bundle. "Or this here . . ."

Drucis chuckled slightly. "He has some fine things to make an elf like you proud."

Odlon replied, "Looks like old Dwarven undergarments to me. Smelly and discolored like your hand-me-downs."

"Oh! You wait," Drucis said, tightening a fist.

Odlon laughed and then in a more serious tone, he said, "All seems well here. No sign of Waxxon's men."

"Nah. Probably more toward the center of town," Drucis said, "where there be less peasants clamoring for handouts."

Riese kept his gaze on the rope-plank bridge overhead that crossed from one side of the town to the other. Two women cautiously walked across the bridge carrying heavy baskets of linens. Not far behind them were two Ironwood archers that paused to look down at the streets. Other sky-bridges detoured from the main overhead bridge, which was where the richer folk of Ironwood probably lived. Archer guards patrolled all the intersecting bridges.

Riese whispered, "It's best we start no brawls out in the open."

Odlon and Drucis followed his gaze.

"You be right with dat," Drucis said. "But still, I don't think Waxxon's men are along the streets. More than likely, they be in the darker streets of Ironwood."

"You know a place?" Odlon asked.

"Aye. Need ye ask?" Drucis replied. "That be in the Redlamp Borough where all the trouble-seekers hide."

Riese said, "Lead the way."

"With pleasure."

Drucis tapped Grey's flanks and moved past Riese. They left Cheap-skate's Way and turned right at Slatter's Row, which headed down a cobble-stoned slope. Once the path leveled, the sounds of the upper town level were no longer heard.

Blazing lampposts flickered, preventing the streets from being swal-lowed in complete darkness. More vendors were here, but they were not nearly as boisterous as those on the street above. Of course, what they had to sell wasn't the simpler wares.

Fluttering bats swooped and dove for insects that swarmed around the blazing lights. Rats darted from the main street into tiny crevices along the building edges or behind empty barrels. Horses were tied outside different taverns or houses of mysteries. Masters of various magic and healing powers had shops where, for a price, they sold their spells to those that had enough gold to pay.

Mercenaries lurked in the shadows to sell their services should someone need an unwanted foe or family member taken out. Others offered to sell swords and daggers they had taken off their victims or happened upon while crossing the slain bodies in recent battlefields.

Several people dressed in dark robes and hoods slinked past in the shadows. Although partially visible, their mysterious movements from building to building were cause for most visitors to be alarmed.

"Watch your gold pouches," Drucis whispered. "Crukas probably knows this area quite well. Thieves scurry here like rats in the bottom of a ship."

The horses' shoes clacked on the cobblestone. Eyes from the shadows watched the trio pass various lodges, taverns, and brothels. Drucis pulled back the reins when they came to the Murky Flask Cellar.

"Here be strong drinks!" Drucis exclaimed, swinging off Grey and tying the horse to a post near a water trough.

Odlon rolled his eyes.

"Keep your wits, Drucis," Riese said in a low tone. "This isn't the time to swim in liquors."

"Aye, I know. But Murky Flask is the best tavern 'ere. Bound to be the place for finding what we came in for."

Riese and Odlon dismounted and tied their horses to the post outside the tavern. Drucis handed a stable master several gold coins to watch their horses. The old man nodded modestly and bowed his appreciation. He was armored with tarnished chain and two short swords hung on his belt. In the faint light, the man appeared old and feeble, but his eyes revealed a rugged nature keen on fighting, and he was no stranger to killing.

Drucis pushed open the heavy wooden door. It creaked as the gap widened. The smell of rum, ale, and burnt oak hung in the humid air. Drucis took a deep breath and smiled.

"Now, we got something," Drucis said.

The dimly lit tavern bustled with drinking patrons. Barmaids brought tall flasks to and from the tables. Candelabras hung over each crudely carved table and kept the room modestly lighted. Drucis headed to the nearest available table and sat down. A wide smile parted his white beard.

Odlon and Riese joined him, but not with the same enthusiasm. Riese looked around and felt uneasy.

"What is it?" Odlon asked.

Riese shook his head. "Ah, just reminds me of Hobskin's Tavern."

Drucis replied, "At least what it *used* to be."

"And what it will be once again," Riese said.

"You plan to rebuild it?" Drucis asked.

Riese nodded. "And destroy all the undead creatures roaming Glacier Ridge."

"Need an extra ax, let me know."

A barmaid came to their table and asked, "What will ye have to drink?"

Drucis and Odlon each ordered strong ales, but when the maiden turned to get Riese's order, her eyes widened, and she became uneasy.

"Is there a problem?" Riese asked.

She quickly shook her head. "No. I'm not in trouble, am I?"

A frown creased Riese's thick brow. "For what?"

She studied Riese for a few moments, and then she said, "You're not with them, are you?"

"Who?"

She nodded slightly toward the back of the room. Riese followed her direction and noticed four of Waxxon's men seated at a table, laughing heartily after one slapped another barmaid's ass. They were drunk and all those seated near the guards' table didn't dare glance their direction.

"No. I'm not with them." Riese ran his hand down his long beard and watched the men for a moment longer.

She breathed a sigh of relief. "What do you wish to drink?"

"Cider. Nothing stronger," Riese replied.

Drucis' mouth gaped open.

She nodded and smiled. "I'll be back quickly."

"Teetotaler? Bah, what's with you?" Drucis asked.

"One of us needs to keep our senses sharp."

Odlon shook his head. "One drink is my limit, and that's really not serious drinking for me."

Drucis laughed aloud. "A whole barrel wouldn't dent me senses!"

The barmaid returned and set the flasks on the table before them. As she turned to leave, Riese asked, "Why are you fearful of those men?"

Her eyes widened. "They have the protection of Duke Q'aran, which means they can have their way with anything or *anyone*."

"Q'aran? Isn't he the son of King Offaerius of Legelarid?" Drucis asked.

"He is," she replied softly. "This town has headed for ruin every since Q'aran was deeded the title to Ironwood."

She lowered her gaze and quietly slipped away from the table.

Drucis gave Odlon a serious stare. Drucis said, "Why would Q'aran let these renegades take charge of Ironwood? Offaerius has more strength than Lord Waxxon."

Odlon nodded. "I agree. There must be more to it than what we know."

"It could be," Drucis said, pausing to take a swig from the flask, "Q'aran seeks to be a fist for Waxxon, using this town as a tariff haven for any travelling to the North."

"Possibly," Odlon said. "But what could he gain from it? His father has the largest armies in Aetheaon. He could shred Ironwood to sawdust if he so chooses."

"Aye. But why waste the time or energy. Nothing here worth King Offaerius to wipe his nose or royal ass with. He'd just think his son a brat like any other, and those type of children, royal or otherwise, usually don't live long lives."

"That is true."

Riese kept a harsh gaze at the four drunken guards. One of the men grabbed a barmaid and wrapped his arms around her, making her sit on his lap. She struggled to free herself, but the man was too strong. Her eyes widened, and she tugged desperately to yank loose of his hold. The man roared with laughter, and so did his three comrades.

"There's one way to find out," Riese said, rising to his feet with his hammer in his hand.

"What happened to keeping a low profile?" Drucis asked.

"I'd say you have a head start on that," Riese replied with a wry smile.

The dwarf frowned, took a big gulp from the flask, and stood. "Well, if it be an all out brawl . . ."

"Not yet," Riese said, "but if they attack, and I expect they will, you two be ready."

Drucis sat down, lifted his flask at the barmaid, and said, "Another!"

Riese crossed the tavern floor in just a few long strides. The various races that were seated at different tables regarded Riese with the same nervousness that they did Waxxon's men, so Riese was comfortable that none of these would rise to aid the Vyking men seated at the far corner table. Should worse come to worse, he hoped they might ally with him.

Riese towered over the man seated with the maiden in his lap. "Let her go," he said.

The man's wide grin narrowed when he looked up into Riese's harsh stare, but his smile quickly returned when he noticed Riese was of Vyking blood, too.

"What's with your peasant-like clothes?" the man asked. "You need to dress as King Obed has commanded."

"I don't follow Obed's commands," Riese replied.

The other three men partway rose from their chairs, placing their hands upon the hilts of their swords. Before they stood, Riese brought his heavy hammer down onto the center of the table. The wood splintered, and the table collapsed. All the men seated around looked up with wide eyes.

He turned toward the Vyking with the barmaid again and firmly said, "Let her go."

The man's hold lessened, and the barmaid screeched as she ran from the table. The seated man brushed back his long wavy hair, straightened his belt, and ran his hand through his short brown beard.

"I don't know *who* you are," the man said, crossing his arms. "But you have one hell of a nerve to challenge me in front of my men."

"You may pick on a lass because she's not strong enough to fend you off, but I'm *more* than your equal."

"More? And how do you come to such a conclusion without first knowing my name?"

Riese smiled and softly chuckled with chiding mockery. "You can't be too powerful since you submit yourself to another's command. I rule my life and bow to no man."

"Nor do I."

"You're nothing less than a dog on Waxxon's leash and wag your tail at his barking orders."

"Careful," the man said. His fierce eyes narrowed. "Or I'll be forced to put you into your place."

"I have no fear of you."

The man studied Riese's eyes intently. Riese didn't blink and held the man's gaze with overbearing confidence and challenge.

He said, "Then perhaps I should offer my name since you can't bring yourself to ask."

"Names have no importance to me, other than my own," Riese replied.

"I'm Prince Manfrid, second son of King Obed."

Riese shrugged.

"Now would be a good time to bow." Manfrid rose and grinned.

"Perhaps you didn't hear me," Riese said. "I bow to no one."

"I heard," Manfrid replied without blinking, "but I wanted to at least give you that one opportunity."

The three men seated in the corner rose to draw their swords. Before they drew them, an arrow pierced through one's right shoulder. He clutched the arrow and spun around, growling in pain. His sword clattered on the floor.

Riese swung his hammer and smashed through Manfrid's closest guard. The hammer caved in his leather chest piece, shattering the man's sternum and ribcage. The Vyking's feet rose inches off the floor and then he dropped lifeless onto his chair.

Drucis rushed across the hardwood floor. His feet thudded as he moved. He leapt, ran across a table, and then he dove. He caught the last of the three men behind the table by wrapping his thick muscled arms around him and tackling him. Drucis pounded his thick fist into the Vyking's face over and over, until the man lay unconscious beneath the oak table. The man Odlon had shot through the shoulder was tugging to pull out the arrow. Drucis then turned, grabbed the arrow shaft and twisted. The

Vyking roared in pain, clutched Drucis' throat, and hefted the stubby dwarf into the air.

Drucis snapped the arrow shaft, drew back and drove the splintered shaft deep into the Vyking's right eye. The tight grip around Drucis' throat lessened. The man toppled backwards, and the dwarf fell with the giant man.

Odlon edged around the table with his crossbow trained on Manfrid's face. Drucis grabbed his ax and stood directly behind Manfrid. Manfrid held his hands away from his sword and daggers.

Manfrid shook his head. "Didn't expect that."

"What? That I came alone?"

"Well, that, plus I never expected you to be teamed with an elf *and* a dwarf," Manfrid said. "Odd combination, don't you think?"

Drucis smiled. "Odd, but effective."

Manfrid shook his head and tisked. With a proper royal accent, he asked, "Why a blacksmith hammer? Why not a sword or ax?"

Riese smiled. "It has a comfortable feel in my hand. I know how to use it, and it has never failed me."

"Very well," Manfrid replied.

"You have two other guards in Ironwood. Where are they?" Riese asked.

Manfrid ignored the question and asked, "How is it that you know so much about me and my party when I know absolutely nothing of you."

"Oh, but you do know me," Riese said. "I am Riese."

Manfrid's eyebrows rose with sudden interest. "All legends I hear of you have never been pleasant. You're a traitor, and betrayed my father's throne by killing General Yerdrick."

"And Yerkrick's brother."

Manfrid winced at the news and in his princely tone, he said, "Adding more to your list of crimes, I see."

"Your death would be worth more than all combined. That would cause more pain for Obed and satisfy me much more than killing him."

Manfrid laughed and waved his right hand elegantly in the air. Though surrounded by Riese, Odlon, and Drucis, Manfrid held his arrogance and dismissed any possible dangers. He acted as if the tavern was his throne room and court, and these that held weapons on him were nothing more than mere peasants.

Manfrid seated himself, brushed away table splinters from his elegant jerkin, and sighed. "If only that were true, Riese. My father despises me, which is why he sent me on the excursion with the incompetent Waxxon that praises himself as a Lord. Pity. The bastard knows nothing about fighting, swords, or how to overtake a town, which is why he requested my father's aid in taking Hoffnung. Now we scour the lands looking for some little cur that poses a threat to the throne if we don't find and kill her. She's of no importance, but Waxxon is a fool. He's too paranoid to forget about the girl and has us chasing rumors of where she's been or going."

Riese leaned closer to Manfrid and said, "And yet, *you* follow *him*."

"Why not kill Waxxon?" Drucis asked, still leveling his broad ax at Manfrid.

"I have my reasons."

"Such as?" Odlon asked, training the crossbow between the prince's eyes.

Manfrid looked around the tavern. Most of the patrons had returned to drinking and swapping tales while the others positioned themselves further from the Vyking skirmish. Even the bartender ignored the brawl, not looking their direction while he talked to two of Ironwood's drunken guards.

Manfrid lowered his voice to a near whisper and said, "With Waxxon to blame for Queen Taube's death and overtaking Hoffnung, he is the prime enemy in all the land. He's hated more than any man. Once he's established his kingdom, and I kill him, who do you think will be their hero?"

Riese nodded while thinking the suggestion through. "That'd work," he said, "but you failed to consider one thing."

"What's that?"

"That you need to be alive to fulfill such ambitions."

Before Manfrid could reply, Riese struck the prince in the face with the hammer's head and knocked him unconscious. He collapsed and fell forward onto the broken table.

"Bind him," Riese said.

"Why?" Drucis asked. "What you got in mind?"

"You'll see soon enough," Riese replied. Looking at Odlon, he said, "Go back to the others, bind Crukas, and enter Ironwood. Make certain Hordus is with you, too."

Odlon frowned. "What? Why?"

"It's time we get to the truth of what's really going on in Ironwood."

CHAPTER 60

Odlon met Roble, Shawndirea, and Crukas on the road in Ironwood Forest. He explained what Riese wanted to do.

Crukas paled. "They'll kill me."

Odlon shook his head. "We'll protect you. As long as you're in shackles, they have no need to kill you. At worst they will attempt to take you into custody, but we will not allow it."

"You don't know Q'aran. He won't hesitate to kill me."

"He has to have a reason," Odlon replied.

"Any idea why he wants you dead?" Roble asked.

Exasperated, Crukas said, "No. I keep telling you that I don't know."

Odlon smiled. "There's a reward for you, right?"

"A substantial one."

"Then they most likely will want a trial."

Odlon dismounted and walked to Hordus.

"What do you need me to do?" Hordus asked.

Odlon removed the shackles from Hordus. He had Crukas hold his hands in front at his waist and locked the shackles.

"You have a pick that can unlock these?" Odlon asked, looking the thief in the eyes.

Crukas nodded with a sly smile. "Of course."

"Good. Have it ready so that once we get inside Ironwood, and I signal you, unlock them."

"What about me?" Hordus asked.

"Riese has asked that you join us."

Roble said, "Where does he want us to meet?"

"Murky Flask Cellar."

"Where?"

"It's a tavern. Just follow me."

WHEN ROBLE ENTERED the Murky Flask Cellar with Odlon and the others, Riese sat beside the bound Prince Manfrid. The prince's nose was slightly twisted and obviously broken. Dried blood covered his mouth and partway coated his short beard. He looked more frustrated than mad but seemed to realize he wasn't in charge.

Shawndirea sat on Roble's shoulder and quietly studied the tavern.

"What are we doing?" Roble asked.

Crukas' eyes darted back and forth. He seemed to expect to be attacked at any moment.

Riese whispered, "Now that Crukas is here, I think we'll discover why they want him."

"Here?" Roble said. "This is a tavern. Those that want him are the ruler or the magistrate."

"Crukas is a master thief. The Redlamp Borough is where thieves tend to hide."

"So?" Roble asked.

"Patience," Riese said. "Whomever really wants Crukas probably knows he is now in Ironwood. They'll expect us to collect the bounty from the magistrate, but since we're here, they'll come to us."

Crukas swallowed hard. His eyes reflected his fear. Roble noticed the lock pick between Crukas' shaky fingers. He was ready should he have to release himself and dart into the shadows. Roble wondered if the thief was fast enough.

Odlon said to Riese, "You have suspicions?"

Riese nodded. "I find it odd that there is a reward offered for the master thief when other thieves roam right outside in the borough, preying upon travellers and drunks without persecution."

Drucis weighed the information and said, "Makes sense."

"So you don't believe the city is the one that wants Crukas?" Roble asked.

"They may have a hand in it, but someone else has a greater desire to get Crukas," Riese said, looking at Manfrid.

"I have no part of this," Manfrid said. "All this over a thief? It's not even *my* jurisdiction."

Riese smiled. "No, what's about to take place has nothing to do with you. I have other plans for you."

"If it be my death," Manfrid said, "then that will be your loss. Killing me won't bring one tear from my father. He won't grieve. I certainly won't be missed by him."

Riese chuckled. "You are his son, a prince. You announced it a half hour ago."

Manfrid offered an embarrassed shrug. "So I did, but the part I intentionally left out was the part of me being his *bastard* son."

"I'd like to believe you," Riese said, "But—"

Hordus cleared his throat and said, "What he speaks is the truth. King Obed does not favor him for any cause."

"You see, dear Riese," Manfrid said, "I'm worth far more to you alive than dead. My father resents me, as does his wife, the queen. Both would have me dead and lost in order to prevent me tarnishing his image. Why else would a prince be riding along with a dimwit like Waxxon in the first place?"

"Good point," Riese said. "So where's Waxxon?"

"Not in Ironwood. Yesterday, he took a band of warriors north to Hoffnung and left me to scout for the little cur should she happen into town." Manfrid touched his broken nose and winced. "Gods, Riese, did you have to strike my nose?"

Riese replied, "Gives you character. But until the swelling goes down, I'd not plan to pose for any busts or coin images."

"Again, you overestimate my worth."

The door to the tavern burst open and several town guards entered with a band of hooded thieves. Riese and the others turned. At the rear of the guards and thieves stood a short stocky man wearing a crown and a flowing crimson cape. He held a short sword and let his gaze pass across all the tables.

Riese glanced at Manfrid questioningly.

"Q'aran," Manfrid said softly.

"Ahh." Riese faced the man. A heavy frown furrowed Riese's brow, but his even grin was a warning to Q'aran that the Duke had best keep his distance.

Crukas moved swiftly around Riese and Manfrid, hiding in the edge shadows of the tavern. Although he moved quickly, he had been noticed.

"Crukas!" a smaller figure standing beside Q'aran shouted. "Show yourself!"

Half drunken patrons rushed around the guards and hooded thieves and ran out the door. The bartender and barmaids followed, leaving Q'aran and his men alone with Riese and the others.

"If you want out of here," Manfrid said, "use me as a body shield."

"Why?" Riese asked.

"He has been led to believe that if any harm comes to me, my father will savage the town and behead him."

"By you, no doubt?" Roble asked.

Manfrid gave a sheepish grin and shrugged. "Again, all you have to do is hold a blade to my throat, and he'll make certain you're released."

"Gladly," Drucis said, pressing his sharp ax blade against the prince's throat.

Manfrid's throat tightened. His eyes widened with genuine fear. He whispered, "You don't have to be overly enthusiastic about it."

Drucis grinned, shrugged, and winked. "Just making it look more realistic."

"Crukas!" a hooded figure near the Duke said. The voice was high-pitched, feminine. She pointed. "There, in the corner, behind those men."

"Guards," Q'aran said and pointed. "Take him. Kill anyone who stands in your way."

"Aye," Drucis said. His hands tightened on the ax handle. "I wouldn't be doing that."

Manfrid raised his hands and said, "They're serious, Duke Q'aran. They'll kill me."

"Crukas is with us," Riese said. "He leaves with us as well."

Q'aran motioned his men back. His eyes stared nervously at Riese and the others. "What are you doing in Ironwood?"

"Passing through," Roble said, stepping forward with his hands on the hilts of his throwing daggers. Odlon stepped beside him with the crossbow trained on the Duke.

"With the most wanted thief in Ironwood? I hardly find that believable. Surely you are here for the reward?"

Riese shook his head. "No. Your gold is worthless."

"Then what?"

"Crukas hired us to get him past Ironwood, so tell me what you want him for."

"He's a thief. That's reason enough," Duke Q'aran said.

"Then arrest those standing beside you, and those that slink through the borough alleys and streets."

"You dare instruct me on how to perform my duties?" Q'aran asked.

"Only because your double-standard belittles your ability to rule," Riese replied.

The small hooded female looked at Q'aran and said, "Arrest Crukas!"

Riese smiled. "Starting to make more sense now. The woman has some hold over you."

Q'aran's face flushed red.

Angered, the small hooded woman turned toward the Duke and said, "We had a deal. Kill them and take him."

Q'aran looked at Odlon's bow, which was aimed at the Duke. Then his uncertain glance went to the others with Manfrid bound in their midst.

"Perhaps you should have brought more men," Riese said.

The Duke spat on the floor, looked at the hooded thief, and said, "If you want Crukas that badly, *you* go take him yourself." He said to his guards, "Let's go."

Q'aran and his men exited the tavern, but the hooded woman and her two companions remained.

"You have something I want," the small female thief said. "If you don't surrender it to me, I will track you outside Ironwood until I get it."

Crukas frowned. He stepped around Riese and said, "Darrath?"

She yanked her dark hood from her head. Her jet-black hair and pointed ears immediately caught his attention.

Crukas gasped. It was she.

Drucis nudged Odlon's ribs with his elbow. With a sly grin, the dwarf said, "Don't be losing your attention on the fact that she's a thief, now. I'm pretty sure you can find better elven women in Faybourne that are honest and true."

Odlon replied with an even frown.

Crukas' facial expressions were hard to read as he studied the dark haired elf thief. For a few moments he struggled between attraction, sympathy, and fear.

"Surprised to see me alive? I imagine you are since you handed me over to them for the reward. But, they didn't kill me." She seethed. Her chest swelled, and so did her anger. "The things I had to do in order to get him to spare me. And even he betrayed me by not taking you into custody."

"What does she want?" Roble asked Crukas.

Darrath didn't allow Crukas to answer. "What he took from our thief guild treasury."

"That was *mine* before I became a part of the guild."

"It became ours when you joined. Everything has a price, and that was your dues."

"Agretor died. The guild disbanded," Crukas said. "I had the right to take back my offering."

"The guild should have voted on it," Darrath replied. "That necklace was the most expensive item ever looted in Hoffnung. We should have taken a vote."

"No," Crukas said. "I never gave that necklace willingly. Had I not handed it over, Agretor and the others in the guild would have killed me for it. There's no questioning the level of their greed when they beheld my treasure. Some of them were probably jealous that I had stolen something they couldn't."

"But you gave it."

"I was still a child."

Darrath frowned. Her eyes blazed with anger. "You weren't a child when you betrayed me and handed me over to Duke Q'aran for the reward money."

"I only did that because you tried to kill me in Glacier Ridge. If I had had the necklace in my possession that night, you would have killed me."

Darrath smiled. "You don't know that."

"Pressing a knife to my throat is a pretty clear indication that you planned to carry it out."

With a shrewd grin, Drucis said, "At least it wasn't an ax, lad."

Odlon glanced at the dwarf and shook his head.

"Could be she was teasing?" Drucis whispered, and looked down to see sweat beading on Manfrid's brow.

Drucis slowly lowered the blade. Manfrid glanced up with a relieved expression and rubbed his throat where the ax crease remained.

"The sad part is," Darrath said to Crukas, "that I held a secret affection for you the entire time we were in the guild together."

Crukas unlocked the shackles and let them drop to the floor. His eyes studied her for a few moments. "I didn't know."

Drucis shook his head. He said, "Ah, don't be falling for that, lad."

Darrath glared at the dwarf, but Crukas ignored him, taking a few steps toward her. He searched her dark eyes and then he said, "I never had any idea."

She shrugged and crossed her arms. "What's that matter now? You're my sworn enemy for your betrayal. I will hunt you down and carve your heart from your chest."

Darrath turned and strode toward the door. The two thieves with her followed closely behind. When she reached for the door handle, she paused and said, "Take him!"

The three scattered like swift moving shadows. A blast of blue light flowed from one of the hooded men's hands as he ran and then turned. The energy burst like a ball of lightning and headed straight for Roble. Shawndirea was quicker, and cast a green energy shield around her and Roble. The blue light shimmered, crackled, and disintegrated as her power neutralized the attack.

Odlon fired an arrow at the robed wizard. With an erratic wave of wizard's hand, he sent the arrow's trajectory sharply to the left. His nervousness spared his life but still proved a grave mistake in his judgment. The arrow plunged into the gut of the wizard's thief companion. The other man's eyes widened, he clutched at the shaft buried in his stomach, and dropped to his knees. Dark blood oozed and coated his fingers. He gasped a couple times and the light in his surprised eyes dimmed.

Darrath gnashed her teeth and rushed toward Riese. She pulled two daggers and dove forward like a leaping mountain lion. Riese positioned himself in a defensive pose to parry her attack while Crukas hurried to get behind Riese.

Riese deflected both blades with his hammer, which was what Darrath had intended, and as he prepared his counterattack, she quickly changed direction. She rolled on the dusty hardwood floor and came up on the other side of Riese and slashed her blades at Crukas' throat. His lips moved quickly. Before the metal of her razor-edged knives sliced his flesh, Crukas had transported himself to the other side of the room. She growled curses. She pivoted forward, off balance for a moment, and right as she turned, Odlon raised his bow.

Instead of slowing her pace, Darrath ran toward the wall. Odlon fired. A second before the arrow would have pierced through her back, she jumped, kicked off the wall, and back-flipped over the arrow. The arrow tip embedded into the wall with a dull thud.

Landing on her feet, Darrath rushed toward Crukas at the far end of the tavern. Roble stood in her path, turned and faced her, and flung two daggers. She moved remarkably fast. Darrath slid, knocked Roble's feet out from under him, and nimbly twisted back into a sprint before Roble collapsed on his back. He winced, immediately regretting that he had thrown the knives.

Roble fell, and Shawndirea jumped to prevent the chance that she'd be crushed beneath him. She lightly dropped and landed on Roble's chest. Angered at the female rogue's blatant arrogance and attack, Shawndirea fired two greenish orbs at the thief, which struck Darrath in the center of the back.

Darrath groaned in pain and sharply took a deep breath. She toppled forward, losing her balance, and crashed into an empty table. The mugs and flasks slid off the table with her and smashed into jagged shards. She fought to roll back to her feet, and splinters of thick glass dug into her leather armor. She winced in pain but shoved herself to stand. Pieces of glass tinkled on the floor as she brushed the looser shards away. The larger pieces appeared to have pierced the armor into her flesh.

Crukas ran for the bar before she found her footing and targeted him again. He dove behind it where the weaponless Hordus was crouched, hiding.

Darrath's wizard companion's eyes widened. His hands rose and bluish sparks flowed. She turned to see an arrow slicing through the air, heading straight for her heart. The arrow went off course and stuck into the far wall. The shaft wobbled madly. Darrath turned and ran toward the door. The wizard turned to follow, but Riese's hammer struck the back of the wizard's head. He dropped lifelessly to the hardwood floor with his robes fanned delicately outlining his thin body.

"Mark my words. I will find you Crukas!" Darrath darted through the door and vanished into the borough.

Riese extended his hand and helped Roble to his feet. Crukas was pale and visibly shaking. Hordus stood from behind the bar and helped the thief stand. Crukas peered around the tavern, hesitant to leave his place of protection. Almost reluctantly, he braved the steps to join Roble and the others near the fallen wizard.

"She's injured," Roble said.

"Aye," Drucis said.

Crukas gathered with their circle and said, "Thanks for keeping me alive. I'm indebted to you."

"What did you steal that she wants so badly?" Roble asked.

"I stole a necklace from a high official's wife in Hoffnung. It's so expensive and well known, there's no way I can ever sell it."

"Then why not give it back?"

Crukas shrugged. "Pride? Notoriety? I don't know. With Waxxon's men now in control of Hoffnung, I doubt the woman is still alive. Even if she is, she probably no longer holds a position of power."

Drucis nodded. "Probably true."

Manfrid walked to the two dead robed men on the floor. Near the wizard's smashed skull, Riese picked up his heavy hammer from the growing pool of blood.

Manfrid looked at Riese with great admiration. "Indeed the hammer is your weapon of choice."

Riese turned the dead wizard over.

"Careful," Manfrid said. "His magic may still linger to protect his corpse."

"It can do that?" Roble asked.

Odlon nodded. "The mysteries of magic are never-ending. Well, at least to those of us who don't wield it."

"Too much to learn," Roble sighed.

"You can live ten lifetimes here and never know the fullness of all there is to know," the elf replied.

With caution, Riese pulled back the man's hood. He was human. His bald head was covered with strange blue tattoos.

"He's a worshipper of Lez'minx," Manfrid said, stepping back. "The woman thief has powerful allies."

Roble gave a confused glance at Shawndirea. She whispered, "A reptilian god worshipped by a sect deep in the Woodnog swamps."

"Does he exist or is he a myth?" Roble asked softly.

Shawndirea opened her mouth to reply, but their attention quickly returned to the corpse.

Blue flames flickered on the dead wizard's fingers. Riese stepped back. The intense flames rose higher. The candles throughout the tavern flickered. The wizard's dead eyes opened. His eyes were bluer than the flames. His lips suddenly moved.

"Don't challenge me, Overlander," a deep voice said from the dead man.

Drucis readied his ax and said to Roble, "Does that answer your question?"

Roble took a deep breath, slightly shuttered, but no words came. He nodded. The room chilled, he thought, or perhaps it was his fear wrestling against the strange reality.

"My power has protected you," Lez'minx said.

Roble cleared his throat. His eyebrows rose in question and said, "In what way?"

"The blessing on your armor has protected you thus far, has it not?"

Riese and the others stared at Roble with keen interest. Drucis held his ax, and for a few moments, he had looked like he might decapitate the dead wizard. But now he lowered the ax. His interest was more in what else the god might reveal.

Uncomfortable to see a dead man speak, Roble swallowed hard and replied, "It has."

"Seek me out, Overlander, and see what other gifts I bestow upon those who worship me."

Something about the deep voice disturbed Roble. Although frightening in tone, it held a subtle seductiveness that made him want to listen more.

"Do you fear me, Overlander?" Lez'minx asked.

"I don't know you well enough to fear you," Roble replied.

Lez'minx softly chuckled. Roble's armor moved as if it breathed within the god's presence.

"You've a lot to learn, Roble," he continued. "Take the wizard's rings. These I've blessed like I have your armor, only with different attributes. In this dark world, you'll need additional help, at least until you've grown wiser."

Roble stared at the dead wizard's rings—one held a large ruby and the other, topaz. He was never a man who wore rings, not even a class ring, but these lured him, making him lust to possess them.

"Seek me out in Woodnog swamps." And with that statement, the blue energy surging through the wizard's dead body vanished.

A chill shot through Roble. He shivered. Looking at the corpse, he whispered, "That was odd."

"Be wary," Shawndirea whispered.

Odlon stepped closer. "That is not an invitation you should take alone," he said.

"I have no plans to find him," Roble replied.

Drucis cocked one eyebrow. "Aye, but he's found you. He won't rest until you seek him out."

Roble kneeled beside the wizard's corpse. He reached for the topaz ring.

"No!" Shawndirea gasped.

"Why not?" Roble asked. "He offered them to me."

"To be his slave? His servant? Is that what you wish to be?" she asked.

Roble removed the ring. "No. I won't wear them."

"Then why take them?"

"Do you not think others in Ironwood won't steal these for themselves, or far worse, to use their power to harm others?" Roble asked.

Drucis nodded. "He's right. The first lowlife that enters the tavern will loot anything of value these two have. He might as well take them."

Roble slid the wizard's rings off while Drucis took the dead men's gold pouches, an amulet, and a small spell book.

Manfrid watched Roble with new interest and smiled. "Overlander? Interesting. What brings you here and how did you become a member of the Dragon Skull Order?"

"It's a long story," he replied.

Manfrid raised his shackled hands and said, "It seems I have plenty of time."

Riese shook his head. "Not as much as you might imagine."

Drucis' brow furrowed. He glanced around the tavern and realized they were the only ones still left inside. None of the barmaids had returned, nor the bartender. A smile crossed his face. Drucis nodded at Odlon and Roble and said, "Bar's open! Let's help ourselves!"

Roble and Odlon followed him to the bar. Crukas walked behind the bar and placed several corked bottles of strong liquor on the counter. Shawndirea stepped onto the bar and requested honey ale. Crukas read different bottle labels until he found some. He poured her a small amount in a silver spoon.

Manfrid appeared hurt by Riese's statement. He said, "If your grudge is truly against my father, keeping me alive and joining me is the best way we can dethrone him. Not to mention, a chance for your redemption."

Tired, Riese walked to the nearest table and sat down with a serious frown on his face. Looking into Manfrid's eyes, Riese said, "I do not seek redemption. I'm not ashamed of anything I've done or the lives I've taken. I've not killed the innocent as King Obed and his men have done."

"Help me take my father's throne," Manfrid said, "And you'll be a man of great power."

"Not interested," Riese said bluntly.

"Then perhaps I could join you in your mission to stop Waxxon and his men?"

"That's not my mission. To remove your father from the throne and his head, that is what I seek to accomplish."

"Don't be a fool," Manfrid said. "Without me, you'll never succeed."

"I've done well thus far."

In his stately voice, Manfrid said, "You're on the outskirts of the outskirts. There are thousands of men between you and where my father reigns. Thousands. One man cannot charge the throne and take my father down. He's too powerful."

Hordus pulled his long silver hair behind his head and tied it. He said, "If that is your true goal, Riese, Manfrid is correct. You could use us and our knowledge to get to Obed."

"I can gather troops," Manfrid said. "Most of those under my charge agree with you. My father is a tyrant."

"I do not trust you," Riese said. "No more than you trust me. Besides, you're willing to make any deal to get free of your death sentence."

"I understand that you don't trust me. How can I prove myself to you?" Manfrid asked.

Slightly angered, Hordus said, "Why kill a bastard prince? What glory is there in that, Riese? Even if you killed Obed, the throne won't fall to Manfrid. You spared me in Woodcrest, and for that, I yield my life to you. I believe you're a man of honor, and I understand your rage. I am in your service."

Hordus took a knee before Riese.

Riese studied Hordus' face for a long while. The old Vyking's words held great wisdom and logic. Riese said, "Basically, you're indicating that I should help Manfrid take his father's throne?"

Hordus gave a solemn nod.

"What's to say that Manfrid won't have me beheaded after he assumes the throne? Or that he'll have me killed during our journey there?"

"I'm in your service as well," Manfrid said. He, too, took a knee. He slid his signet ring from his finger and handed it to Riese. "I swear to you on my grandfather's grave that I will not betray you. I will, however, richly reward you when our deed is done."

"I'm not interested—"

"In riches," Manfrid interrupted. "I respect that, but once the battle is over, you'll need a place to retire. I can give you that."

"And why would a prince yield himself to a common blacksmith?"

"You're much more than a blacksmith, Riese," Manfrid replied. "You're a better warrior than most of the men I have led. Proof of that lies at the table yonder. You're even better than myself, and that's not a compliment I'd normally give."

"You do know that I still don't trust you," Riese replied. "I will always look at you with scrutiny."

"I understand, but I can get you out of Ironwood alive," Manfrid said. "Do you honestly believe that Q'aran won't have dozens of men waiting for us when we leave the tavern? He knows I'm in here with you and keeping me alive will be in his best interest."

"He may well attack with you in our custody anyway."

Manfrid gnawed at his lower lip for a moment and then said, "Possibly, but I do know another way out of Ironwood."

"The sewers?" Riese asked.

"Okay," Manfrid said, "Then I know *two* ways."

"What is the other?"

"For that, we have to come to some agreement on how we join forces."

"I'll have to think about that."

"You have my ring, which states my authority. That token will show that I've placed complete trust in you."

"Others may think I forced you to give it up."

Manfrid smiled and shook his head. "Not without the removal of my finger, they wouldn't. Even you should know that."

Riese looked at the ring and thought. What the prince said was true. No man or woman of royalty freely gave up a signet ring without insisting the taker also cut off the finger that bore it.

"Let me think about it."

"I wouldn't waste much time," he replied, returning to his stately tone. "They may be heading into the borough to corner us as we wait."

<h1 style="text-align:center">CHAPTER 61</h1>

Darrath clutched her chest as she ran through the dark alleyway in the borough. Warm blood dripped from where large shards of glass remained embedded. Her fingers were coated with crimson. She staggered, nearing unconsciousness, and placed her hand against the corner of a building to steady herself.

Pain rippled through her. She gasped. Death wasn't something she welcomed. Not yet. She wanted revenge, to kill Crukas and take the necklace for her own, but she grew weaker by the minute. Her bloody fingers touched the jagged tip of glass that stuck out of her leather vest. A gentle tug made her gasp. She realized removing the glass meant immediate death. She needed help and quickly.

Darrath took two more steps and found herself outside the door of another tavern where two Ironwood guards stood. She said weakly, "Take me to Q'aran now."

She dropped to her knees, and the two men caught her and helped her stand between them.

One guard said, "Q'aran is right outside Redlamp Borough."

"Get me to him quickly then," she said in a near whisper.

They hoisted her between them and hurried up the dark winding cobblestone pathway. Two lines of armored guards with swords drawn waited on the upper roadway with Q'aran seated on his mount at the rear.

The two guards carried Darrath past all those waiting Q'aran's orders.

Q'aran looked down at her. "Darrath? What happened?"

"Get me a healer," she said weakly.

"When they emerge from the Murky Flask, they're dead," he said sternly.

Darrath shook her head. "No. Let them leave."

"What? They've nearly killed you. They have Manfrid as well."

"Manfrid's not your concern," she said. "Let them leave Ironwood unharmed. Have a scout follow after them. But don't kill them. When I've regained my strength, I'll find Crukas myself."

"Why? I can end them here."

"True, but doing so will cost you a great fortune."

"I don't understand," Q'aran said.

"If you kill Crukas and the others, what he stole is gone forever."

"And what exactly does he have that is so valuable?"

"I cannot say just yet. But help me with this, and I promise to make you an even wealthier Duke."

Q'aran studied her eyes for several minutes. "Very well."

Darrath coughed and warm blood coated her teeth. "Get me to a healer before it's too late. If I die, my secrets die with me."

Q'aran waved his hands to the two guards, and they hurried away.

DRUCIS DOWNED another flask of strong wine. "Ahh! That's more than plenty."

Odlon smiled in agreement. Crukas sipped from his wine flask, and then he corked all the half empty bottles.

Riese explained what Manfrid's plan was to get out of Ironwood.

Roble said, "Can we trust him?"

Drucis slid his ax off the bar. "He best not try to betray us."

Manfrid said, "Like before, just keep a blade on me."

"If you be misleading us—" Drucis said.

"Then kill me," Manfrid said. "It's not a difficult decision. I know. And since I truly wish to see my father overthrown and my life spared, I will not betray you."

"Good." Drucis gave a firm nod but his narrowed gaze didn't lessen.

Riese said, "I think it's time for us to leave." He glanced at Manfrid and asked, "Which direction should we take?"

"We should stick to the back alleys of the borough and head toward the sewers," Manfrid replied.

"The sewers?" Drucis asked with a harsh frown.

Roble shook his head. "I'm not leaving without my horse."

"Nor I," said Drucis. "Ol' Grey is too old to abandon. Besides, I'd rather fight to the death than crawl through the stinking sewers like a grubby ol' maggot."

~

At Drucis' insistence, Riese, Roble, and the others decided to mount up and head back to the upper road to confront whatever resistance Q'aran had positioned.

Manfrid was seated on Bleys while Roble kept a dagger pressed against the Vyking prince's throat. Odlon held his crossbow aimed at Manfrid as well. To their surprise, the cobblestone street that led out of the Redlamp Borough was deserted. No patrons, workers, or guards were seen.

"Something's not right," Drucis said.

"I have to admit," Manfrid said, "that this even seems a bit suspicious to me, too."

Riese eyed the upper bridge-ways of Ironwood, and although guards marched across the planked walkways, none paid them any mind.

They continued through the Cheapskate Way and back through the front gates where Roble was certain confrontation awaited.

Again, nothing. Even the poor traders and merchants had vacated. Most left their wagons and unsold goods.

"Never seen Ironwood so . . . empty," Drucis said.

Odlon shook his head. "No."

Riese kept his attention on the higher roofs, the balconies, and the overhead bridges. No one was watching their departure.

Shawndirea balled a small green orb between her hands.

"What are you doing?" Roble asked.

"Detecting magic."

"Find anything?"

"Other than my own? No. Even the rings in your pocket from the wizard have grown cold."

"You think Q'aran is just going to let us leave?" Roble asked.

Drucis cleared his throat and said, "Appears that way."

"That makes no sense," Roble said.

"Are ye looking for a fight?" Drucis said with a broad grin.

"No. But with his numbers, he has a superior advantage and yet, it seems he is afraid of us."

Odlon shifted in his saddle, keeping the crossbow aimed at Manfrid. The elf said, "Q'aran didn't seem like he wanted Crukas anyway. Darrath thought she had a hold over him and found out differently. Q'aran holds position in title only, and the less trouble he involves himself with, the longer he'll live."

"That's true, I suppose," Roble said. "If most of the town feels the same toward Q'aran as the barmaid does, it's doubtful he has many willing to die for him."

"Few deal with the politics and allegiance in a town like Ironwood," Manfrid said. "Most are too preoccupied keeping food and a roof over their heads to worry about who presides over whom. Unless, of course, the ruler is a tyrant like my father."

"Thousands follow him," Drucis said.

"Only by fear," Manfrid replied.

Drucis scoffed. "Your kind is known for their plundering along the shorelines."

"Ask Riese why they do that."

Drucis looked at Riese.

"We are taught at a young age that what our king says, we must obey without question," Riese said, deep in thought. "Otherwise painful death is warranted. As children we were forced to watch captured turncoats be burned alive to spare their souls. Some were beheaded. The only true honorable death came from dying on the battlefield, serving our king and our gods."

They passed through the gates and into the towering rusty-colored giant trees. No guards awaited, so Roble removed his dagger away from Manfrid's throat and Odlon lowered his bow.

Through the thick forest they traveled several hours before the forest turned darker and the trees twisted and forked their spindled branches toward the dark overcast sky. They didn't pass any riders in their journey further away from Ironwood, which brought a brief sense of relief to Crukas. That is, until Manfrid caught sight of the single scout riding at the farthest edge of the path.

"We're not alone," Manfrid said.

Drucis and Odlon turned in their saddles and peered back.

Drucis smiled. "Appears someone wants to see where we be heading."

Odlon nodded and pointed where the path grew the darkest. The path forked at the foothill of a great mountain rise. "Ahead, he will become confused."

Roble looked at the elf and said, "Why is that?"

Odlon gave a slight grin. "That is where we part ways. We head toward Woodnog, and you take Shawndirea to Elvendale."

Shawndirea kissed Roble's cheek. Excitement shot through her. "I'm almost home!"

Roble was filled with mixed emotion. He was happy that Shawndirea was close to her kingdom where she could get her wings restored, but he'd miss the company of Drucis, Odlon, and Riese. Crukas wasn't as much a loss, but lacking a circle of friends, he felt less protected.

The slope of the mountain ridge blocked the sun. The trees at the branch in the hard road were thicker and kept the shadows deep and the ground moist. Strange insects buzzed. Birds quieted as their party separated into two groups.

"Roble, blessings to you in your journey to Elvendale," Odlon said.

Roble nodded. "And to you."

"Once you're done in Elvendale, meet with us in Woodnog."

"Sounds a bit familiar," Roble said with a slight grin.

"Not a spiritual invitation," Odlon replied.

Roble peered up at the steep mountain ridge. "This place is shrouded in shadow."

Drucis said, "Aye. The Black Chasm is nestled on the other side of this mountain range. But don't worry, it's not like you'll fall into it."

Roble became uneasy.

"It's very difficult to reach," Odlon said. "Simply keep to the path to Elvendale, and you won't go near it."

"But be wary of what may come *out* of it," Drucis said, running his hand through his white beard.

Shawndirea bowed to all of them and said, "Many thanks for aiding us in getting me home."

Crukas stayed with Roble and Shawndirea. He decided to go to the Kingdom of Legelarid where he'd be further away from Riese. Although Riese had mellowed and no longer desired to see Crukas hang, Crukas wished to be in a place where recognition wasn't likely. Legelarid hosted the largest population in Aetheaon, making it easier to vanish into the crowds.

Odlon, Drucis, Manfrid, Riese, and Riese's son headed to Woodnog where they planned to round up other warriors and Dragon Skull riders to find Lady Dawn while killing Waxxon's men along the journey.

CHAPTER 62

*R*oble stopped Bleys outside the gates of Elvendale. Shawndirea sat on his shoulder. Crukas kept walking.

"Aren't you staying the night here?" Roble asked.

Crukas shook his head. "No. I wish to make it to Legelarid by midnight. Besides, I'm not fond of the tricks Fae play on humans."

Shawndirea giggled.

"Is he serious?" Roble asked her.

She nodded. "Of course."

Crukas turned to walk on and said, "You'll see soon enough."

"Be safe, Crukas," Roble said.

Without turning back, the thief said, "Thanks for honoring your word, Overlander. I had my doubts about you at first, but you've proven yourself to be a man of honor. I hope that time in this realm won't tarnish that."

Roble nodded slightly and thought, "Me, too."

"May our paths cross again," Roble said aloud.

"Eventually all paths do," Crukas replied.

He watched the thief keep walking until he rounded the next bend on foot. He glanced at Shawndirea and smiled.

"What?" she asked.

"I kept my word to you as well."

She kissed his cheek. "I never doubted you."

"Even in the beginning?"

Shawndirea made a near pinch symbol with her index finger and thumb and then she said, "Well, maybe a little. But you've done what you promised. Now you can return to your home and leave me here."

"Why would I do that? You said that we're meant to be."

She smiled. "You've yet to step into Elvendale, so you still have a chance to turn back, if you harbor any doubts about us or living in my realm."

Roble shook his head. "I have no doubts. I know that I have nothing left to go back to if I don't have you."

"I feel the same. But once you cross into my kingdom, you are sealed with me."

"How? You said that you would never cast a spell on me."

She shook her head. "I won't. That's not what I mean."

"Then what do you mean?"

"Before I left Elvendale on my quest to find my life partner, I swore I'd never enter Elvendale again until I found him . . . you. No spell will be placed upon you, nor have I ever bewitched you with a spell. But by you entering with me, you're letting my goddess know you've pledged to live your life with me. Is this what you truly want?"

Roble studied her emerald eyes, her nervously shy glance, and the perfect pout on her lips. He replied, "Of course, this is what I want."

Flattered, her beautiful smile brightened her face. She waved her hand with a gesture to move forward and said, "Then so be it."

He nudged the horse's flanks, and Bleys stepped from the path into Elvendale. A heavenly fragrance permeated the air and for the moment, all his stress vanished.

Down the sloping grassy path, the meadows blossomed with pastel flowers. Thousands of butterflies drifted from flower to flower upon the gentle breeze that carried them. He marveled at the beauty. His heart raced to see the vast differences in the butterflies. Unlike when he collected in the Overlands, where butterflies were categorized into various species based upon their colors and sizes, these were unique creatures.

Roble pulled the reins slightly, and Bleys stopped.

"This is home," Shawndirea said.

"Spectacular."

She kissed his cheek hard. "Thank you for bringing me home."

"Where can I tie Bleys?"

"Just let him roam," Shawndirea replied.

"I don't want him to damage the flowers or butterflies."

"They'll be fine."

Roble climbed down and patted the side of Bleys' face. The horse snorted and then lowered its head to graze.

"And now, where do I take you?" Roble asked.

"That depends," she said.

"On what?"

Shawndirea smiled and slightly blushed. Her eyes held a bit of fear as she struggled to find the proper words.

Roble looked at her, saw her confusion, and then he asked, "What is it?"

"I guess you have a decision to make," She said, taking a deep breath. "Do you wish to remain here with me awhile longer before I make your introduction to my mother?"

"Certainly," He replied. "I'd love to see more of your homeland. This is far more beautiful than I imagined."

"Will you ever seek to return to the Overlands?" she asked.

He looked into her sparkling green eyes. Her eyes pleaded for an answer, and she looked like she held her breath, waiting for him to respond.

"Other than returning to tell my sister that I'm okay and not to worry about me, I want to stay here with you."

Tears moistened her eyes. "I'm glad that you feel that way, but are you certain?"

He nodded. "I have no doubts. There's so much I can see here that I can't there. And I know if I return without you in my life, nothing there can fill that void."

"I believe we'll be happy together."

"Where do I need to take you?"

She pointed to a small grove of trees. "I need to take *you* there."

"Me? Why?"

"To make you my size."

Roble chuckled. "Why not make you my height?"

"In time. But in order to introduce you to the Courts and my mother, you must be my height to enter."

"I see. Do you think she'll accept me?"

Shawndirea replied, "Doubtful, but don't take it personally."

"Then why have me enter the Courts anyway?"

"To follow royal procedure. Since I'm destined to one day assume the throne, I am to bring my prospective husband before the courts."

"And if she rejects me?"

Shawndirea shrugged. "I'll forfeit my right to the throne."

"Don't do that."

"You need to understand that I've never wanted the throne."

At the center of the grove was a circle of scarlet mushrooms.

"Step into the center, and set me at your feet," she said.

Roble did what she requested. She spoke several words softly. A turquoise hummingbird zipped through the forest, slowed and hovered an inch from her, and she took what looked like a slender twig. After she took the object, the hummingbird zipped away. In her hands, the tip of the twig glowed bright green.

"What is that?" he asked.

"My scepter. I'm in my kingdom now, so its power is at strongest. Are you ready?"

He nodded.

Shawndirea closed her eyes and raised her hands. The ground around her feet shimmered and glowed. The emerald scepter glowed a brighter. Other Fae came from their hiding places and joined her.

A rush of warmth and power surged through Roble's body. The power overwhelmed him. He tried to keep his eyes open, but a blinding light stung his eyes. He felt dizzy. His stomach became nauseous. When the power raised another level of intensity, he lost consciousness.

He awakened two hours later and opened his eyes. Everything was blurry. His head rested in Shawndirea's lap. She gently stroked his hair and face. Her radiant smile was the first thing that came into view.

The sun was lower on the horizon, and dusk was less than a couple hours away.

"How do you feel?" she asked.

"Light-headed but okay."

He pushed himself into a seated position.

"Careful," she said.

"Yeah, I'm not trying to rush myself. How far are we from the Courts?"

"Not far," she replied, "But I've arranged for transportation. There's no way we'd reach the halls before darkness fell upon us."

"Transportation?"

She nodded and pointed at a massive moth resting on a scarlet mushroom.

"Wow."

"I hope you're not afraid of heights."

"Never really thought about that, until now."

THE MOTH LANDED outside the Courts grand doors. She took him up a side flight of stairs and down a long gloriously jeweled hallway. She opened a side door and led him inside.

"Where are we?" he asked.

"I need to find you suitable clothes before you enter the Courts. This is where my father's belongings were stored. Let me find you something. After searching through the closet, she returned with a silk shirt and pants. He hurried and changed clothes.

After a half hour, Shawndirea led him back down the stairs and hurried toward the tall doors of the Courts. Various gems glittered from their insets on the tall golden doors. Two guards raised their halberds defensively until they recognized Shawndirea. They lowered their weapons and bowed slightly.

"Young Queen," one said. "What brings you to the Courts?"

"I'm here to see my mother and to announce my engagement."

The elven guards' eyes widened. They stared at Roble in question.

"Yes," Shawndirea said, "this is my husband to be."

The guard swallowed hard, turned, and pushed the door inward. "One second, your grace. I will break the um . . . news."

He left the door slightly ajar. A few seconds later, everyone heard a high-pitched shriek.

"A human? Send them in!"

CHAPTER 63

Queen Istrell's face darkened with anger, spite, and disapproval. She glared at Roble and then her eyes shifted toward Shawndirea. The darkness in her gaze didn't lighten.

"You wish to abandon the throne to marry him? A human?" Istrell said with such a harsh tone one expected her to spit on the floor soon thereafter. Her lips quivered with distaste much like a child's when it has something vile on its tongue. She forced her next words and said, "Really, child?"

"I love him," Shawndirea said.

"After what he did to your magnificent wings? Child, surely you've more self-respect than that?"

"He risked his life to get me home," she replied.

"As well he should since he destroyed your beauty."

"It was an accident. I'd say that he's more than compensated for his mistake."

Istrell wrung her withered hands and shook her head. "With humans it is always *an accident*. Humans never respect what nature has to offer. They dig deeper, either mining or destroying whatever lies in their way just to find more gold."

"Not all, mother."

"And does this human also *love* you?" Istrell asked.

"I do," Roble replied.

Istrell's nostrils flared. Her eyes widened. "Silence! I have not given you permission to speak in my court."

Roble offered a slight bow to signal apology.

"He does love me," Shawndirea said. "It is not his fault that your heart has grown cold and bitter after the loss of your husband, my father."

"How dare you!" Istrell said, her anger boiling. "You best mind your tongue, my child! I will not tolerate insolence from you."

"If you forbid me to marry him, you have lost a daughter."

Istrell gasped and fanned her face with such a feign gesture that she and Roble knew the queen openly mocked her.

"Really, mother?" Shawndirea's hands balled into tight fists. A tinge of green glowed around them. "Think of how long I was gone this time. I almost chose not to return to your halls."

Istrell smirked. "Then *why* did you, child?"

"To be healed. To have my wings whole again."

"I won't grant that to you, not if you choose to be with this human."

"I don't need *you* to grant this."

Istrell's eyes narrowed. "Then how do you expect such a blessing?"

"That power lies within me."

Istrell chuckled. "If that is true, why haven't you done that yet?"

"Because seeking your blessing for my marriage to Roble *seemed* more important at the time."

Istrell swallowed hard, thinking on the words. Her eyes softened, but only for a moment. She cleared her throat and glared down at Roble again.

"You say that you love my daughter?" Istrell said.

Roble nodded.

"My question means that you may speak," she said.

"Yes, with all my heart."

Another smirk curled the queen's lips. "Words *so* easy for a human to say. Care to put some action or risk behind them?"

"You're challenging me? My word is not enough?"

"Humans are filthy, untrustworthy individuals, prone to say anything that will gain them something they desire. My daughter deserves to marry someone brave, daring. I need to know that she hasn't foolishly chosen someone incapable of protecting her."

"I'm willing to prove myself," Roble said.

"Don't," Shawndirea said.

"No," Roble continued, "name the challenge. What does it take of me to prove my love for your daughter?"

"Very well," Istrell said with amusement in her eyes and a devious smile on her lips. "This is what I require of you. We have a situation growing in our world, and since you've journeyed through some of the territories, I'm certain you've heard of the Black Chasm by now?"

"Mother," Shawndirea said.

"Hold your tongue, child."

Roble nodded. "I have heard of the Black Chasm and about the unknown mysteries that are hidden there. What do you ask?"

"A party of warriors is gathering to ride through the strange dark misty fog that engulfs it. I would have you lead their charge. Report to me what lies inside the chasm, and I'll grant you liberty to marry my daughter. What say you?"

"That's suicide!" Shawndirea shouted. Her voice rang throughout the palace rafters. The butterflies on her wings burst into flight, drifted for a few moments, and slowly settled on her. A few fluttered around her face to comfort her.

"The choice is his," Istrell said. "Be he a man of bravery and integrity or is he a *coward*?"

"I'll do it," Roble said, anger rising in his tone. His eyes narrowed at Istrell to which she seemed greatly amused.

"Do you swear it?" the Queen asked.

"Roble," Shawndirea said, "no."

"I swear it."

Istrell studied Roble's eyes. His eyes didn't stare with dishonesty. He never broke their gaze. His body didn't flinch. Fear didn't alter his breathing. He remained calm in spite of Shawndirea's adamant protests.

Istrell smiled. "Perhaps she judges character better than I do. Time will tell."

In fury, Shawndirea squeezed her fists tightly. "I'll not allow you to do this, mother. What you're asking is for his death!"

"He has sworn his oath to me, child. To break that oath *is* death."

"To honor it is death! Mother, I swear to you that if he dies because of this, you're *dead* to me. Dead! Do you hear me?"

"Roble," Istrell said, ignoring Shawndirea's outbursts. "Tomorrow morning my guard will guide you to a neighboring town where you'll join the group. The Black Chasm is only a day's journey. Rest well and say your goodbyes in the morning."

Roble bowed and said, "Your Highness."

He took Shawndirea's hand and turned to walk away.

"You can't do this," Shawndirea whispered. Tears flowed down her cheeks. Hurt possessed her. "You can't. You'll die."

"I have no choice, dear," Roble said. "I want to gain her blessing. Otherwise she will always detest our marriage. Besides, I love exploration."

"No." The pleading in her voice became desperate. "You don't know her.

I do. Even if you succeed with this *exploration*, as you call it, you'll never gain her blessing. You won't. She hates humans."

"Then I will have to prove myself to her."

Shawndirea tried to speak, but her voice broke into heavier sobs. She held his hand tightly and covered her eyes with her other hand. At the end of the great hall, she stopped walking so he stood at her side. She wiped away tears and flung herself against his chest and sobbed.

"For so much you have done to get me home," she whispered, "you'd sacrifice yourself just to prove your love for me? I love you so, but I can't bear this pain inside."

Roble wrapped his arms around her and kissed the top of her head.

His silken shirt was soaked with her tears. It was then he truly knew how deeply her love for him was, and how much he'd go through just to prove his love for her because he loved her equally.

"I'll be okay," he said softly. "I promise. Don't worry. I love you."

She peered up at him with sad eyes. "This isn't a game. Most who have ventured into the chasm have died. And anyone that survived going in and coming out, they were not the same. They were different, mindless creatures. A power of darkness surges within those shadows known as the Black Chasm. The force controlling that area terrifies everyone, even my mother. Please reconsider your oath."

"Any ideas why this chasm appeared?" he asked, wiping tears from her eyes.

"The ruins of the City of Mortel are possibly still there."

"There's a city there?"

Shawndirea sighed, still trying to calm herself. "One son of King Offaerius was granted the land, but it was meant to be for hunting. Instead, his son, Tyrann, hired an architect and workers to build his castle. When Offaerius learned of this, he became outraged and insisted Tyrann stop the construction."

"Why?"

"Offaerius believed this was a threat to the Kingdom of Legelarid, even though Tyrann held no armies, no loyal allegiances to other cities in Aetheaon or any other continents."

"There must be more to it than that?" Roble asked.

"Perhaps it was because Tyrann's mother had been of the Shi'marush clan from the Isles of Bloodmoore, deep in the South Seas. According to bard's tales, this is a region where a strange race of people resides. They are considered people of the night. Their isles are shrouded with misty darkness, much like the Black Chasm."

Roble ran his hand through his short beard. "So his queen is from Bloodmore?"

"No. His mother was the daughter of Bloodmoore's matriarch and became Offaerius' mistress when she visited his kingdom. The queen never knew of the affair until a year after Jez'baal had returned to Bloodmoore. A ship docked and with the cargo a midwife delivered Offaerius his illegitimate son, Tyrann."

"Not a present he quite expected, I suppose."

"No, but he did receive the resentment from his wife. However, he treated Tyrann as a prince, favored amongst his own children even though he was different."

"Different? In what way?"

"He favored Jez'baal. Dark eyes, pale skin, and coal black hair. But he had other differences, too."

"Like what?"

"A keen sense of the occult. Dark magics. Animals and demons communicated with him, or at least it seemed like that. The queen was terrified of him and had, according to the tales, tried to kill him several times during his youth without success. After the third attempt, she died from some type of mysterious plague."

"So he lives in the Black Chasm then?"

"Not quite," Shawndirea replied.

"What do you mean?"

"After his castle was completed, Offaerius sent several knights to inspect Tyrann's new home. Only when they arrived, they discovered an entire city surrounded the castle. No people lived there. At least not yet, but the magnitude of what he had crafted, some suspect through his magic or demonic connections, appeared to be to establish a civilization loyal to Tyrann.

"The City of Mortel contained a temple with Tyrann's image on a huge tapestry above an ebony altar. When Offaerius received news of this, he was further outraged and sent dozens of knights back. Two of the knights confronted Tyrann in the temple and sought to take him into custody and return him to Legelarid. He refused. Needless to say, they killed Tyrann inside his temple right upon the ebony altar. Or so they thought."

"So he is alive?"

Shawndirea nodded. "He set them up. By killing him inside his temple, on the very altar where his followers would worship, he became immortal. When the knight that had run him though with his sword pulled it out, Tyrann rose and pronounced a curse upon the men. All except one, died.

He survived only to return to Offaerius and tell the tale. The others, so the tale goes, became warriors under Tyrann's power."

"Is there any proof?" Roble asked.

"Sadly, these are the tales and legends that bards sing in the taverns. While there may be some truth to it, we don't exactly know. That's why I'm begging you not to go. We don't know what's there or the strength of Tyrann's power. Like I told you, any that returned from going in, never returned the same way. I love you the way you are now. Please?"

"It's going to be okay, Shawndirea. We still have tonight," Roble said, quickly changing the subject, more to ease her mind than to avoid the subject entirely. Although now, he was more apprehensive than before, knowing the legends. "Care to show me your kingdom? But first, I want you to get your wings back. Before I make that journey into the Black Chasm, I need to see you in your full beauty. I have to know, if nothing else, that our journey to your homeland was successful."

She glanced back at the rugged frame of what had been her glorious wings. She nodded. "Thank you for everything you sacrificed to get me here. I know picking you to be with me was not a foolish choice. I'd sacrifice my wings to be with you."

"I'm not worth that," he replied.

"To me, you are, and again, that's why I plead for you to not follow through with my mother's quest. She only chose such a thing because she doesn't want you to be with me. Your death ensures that we won't be together."

"I'm not dead yet," Roble replied. "Nor do I intend to die on this exploration."

"Very well," she said, taking his hand. "Come see the glories of my kingdom."

Shawndirea strolled through the kingdom and showed him the fountains, the pools, the extravagant flower gardens filled with hundreds of spectacular butterflies, and she told him the history behind each monument and statue of those that had reigned over her kingdom long before she was born.

Roble squeezed her hand when she showed the statue of her father, the former king. He said, "And you don't want your name and likeness to follow in your father's lineage?"

"My father was an honorable person, and he had none of the vileness or resentment that has soured my bitter mother. I know he would have been proud to see me marry you."

"Do you ever wonder if her resentment to humans is due to the loss of him? Did she love him so much that she feeds on hatred to bury her pain?"

Shawndirea shook her head. Her eyes remained saddened. "No. My father took quests and travelled to other lands to be far from her. He filled his life with adventure, which isn't something a king does often.

"My mother has always been a lady filled with malice. She rules in a cynical nature. It doesn't matter if someone wants to have dreams. She will do everything possible to destroy them. Aerlene, my aunt, is her sister, and my mother has told our kingdom for as long as I can remember that she was dead."

"Dead?"

Shawndirea nodded. "Yes. I believed it until I met her in Woodcrest."

"Why would she tell others that her sister was dead?"

"Because that is what she wishes for her. They had a dispute, and my mother was so angry after Aerlene left the kingdom that she announced that Aerlene had been killed by a goblin."

Roble shook his head. "I often wished I had come from a large family. My sister Lib is the only sibling I have. In ways, seeing all the turmoil and politics that run through siblings is enough to make me thankful that she is the only one I have. But we've always been the best of friends. We'd never turn on one another."

Shawndirea smiled. "But you're not of royalty, love. Such blood is often tainted with jealousy, lies, and backstabbing. That's another reason I abhor the thought of taking the throne. I want a loving husband and wonderful children to rear." She crinkled her nose and pointed a playful finger at him and said, "That's why you best not get yourself killed."

Roble smiled. "It's not in my plans to die. She never said how far into the chasm we had to travel. She just wants an investigation. That's what she'll get."

"You're right! She didn't say how far inside you had to go."

"See? All is not lost."

She faced him with a broad smile. She studied his face and her smile slowly faded.

"What's wrong?" Roble asked.

"It won't happen like that though, will it?"

"What do you mean?"

"No. It won't. Even though we've not been together that long, I understand you better than you think."

He frowned. "I don't understand."

Shawndirea pursed her lips. "You're a scientist. You like to explore and discover new things. You'll attempt to view as much of the Black Chasm as possible. No amount of persuasion from me or anyone else will deter your lust to discover something new."

"I never hinted anything of the sort," Roble said.

"You don't have to. It's instilled inside you. It's who you are. No matter. There's no point discussing anything more about it right now. Come," she said, taking his hand again. "Let's get my wings back."

Roble took her hand, but his heart ached. Was he destined to do exactly what she insisted he would? Of course, being a scientist had always made him keep searching for discovery and new information. He thrived on it. But this journey wasn't something he wanted to do. He didn't want to leave Shawndirea, but his pledge bound him to the task. He really only planned to enter a short distance and turn back, but the more he thought about her statements, the more he believed her instincts were probably correct. He suddenly feared that he would keep exploring the chasm until he knew everything about it and why it originated where it had.

And since the chasm grew over the City of Mortel, all they had were the legends and tales. He might look until he found the truth since no other ever had.

Roble followed her down a long, winding set of ivory stairs. Flowering vines and shrubs lined both sides. The intoxicating mixture of jasmine, vanilla, and citrus scented the air. Butterflies, damselflies, and little dragon sprites drifted from flower to flower. As they stepped off the last step and into a vast field filled with thousands of pastel-colored flowers, a miraculous event unfolded right before Roble's eyes. The butterflies swarmed her with their little kisses and a mournful fluttering at the sight of her damaged wings.

Without warning, the iridescent blanket of swarming butterflies gathered on the stubs of her broken wings. Green light shone around Shawndirea's feet. Light illuminated around her like a glowing bubble and then blasted with such radiance that Roble was forced to cover his eyes. When the light faded, and he looked at her, her wings glittered in the greenish-turquoise like they had on the day he first met her. Tears filled his eyes.

Shawndirea flexed her shimmering wings. Such spectacular colors twinkled from being kissed by the sunlight. She smiled in spite of her mournful tears.

"You are the most beautiful sight I've ever seen," Roble said.

The butterfly swarm drifted upward and scattered, returning unharmed by the light to drink nectar from the flowers. Her wings didn't quite resemble the colors he had seen on the day he captured her with the butterfly net. But being her height, he believed, allowed him to get the full glory of her true colors.

"How?" he asked.

"I'm the Butterfly Queen. They saw my injuries and in their own kindness donated part of their wing scales to me. Their compassion, joined with my magic, rebuilt my wings."

Shawndirea ran to Roble and grabbed his hands. He pulled her close and kissed her. When he looked into her eyes, he read so many emotions, but the greatest thing he sensed was the bond of love between them.

She said, "Come with me."

"Where?"

"The spell that has allowed you to be my height won't last until morning. If the possibility exists that this might be our last night together, I would have this night with you in my chambers."

"Without her blessing?"

She crinkled her nose and kissed him firmly. "We're adults. With the circumstances as they are, I would have you *without* her blessing."

Roble smiled at her. She took his hand and led him across the fields of flowers filled with flittering butterflies until they came to a large oak. She spoke words in her native language and a door materialized on the wide tree trunk. She opened it and led him inside. When the sun rose the next morning neither had slept.

CHAPTER 64

Exhausted, Roble exited the invisible door and stepped out onto the flowery field. Since he was about to scout the Black Chasm territory, he wore the Dragon Skull Order armor instead of Shawndirea's father's silken clothes.

The moment the sunlight touched him, the spell cast over him and his clothes ceased. He returned to his normal height. He knelt and started to pick her up.

She laughed and ascended into graceful flight, gliding before his face in all her regal splendor.

"I want to return to your size," he said. "I don't like this size difference."

"When you return from the Black Chasm, I will be your height," she replied.

"Don't you mean *if?*"

Shawndirea frowned and playfully shook her finger at him. "If you can be optimistic, so shall I."

"Glad to hear it. But doesn't that mean you're giving away your right to the throne?"

She smiled and nodded.

"Why?" he asked.

"It's not worth the agony to oversee a kingdom's problems. Besides, Dirk loves controversy and control. He's better suited for assuming the kingdom."

"And that doesn't bother you? That he'll have authority over you and others?"

"Not at all."

"His reign, should he take power, may be far worse than you think."

Shawndirea shrugged. "Perhaps, but it's a risk I'm willing to take. Once we're wed, none of the Fae will accept you as a king."

"As long as you're certain this is what you want."

"I have something to give you," she said.

"What?"

She handed him a folded square of cloth. He unfolded it and it was about the size of a handkerchief.

"What is this?" he asked.

"Some enchanted cloth. It never hurts to have some added protection, much like your armor."

Roble smiled and tucked the cloth into his vest.

A male faery dressed in a thin layer of fancy armor drifted through the air and hovered before them. On his belt he wore a sheathed dagger and sword.

"Roble?" the male faery asked.

"Yes?"

"I've been sent to escort you to Westwyrm to meet with your squad to explore the Black Chasm."

"You are?" Roble asked.

"Cildaer. If we hurry, I think we can be there before the midday sun."

"Okay."

"Do you think you can keep up with me?"

Shawndirea frowned and said, "Cildaer. No pranks and no hide-and-seek. Always stay within Roble's view, or you'll have me to contend with later."

Cildaer blushed and tugged at the collar of his fancy armor. He sighed and motioned Roble with his tiny hand, "Come on."

Shawndirea rose before Roble and kissed his lips. Trying not to cry, she said, "Return to me, my love."

"I will. That's a promise."

Roble climbed upon Bleys, gently tapped the horse's flanks, and followed Cildaer from the flowery paradise into the evergreen forest filled with mossy rocks and gentle flowing brooks.

THE JOURNEY from Elvendale to Westwyrm wasn't a rugged journey, and while riding through the beautiful trees, Roble thought of Shawndirea, her fears, and their future together. He didn't want to disregard her worries as unimportant because she continually warned that he needed to take stronger precautions.

The closer he rode toward Westwyrm, the darker the skies became. A warm breeze rustled the treetops, but the wind didn't hint of a thunderstorm or even a drop of rain. The warmth was more like summer near a beach.

He couldn't help but think about what lie within the Black Chasm. In all he and Shawndirea had experienced together, she had never expressed such emotional worry and absolute fear. Part of him wondered why he had decided gaining Queen Istrell's approval meant more to him than what it should have. He understood why Shawndirea didn't have or ever would have a close relationship with her mother. He had gained an immediate distaste for Istrell's attitude and how she tried to exert dominance over her own stubborn and resistant daughter. Perhaps that was the problem; they were too much alike.

No, he thought, shaking his head. Shawndirea was much stronger than her mother credited her.

Istrell wanted to usurp her power and position over her own daughter, and when that didn't work, she tried to guilt her daughter into being the next queen, knowing quite well Shawndirea opposed.

Cildaer glided slowly ahead of the horse. Boredom overtook him, so he said, "Westwyrm once was a more fearful place."

"Why?" Roble asked, enjoying the warm breeze that ruffled his hair and beard.

"Two dragons kept travellers from venturing here. They weren't monstrosities, but pesky nonetheless. Stealing sheep from shepherds for food and occasionally they flew over small villages and set roofs on fire to appear more intimidating than they actually were. They never went full onslaught and wiped out a town. They just wanted to be appear menacing."

"Odlon told me that there weren't any dragons anymore."

"He's right. Those two are now dead."

Roble felt saddened that he'd never see a dragon, and it was odd that here they had existed more than in just stories. Hell, he'd raise sheep to feed a dragon in order to study and research, but according to the tales, none existed any longer.

"What happened to them?"

"Politics," Cildaer replied.

"Politics?"

Cildaer nodded. "King Offaerius of the Kingdom of Legelarid offered the hand of his daughter to any prince that could bring the dragons' heads to him. Many kings throughout the land lost sons due to this challenge and were angered at their losses of future heirs. However, Prince Bhelgan of Nagdor survived the challenge and returned to Offaerius' throne with the heads. It was laughable, to say the least."

"Why?" Roble asked.

"You really aren't familiar with our cities and kingdoms, are you?"

"No, but I am learning."

Cildaer sighed, rolled his eyes, and continued, "Bhelgan is a dwarf, and Offaerius is elven. Not exactly a match made by the gods, is it?"

Roble grinned. "I imagine not."

"Indeed," the faery said.

"Did King Offaerius honor the reward?"

"To a dwarf?" Cildaer said, his eyes widening suddenly. "How absurd! Bhelgan refused the marriage, and Offaerius was happy to oblige, size not being the culprit here, but their religious clashes, cultural differences, etc. No, neither would have it, but Offaerius did pay a hefty bit of gold for Bhelgan's troubles. A few barrels of ale to boot as well. He was *really* happy about that exchange then."

Roble chuckled. And yet, the dragons died for gold? As sport? He shook his head.

The narrow road through the trees arched upward onto a winding tree-lined ridge. Where the road curved sharply to the left, they were able to see the Black Chasm from above. The purple-black mists swirled with flickering electrical surges that resemble strange lightning. No rumbling sounds echoed in the small canyon below.

"What do you know about the warriors I'm meeting at Westwyrm?" Roble asked.

Cildaer shook his head. "No one's given me that information."

Roble glanced back at the Black Chasm. He envisioned the best of the best warriors fighting their way with him to find out what lay inside of the chasm. So many sought fighting as means to prove themselves, which generally brought the most intimidating people he had seen. Riese was a prime example. A dozen or so men like him, and Roble didn't have to fear much. Most trophies were in titles more so than gold.

Even though Odlon had given him some practice with the sword, Roble still didn't feel comfortable using one in combat. He packed his knives and even had brought more that he had stashed in his saddlebags, his boots, and his belt. The worst thing about using throwing knives as weapons was each could only be thrown once, so he needed to hit his mark accurately whenever he used one.

When the narrow road wound around the ridge, he studied the Black Chasm one last time. If there were buildings within, he couldn't see past the swirling mists. Troops? He had no idea. The most troubling part of viewing the chasm was the sense that something within watched and waited.

"Not much further," Cildaer said.

"So what's at stake here for Queen Istrell?" Roble asked.

"What do you mean?"

"She seemed insistent that this mission was of the utmost importance," Roble said.

"In a lot of ways, it is. No kingdom that has sent warriors in has discovered the true nature of this chasm or the source behind its power. None have returned alive, either."

He thought about the tales Shawndirea had told him. "Does Queen Istrell not know the tales?"

Cildaer laughed with great amusement. "Only fools believe drunken tales."

"So the queen believes this group can succeed where others have not?"

"Again," Cildaer said, "Not information I've been informed of. I'm just your escort. Sorry."

Cildaer led Roble into the tiny settlement of Westwyrm and introduced him to the eight men he'd be leading into the Black Chasm. Not only was he disappointed with their number, he couldn't believe the group that stood before him.

Dread shot through Roble's mind. He looked at the ragtag squad of human warriors that were gathered together. He suddenly realized what Shawndirea had expressed to her mother was correct. This *was* a suicide mission. He was quite certain Istrell knew this and was pleased that he had offered to join them.

This poor excuse of a squadron was merely a group of unknown misfits no one would miss if the Black Chasm swallowed them forever. Roble missed Odlon and Lehrling, and had they accompanied him to Elvendale, they probably would have swayed him into not accepting the challenge Queen Istrell had deliberately set before him. Indeed, the queen didn't want him to survive this mission. Killing him prevented her daughter from marrying a human. Her prejudiced hatred toward humans was so strong that she really didn't care if Roble died proving his honor and love for Shawndirea. At least if he died, that brought him out of the picture. Forever.

Realizing that he had been set up, anger rose inside Roble. Beneath his breath he swore that if he survived the Black Chasm, he'd find a way to turn the tables on Istrell whenever the opportunity arose.

None of the squadron before him had a full set of gear. They were malnourished, weak, battle rejects, if such a rank existed. Their shoddy weapons were tarnished with rust, cracks, or dullness. Few even possessed shields, and those that did had battered ones that might survive one solid blow before falling apart. The horses' hooves were split, untrimmed, and unshod. Two had lame mules and another one rode a fat, bloated pony. The only part about these men that gleamed was the flickering hope set in their eyes.

"This is it?" Roble asked the faery.

Cildaer said, "Afraid so. Good luck."

Before Roble could reply or ask for further directions or instructions, the faery darted through the trees and headed back to Elvendale.

Roble faced the others as they mounted up. He asked, "What has prompted you to join this expedition into the Black Chasm?"

"Gold," one said.

"Treasures," said another.

A tall slender human said, "Land grants."

Puzzled, Roble frowned, looking at the eagerness on these men's grimy faces. None seemed alarmed about *what* the Black Chasm was or what might await them on the other side of the veil. They had all been misinformed and apparently on purpose. The offer of great riches overrode desperation, and men like these probably journeyed from town to town searching for handouts.

"By whom?" Roble asked. "Who told you such things would be awarded to you for venturing into the chasm?"

The slender man reached inside his vest and pulled out a rolled up piece of yellowed paper. He unrolled it and tapped his filthy index finger on the paper.

"Here, see?" he said, pointing. "It says that this is the meeting point."

Roble nodded. "It does, and that the leader of your group would be here."

"That's you, isn't it?"

"I guess so."

The flyer did offer the promises the men sought, but nothing about the real dangers of the Black Chasm were listed, which might not have deterred them even if the risks were written there. These men didn't have anything valuable to lose. Their lives weren't worth much if they didn't find treasure, so they gambled everything. Sadly, even a hundred men like these weren't worth a lot should a battle ensue once they entered the chasm.

"I suppose we should head to the chasm," Roble said without enthusiasm. He wondered if Shawndirea was right about just abandoning the journey and heading back. But, he couldn't. He had given his word to prove his love for Shawndirea, and perhaps a part of him now wanted to succeed simply to spite Queen Istrell. After all, he figured Shawndirea would have done the same.

CHAPTER 65

From their approach to the Black Chasm, Roble watched the swirling black, purplish mists that loomed along the base of the surrounding cliffs. The movement of the misty shroud reminded him of a massive tornado but without the roaring winds. The silence that surrounded this chasm intimidated, being combined with the eerie towering mass. Its power didn't rely upon its movement across the land because it hung over this chasm, almost like it was rooted to the spot, but the most worrisome characteristic was its drawing power.

Roble had to admit that even without the dare Queen Istrell challenged him with, he probably would have still wanted to know what was inside. That was simply part of his nature as a scientist. His curiosity demanded that he turn every stone to see what lie beneath them, and this chasm held so many mysteries that he couldn't turn his attention away. He didn't see why he had tried to deny Shawndirea's accusation of his blatant need to seek answers even in the most dangerous places like Devils Den and now the Black Chasm.

A smile crossed his lips. She knew his nature and that flattered him while it frustrated her. Those differences between them would probably always remain, provided he survived this exploration.

Roble turned and looked back at the ragtag treasure hunters to find that the greed that had outlined their facial features had succumbed to their sudden fear of the unknown.

"We can always turn back," Roble said.

Their fear faded, replaced with quick, seething anger. Their hands were on their crude weapons in a blink. "Are you reneging on the campaign?" The thin toothless man asked.

"No," Roble replied.

"Because if you are . . ." another said, drawing his rusted sword.

"It was only a suggestion in case you were having second thoughts."

They shook their heads.

"Very well," Roble said, "prepare yourselves for whatever awaits us on the other side."

"What'eva it be," a dwarf said, "will taste death before I do."

Roble shook his head and looked at the towering misty wall that defied all logic. Greed often was stronger than fear. Not always, but when people lacked essentials but didn't want to give up, they often did foolish things. No words would dissuade these men into turning back. They'd die before admitting their defeat. None of these men could survive turning around and living with the questions of what wealth they had forfeited by not entering the Black Chasm. Not knowing would continue to gnaw at them.

But the look in their eyes when he had suggested turning around was frightening. For the first time, Roble understood what caused mutinies on ships at sea. Greed for greater wealth was the ultimate blindness that caused men to cheat, kill, or destroy.

Roble led the way to the Black Chasm wall. He expected, and *hoped*, the wall to be impenetrable but no resistance met them. They passed easily through. It was too easy, Roble thought. He wondered what traps and possible ambush awaited them. But much worse than he imagined lingered within the shadowy mists. Without intervention the quest for discovery was dead before they began.

Queen Istrell stood at her magical summoning crystals. She couldn't believe the contempt Shawndirea had displayed in the High Court. Her daughter had deliberately disobeyed her many times before, and although an adult, Shawndirea needed to be punished for her actions.

She took the black mirror and focused upon it until the silvery glass shimmered. Materializing in the glass was Shawndirea. Her daughter sat upon her bed in her chambers, weeping and wiping her tears away with a cloth. Little butterflies flittered around the room, landing on her face, licking at her tears and trying to soothe her.

Part of Istrell's heart swelled to see her daughter in agony, simply because her unruly daughter had challenged her in the courts.

"How dare you bring a human into my courts," Istrell whispered, watching her daughter heave and sob.

Seeing Roble stand in the courtroom had left a horrid taste in Istrell's mouth. The nerve Shawndirea had to entertain the idea of tarnishing her future bloodline. She set the mirror down and placed her hands upon the crystals. Power shimmered through them and radiated up her skinny, wrinkled arms. Her eyes turned back in her head, and for the first time, she was able to see Roble on the inside of the Black Chasm. She wondered why the veil had suddenly allowed her vision to move past the swirling mists.

Roble rode his horse while the others followed behind. All of them covered their mouths and noses with thick cloth. Thick smoke billowed from small holes along the gray rocky path they rode upon. One rider collapsed from his horse. His limp body sprawled on the path. He didn't appear to be breathing. Roble glanced back and sadly shook his head. He clamped the cloth tighter to his face and leaned lower. None of the others bothered to look at their fallen comrade, but they too, looked weakened, perhaps poisoned, and perhaps dying.

The horses faltered, stumbled, but kept fighting to move forward.

A smile curled Istrell's lips. For as long as the chasm had been in the vale, she had tried to see what was inside. Now she could witness what had eluded her for so long.

Skeletons of dwarves, humans, and elves were scattered around the path. These were the remains of former explorers. A couple of horse skeletons crumpled across the dark ground. Skeleton heads were placed on tall skewer poles like a foreboding forest and as a warning that any who entered the Black Chasm would share the same fate.

The rocky path resembled volcanic rock, black and sooty. Vapors and dust rose with each step the horses took. No grass grew anywhere within the chasm. Strange gray briars and weeds were scattered in small clumps. The path ascended slightly and leveled at a short bridge. Beyond Roble stood pillars made from the same stone that composed the road. Roble's horse stopped outside a massive double set of sealed castle doors. An oozing channel of black fluid flowed around the outer edge of the castle walls. It bubbled like thick tar. Lavender gases rose from the moat in a mist.

No one stood above the tower gates.

Odd, she thought.

Roble turned his horse, left the gate, and started around the edge of the black moat. The remaining seven men followed until two more horses collapsed on the ground dead. The two riders swung off right before they would have been pinned. Roble's horse stumbled, and he quickly dismounted. He took the cloth he covered his face with and placed it over the horse's while he led the horse by the bridle cheek strap. He rubbed the side of its nose.

Two of the men dropped on the sparsely vegetated ground. They gasped for several seconds before their bodies seized in tight spasms. They moved no more.

Poison?

"How far will you venture, human?" Istrell whispered while watching with keen interest. She wanted to know what else was in the chasm, but she knew if he continued much further, he'd die, and then she no longer had to worry about her daughter's ridiculous wedding plans. Shawndirea would have to take the throne, despite her rebellious objections.

Another man fell, dying seconds later.

No sentries guarded the castle, and she understood that with the poison, an army didn't need to keep intruders out.

The veins in Istrell's arms swelled. Sweat streamed down her face. The overpowering flow of energy from the crystals surged through her. Never had she connected to such power. The magical conduit alarmed her. She feared she'd lose consciousness before she discovered what else occupied the black chasm.

Roble held the cloth over his horse's mouth and nose. His face reddened while he apparently held his breath to allow the horse to be protected from the poisonous gases. He heaved, coughed, and almost choked. Quickly he placed the cloth over his face for several seconds before trying to keep the horse alive. She realized what the cloth was and who had given it to him.

The enchanted cloth was Shawndirea's and given to her by Zauber for when she ventured into dark caverns that housed poisonous mushrooms that she sometimes gathered to trade for other herbs. The cloth resisted most all poisons but didn't seem to completely aid Roble inside the chasm.

A few minutes later, Roble was the only human still alive, but he wasn't making his way out of the chasm. He was heading deeper into the misty fog. Ahead, she noticed a large shadow moving but couldn't see what the shadow lengthened from.

For no explanation, her contact was cut off.

Istrell dropped to her knees, gasping for air, and soaked with heavy sweat. Her heart hammered in her chest. What had blocked her view? Why was the connection severed? She leaned forward on her hands and knees, panting for air. Her mouth was dry. Darkness clouded her vision, but she fought the urge to collapse. If Roble were braver than she had thought, she'd at least like to know he survived.

Nauseated and fatigued, she reached up and grabbed the crystals. She pulled herself to her feet and took several deep gulps of air.

Istrell called upon the power of the crystals, but they remained cold. No magic flickered. No pulse or twinkle. Nothing.

Still breathing heavily, Istrell remembered her daughter's words, "Mother, I swear to you that if he dies because of this you're *dead* to me. Dead! Do you hear me?"

Queen Istrell's hands shook with fear. Shawndirea's words were a solemn threat and not uttered lightly. Her daughter's rebellion was mellow compared to the endless grudge her daughter would carry out. Somehow, Istrell needed to help Roble, but she didn't know how.

She summoned the crystals again, but they remained cold. She grabbed the mirror and held her focus, but the glass didn't shimmer. It, too, refused to acknowledge and obey her power.

With everything she had, she commanded, and then pleaded but the power seemed sapped. She dropped to her knees again and sobbed. Her power was somehow gone.

~

ROBLE STOOD ALONE BESIDE BLEYS. The horse trembled but understood the danger they were both in. Bleys took turns breathing through the cloth with Roble, and the odd thing was, the horse held his breath until Roble placed cloth back over its nose as if Bleys knew the air was poisonous. Near the corner of the castle wall was another set of dark pillars. Something large and winged moved between two pillars.

Roble readied a knife in his left hand and waited. He wasn't certain what had passed by, but he'd get at least one throw before the gases probably claimed his life like it had the rest of the ragtag treasure hunters.

He hated that he had led the group to their deaths, but by what he estimated, they were probably better off not struggling with their day-by-day begging. Their reward was death and the absence of hunger, thirst, and pain. Did he feel guilty for their deaths? No. He had tried to turn back, but they insisted with unspoken threats that he head into the Black Chasm anyway.

The winged creature stood between the two pillars, giving Roble a full view. It was, as best he could describe, a demon of some sort. Black veined wings that were unfolded and made the beast completely fill the gaps between the pillars. It had hulking arms, chest, and legs. Thick claws protruded from its fingertips.

More wings shifted and moved behind it.

Even if his dagger could penetrate this beast's skin, which he doubted, there were others to contend with.

The demon roared with a wide mouth, revealing rows of jagged yellow teeth. Others roared behind it. And behind them was a line of at least a dozen knights seated upon mounts. Their eyes glowed a vivid blue through the eye slots in their skeleton-faced helms. Were these the knights Tyrann had cursed? Their black armor glistened like wet onyx.

Roble turned and looked back toward the path they had entered. The band of treasure-seekers bodies twitched. The men were coming back to life. When they tilted their heads upwards and glanced in his direction, their eyes were radiant blue like the knights beyond the gates. He shook his head, and for a moment, he wondered if the poison was affecting his mind. Perhaps.

Roble thought of Shawndirea and tears moistened his eyes. She had warned him, pleaded with him, and yet, he stubbornly decided to honor his oath to her vile mother. He shook his head in regret. He was too far from the chasm wall to exit, and he had attracted the attention of the large black demons that slowly moved through the two pillars and fluttered toward him. And even if he managed to miraculously kill or deter their attacks, the knights awaited him. He didn't see any way to survive.

He looked at Bleys and said, "Which way do you want to die?"

The horse whinnied and nudged his hand.

"Yeah, me too," Roble said. He folded the cloth and tucked it into a pocket. "Poison looks like the less painful route."

He inhaled one deep breath, choked on the air, and sputtered. He and Bleys dropped to the ground. Pain radiated through his lungs almost like he was breathing liquid flames. His vision was dimming, but he kept his attention on the three large demons approaching. The dead men on the path behind him staggered to their feet. They were alive, but much no longer human or dwarf.

Roble reached over and patted Bleys' nose.

A shimmering blue light exploded in front of him causing the demons to shriek with bone-chilling cries. Their wings buzzed like giant locusts and they quickly retreated back to the walls. The light prevented him from seeing anything. Fingers wrapped around both wrists and dragged him into the light. Seconds later, he lost consciousness.

CHAPTER 66

Queen Istrell rested on her knees and hung her head at the base of the crystals. She sobbed.

"I'm so sorry, Shawndirea," she whispered. "I hope that one day you'll forgive me for my foolishness."

Her hair was soaked with sweat, but she didn't have the energy to stand. She lay down and drifted to sleep.

TWO DAYS LATER, Roble awakened in a bed. His eyes opened slowly. After blinking several times, he looked around and didn't know where he was.

He rolled over and gazed into the wide eyes of an elderly woman seated at the side of his bed. "Where am I?" he asked.

"Easy," she said. She smiled, rose quickly, and headed for the door. "Wait here."

"Who are you?"

"Timirius."

The woman hurried out of the room and returned a few minutes later. Behind her, standing in the door, was Shawndirea. She stood about five-foot six inches from his estimate, but it could be that he had shrunk back down to her size. She smiled in spite of the tears flowing down her cheeks.

"You're awake," she said, crossing the floor in hurried steps. "Thank the gods."

"Where am I?"

"In a cottage on the outside of Elvendale," Shawndirea replied.

"How did I get here?"

She shook her head. "I'm not certain. Word was sent to me that you were found on Corwin's Pass."

"Corwin's Pass?"

"Yes. You were almost dead."

"I would be had you not given me that enchanted cloth. The air there is a fog of poison."

Shawndirea smiled. "The cloth probably helped a lot, but I believe your armor also protected you."

Roble touched his chest and realized he was wearing a sleeping gown. "Where is my armor?"

Timirius pointed across the room. The armor hung on a rack.

Shawndirea placed her hand to his cheek, leaned down, and kissed him. "When I got here, I feared you were going to die. You were barely breathing when I got here."

"That close, eh?"

Tears moistened her eyes. "Yes. What's inside the chasm? Can you remember?"

"I do, but I'll tell you after I feel better."

She nodded. "We'll have a scribe write it all down and send it to my mother. Neither of us shall enter her Courts for a *very* long time."

"That's good. A report should suffice."

"It will have to."

"What about my horse?"

"They have him at the stables. He's healing and should recover fully."

"Great."

"What about the men that ventured into the chasm with you?" she asked.

"All dead," Roble said, shaking his head. "They were all dead before I fell to the poison. But you were right."

"About what?"

"Your mother set this mission up to fail. None had adequate armor or weapons. I highly doubt any of them had combat training. The men that I led into the chasm wouldn't survive fighting chickens."

"That bad?"

He nodded. "Worse, but at least they didn't run."

"So they had some bravery?"

"No, their greed was insatiable. That was why they came."

She took his hand and squeezed. "Greed?"

"Yes. They were led to believe they could mine or hunt for treasures. One thought he could have land deeded to him."

Shawndirea pursed her lips and then sighed. "My mother . . ."

"Now what do we do?" he asked.

"We find a place to settle and a priest to wed us."

Roble smiled. "You know of any places?"

"Lots of them."

He squeezed her hand and said, "Am I your size or are you now mine?"

"I'm yours in size and companionship."

Roble eased up into a seated position. His head felt woozy. His vision blurred. The elderly lady brought a pot of tea and some bread and honey.

"How long have I been here?" he asked.

Timirius replied, "Two days."

He shook his head. "I feel like I coming out of a severe hangover."

Shawndirea frowned. "What do you mean?"

"Ah. Don't worry about it."

"Do you remember how you escaped the Black Chasm?"

"The last thing I remember were the black flying demons heading for me. I collapsed and this shimmering portal or something appeared on the ground beside me. Before I lost consciousness, I felt hands grabbed me and pull me through."

"Did you see who it was?"

Roble shook his head. "No. That's the last thing I can clearly recall. But isn't Corwin's Pass a good distance away?"

"There's a rough mountain ridge between the chasm and where they found you. My guess is that someone used a magical teleportation spell, which requires a lot of power and drains one's energy severely."

"But who would do that?"

"Your guess is as good as mine."

Roble chuckled. "You know far more people capable than I do."

"True. But I don't have any idea who else knew you were there or why they'd expend that much energy to save you. I'm just thankful that they did."

"Me, too. Who found me on Corwin's Pass?"

Shawndirea spread honey onto a rough slice of bread and handed it to Roble. She said, "A travelling peddler. He was on his way to the Kingdom of Legelarid, found you, and dropped you here. This was the first cottage he came to."

Roble chewed the bread slowly. After a couple of minutes, he said, "What was his name?"

"He never said apparently."

"He should be rewarded."

Shawndirea nodded. "I will send word to Legelarid for him to be found so we can know his name. Then we will give him some gold for his aid."

"So how did you know I was here?"

"A blue raven brought me the message. The small scroll was tied to its leg. After reading that you were here, I came immediately."

Roble frowned, rubbed his eyes, and then looked into hers. He said, "You think the peddler sent the note?"

"Not likely."

"Then who?"

Shawndirea smiled. "The mysteries continue to increase, my love. My guess is a wizard since the raven message generally is like a calling card. But I don't know a wizard that owns a blue raven. I don't think such a raven exists in the wild."

She reached into her pocket and pulled out another note. This one was still sealed. She handed it to Roble. "This one arrived for you yesterday."

Roble took the note, broke the seal on the back of the folded parchment, and unfolded it. He read the message and looked at her.

"What does it say?" she asked.

"Odlon requests that I journey to Woodnog to train and discuss a possible search mission to help him form a group to find Lady Dawn. Apparently Lehrling is well enough to travel and is headed to Woodnog now."

"Not before our wedding, dear," she said softly. "Besides, I think you need a couple more days to recuperate."

"Yeah," he said, rubbing his temples. "I'm not quite ready for riding to Woodnog."

SHAWNDIREA STOOD beside Roble inside a white marble temple hall. A priest dressed in white robes stood before them as they exchanged their vows. Thousands of butterflies flittered around the hall. She and Roble kissed one another passionately, and then they headed outside the temple. The massive cloud of butterflies followed them.

He helped Shawndirea climb upon her horse. And then he got upon Bleys. They rode for half a day until they came upon a ridge of dense trees. She stopped her horse and pointed.

"This is where we will live," she said.

Roble eyed the place suspiciously. The trees were tall and massive and the underbrush was thick. He didn't see anywhere to build a cottage.

"Here?"

She nodded. "There's more here than meets the eye."

Shawndirea chanted a series of words in a language he didn't understand but hoped she'd teach him. On the front of the largest tree trunk, a door appeared. His eyes widened, and she smiled with amusement.

"How?" he asked.

"I have been building this house for many years. It's camouflaged so we'll always be safe from intruders. Some dryad kin also protect the trees. Less likely unwanted visitors will venture here long and certainly cannot without notice."

She opened the door and said, "Come inside. Let me show you around."

"What about the horses?" he asked.

Shawndirea whistled. Nearby a servant stepped from the thick ivy vines, took the horses by the bridles, and led them back through the oddly cloaked vines. As they disappeared, she looked at Roble and said, "We also have stables here, too. When you're ready to head to Woodnog in a few days, I'll show you."

"I look forward to it."

Shawndirea smiled, winked, and took his hand in hers. "Good. Now, let me show you our home."

THE END

AUTHOR'S NOTE:

Thank you for purchasing this novel. If you enjoyed this book, please check out my website and join my mailing list at www.leonarddhilleyii.com to receive a free digital copy of Forrest Wollinsky: Vampire Hunter.

If you could also take a moment and leave a review, it is greatly appreciated!

Blessings to you and yours.

ABOUT THE AUTHOR

Leonard D. Hilley II grew up a quiet, shy kid with an inquisitive mind. Learning to read at an early age, he fell in love with books. He read every book he could get his hands on and stacks of dark comics about ghosts, monsters, and creepy things that stalk the night.

Like a lot of boys, he caught beetles, wooly bears, butterflies, and had an ant farm. When he was ten, his interests in science increased even more after seeing a professor's insect collection. Soon he set out on his quest to build his own collection. He also learned to rear butterflies and moths to obtain perfect specimens. He learned botany, gardening, and set his goal to become an entomologist.

At eleven, he saw Star Wars. His imagination soared. Soon after, he discovered Roger Zelazny's Chronicles of Amber. Six months later, he had written the first draft of a novel. A novel he later discarded, but the characters stuck with him. Years later, these characters came to life in Shawndirea, which Hilley intended to be a novella for Devils Den. The characters, however, refused to be ignored and took the opportunity to unveil Aetheaon in their first epic fantasy. Lady Squire: Dawn's Ascension was quick to follow.

Shawndirea was Hilley's farewell to butterfly collecting, and those who have read the novel understand why. He has taken Ray Bradbury's advice to heart: "Follow the characters." He does. He follows, listens, and take notes—often never knowing where they're going to take him, but he's never been disappointed in the results.

Hilley earned a B.S. in Biology and an MFA in Creative Writing to combine his love of science and writing.

Sci-fi Titles: Predators of Darkness: Aftermath, Beyond the Darkness, The Game of Pawns, Death's Valley, The Deimos Virus.

Epic Fantasy: Shawndirea (Aetheaon Chronicles: Book One), Lady Squire (Aetheaon Chronicles: Book Two), Frosthammer (Aetheaon Chronicles:

Book Three), Shadowfae (Aetheaon Chronicles: Book Four), and Devils Den.

UF/PR: Succubus: Shadows of the Beast (Nocturnal Trinity Series: Book One), Raven (Nocturnal Trinity Series: Book Two)

YA UF/Paranormal: Forrest Wollinsky Vampire Hunter; Forrest Wollinsky: Blood Mists of London; Forrest Wollinsky: Predestined Crossroads.

ALSO BY LEONARD D. HILLEY II

UF/PR:

Succubus: Shadows of the Beast

Raven (Nocturnal Trinity Series: Book 2)

A Touch of the Familiar (Nocturnal Trinity Series: Book 3)

Forrest Wollinsky Series:

Forrest Wollinsky Vampire Hunter: The Beginning

Forrest Wollinsky Vampire Hunter: Blood Mists of London

Forrest Wollinsky Vampire Hunter: Predestined Crossroads

Epic Fantasy:

Shawndirea: Aetheaon Chronicles

Lady Squire (Aetheaon Chronicles: Book 2)

Frosthammer (Aetheaon Chronicles: Book 3)

Shadowfae (Aetheaon Chronicles: Book 4)

Devils Den (A Justin McKnight Adventure)

Science Fiction:

Predators of Darkness: Aftermath

Beyond the Darkness

The Game of Pawns

Death's Valley

The Deimos Virus

YA Mystery:

Dee's Mystery Solvers: Witch Cat

Dee's Mystery Solvers: The Beating Heart Beneath Hollow Hill

Dee's Mystery Solvers: Buried Treasure

www.ingramcontent.com/pod-product-compliance
Lightning Source LLC
Chambersburg PA
CBHW032156180726
48284CB00001B/70